THE OFF SEASON

ALSO BY COLLEEN THOMPSON

Fatal Error
Fade the Heat
The Deadliest Denial
Heat Lightning
Head On
The Salt Maiden
Triple Exposure
Beneath Bone Lake
Touch of Evil
The Best Victim
The Night Holds the Moon (with Parke Roberts)
The Jersey Devil Made Me Do It (a Pretty Little Liars novella)

Harlequin Intrigue

Capturing the Commando
Phantom of the French Quarter
Relentless Protector

Harlequin Romantic Suspense

"Lethal Lessons" (novella) in *Deadlier Than the Male* (Silhouette Romantic Suspense)
Passion to Protect
The Colton Heir

Lone Star Redemption
Lone Star Survivor
"Rescuing the Bride" (novella) in
Cowboy Christmas Rescue

Writing as Gwyneth Atlee

Touch of Fire
Night Winds
Canyon Song
Against the Odds
Trust to Chance
Innocent Deceptions
Dangerous Attractions (originally published under
the pseudonym Colleen Easton)

THE OFF SEASON

A NOVEL

COLLEEN THOMPSON

This is a work of fiction. Names, characters, organizations, places, events, and incidents are either products of the author's imagination or are used fictitiously.

Published by Montlake Romance, Seattle

www.apub.com

ISBN-13: 9781503937864
ISBN-10: 1503937860

Cover design by Shasti O'Leary Soudant

Printed in the United States of America

CHAPTER ONE

Christina Paxton's two-year-old looked up, studying her with a serious expression before her daughter's thin voice sliced through Christina's 2:30 a.m. stupor. "Murder me. Bad people."

Christina blinked hard, every fine hair rising along her arms, behind her neck. Her daughter, Lilly, hadn't said that, couldn't have. As a doctor, Christina knew better.

I'm dreaming on my feet, that's all. Or hallucinating, maybe. As tough and unflappable as she tried to convince others she was during her long shifts in the ER, the brain could get by with so little sleep for only so long before it started fraying at the edges.

It's the storm, that's all, she told herself as the wind's cold breath rattled windows sugared with ice crystals. That had to be it. She'd heard the wind blowing in off the dark expanse of the Atlantic, which was hurling itself against the beach across the street. The rushing and the crashing made her feel small inside this huge house, and more alone than she could bear.

But she *would* bear it. She had no choice, so she swallowed back a lump and helped Lilly pull up a fresh pair of the training pants they were still working on keeping dry through the night. As the bottoms of

Lilly's pajamas followed, Christina wanted to ask, "What did you say?" but she couldn't find her voice.

If she just tucked her daughter back into bed, maybe they could both grab a few more precious hours of sleep before the alarm went off. But Lilly was staring again, studying her mother with such fierce concentration that it sent a chill clean through her. Unlike the brown eyes of both her parents, Lilly's eyes were a deep, crystalline blue that Christina always imagined had been passed down from her own birth mother. Not that she could recall any other details of the woman's face, not after thirty years.

Still, some memories remained branded in her brain, despite the fact that Christina hadn't been much older than her daughter was now on the snowy night her mother dragged her and her baby sister from the warmth of wherever they'd been staying, then disappeared into one of Philadelphia's roughest neighborhoods. Christina still had nightmares of the icy flakes finding purchase on her thin clothes where she'd huddled, the freezing metal of the dumpster burning as she pressed her back against it. She remembered shaking in the cold, wrapping skinny arms around the four-month-old sister she'd been ordered to look after, and holding on for dear life.

Now, inside the big Victorian she'd been house-sitting since moving back to the little South Jersey shore community where she'd been raised, fresh chills skated over her nerve endings, and she pulled her terry robe a little tighter. Outside, a storm blown in off the Atlantic was doing its best to sandblast the paint off the 140-year-old structure, deepening her dread.

"Mur, mur, mur-me," Lilly crooned to herself. "Murder me."

Christina's heart dropped like a hammer. "What are you singing, baby? Where did you hear that?"

She held her breath, waiting for her daughter to start chattering about the latest Disney princess or Christina's friend Renee's three-and-a-half-year-old son, Jacob, who served both as Lilly's best buddy and as her arch nemesis. She ached for her daughter to return to the linguistic shorthand typical of toddlers and other tyrants. *Movie now! No bath! Want mac 'n' cheese! My blankie!*

Instead, Lilly frowned, her little forehead creasing in a surprisingly adult expression. "Kill me," Lilly said, words that sounded obscene, spoken in her sweet voice. "No leave babies."

An icy fist formed in Christina's stomach, knuckling her vertebrae. It was hard to drag a breath in, but from somewhere she heard her most sensible mom voice speaking. Because this couldn't be real.

"Don't be silly, sweetie," she said. "It's much too late to play pretend now."

"No pretend, Kay-dee."

Christina flinched, the night swirling around her. Because no one called her Katie. Not since her adoptive parents renamed her Christina when they'd brought her home, rather than using what was written in block letters on the tag of the T-shirt she was dressed in the night she'd been found.

A new name for a new start, the woman she would always consider her real mother had insisted. Christina had grabbed it like a lifeline, never looking back, going by the full first name—never Chris or Christie—ever since.

"Mommy-Kaydee," Lilly babbled, one chubby hand moving in a circle. "Katie-Mommy."

No way had her daughter just spoken a name Christina hadn't heard in decades—or gestured to illustrate how Christina had switched roles. "Wake up," she murmured to herself, panic crowding her throat. "You have to wake up now."

In spite of her denial, the weight of her daughter's solid little body felt real in Christina's arms. As did the trembling that found its way into her own voice. "Let's get you back to bed now, honey."

She tucked her daughter back into her bed—they'd left the crib behind in Dallas—and pulled up the blankets, knowing that if he had been there, her husband, Doug, would have given her a hard time about her fixation on keeping their daughter warm enough. A pediatric surgeon eighteen years her senior, he would have cited cases of infant suffocation, of SIDS deaths linked to co-sleeping or too many covers. She could almost hear him saying, *Trust me on this. She's fine.*

But Doug would never lecture her again, would never again offer his brand of comfort edged with condescension. As if she didn't see more death on a weekly basis in the emergency department than he ever had in surgery.

As if she hadn't cut her teeth on it that snowy night her four-month-old baby sister went still and cold in her arms.

In the dim light of the little elephant lamp that her adoptive mother—a well-respected local property manager whose business mainly catered to wealthy, out-of-town clients—had brought to the home she'd arranged for them to house-sit, Lilly's long eyelashes fluttered, and her breathing slowed and deepened. Christina stood there in the darkness, rubbing her daughter's silky blonde head until she was asleep.

Too shaken to go back to bed, Christina stayed with Lilly a long time, staring through the narrow spaces between the wooden blinds. Gazing out as flakes spun crazily past a lonely streetlight, flakes that looked so pale against the black void of the sea.

She wasn't sure what dragged her gaze back to the shoreline, but at some point she blinked and focused, abruptly realizing there was a vehicle parked on the street below that she didn't remember seeing earlier. A big, dark-colored SUV, lightly coated with a layer of frozen sleet and snow. She rubbed the chilled flesh of her arms, remembering the recent rash of break-ins she'd heard about along this stretch of unoccupied vacation properties, the senseless vandalism—drywall smashed, sinks plugged with all the taps left running—that had cost the owners far more than the thefts. It was the reason Christina and her daughter were living here rent-free this winter—to make more than two million dollars' worth of off-season real estate a less attractive target. The old security system had been repaired, too; she remembered setting it after taking out the dog this evening and coming up to bed.

She thought of calling the police, asking them to send a patrol to check the strange vehicle, but what self-respecting criminal would be out on a night this raw? It was probably just some neighbors coming in for the weekend to check their property. So instead of picking up the phone, Christina flipped a couple of lights on and off on the remote chance that some idiot was out there trying to decide which house offered the easiest pickings, then dismissed the worry before trudging back to bed.

Exhausted as she was, she lay awake a long time, with the words she'd surely imagined her tiny daughter speaking whispering through her restless mind.

Waiting around, even in the best of circumstances, had never been Harris Bowers's strong suit. He'd been born restless, prone to move, to act—often without bothering to think through the consequences first.

Over the years, this tendency had cost him deeply. God only knew he had the scars, inside and out, to prove it.

Yet the most recent and most serious among them had served a purpose. To remind him of the price of his impatience. The same blast that had slowed his step and left scarred patches on the right side of his chest and his right arm and shoulder had forced him to take the time to think things through, to plan out his actions before rushing into the thick of things with his gun blazing and his pulse pounding like a war drum at his temples.

But he damn well didn't have to like this newfound caution, especially when it involved freezing his balls off in the darkness, thanks to the Tahoe's half-assed heater and the three inches of new snow blanketing this neighborhood, where the kind of mansions rich people called beach cottages sat across from a beach area that only the toughest shorebirds visited in January. He thought longingly, too, of the coffee he'd denied himself during his night's vigil—a jolt that was going to be his first order of business as soon as the sun boiled its way up from the cold Atlantic depths.

Turning his face toward the houses he would never be invited into, Harris performed one last, long visual sweep. A flicker caught his gaze and held it: a light coming on in a second-story window from the only house currently occupied along this stretch of Cape Street.

Reflexively, his left hand touched the butt of his SIG Sauer before he spotted the woman, her slender figure silhouetted as she looked out over the street.

His sluggish blood stirred to life, his heart pumping as if he'd just mainlined half a pot of bitter station brew. Had she seen him sitting here, his vehicle idling in the darkness? Did she have any idea of the memories the news of her return to town had sparked?

He thought back to those hot nights, to walking and laughing on the boardwalk. Wandering among what a couple of shore kids like them called the *shoebies*—those socks-and-sandals day-trippers who packed their hometown every summer. The two of them playing the rigged carny games and burning through greasy delicacies, with the supercharged metabolisms eighteen-year-olds took for granted. For just a moment, he was flung back to that season, the air thick with salt and humid heat, the scents of deep-fried funnel cake and french fries, and the laughing cries of the thieving gulls who'd swoop in to steal the food from their hands if they let down their guards a moment.

And then there was the night, a memory smooth and clear as sea glass, when he'd taken her to a rental place, one of a row of crooked bungalows up on stilts—later bulldozed after Hurricane Sandy—that his uncle had co-owned with some boozer cousin. Truth was, Harris hadn't asked permission but had swiped a key one evening when he knew it wasn't rented, then gone over to make sure there were clean sheets on the bed and even a bouquet of white-and-yellow daisies with purple irises, because it was a girl's first time only once, and he'd figured it might take some extra wooing.

Her first time, and their only time together, sat in his memory like a lead weight, frozen as the snowy pellets that splashed down to melt in the salt water. Cold as the conscience of a kid too green and too pig-stupid to realize that revenge was a blade that cut both ways. A blade that would end up leaving him the person gutted, while she'd ended up with an MD tacked onto her name and some rich old guy for a husband.

Still, she'd ended up back here, wrecked on home shores, just as he was.

Harris reached into the Tahoe's center console, where he picked up a pair of good binoculars, not even pretending he was staring at anything but her.

~

A few short hours later, the alarm pulled Christina from a dream. Bobbing along its surface, she silenced the annoying tone and reflexively reached to her left. Her hand bumped a warm, breathing bulk beside her in the predawn darkness, and she started, exhilaration and pure relief shooting through her veins.

"Doug!" she cried out, jerking upright, so thankful to have wakened from an eight-month nightmare that she felt the burn of tears.

Hand shaking, she switched on the light, and reality impaled her. The white glow from the windows, thanks to last night's snowfall, the absence of her husband . . . and the presence of the retired racing greyhound he'd adopted last year as a running partner, who'd sneaked up beside her on the comforter. Again.

"Move it, Max," she scolded, pointing to the hundred-dollar heated dog bed she'd bought after moving in early in December.

The big fawn-colored dog looked up pleadingly, then rolled onto his back, his spine curving like the letter *C* as his long legs stuck up like a road-killed whitetail's.

Christina knew that she should ignore the pang of loneliness she felt and force the issue, instead of stroking his thin, sleek coat. But after getting up with Lilly last night and lying awake for so long afterward, she was too exhausted to—

Lilly. Last night.

Christina's scalp prickled with a memory of her daughter's china-doll eyes shimmering as though filmed underwater. Nausea rose with an echo of her sweet voice. *Murder me . . . No leave babies . . . No pretend, Kay-dee.*

"Impossible," she said aloud, talking to herself the way she'd speak to a delusional patient. It was only a bad dream triggered by cold weather. And the fact that Lilly was quickly approaching the age Christina had been on the night that forever changed her life. Or maybe it was proximity, knowing that after years in Texas—years she'd spent making excuses to avoid visiting any more often than she had to—she was back within a hundred miles of where it had happened.

Details filtered through her fog, the cold seeping in and the memory of her daughter in her arms morphing into the memory of her own baby sister as the snow came down around them.

Christina remembered a car out there that night, recalled her own hope fading with its receding taillights. Or were her memories getting mixed up with the sight of the strange vehicle she'd spotted last night on the street?

Throwing off the covers, she went to the window and looked out again. But the SUV had gone, leaving behind nothing but a splotch of bare, dark asphalt. As if the vehicle had sat there for a long time, arriving before the snow came and leaving after it had ended.

A gust off the churning water gave rise to a twisting specter, white with frost and vaguely feminine as it danced across the dark spot. Christina shivered as the snowy form dispersed, her imagination whispering forgotten words in her ear.

You take care of her and wait here just a minute. Mama'll be right back. Her breath caught.

But it was only another shard of a nightmare caused by how little sleep she was getting between Lilly and the new job, the stress of fresh grief, and the grueling cross-country move back from Texas to New Jersey. A woman of science, Christina clung to the rational explanation.

At least until the next time her mother spoke to her.

CHAPTER TWO

As Christina swallowed her last bite of toast, Renee bounced in through the back door with curly-haired Jacob wrapped in one arm and a striped tote draped over the other. The shiny, strawberry-blonde waves Christina had envied since they'd first become friends in junior high school swung over Renee's shoulder as she chirped, "Morning!"

Her petite friend's perkiness this early made Christina's head ache, but they'd known each other for so long that she wasn't going to strangle her friend for the offense. For one thing, since renewing their long-dormant relationship, Christina had become aware of a certain desperation behind her friend's size 2 brand of cheer, a brittle edge suggesting that last year's divorce had been no easier on Renee than Christina's loss had been for her. It helped, too, that Christina had already had her first cup of caffeine, thanks to the barista-worthy coffeemaker that was her favorite thing about the house's gorgeously remodeled kitchen.

"Lilly's still sleeping," she reported, grateful that she wouldn't have to deal with any toddler crankiness this morning. Still, a remnant of unease flickered behind the thought, a lingering relief that her daughter wouldn't open up those shining eyes and call her *Kay-dee* and not *Mommy*.

Christina filled her travel cup with a second hit of coffee, rich and dark and strong enough to burn away the chilling realization that she'd sunk to a new parental low. Afraid of her own daughter because of what she was certain had been nothing but a nightmare.

After slinging her bag atop the granite island, Renee set Jacob down and asked him, "You want to watch your show?"

Instead, he took a step toward Christina and held up a green toy dinosaur, mischief in his hazel eyes. *His father's eyes,* she thought, before pushing aside a memory of Harris Bowers's face.

"Rawr!" Jacob said, his shoulders hunching toward his ears.

Christina waved her hands and squealed, "Oh no! Not the mighty T. Rex! Who will save me? Maxie?"

From the family-room sectional where he was sprawled out, the big dog looked up and thumped his tail against a cushion. Instead of coming to her rescue, he yawned and laid his head back down.

"Lazybones!" Jacob laughed, forgetting his game as he made a beeline for the TV. He turned on a kiddie show, then heaved himself onto the sectional, draping an arm around the greyhound while they watched.

Figuring that dog and boy would soon go back to sleep, Christina stirred a splash of cream into her coffee and told Renee, "Those two have the right idea."

She found Renee eyeing her as critically as she so often had during their junior high years.

"You look terrible," Renee said bluntly. "Did you sleep at all last night?"

Christina snapped the to-go top on her cup with a bit more force than necessary, then peeked at her reflection in the microwave to check her usual slapdash makeup application and the ponytail she wore to keep her hair out of her face while working.

"I slept," she insisted, despite the dark circles under her eyes.

Renee slipped an arm out of the sleeve of her jacket with a snort of disbelief—or was it disdain? "Sure you did, but did any of that sleep come in more than twenty-minute stretches?"

Christina shrugged. "Can't have everything, I guess."

"Can't have *anything* if you keep stumbling around looking like you ought to be admitted to the hospital instead of treating patients. Call your sister," she said, lapsing into her old tendency to issue orders. "Have Annie stay over for a couple nights, and have her get up with Lilly if you need her to, while you take something so you can get some real rest for once."

"I'm late for work," Christina told her, too on edge to deal with the unsolicited advice. Especially the advice to lean on the same sister whose seemingly miraculous resuscitation had planted the seed for med school in Christina's own mind long ago. "You know, where people worry more about whether I can stitch 'em up or get their kid to stop projectile vomiting than how recently I've tweezed my eyebrows."

Renee winced at the sharpness, hurt blooming in her blue-gray eyes. "You're right, of course. Don't mind me. I'm just worried, that's all."

Christina stared at her, uncomfortably reminded of how much her friend needed the babysitting money since she'd lost her teaching job not long after her divorce. Her divorce from a man Christina still regretted not warning her about.

"I'm not mad, Renee. How could I be?" Grabbing her tote and cup, she offered a one-armed hug. "You're a real lifesaver, coming over. Have any trouble with the snow?"

Renee shook her head. "Main roads are all plowed." She shrugged. "And, anyway, I've got the Jeep. The one good thing Harris left me."

Hiding her discomfort at the mention of Harris Bowers, Christina nodded toward Jacob's sleeping form. "Not the only good thing." He really was a great kid—smart, sweet-tempered, and compliant—where Lilly was a live wire, to put it mildly. But then, Renee was such a natural in the mothering department, her self-assurance the polar opposite of Christina's awkward efforts.

Soon she was on the road, driving the sleek, black Mercedes she suspected she would always think of as Doug's car. Though she'd never thought of herself as the luxury-sedan type, the comfort of its heated leather embrace felt like the only thing keeping her from tears that icy morning . . . tears that threatened to overwhelm her as she allowed herself to consider that last night's *dream* might have had a darker explanation. That if Doug were here, he would remind her that this wasn't the first time she'd heard voices, after all.

That night Christina lay in bed, awake for hours, though her body was aching with exhaustion. Cocooned within a silence so absolute it felt like death, she found herself trapped with her regrets, her doubts, and the bone-deep need to hear the rumble of her husband's snores beside her.

When he was alive, it had driven her crazy—the sheer volume, with the stops and sputters she'd warned him many times indicated that he should be evaluated for sleep apnea, especially considering his family history of early heart disease. On at least three occasions that she could recall, he'd set up an appointment, only to cancel when some emergency reshuffled his busy surgical schedule.

She wondered now, as she had so often, whether he would still be alive if she'd forced the issue—or whether he would have at least reconsidered the wisdom of swimming a damn lake, without a word to her or anybody, in preparation for the triathlon he'd planned to enter. Of swimming so far from the shore that, once the chest pains had started, there could be no swimming back.

A lump formed in her throat as anger, like a red-hot coal, burned its way through her flesh.

You were supposed to be here for us. Supposed to help me raise our daughter, to keep her safe in case I ever . . . it ever happened again.

Feeling like the worst person on earth for being angry with a man she would have given anything to bring back, she climbed from the bed to take one of the nighttime pain relievers she'd been trying to wean herself off. From experience, she knew it would make waking up in a few hours like a slog through hardening concrete, but a little sleep beat none at all—and there was always coffee.

Sometime later, she was almost out when she heard the rustle of movement from the baby monitor sitting on her nightstand. For a moment, she held her breath, praying that her daughter would go back to sleep. As the monitor went quiet, Christina whispered a prayer of gratitude, then gradually wound down until she was dreaming of snowflakes spiraling around her. And a cold so deep, her toes and fingers lost all feeling, her bones aching and her—

"I need you to come find me, Katie."

The words jerked Christina awake—an adult voice that had her struggling to escape the tangled sheets. Her heart booming in her chest, her instincts shrieked that there was an intruder inside the house, in her daughter's room.

She hesitated, noticing that Max, who had once more crept up to sleep beside her, seemed to be out cold. Laid-back as he was, he sometimes slept through Lilly's fussing, but normally he would have rushed to investigate any strange noise in the house.

Before Christina could decide whether what she'd heard was real, he abruptly lifted his head, the tips of his ears shaking as he stared at the monitor. A growl started low in his throat, a low rumble she had never heard before.

"If you don't come, baby"—the voice came through the speaker loudly, clearly, undeniably—"you'll both stay lost forever."

Vaulting from the bed, Christina bolted toward Lilly's room two doors down, where she was dead certain she would find the stranger who was her mother alive and standing at her daughter's bedside. Christina would rip the hair from the woman's head, claw her face to ribbons, kill her with her bare hands if that was what it took to get her away from Lilly. Away from both of them and out of this house, out of their lives forever.

Christina flipped on the hall light outside Lilly's room and flew inside, ready to fight for her daughter's life.

But Lilly lay fast asleep in her bed, her small back rising and falling gently beneath the plush-footed pajamas she was wearing. Her flesh pebbled with chill bumps, Christina desperately looked around. But all was still and peaceful, though the hand she laid atop her daughter's silky head was shaking. Christina's breath came in ragged gulps as she imagined Lilly standing outside on a night far colder than this one, imagined her vulnerable and alone, save for the tiny burden she struggled to hold on to.

As Max followed her into the room to halfheartedly sniff around the floorboards, Christina whispered a message to the woman she wanted to believe was no more than a figment of her own imagination. "You stay away from her. She's mine. Stay away from both of us, or I swear to you, I'll—"

A cry caught in her throat as she heard the creak of wood. The house settling? The groan of an old memory? Or was someone waiting nearby, waiting to take Lilly when Christina retreated to her room?

Rather than rushing to investigate, the dog stared up at her, his head cocked in a look of vague confusion. A moment later, he yawned silently, bowing and stretching his long body before padding past the night-light and back toward the master bedroom.

But Christina didn't need his confirmation. She knew she'd been wide awake when she'd heard—they'd both heard—that strange voice, tinny and distorted, coming from inside this house. Certainty flooded her brain, an unshakable conviction that those words had been as real as the string of reported break-ins, as real as the SUV she'd seen parked outside the house the previous night.

Her heart stumbled at the thought, and she bent to scoop up Lilly, who moaned in protest and buried her face against her mother's shoulder. Arms wrapped tightly around Lilly's waist, Christina hurried back into her bedroom, pausing to close and lock the door behind them.

Her daughter was out again as Christina laid her on the bed beside the world's worst watchdog and picked up the landline to dial 911.

But what on earth would she report? A footstep she'd thought she heard? The voice of a woman who hadn't cared enough to look her up over the course of thirty years?

A wave of anxiety broke over her, but she fought free of it, knowing this was different from the hallucinations that had once scared her out of her mind. *Make the call.* Her hand tightened on the phone as she pressed it to her ear and sucked in a sharp breath.

The line, along with any further hope of sleep, was dead.

With his eyes glued to Christina's house, a few doors down from where he'd parked to assess the situation, Harris stepped off the edge of an unseen curb. Icy slush poured over the tops of his leakproof tactical boots, but he didn't break stride. With his wet feet squelching and his weapon in his left hand, he flipped on a flashlight that could double as a baton, providing that he could maintain a grip with his right.

Part of him wished there had been someone else he could have sent, someone with two reliable hands to respond for him. But when the call from the alarm company came in, informing the dispatcher that the landline at 127 Cape Street had failed, and the resident could not be reached via the alternate cell number, he couldn't bring himself to put the rookie on it. Or fucking Fiorelli, a burnout longtimer more likely to be parked somewhere snoring in his department cruiser than listening for calls.

As Harris crossed the yards of multi-million-dollar shorefront mansions, he swore to himself he would figure out some way to can the useless bastard without getting himself fired in the process. Though Seaside Creek's newest city-council member might not need any excuse besides the recent rash of vandalism—destruction that had recently turned violent.

Harris's gut clenched as he remembered what had happened a few blocks away after an elderly homeowner had surprised the culprits in the dead of night. Hurrying his own steps, he hoped to God that this particular call would prove to be another false alarm, one of many that kept his tiny police force—a skeleton crew during the long off season—hopping. The salt air and winter storms were hell on security systems—on *every* kind of wiring—and the area's cell-phone service was a straight-up joke most any time of the year.

Still, he kept picturing Christina lying on her kitchen floor, her light-brown hair fanned out in a pool of blood. His heart stumbled at the image, the fear twisting through him that he might already be too late. That he might fail a woman he'd once hurt so badly, a memory that made him grimace every time it crossed his mind.

His breath fogging in the cold air, Harris came in through the front gate to walk around an extravagant blue-and-white two-story he cursed for its highly ornamented wraparound porches. Porches whose shadows could easily conceal any number of unpleasant surprises.

Avoiding the light from a nearby street lamp, he strained his ears—though he no longer heard much out of the right one—realizing that the alarm's outdoor siren wasn't wailing as expected. Had it automatically timed out and shut off, or was there some issue with the system?

He wondered, was it possible that Christina and her little one were both upstairs sleeping, unaware that he was about to scare them half to death?

Better me than armed intruders, he thought as he proceeded.

CHAPTER THREE

Good to have a strong blade, one capable of slicing through skin and sinew, of hacking all the way to bone. Though for now, the target wasn't human, it was exciting to think it soon would be. To envision the first trickle of crimson turning to a waterfall of blood and see the startled look on her face, the fear and rage and horror when the bitch saw what he'd done.

Working its way upward, the point bit into a harder surface. Digging deep into the gleaming black paint, it made satisfying *scritching* sounds with every inch it covered. And there were going to be a fucking lot of inches before this was all finished. Wounds carved into rubber, words cut into steel . . .

But only one such tonight, one word to show her all she really was, once you sliced your way past all the stuff she had no right to, past the MD she hid behind—like she was some big-time doctor, and the rest of them were nothing.

And if that single word was not enough to get across the message, there were more and more and more things that might be done. Along with the certain knowledge that a knife so well made and so sturdy could do far more than send a message.

A weapon such as this could stop a beating heart.

It came from his right side, the side forever scarred by another occasion when Harris had foolishly failed to call for backup. Only this time, he had the warning of a glint off metal.

This time, he had a split second to jerk back out of the way of whatever was swinging toward his head—or *fall* back, after one foot slipped on a patch of slush that had refrozen with the night's chill.

It was enough to bring him down hard, his ass crashing on the icy walkway. But he was already shouting, "Freeze! Police!" with his left hand rising to aim the barrel of his pistol at . . .

Dimly illuminated by the streetlight, a tiny toddler stared with wide eyes as the slender woman holding her twisted to shield her child from the line of fire. "No, please!"

At the same time, some kind of metallic stick—the golf club she'd been holding—clattered onto the ice beside him.

"It's all right, Christina," he said, making an effort to sound a hell of a lot calmer than he felt, considering the pounding in his chest. When she froze, he lowered his weapon and grunted to his feet. "I'm not here to hurt you. I'd never—"

But the dark eyes staring back at him reminded him that it was far too late to make that promise. Dressed only in thin pajamas, she was shaking so hard he was half-afraid she'd drop the little girl.

"Then why—why break into my—?" she demanded. "How do you know my name? What is it you want?"

"I'm not here to break in, either," he assured her, realizing that with his back to the light, she could only be reacting to a looming silhouetted figure in a leather jacket holding a weapon on her. Not to him or what they'd once been to each other, however briefly.

Grimacing at his mistake, he holstered the SIG Sauer to reach for his ID wallet and flip it open. "I'm a cop, Christina. Harris Bowers, chief of police. See?"

She peered into his face, searching his eyes before dropping her gaze to his mouth—a glance that hit him like a gut punch before flicking to the badge itself.

"H-Harris?"

Maybe it was the shock of seeing her up close again, of hearing his name on her lips, but he thought she sounded glad to see him. Or at least relieved.

She collected herself in the space of a heartbeat, her voice cooling. "Oh, th-that's right. Renee told me you were a cop."

He winced, imagining the two women comparing notes, scoffing at the idea of Seaside Creek either honoring or handing a pity post—depending whom you asked—to the man who'd screwed them both over so royally. Dissecting his failings over a glass of chardonnay. Or maybe the whole bottle, after Renee had learned that he'd once had a summer fling with her best friend. A *fling* designed to hurt a girl whose brown eyes had looked up at him with an openness he'd crushed out like a lit match—an act that had circled back to cost him more than she would ever know.

Your own damned fault, not hers, he knew. Yet behind it, a trace of the old bitterness that had fueled his unforgivable game lingered.

"We had a call from your security company," he said, determined to show that he could at least conduct himself like a professional. "You didn't pull the panic alarm, did you?"

It was the only thing that explained why she'd be out here with the kid, shivering and barefoot, but she was shaking her head.

"I tried after I realized the phone was dead, but the siren never went off. Then I realized I'd left my cell in the car, so I waited a little while before I decided to risk coming out." Shaking her head, she groaned. "I don't even have my damn keys. I'm such an idiot—"

"You're shaken up." He thought of the young MPs he'd once led, half out of their minds on their first overseas deployments. He wished he could go back in time to teach them that the worst dangers rarely showed up when and where they were expected. "It happens."

Holstering his gun, he stripped down to the black sweatshirt he wore with jeans, and then wrapped his jacket around her and the tiny blonde girl. A cute kid, maybe a year younger than his own son, she leaned her head against her mother's shoulder and popped two fingers into her mouth.

"What made you pick up the phone in the first place?" he asked. "You hear something?"

She hesitated a moment before taking a deep breath and saying, "There—there was a woman talking. On the monitor. It woke me."

"Baby monitor, you mean? You keep one in the kid's room?"

She nodded, her eyes glassy with what looked like shock. Adjusting the child in her arms, she clutched the front of the jacket to keep it from slipping off her shoulders. "I was sure this woman was in Lilly's room, but when I ran in, there was no one." She grimaced, then admitted, "It—it could've been a dream, I guess."

"Or maybe it was just a freak thing," he allowed. "Your radio accidentally picking up a conversation from somebody else's house." But whose? With none of the nearby places occupied, the theory seemed unlikely.

"It's digital, not radio."

That made a lot more sense. "There could've been some kind of glitch. Or it could've been hacked into."

She blinked, her dark eyes widening. "Hacked? You mean, like someone scaring me on purpose?"

"Maybe." His investigator's instincts perked up. "Somebody come to mind? Someone who might want to do that?"

"I can't imagine they would, now that—no." She shook her head. "Besides, I heard footsteps, someone walking. Or maybe it's all just my imagination."

He filed away the response she'd bitten off, intending to ask her about it later. Because in his experience, the reactions that popped out before denial kicked in were often worth exploring. But not right now, when he heard what sounded like tears choking her voice. He'd heard other things around town as well: How she'd come home to be closer to her family after the unexpected death of the surgeon she'd married. How her mom, whose own more modest home was undergoing renovations, had set her up to stay in an area as silent as a graveyard throughout the long off season, if you didn't count the ever-present hiss of surf on the dark shore.

No wonder Christina was spooked. Though it still didn't explain the alarm system's malfunction or why the phone line had gone out.

"I'm going to check things out inside. But first, let's get something for your feet—"

"My boots, yes, sure," she said, raising first one bare foot and then the other, as if she had just noticed that her feet were freezing. "They're right inside the back door. I should have grabbed them on my way out. Like I said, I wasn't thinking."

"It's okay. Let me get them for you. Then I'll need you to take your daughter—Lilly, you said?"

Christina nodded, and at the sound of her name, the toddler lifted her blonde head from her mother's shoulder to stare at him with a look that threw him right back to the war zone, to the haunted eyes of kids who had seen way too much.

He shook off the odd thought, irritated that he was letting the past invade a present where he was determined to be on his game. To prove something to himself, even if he could never hope—or deserve—to prove anything to Christina.

He quickly retrieved the boots for Christina and steadied her with a hand on her arm as she slipped her feet into them.

"I need you to take her to my Tahoe there," he said, pointing to where he'd left the SUV. "I'll be watching till I see you're safely inside, and don't forget to lock the doors."

"Thanks," she said quietly. "I appreciate your coming, Harris."

"No need for thanks," he said gruffly, nodding toward the SUV. "Heat's on the fritz, but I left the engine running, so it should be at least a little warmer inside."

Her gratitude sliced through him, along with the realization that she had every right to be surprised that he'd personally shown up. Something passed between them in that moment, the resurrected ghost of a connection he had put down like a rabid dog. A betrayal it was far too late to do anything about.

So Harris didn't, wouldn't, tell her he'd been driving the neighborhood and staking out her street nearly every night since Walt Gunderson had been attacked. That he'd been worried about her staying out here on her own, even though he suspected the thieves' run-in with the old man had been accidental.

As he turned toward the door again, Christina clutched his elbow, her grip surprisingly strong.

"Please be careful in there, Harris," she warned, an unexpected fierceness burning off the fear in her voice. "I might've wanted you dead once, but not tonight."

No sooner had the words slipped from Christina's mouth than she felt a desperate need to snatch them from the air and stuff them back down her throat. But clearly, they'd already hit their mark. She saw it in Harris's stiff nod before she turned and walked away.

So much for pretending she'd forgotten all about what he'd done. As if any woman would ever forget the man who conned her out of her virginity, whose sweet lies had carved bloody slivers off her heart like the sharpest scalpels.

But she wasn't herself this evening, not with every nerve stripped bare. Maybe it was the nighttime pain reliever she'd taken earlier, lowering her defenses. Or maybe it was raw fear that had exposed the person behind the polite, professional facade she'd been using to keep her new coworkers—and everyone—at a safe distance since her return.

She carried Lilly to the idling SUV, stopping short when she realized it was the same vehicle she'd spotted outside last night. Had Harris been here staking out the street, or had it been a different officer? Wouldn't the police chief have more important duties?

Maybe he was just keeping an eye out, since Renee and their son, Jacob, spent so much time at the house. Though Renee had never spoken directly of the circumstances that had broken up her marriage last year, she'd dropped hints about another woman, and had once remarked that Harris couldn't be trusted. As if Christina hadn't learned that lesson for herself—though she'd been too humiliated ever to say a word to anyone about it.

Lilly shivered, breaking the spell, and Christina climbed into the unmarked vehicle's passenger seat and locked the doors. Teeth chattering, she fiddled with the vents, directing the lukewarm air onto the child in her arms. Wondering whether she could figure out the police radio in front to call for help if Harris didn't come back.

Her stomach tightened at the thought, and she assured herself he'd be fine, with his experience and training. But her own experiences in the ER, the faces of the dead and dying, reminded her that both qualities had their limitations.

Fifteen minutes passed, then twenty. Her gaze skimmed the shadows, which only deepened when the overhead clouds parted, and a full moon cast its cold light on the frothing shore below. Snuggling against her chest beneath Harris's jacket, Lilly was sleeping heavily by the time Christina finally spotted his tall, lean frame jogging toward them. Probably half-frozen, wearing only his sweatshirt, and limping, too. Was it from the fall on the back walkway, from when she'd tried to take his head off with the golf club? Or was the injury an old one, from the explosion that had made headlines about five years back?

She unlocked the door, and he climbed in behind the wheel.

"Is everything all right?" she asked.

"Far as I can tell," he said. "There's no sign of forced entry. Nobody inside, either. Well, other than one big dog—or a really scrawny horse."

"That's just Max." A news story from last week popped into her mind, an incident where Newark cops had shot a family pet after kicking in the wrong door after midnight. "You didn't hurt him, did you? He doesn't even bark."

"Wagging his tail at me and grinning the way he was? C'mon, Christina. Give a guy a little credit." The corners of his mouth quirked upward, an unwanted reminder of the boyish charm that had lured her like a bluefish, heedless of the hook.

She blew out a breath, feeling both relieved and foolish. "Then this was all for nothing, dragging you out here at this hour."

He turned to look straight ahead, his Adam's apple working. "Least I can do . . ."

For a moment, she held her breath, certain he would bring it up. That he'd apologize or say something to make the moment even more difficult.

Instead, he shrugged it off. "It's the job they gave me, after all."

"The way I hear it, you're a hero." When she'd first heard the details of how he'd nearly lost his own life protecting others, she'd been blindsided by a rush of pride for the same boy she had spent so many years hating. In a way, she realized, it had felt like a vindication, the knowledge that the potential she'd seen in him had been more than a case of raging hormones—or naïveté.

He made a scoffing sound, still not looking at her. "Well, this *hero* needs to catch some burglars before somebody else gets hurt."

"Somebody *else*?"

"You didn't know? There was an older man three blocks from here." He filled her in on the specifics.

"I don't understand." She shook her head. "Why haven't I heard about this? I mean, I work at the med center, right in the ER." That was no guarantee, what with HIPAA laws protecting patient information. But in a community as small as Seaside Creek, news of a brutal assault in the neighborhood where she lived should have filtered back to her, even if the poor man had been brought in on one of her off days.

"They took him to Presbyterian, over in Woods Crossing," he explained, referring to a private hospital about thirty minutes inland. "And, anyway, we haven't publicized it."

"Why on earth not?" she demanded. "Shouldn't I have known if my daughter and I were in danger?"

At the anger in her tone, Lilly shifted with a whimper.

"Let's say we talk about this inside," Harris said, laying a hand on Christina's arm, "where you'll be more comfortable."

She flinched away from his touch, and their gazes clashed as awareness arced between them, a reminder that she would never be comfortable as long as she remained in his still-too-handsome presence. That while two days ago she might have passed him on the street with no more than a cool nod, the words she'd heard these past two nights had left her too shaken for pretenses . . . the words still ringing in her memory, words that couldn't be explained away by any glitch in a monitor.

I need you to come find me, Katie.

But where was she to look, when the investigator she'd hired two years before had turned up nothing? And what if she didn't find the woman who had once dragged her to the dumpster and demanded that she stay there and take care of the baby?

What if the only thing Christina found was proof that she was no more fit to be a parent than her mother had been?

CHAPTER FOUR

It took longer than the five minutes Christina had promised Harris before she came back downstairs. Though Lilly settled with merciful speed once she was tucked into her own bed, Christina stood watch over her daughter for some time before leaving Max curled on the rug beside her—as if the big lug offered anything more in the way of security than a tripping hazard.

Leaving the door ajar, she stopped by the master bedroom to change into comfortable jeans and a thick blue cotton sweater. Two pairs of socks, too, along with her coziest lined slippers. But no matter how much clothing she piled on, she couldn't escape the chill that had burrowed down inside her. Couldn't stop shivering as her mind continually replayed the events of the past hour.

Steeling herself, she headed downstairs, only to pause midway when Harris's voice echoed from the entry. He was instructing someone, presumably one of his officers, to check all possible points of entry, the phone line, and the detached two-car garage as well. In one sense, it was a relief to know he was taking her complaints seriously. Still, her hand tightened on the banister at the idea of the police creeping around the old Victorian, scrutinizing everything . . . including her sanity.

Face burning, she forced herself to swallow and descended a few more steps. Far enough to see that there were three of them inside the front door, Harris with his back to her and two uniformed officers intent on what he was saying.

"Stick together, both of you, and keep in mind we may be dealing with multiple suspects, possibly armed," Harris told the mismatched pair.

"You can't really think they'd still be hanging around." The speaker was middle-aged and male, with drooping jowls and thinning hair in a shoe-polish black that couldn't possibly be natural. The straining buttons of his dark-blue shirt brought to mind the cardiac patients that came into the ER all too regularly, especially considering the splotch of greasy yellow-orange—her bet would have been congealed cheese from a fast-food burger—on his collar. "What with two marked patrols cars and—"

"Three live cops," Harris finished, with some heat. "And I mean to keep it that way. Always."

The second officer, a woman nearly a head taller than Burger Cop, broke the loaded silence that followed by clicking her flashlight on and off with her thumb, as if the male posturing left her bored. With her dark-brown hair pinned back and her impressive height—she stood eye to eye with Harris, who easily topped six feet—she reminded Christina of a warrior princess from a bygone age.

"So let's do this," she said.

Once the two officers closed the door behind them, Harris turned at the creak of a stair. "I was about to check on you," he told Christina. "Everything all right?"

She nodded. "Could I—it's so cold out there. Would you like some coffee? I'll make enough for the officers as well."

"That'd be great, and I'm sure they'd love some once they're finished." A smile stretched one side of his mouth. "Well, if *you're* the one who offers. If it was me, Fiorelli'd probably send it out for testing for heavy metals and rat poison."

The knot in her stomach eased a little. "Really. I'm a doctor. You wouldn't expect me to use anything that'd leave behind such obvious evidence."

He speared her with a narrow-eyed look that left her wondering—was she out of her mind, joking about poisoning the police?—before letting her off the hook with a fuller smile. A smile so rakishly appealing, it put Christina instantly on guard.

"So what *would* you use?" he asked as he trailed her into the kitchen. "If you were of a criminal persuasion, that is?"

She shrugged before admitting she hadn't given the idea much thought. "I'm too busy worrying about keeping people alive."

He leaned against the counter while she took out fresh beans for the Coffeemaker of the Gods to grind and brew. "Well, then, there's one thing you and I both have in common."

She swallowed hard, trying not to think back to other things they had once shared. The way they'd laughed together so easily. Her startled gasp, and the sigh that followed, when he'd slipped up behind her to cup her breasts, the first time in her life that anyone had touched her like that.

"You—you like it strong?" She shivered despite the flush of heat that scorched her skin.

"That'd be great. Strong as you like."

A whirring sound was followed by a series of satisfying hisses and burbles. Harris gestured toward the little breakfast table, an invitation that sent her heartbeat off-kilter and made her wish she'd never hit the panic button.

As a rich aroma wove its way into awareness, he took the seat across from hers, the golden-green of his eyes reminding her of flecks of sunshine filtered through the leafy canopy of a summer woodland. The thought sent her mind spinning to a state park she'd visited with a strong and healthy Doug last year, a happy memory steeped in pain . . . and now guilt as well.

"So let's start from the beginning," said Harris. "Can you tell me more about this voice that woke you? A woman's voice, you said?"

Christina's lungs scooped shallow breaths, and her cold hands ached to curl themselves around the comfort of a warm mug. She had to tell him something. "Yes, a stranger's, and I swear, in that first moment, I thought she was in my room."

"Did she sound young? Old?"

The words replayed in Christina's brain: *I need you to come find me, Katie.*

She shrugged. "Somewhere in between, I guess. The voice was kind of distorted, so it's hard to say."

"Caucasian, you think? From around here? As much as you can tell, I mean."

If you don't come, baby, you'll both stay lost forever.

"No particular accent I picked up on," she forced herself to say, "but I'd just been woken from a sound sleep."

Snow, swirling past a dumpster.

"Are you okay, Christina?"

She rubbed the goose bumps on her arms through the thick sweater. "Yeah, I guess. Just thinking of a nightmare I was having when she woke me up."

"Could she have been part of it?" He shrugged. "Sometimes I have bad dreams, and I'd swear I hear *him* talking. In real life, I mean."

"Him?" She was remembering things she'd heard, way back in school, about Harris's father. About the drinking and the rages, the wife who'd shown up to school functions with bruises on her face, though she could never be persuaded to speak a word against him.

"Yardley, the young MP from my own training class," Harris said, his mouth twisting into a grimace and his gaze sliding away. "The one I didn't stop in time."

"But you did stop him." Christina had heard reports about how many lives could have been lost had the twenty-year-old with the bomb strapped beneath his uniform jacket made it into the graduation ceremony before Harris noticed his erratic behavior.

"Tell that to the four he killed. And Private Yardley's family."

A sigh slipped free as she realized that the scars from that day ran far deeper than the few patches of grafted skin she'd spotted on Harris's neck and his right hand.

He looked back, searching her face. "You've been under a lot of stress lately, I understand, what with your husband and the move and a new job."

"It wasn't just a bad dream." The words came out sharp, defensive, but she couldn't listen to him accusing her of hearing things. Not now. "I was wide awake the second time. Her voice was coming loud and clear through the monitor."

Harris raised a palm. "Okay, okay. You really heard her. So what was it she said?"

"I—" She racked her brain for something she could tell him. Something to explain her panic without giving him reason to dig into her history. "I don't recall, exactly."

Suspicion flashed through his eyes, only to be tucked away so quickly that she wondered whether she'd imagined it.

"Then what was the gist of it?" he pressed.

Her hands were shaking so hard, she pulled them out of sight. Glancing toward the coffee machine, she said, "Let me check on that."

"You're very pale," he told her. "I'll get it."

Pushing back his chair, he walked to the counter and gestured toward a row of sturdy white mugs hanging on cup hooks beneath a cabinet. "These okay to use?"

"Sure," she answered, crystals of ice slowing her thoughts to a crawl. But the pressure was growing, and she had to come up with something, anything, to tell him.

He nodded toward the mug he'd just filled. "How d'you want this? Black all right?"

She would've preferred a little of the real cream she kept in the fridge, but it was all she could do to nod. "I think," she heard herself saying, "she said something like, *I'm right here, waiting for you.* That's when I jumped out of bed and ran into my daughter's room."

Though her mouth seemed to be functioning independently of her brain, she decided that, as lies went, this wasn't such a bad one. Except that Harris finished filling the first mug and gave her an assessing look that had her blurting, "Look, maybe you were right before. It's just some prankster who's hacked into the house's Wi-Fi for kicks."

"Speaking of Wi-Fi, the one you're using here—did the homeowners leave a password for you?"

She nodded. "They keep it printed on a card taped behind the pantry door over there—for the summer guests who rent this place."

He went to check it out. "Great. See how the edges of this card are bent, and it's yellowed? That's telling me that anybody who's had access to this place, from past visitors to whatever painter, maid, or pest-control guy who's ever worked here, could have access, and not only to your monitor. Your cell, computer, anything you've used here."

"I—I never thought to—"

"As long as it's working, people take technology for granted," he said. "But speaking of technology, you know anything about those security cameras? I saw one pointed at the front door and another in the back."

"I—um—I'm not sure how they work or where they record to, but I can give you the homeowner's number, or I have the number of the alarm-company people if you'd rather have that."

"We have both on file at the station. I'll make the calls when I get back there, see if we can get access to any footage shot tonight."

To prove that I was dreaming? Is that what he's really thinking?

Before she could voice the suspicion, there was a solid rap at the front door.

"Chief, you got a minute?" There was palpable tension in the female officer's voice as she stuck her head inside.

"Right there," he said, setting Christina's mug in front of her on his way out of the room.

She wanted to follow him, to know what was going on. But her knees felt too loose to support her, so she picked up the steaming cup and blew across the coffee's surface. As ripples expanded across the dark sea, part of the murmured conversation reached her ears.

"Fiorelli had it all wrong. Lady doc's not just spooking at shadows," the officer told Harris. "From the looks of the garage, there's definitely been someone here. Someone I'd say she's got good reason to be scared of."

This much Harris knew before he zipped up his jacket and followed rookie officer Aleksandra Zarzycki back outside, where the soft hiss of ever-present waves carried in the stillness. Something tonight had left Christina badly shaken. Fear radiated from her like waves of cold lifting off a chunk of dry ice. But he was sure, too, she was holding back on him, afraid to trust him with the whole story.

Or, who knew? Maybe it was a story she was afraid to tell herself. Happened all the time—people struggling to keep some ugly truth at bay by refusing to speak of it. Denial was the life vest that kept a lot of souls afloat.

As Harris crunched through the frozen slush behind Zarzycki, he tried not to count the lies he'd told himself. Yet they lined up in formation, each one more transparent than the one before. *Decorated marine. Devoted husband. Good father.*

Inside a well-lit garage that once might've been a carriage house, he found Fiorelli shaking his head at the condition of a late-model black Mercedes. A mile-long sedan, it all but screamed *money*, with its sleek, aerodynamic lines.

Except at the moment, Christina's car was listing badly, sitting unevenly on flattened tires.

"Seems some asshole's got a hard-on for rich folks," Fiorelli announced as he gestured toward slashed sidewalls. "First, their fancy houses, and now the high-end cars."

"Maybe," Harris allowed, wondering, not for the first time, if the extensive vandalism they'd seen in the previous break-ins had been more the point than the burglaries. Though everybody knew Seaside Creek would be circling the drain without the wealthy homeowners and summer visitors fueling its economy, that didn't stop a lot of homegrown have-nots from scorning those who, at best, ignored and excluded them. And, at worst, treated every local like the hired help.

"Or maybe this particular somebody has a beef with women," Zarzycki added, scowling down at the driver's-side door panel.

When Harris joined her, he winced to see her looking at the crude word someone had carved—the mother of all crude words for a female—into the glossy black paint. Though he'd worked with plenty of women MPs over the years and respected their professionalism, some latent reserve of chauvinism—or maybe it was chivalry—kicked in. "Sorry you had to see that."

Fiorelli gave a bark of scoffing laughter, his breath rising like smoke in the frigid air. "Yeah, like Alphabetty never heard that back when she was a big, bad, broad-ass marine."

"I've asked you not to call her that name," Harris ground out. "Repeatedly."

"It's no big thing." Zarzycki shrugged, her half smile contrasting with the narrow-eyed look she gave the sawed-off Italian. "I've been called worse, by better people."

Fiorelli grinned at her, something that looked surprisingly like real affection plastered on his ugly mug. "Betcha have, at that. She's all right, Chief."

Harris backed off, reminding himself that Aleksandra Zarzycki, whose A-to-Z of Polish names had inspired the nickname Alphabetty a half hour into her first shift, was up for whatever the department's good old boys could dish out. A former MP just as he was, she'd proven tough and smart enough not to let anybody run her over.

"And, anyway," Zarzycki continued, "this stuff with the car, it feels more directed to this particular resident. For one thing, look at the rest of the garage." She gestured toward a ladder hung on hooks and neatly arranged shelves containing cans of paint and boxes of lawn tools, a treasure trove for vandals, all untouched. "Besides, in my experience, this is the kind of word a woman gets called when she's not up for whatever some man has in mind."

"A piece of ass, you mean." Fiorelli rubbed the roll beneath his chin, clearly warming to the theory. "Could be a jilted lover, maybe, or some guy who wants to do her."

"Dr. Paxton only just moved back from Texas last month." Harris couldn't imagine she was settled in yet, much less thinking about allowing a new man into her life. Not a woman like Christina. "And she's a recent widow, with a little kid."

"Rich widow, from the looks of her ride," Fiorelli pointed out. "You know one of these things costs way over a hundred grand? More than my damned house, some of 'em."

"You're kidding." Zarzycki's blue-eyed gaze swept over the big car, a new respect in her expression. "Guess I should've studied harder, gone the med-school route instead of running off to the recruiter."

"Cost her a pretty penny to get that shit buffed out and repainted, too, I can tell you," Fiorelli went on, reminding Harris how the guy drooled over car magazines at his desk and rode around in a vintage muscle car with a shaggy black doofus of a dog on his days off. Because everyone should have a hobby besides being an annoying little bastard.

"Or her insurance, anyway," Harris said before changing the subject. "You see a security camera out here?"

"Nope. Must've figured the garage was safe enough since it was kept locked. You see the keypad out there?"

He made a mental note to ask Christina whether she'd secured it earlier. "Camera on the back door might've caught it if it's working."

"Maybe," Zarzycki said. "Unless it's the kind dependent on the phone line. Speaking of which, you might want to have a look at this, Chief. See what you make of it."

While Fiorelli stayed behind to take cell photos of the damage to the car—and slobber over *that fine Nazi engineering*, as he put it—Zarzycki led Harris to the rear corner of the house, where a cable rose from the ground to connect with a metal utility box. Shining her flashlight just beneath it, she steadied the beam, giving Harris a few moments to study the partly stripped, corroded wiring.

"Before we found the car," she told him, "I would've said it had been rusting for a long time before it finally gave up the ghost. But considering the c-word, I've gotta go with Option B. Some bastard yanked out the loose wire because he meant to scare her."

"Except there must be some kind of system backup that automatically triggers a call from the monitoring company when it detects a cut line," Harris said, thinking that Christina's frantic activation of the panic alarm might have been beside the point. "And I'm not sure you're right about this being some frustrated lover. She tells me there was a voice over the baby monitor. A female's."

"A woman, hmm?" Zarzycki frowned. "Somebody not liking the attention the pretty new doc's getting from her man?"

Harris murmured in agreement, thinking that could be right, whether or not Christina had welcomed any of it. Or Fiorelli, who knew this town and its inhabitants as well as anybody, could have a point, too. Maybe their vandalism-prone burglars had switched up their MO a little, but they could still be getting off on sticking it to randomly selected rich folks.

"So, this dead husband of hers," Zarzycki continued. "We know anything about him?"

"Older surgeon. Part of a thriving practice in Dallas when he went out for a swim with a bum ticker." Or at least that was what Renee had told him.

"Back when I was in Iraq, I had this uncle die," Zarzycki told him. "He'd been married to my aunt forever."

"And this is relevant because . . . ?" Harris prompted, impatient to get back inside, partly for the coffee. But mostly because he had a boatload of new questions for Christina.

"Turns out he had another kid. Some kid from an affair that nobody in the family knew of. Thing is, he'd put this kid's name on his insurance papers. Made him a beneficiary right alongside of his own wife and my cousins."

"That must've come as a shock."

"Oh, yeah, and not a happy one, even though that little policy was hardly worth the squabble. Or the legal fees and the bad feelings. But my point is, when someone dies, their secrets ooze up to the surface. And a lot of 'em create hard feelings. Especially when there's money on the line."

Harris nodded, wondering what the hell a bright young woman like this was doing wasting her time in a backwater department so small it had only one dedicated detective—currently out, recovering from back surgery—and no room for advancement. And wondering whether she could be right about something from Christina's past coming back to haunt her. Something that had followed her all the way from Texas.

Before heading back into the house, Harris tapped at the oversize front door, painted to match the house's trim in a shade he suspected had one of those fancy, historically inspired names that women and antique nuts went for but that he would just call blue. When Christina didn't answer, he stepped inside, closing off the chatter of the surf behind him.

He called her name, thinking that as nervous as she'd been, she'd probably run back upstairs to check on the kid or something.

Instead, he found her at the kitchen table, exactly where he'd left her. Except she'd slumped forward in her chair, her head resting on the arm partly wrapped around her half-full mug. With her eyes closed and her breathing heavy, she looked so damned peaceful.

Hard to believe she'd conked out like that, but sometimes stress hit people that way. Unable to cope with a situation, they simply shut down. Especially at—his glance touched on the microwave clock—4:23 a.m.

Wishing he could spare her this bad news, he laid his hand on her shoulder. "Christina."

With a murmur of complaint, she stirred. The silky texture of her hair sliding beneath his palm drove a fragment of memory like a splinter beneath his flesh. He heard the summer waves outside the screened window of his uncle's rental cottage, felt the warmth of damp air heavy with the smells of salt and fish and seaweed. Saw her big eyes looking up at his, her light-brown hair fanned out on the pillow. "I think—I think I love you, Harris," she whispered, "as much as it scares me."

He jerked his hand away and stepped back from the table, pulse throbbing at his temple. He had to get his head straight, put the past behind him. Or at least remember that whatever pain he'd caused her had come back on him a thousandfold.

"Christina." It came out gruffer this time. "I'm gonna need you to wake up now."

"What?" She straightened abruptly, brown eyes flaring in alarm.

"Sorry. Didn't mean to startle you," Harris said. "You okay? You need some more coffee or—"

She pushed her hair behind her ears, her eyes snapping into focus with impressive speed. "What was it the officer found in my garage?"

"Your car." He grimaced. "I'm sorry to tell you somebody's vandalized it."

"*Doug's* car?" A deep flush rose from her neckline. "Why would anybody—I should go see." Pushing back from the table, she stood, looking unsteady and uncertain.

"You don't—there's no need to go out there."

She frowned at him. "What is it? What did she—what did this person do?"

She, she had said. "Four slashed tires," he told her. "And some carving on the driver's-side door panel."

"Carving?"

He nodded. "Obscenity, I'm afraid. The kind directed at a woman."

"I've heard the word *bitch*, Harris."

He winced. "Not that. The, um . . . the other one."

"*That* one? Really?" Christina's eyes sparked with indignation, her cheeks flushing. Shaking her head, she said, "I don't get any of this. The woman on the monitor, the damage to the car. I can't think of anybody who would—"

"Can't you?" he asked, deliberately giving the question a little hang time. "Are you sure about that?"

"Of course I'm sure. I have no idea, unless somebody has a grudge against the kind of people who own places like this one. But this house isn't even mine. I'm only staying here because my mom arranged it with her rich clients."

Rich was a relative term, he'd learned. He remembered how he'd once thought of her and her parents—her dad a respected local pharmacist and her mom the owner of her own business—as rich, miles above a Creekside kid like him. Even Christina, who was living far better than what he now realized was an average, middle-class level, didn't seem to see herself as wealthy, apparently oblivious to the fact that others would.

"I understand, but whoever did it—they might have the wrong idea. After all, a car like yours . . ."

She crossed her arms and huffed out a breath. "That stupid car. It was Doug's baby, never mine, and I meant to sell it after he—but my old Highlander's transmission went out right after the funeral. Then things got so hectic, and I—"

He held up a hand. "You don't have to justify driving a nice car. Not to me or anybody."

She speared him with a look. "You wouldn't think so, would you?"

"There was something else, too," he informed her, "out behind the house. Phone line looks like somebody could've jerked it loose."

She dropped back into her chair and crossed her arms. Her face going pale, she said, "Then s-someone really *was* here. Inside the house, with Lilly and me?"

"There's no evidence of a break-in," he reminded her, knowing he'd be just as rattled by the thought of an intruder inside his own house when his son was sleeping over. "Have you noticed anything out of place?"

She shook her head.

"That side door into the garage. Did you lock it tonight?"

"Usually, I try to," she said. "But this evening, I was running late and in a hurry, trying to get some groceries in so Renee could get home. Then Lilly heard me and—so, no, I'm not sure. I'm afraid I've been a little scattered lately."

She lifted her mug to her mouth.

He took a sip from his as well, meaning to give her a moment to regroup. Except that the dark, rich brew sent such a shock of pleasure through his system. "Understandable, but I'll tell you one thing. You make a hell of a cup of coffee."

She managed a faint smile. "Coffeemaker here's amazing. And I found the owners' secret stash of magic beans in the back of the freezer."

"If you're confessing to a crime—"

"Too late," she said. "You're drinking it. Which makes you an accomplice."

"Accomplice, no," he said before savoring another mouthful. "Accessory after the fact . . . maybe." *Gladly.*

"Don't worry," she confessed. "I already e-mailed the owners, begged forgiveness, and offered to replace the coffee. They just laughed it off and told me to enjoy it."

"I don't doubt it. You were always such a rule-worshipping good girl."

Her smile faltered. "Yeah. But then, I learned early on about what happens when I—when I stray outside the lines."

A strained silence poured into the space between them, a quiet so complete his breathing swelled to a roar. With the past pressing in around them, he forced himself to focus on the faint sounds from outside. His officers' murmured conversation as they went about their work reminded him why he was here.

"So why would someone want to trash your car?" he asked, circling back to see if he could get a different answer. "Or scare you over the baby monitor? Because this kind of thing feels different, way more personal than the break-ins we've been dealing with around here these past few months."

She looked down to her coffee. "Truly, I have no idea."

Remembering her cut-off response earlier, he asked, "Any troubles at the new job? Somebody put out that you got the position?"

She gave a huff of disbelief. "Are you kidding? They'd been advertising for a while, everybody working tons of overtime. They practically had a party when I showed up, and everyone's been friendly."

"Any of them, well, *too* friendly?"

"You mean, like sexually?" She wrinkled her nose. "Nothing like that. Nothing. And, trust me, I'm still in survival mode, struggling to keep my head above water. I'm definitely not looking and don't plan to be for a very long time. If ever."

He nodded, understanding. Survival mode had been his life, both before and after Renee.

"Sorry, but I have to ask," he said, thinking about Zarzycki's uncle. "Your husband . . . I understand he was older?"

Her eyes rose to meet his. "What would that possibly have to do with—"

"How long were you two married?"

"Three years," she said. "And before you ask, we met on this white-water rafting trip another resident had talked me into. I'd never been before—I ended up in the river, half-drowned and freezing before Doug pulled me out. He was an avid sportsman, so he had one of those space blankets."

Her eyes misted with the memory, and he could see that her loss was still a raw wound. That she'd married the guy for love, not money.

"And the rest is history," Harris finished for her, his voice gentle.

She nodded, her mouth tightening.

"And what about that other guy? The one who'd invited you on the trip?" Though Harris was only guessing the friend had been male, he saw from her expression he'd been right.

"We were friends, that's all. Besides, that was years ago."

"Any other boyfriends? Disappointed guys? Past lovers?"

Her spine straightened, and two pink patches stained her cheeks. "No one who'd bother coming after me, especially back here in New Jersey. And I certainly wasn't—I never ran around on my husband, if that's what you're getting at. Not everyone's the cheating kind."

Her tone stung like a hard slap. What the hell had his ex told her about him? Wasn't the truth damning enough?

"Listen, Christina," he said, doing his best to keep his voice steady. "I wasn't saying you had. But I have to ask these questions if you really want to get to the bottom of what's going on, and make sure you and your child are both safe."

"Of course," she said, her hands tightening around the white mug. "But I have nothing to say about my sex life. Mostly because there's absolutely nothing to report."

He nodded, thinking she was being honest, even though he knew he was likely the last person in the world she'd want to speak to on the subject.

"Your husband left an estate, I'm guessing," he said cautiously. "Beyond the car, I mean?"

She hesitated before admitting, "Doug's practice was quite successful, and there was some family money, too, an inheritance that had all come down to him as an only child."

"I see," Harris said, letting it sink in that since he'd last seen her, the gap between the two of them had only widened. Other than Fiorelli, who'd felt shafted when Harris was offered the open chief's position two years back after only a short time on the force, and the newest city councilman, he had the respect of the community. A decent salary, too, far better than the crumbs his old man had always worked for, when he could hold on to a job. To her, though, his life—a new life he'd built upon the wreckage of his old one—must seem like nothing, though he couldn't imagine why he would give a damn what she thought. He only knew that he did, as screwed up as that was.

"So this inheritance," he went on. "You squabble with the family for your share?"

"I don't know which is more offensive," she said, pushing back from the table and coming to her feet. "Your insinuations that I've been involved with some coworker, or that I screwed around on my husband, or that I fought over money like some kind of a gold digger."

He stood as well, realizing he could have phrased his question a hell of a lot better. "I wasn't trying to suggest—"

"Save your questions for your suspects, not me. Get out there and—I don't know—go take fingerprints or something," she demanded.

"Unless maybe you have your own issues with people you think have more than you. *Still.*"

Temper throbbing in his temples, he said, "I'm not some eighteen-year-old kid anymore, *Dr.* Paxton. I'm an experienced cop, doing my job on no damn sleep for your benefit and safety. And all I ask in return is a little cooperation and some honest answers. Not some ridiculous old grudge you've been nursing since—"

"Trust me, Harris," she warned, her eyes boring into his, "you don't want to go there. But I'll tell you where you can go. Out the door right now. Because we're definitely done."

CHAPTER FIVE

Harris leaned against the door frame and stared straight into her eyes. "Not yet. I'm not going. We aren't finished."

Heart thumping wildly, Christina stared back, half-surprised that it had taken so long for her polite facade to crack.

"All right," he said. "This is how we're gonna do things. I'll head outside and make sure everything's being handled as best it can. And if I think of any more questions for you, I'll send in Fiorelli or, if you'd prefer a woman, Officer Zarzycki."

"Either will be fine." *As long as it's not you.*

"And one more thing before I go," he told her. "I know you're under stress. Just like I know it's uncomfortable, the two of us meeting again all these years later. But I swear to you I'm going to find whoever scared you tonight and damaged your car, no matter where the search leads. Or how much you'd like to stab me with a handful of syringes."

The sincerity in his voice made her feel small for having berated him when he'd offered nothing except kindness since his arrival.

"Thanks," she managed, the word rough with emotion.

She could still feel the pounding beneath her breast, all these years since the night she'd dredged up the courage to admit her feelings to him. After he'd made love to her so tenderly, with a reverence in his eyes that had quieted her doubts about the suddenness of his attention. But the intensity of her own feelings, the desire to blow off her scholarship and stay in Seaside Creek with him, had scared her even more. How could she stand to be away from him, she'd wondered, hours away in Massachusetts?

"Love me?" he'd scoffed, his face transformed by a mocking sneer. "Let's not get crazy. This was just a little summer fun to see you off, that's all."

She felt sick, remembering the burn of her humiliation, the way he'd never called her—not one time after that night. Worse yet was the malice she'd heard in his words, the certainty that she'd been deliberately set up . . . out of spite, she had eventually understood when she'd heard a rumor that he'd been competing for the same scholarship she'd been awarded. A scholarship that had been his only shot at getting out of Seaside Creek to attend college.

He nodded an acknowledgment of her thanks. Then he headed through the front door without a backward glance.

Unsettled by their conversation, Christina took her coffee upstairs and checked on Lilly again. In spite of having been wakened earlier, her daughter was already stirring, her tiny body gearing up for another hundred-megawatt morning.

Her vision swimming with exhaustion, Christina sighed, imagining all that energy unleashed upon the household, from demands for potty and breakfast, to whatever outfit Christina hadn't gotten around to washing. And then there was her shift today, the stream of patients who needed and deserved her full attention. How was she even going to get there, with her tires destroyed and her car—the car she remembered Doug hand-waxing so lovingly on weekends—now an obscenity on wheels?

Hanging her head, she felt her breath hitch, followed by the burn of all the emotion she'd been holding back for so long. Tears leaked past her defenses, prompting her to head into the bathroom, where neither Lilly nor any of the officers could spot her weeping.

Sometime later there was a knock from downstairs, followed by the sound of someone coming inside. Wiping her face with a wad of tissues, she held her breath, dreading the thought of facing Harris with her red eyes and blotchy face.

Her name floated up the stairwell. "Christina? Christina, are you okay?"

Renee. Christina sent up a prayer of thanks. Was it six fifteen already?

Rising from the bed where she'd been sitting, Christina called, "I'm in my room. Come on up."

"Just a sec," Renee said, and Christina heard the buzz of conversation downstairs. A tense conversation, judging from the sharpness of her friend's voice. "What on earth's wrong with you, Harris? You should've called me right away so I could be here for her."

Christina couldn't make out Harris's reply, only its low tone. But whatever he said seemed to tick off his ex-wife even more.

"Of course it didn't occur to you that she might need her best friend. Here, take your son, and let me—"

The rest was lost in the echo of her feet coming up the stairs. Making a beeline toward the master bedroom, Renee stopped in the doorway, concern written on her face.

"Oh, sweetie. I'm so sorry," she said before rushing forward and squeezing Christina in a hug. "I would've come if I'd known. No matter what the time."

Christina sucked in a shaky breath, struggling to keep from dissolving into tears once more. "I have to—I can't miss my shift."

"Don't be ridiculous. You're calling in sick. Harris told me you've been up all night. You have to get some rest."

"But Lilly will be up soon. I can't just—"

"I'll stay, of course, and watch the kids. And after a while, if you want, I'll take them over to the Kid Zone."

The Kid Zone was an indoor party place, with ball pits, climbing structures, indoor mazes. One of those places where you could buy the kind of food and drink guaranteed to amp up preschoolers, then burn off their excess energy while you sat there wishing you'd brought earplugs.

"Would you?" Christina asked, her vision going watery with gratitude. "That'd be great. Then I can call the phone company and my insurance and the owners and then—"

"Sleep's your first priority, after I get a decent breakfast in you."

Christina shook her head. "Thanks, but I'm not hungry. And I'm sure the police have more questions. I should go down and see if Harris needs—"

"Harris can darn well wait. Or go find himself a suspect in his old stomping grounds. I swear, those Swamp's End people let their brats run wild, then act all surprised when they get themselves in trouble."

Christina couldn't help cringing at Renee's reference to Creekbend, which the locals had been calling Swamp's End since as far back as she remembered. A low-lying area prone to mosquitoes, floods, and poverty, it had picked up uglier names during its decades-long downhill slide.

She recalled that Harris had lived there in an asphalt-shingled bungalow her school bus had passed each weekday before the horrific rollover accident that had claimed both his parents' lives during her freshman year of college. Like every kid from her neighborhood, with its neatly kept older houses and its air of respectability, she'd absorbed the unspoken rule that you didn't bicycle over to play anywhere around there, that you stuck to your own side of the bridge unless you were a member of that fiercely proud and tightly knit tribe.

And you didn't bring up that past, either, especially not when at least one person around here found you obnoxiously well off. She pursed her lips at the thought, wondering if Harris could be right about the reason behind the damage to her car.

As terrible as the thought was, she clutched gratefully at the possibility, finding it far easier to accept than the idea that she'd really heard her birth mother in the house. This morning, with the weak winter sun edging over the lip of the Atlantic, the idea seemed impossible. As impossible as the thought of her daughter channeling messages from beyond the grave.

And if it was stress that was causing such delusions, Christina told herself she had a responsibility to do something to clear her head. And do it before she became a danger to her patients . . . or her daughter.

"You're right. I'm calling in," Christina said, hoping the crusty veteran nurse in charge of ER scheduling wouldn't take it out on her for the next six months. "But I'll head downstairs first. I want to thank Harris and the officers."

"Just make the call," Renee said, looking pleased that her bossiness had had the desired effect, "and I'll get started on the pancakes. Or would you rather I made eggs or waffles?"

Christina frowned, irritated that Renee had ignored her earlier refusal. And even more annoyed when her stomach gave a growl and Renee grinned triumphantly at her. "All right, so I need to eat. But a yogurt'll do just fine."

Renee crossed her arms and raised an eyebrow, and Christina felt a stab of her old junior high anxiety under the weight of the queen bee's disapproval—a status her friend, whose divorced mother had always worked two or three jobs to make ends meet, managed by force of personality alone.

"Fine, then. Waffles would be great," she managed. "Thanks."

With Lilly still asleep, both women headed downstairs. Christina was surprised to find Harris sitting on the family-room floor helping his curly-haired son build a tower from the squishy foam blocks Christina's mother—the mother she selfishly wished would hurry back from the European dream vacation she'd left for earlier this week—had bought Lilly.

Not seeing the women, Harris focused on his son, a genuine smile warming his tired face. But Christina glimpsed a trace of pain, too, possibly from his right leg, which he held straight out before him on the floor.

Or maybe it wasn't physical discomfort but sadness she was seeing. The sadness of a father relegated to part-time parenting, even if the split had been his doing.

Breaking out in a huge grin, Harris grabbed a plastic pterodactyl and sent it swooping toward the tower with a hawklike cry.

Jacob laughed and clapped his hands, saying, "Knock it, Daddy! Knock it down!"

When the blocks tumbled, both father and son made explosive sound effects and briefly wrestled. Christina smiled, remembering how she and Annie had both loved it when as kids they could coax their adoptive dad—who'd lost his battle with melanoma not long after his granddaughter's birth—into such rough-and-tumble. She felt a pang, too, remembering how she'd tried to talk Doug into giving Lilly more of his attention.

You forget I've been through this twice already, he'd told her, referring to the children of his first marriage with that indulgent, slightly paternalistic smile that had sometimes made her want to scream. *But don't worry, I'll spend plenty of time with Lilly when she grows up enough to get more interesting.*

But, for him, that time would never come.

Renee, standing beside her, shook her head and muttered, "Look at him, putting on the Doting Daddy show for you. Where was all that when we lived together? Where was he?"

Though her voice was low, the venom in it must have carried, for Harris whipped his head around to grimace in their direction.

Embarrassed to be caught between them, Christina cleared her throat and asked, "Did your officers get coffee?"

"They did, and they both thank you," Harris said. "Except I'm afraid you've permanently ruined them for the supermarket stuff we brew at the station."

She forced a smile, grateful he'd chosen to pretend their earlier argument hadn't happened, then noticed Renee swinging a sharp look her way, clearly considering her friend's lack of overt hostility a betrayal. She'd have to get over it, Christina decided. She had enough issues with Harris already without being dragged into the ugly aftermath of their divorce. Besides, there was Jacob's relationship with his father to consider. She hoped Renee could restrain herself from venting her hurt and anger in front of her sweet son.

"Will I be able to have my car repaired?" Christina asked while Harris worked his way to his feet. "Or do you need to run some tests or something?"

"You can go ahead and call your insurance. We've already finished taking photos. Prints, too, but I'm not sure if we got anything helpful. When it's convenient, I'd appreciate it if you can stop by the station, where we'll fingerprint you for comparison."

"Of course," she said. "I'll take care of it as soon as I—"

"I'll bring her over once she's slept," Renee cut in, giving her another pointed look. "And I mean *really* slept this time, not just a ten-minute catnap."

"Sounds like a good idea," Harris conceded. "Meanwhile, we'll be questioning anyone we can find at home within a three-block radius."

"That should take all of five minutes," said Renee, and Christina had to agree, considering all the absentee owners in the historic district.

Harris shrugged. "Still, we'll do it. And we'll be checking the security cameras of businesses along the main arteries through town, too, along with a few we've set up on our own to try to get on top of—"

"Crimes against poor, pitiful rich people?" Renee asked.

Harris swung a hard look her way. "Crimes against taxpayers in my jurisdiction. Or would you rather I left your friend here a sitting duck for next time some jackass decides to take a screwdriver to her vehicle—or her?"

"Jackass!" Jacob laughed at the one word he'd homed in on, earning Harris an even blacker look from his ex-wife.

Before things could deteriorate any further, Harris took down Christina's cell-phone number and told her he'd update her as soon as he knew anything. "Meanwhile," he added, "we'll be stepping up patrols in the neighborhood, so don't be alarmed if you see a department vehicle parked nearby the next few nights."

Yours again? she wanted to ask, but instinct warned her not to splash more fuel on the fire of Renee's animosity. Besides, it didn't really matter which officer it was, as long as she and Lilly would be safe here, at least from the vandal.

But who could keep her safe from the voice she'd been hearing? A voice she couldn't entirely stop suspecting had been spun from the darkest reaches of her own scarred mind.

~

As on edge as she was, Christina didn't expect to fall back asleep, didn't really mean to. But Renee showed such compassion, insisting on serving her breakfast in bed, with a cold glass of milk to wash down the waffles, that Christina felt duty-bound to try.

Most likely because she'd been asked not to, Lilly—now dressed in the outfit they had laid out before bedtime—slipped upstairs to snuggle and kiss Christina's face, her lips sticky from her own meal. But she was too wiggly to settle, her blue eyes alive with mischief.

"Mommy take nap." She climbed from the bed to twirl around, the skirt she wore over purple leggings flaring like a ballerina's. "*Mommy* sleep, not me!"

Christina smiled. "That's what Miss Renee tells me. And we always listen to her, right?"

Lilly nodded solemnly before crinkling her nose. "Or you gonna get time-out."

Christina snorted, amused to imagine herself being ordered by her petite friend to the designated corner chair in the family room. Though come to think of it, Renee would probably have better luck getting her to sit still for five minutes than either of them had had so far with Lilly.

"Guess I'll take my nap, then," Christina said before she heard Renee calling upstairs for Lilly to come back down. "And you'd better stay with Jacob now. Or time-out will be too crowded for both of our patooties."

Lilly laughed like a pint-size maniac, then darted back to give her one last kiss. "Nighty-night. And when you wake up, come find me, Kay-dee-Mommy!"

Christina stared, unable to form a coherent thought, much less a question before Lilly closed the bedroom door behind her.

Come find me, Katie.

Shivering, she could only listen as the turquoise-and-hot-pink boots her daughter was practically living in this winter clumped down the hall toward the steps.

I should get up and go after her, make her explain where she first heard that. But Christina's limbs felt like lead, her eyelids heavier still. For a split second, she suspected Renee had drugged her milk in an attempt to force her to rest. But the idea was so preposterous, she put it out of her mind, assuring herself that the long nights had finally caught up with her instead. Or perhaps she was only seeking to escape the words still crashing through her brain. Words warning, sometimes in the strange woman's voice and other times in Lilly's, of the dire consequences should she fail to find the biological mother who'd been missing for three decades.

Sometime later, she jerked awake from a disturbing dream where she'd been called into the trauma bay, only to find her husband lying on the gurney, his abdominal cavity laid wide open with a medical examiner's Y incision. Turning from the horrific sight, she remembered looking back, telling herself it couldn't be real, and seeing Harris's bomb-blasted corpse lying there instead.

Beside her on the nightstand, her cell phone was buzzing. As Christina struggled to shake off the nightmare, the strange brightness of the bedroom had her blinking in confusion, uncertain what day it might be, let alone what time.

She swiped the "Answer" button, her vision still too bleary to read the caller ID. "Hello?"

In the silence that followed, the details of last night's terror came roaring back to mind. Her pulse thundering in her ears, she was seized with the conviction that this was no telemarketer calling.

"Christina? Is that you?" asked Christina's younger sister, surprise in her voice. "This time of day, I was sure I'd be talking to your voice mail. Did you—did you change up your work schedule?"

"Annie." Relief spilled into Christina's chest, warm and welcome, before her stomach squeezed out an ice-cold warning. "Is everything all right?"

"No, it isn't. Didn't you get my texts?"

"What texts? I was sleeping. Last night was—" Christina decided she didn't want to get into it. Not now. "I've got the day off. So what's going on?"

While waiting for an explanation, she saw that it was a little after noon already. Normally, Annie would have been at one of the many temp positions that never seemed to lead to full-time offers. She recalled her sister saying she'd be working as a receptionist for the next two weeks. Unless things had already fallen apart somehow.

Bracing to hear another list of the ways in which her sister's latest boss was a *pure idiot* or the job *impossible*, Christina nearly dropped the phone when Annie said, "Our—our mother called me."

"She called—was it from Italy?" Overwhelmed by the uphill battle of her own day-to-day responsibilities, Christina had quickly lost track of their mom's itinerary. "Or is it Portugal today?"

When she heard no answer but her sister's rapid breathing, fear had her own breath catching. "Is Mom all right? You're scaring me."

"She—she's fine, as far as I know," Annie said, her voice more strained by the moment, "but I'm not talking about her."

"You're not talking about—?"

It hit Christina then that instead of the thumps and squeals of playing, fussing children or the muffled drone of the TV she should be hearing from downstairs, there was only silence. Were Jacob and Lilly napping? Or had Renee taken them out as she'd promised, leaving Christina in this big old house alone?

She climbed from the bed, her skin erupting with gooseflesh. But before she could leave the room to check out her suspicions, she paused to shake her head. "Wait. If you weren't talking about Mom before, then who?" Her grip on the phone tightened. "Who did you mean when you asked if she's called me, too?"

Dread pooling in her stomach, Christina waited for an answer. But she knew already. She could feel it in the screaming silence from the first floor, in the memory of the words from her daughter's room last night.

"Our—our *mother*, Christina." Annie's voice sounded small and hesitant, the pale shadow of a girl—though now a woman, physically—who never took a single step without endless internal debate. Who'd avoided committing to anything, from a college major to a job or one of the men caught on the flypaper of her fragile beauty. The wrong men, time after time, most of them the kind who believed Christina's delicate, golden-haired sister needed saving. The kind who inevitably grew discouraged when she couldn't decide on any of them, either. "You know, the one who—who left us out there. Or at least a woman claiming she's—"

"Our *birth* mother called you? On the telephone?" Christina was rocked by a wave of dizziness. Because if Annie had heard from this woman, those incidents she'd been telling herself couldn't possibly be real must be. They couldn't both be hallucinating.

"*Someone* did," her sister said. "And she claimed to be—she said it wasn't her fault, what happened to us that night."

"What—what else?" Christina asked, too shocked to admit she'd experienced something similar. And uncertain whether to be relieved or horrified that she was no longer so alone.

"She claimed that she was forced to leave us." Annie's voice trembled. "She told me she was taken."

"Taken," Christina echoed, her stomach knotting with the memory of her daughter using the word *murdered* instead. Or had it been the baby monitor she'd really heard that night, too, instead of a twenty-eight-month-old toddler? The idea took hold, and once more, she imagined some criminal deliberately hacking into the device, someone eager to game both her sister and herself.

Was it for money? But Christina's thoughts turned to her car and the crude word carved into its side. The malice in that act made the silence from the floor below even more unnerving.

"Yes, *taken*," Annie said as Christina hurried to the staircase. "I tried to get her to say more, at least to tell me if she's safe now. But all she said was that she n-needed us to come find her."

Christina's heart stuttered as the familiar words sank in. "Find her where?"

At the sound of her feet on the treads, Max came wagging from the family room to meet her on the landing. Ignoring the big dog, Christina edged past him.

"I don't know," said Annie. "I couldn't think. I didn't—"

"So what did you say to her?" Christina headed for the kitchen, then reached for a scrap of paper left sitting on the counter. She recognized Renee's loopy handwriting, still girlish as ever, at a glance.

"I told her I needed *her*, that we both needed her back then. But not now, and that the last thing I have time for in my life is someone playing sick games."

Christina skimmed Renee's note, her stomach unclenching at its promise to be home from the Kid Zone by two o'clock or so.

"You still there?" Annie asked, doubt spilling back into her voice.

"Good for you," Christina said, proud that her sister had grown past the days when she'd dreamed up childish stories of their *real* mother, making her out to be the kidnapped princess in some dark fairy tale. "But did you ask her name? Did she say?" *Just in case this nutcase really is our mother . . .*

"She just kept begging me to listen. I—I was so upset, I cut her off, and when she tried to call me right back, I turned off my phone. Do you—was I wrong to do it?"

Christina cringed at this cry for approval. But she couldn't deny it to her sister. She never had been able to.

"Of course you weren't wrong," Christina said, falling back into the familiar habit of rescuing Annie—and her sister's of looking to her to do so—that had been permanently ingrained in each of them so long ago. "But we're going to need more information. Did you look back to see the number? Maybe we can track her down." Or maybe, Christina thought, she should call back the private investigator she'd hired and have him deal with this lunatic.

And there was always Harris, though the thought of trusting him with the story she'd told only to her husband turned her stomach.

"I—no, I didn't," Annie said. "I didn't think. I just tried to pull myself together. But in the end, it was no good. I had to go to bed."

"I wish you'll called me right away."

"I—I was worried you might be mad I hung up on her."

"Why would I be upset?" Christina asked her. "We have no idea who this woman really was or what she could've wanted. But maybe I should try to find out, in case she decides to hassle you again. Did you get the phone number?"

"I—no. I didn't notice."

"Could you check your phone's recent calls, then, while you have me on the line?"

"I'm not sure how to do it. Let me try—"

When the call disconnected, Christina rolled her eyes at her sister's hopeless technical skills. Figuring Annie would call back, Christina walked to the front window and opened the blinds, then squinted until her eyes adjusted.

The remaining snow had melted, leaving behind puddles and muddy patches that reflected the winter sun. Across the empty street, the gently sloping beach—a wide ribbon now, at low tide—had attracted a host of long-legged shorebirds, all busy pecking the mirrored strip bordering the relatively calm Atlantic.

There was something hypnotic in the feathered hunters' rhythm, the way they trotted farther out when the blue-gray water ebbed, and then ran for drier sand as it washed their way again. Christina stood taking it in for several minutes, struggling to focus on nothing but the rush and retreat of her own breathing. She realized that during the entire six weeks she'd lived here, this was the first and only time she'd allowed herself to enjoy this privileged view.

I should show Doug.

The thought had bubbled to the surface, a lost artifact of her marriage. But instead of making her sad, she felt the sharp bite of her own anger that he would never be around to share anything with again. Even when he'd been alive, he'd rarely been available, instead spending long hours at work and gripped by his increasingly obsessive interest in running, bicycling, and swimming. In the triathlon training that had killed him . . . *because he had to get away from you.*

Grateful when the phone interrupted her thoughts, she snatched it up again, only to see that it wasn't Annie calling, but Renee's photo flashing on the screen.

"Hi, Renee, is everything all—"

"I called the ambulance! It's—" Renee cried, the words so garbled they were almost impossible to understand. "Where are they? I can't—"

Christina's heart leaped through her chest. Was Lilly hurt? How badly? How would she survive if her daughter, too, was—

"Where are you, Renee?" she asked, speaking with a calm that belied her racing pulse. "What's going on?"

Her grip tightened as Renee sobbed into the phone. Christina struggled to comprehend what she was saying, but she could only pick out a few words . . .

Her daughter's name among them.

CHAPTER SIX

"Christina, this is Harris," he told her after pulling the phone from his incoherent ex-wife's grip. He wished he'd been able to stop her before she'd made the call. But what he'd seen on entering the Kid Zone, after racing there following a frantic call from the manager, had slammed him like a two-by-four across the shoulders. "I'm sending an officer to your house, lights and siren."

"Is it Lilly? Is she—has something happened to my—"

"Lilly's fine," he assured her. "It's Jacob." *My son. My best buddy.* He glanced toward the spot where a registered nurse who'd happened to be there with her own kids was kneeling at his three-year-old's side while Renee sobbed and clutched his hand. The shock of seeing Jacob, pale and unmoving, snaked across Harris's nerve endings, all of them sparking like downed wires.

"What's going on?" Christina demanded. "Harris, talk to me. Was there a car wreck? Or are you at the—"

"The Kid Zone, yeah." He shook his head, distracted by the flashing lights and the beeping backup warning of an ambulance approaching the glassed-in front entrance. "Sorry. EMTs just pulled up. It was a fall, Christina, off one of those padded tube things—I can't even imagine how he got up on top of it, much less slipped off and hit his head, but there's a huge lump on the side. Blood, not a lot, but—"

"Is he conscious? Moving?"

Her seriousness, her focus, reminded him that he was talking to an experienced emergency physician.

"He hasn't said a word," Harris told her, "but he—he moaned and pushed me away when I tried to blot the bump with a handkerchief so I could see it."

"Those are both good signs," she said. "Vocalization. Response to painful stimuli."

"Then he'll be all right?" Part of him knew she couldn't tell him that, not without examining Jacob for herself. But Harris was fighting hard to hold himself together. To hang on to the hope that the last person in the world he loved without reservation wouldn't be torn from him.

"He will be, Harris, if I have anything to say about it," Christina vowed. "I'll call the hospital on the way over—you *are* using Shoreline, right?"

"Yeah."

"Great," Christina went on. "I'll make some calls and try to get Alana Marshall over there to consult. She's a pediatric neurologist, one of the best I've ever worked with."

"And you'll look in on Jacob there, too?" He was surprised at how badly he wanted Christina's opinion. Wanted the unvarnished truth about his son's condition, no matter how difficult it might be to hear.

"I'd be glad to. But what about Lilly? Is she all right?"

He spotted the delicate blonde girl, standing frozen in place about ten feet behind where Renee and the nurse knelt at Jacob's side, staring with those pale eyes that somehow reminded him of a much older woman's. An old soul, his mother would have put it. Or was the toddler simply mesmerized by the confusion? When two EMTs hurried inside with their equipment, she didn't budge as the men cut around her.

"She seems okay," Harris told her mother. "I'll bring her with us to the hospital and make sure she's looked after. Renee—Renee's pretty distracted right now."

"Of course she would be—both of you," Christina said. "I'm so sorry this has happened, Harris. And I promise you, I'll help in any way I can. I adore Jacob. He's a great kid."

"Yeah," he said, voice breaking. "He's everything I've got."

"I get that. Believe me." The compassion in her voice served as a reminder that she, too, had recently lost a spouse.

"The patrol car's just pulled up," she added.

"Thanks, Christina. Thanks for meeting us," Harris said before ending the call. As he hurried to return Renee's phone and see what the EMTs were doing with Jacob, Lilly caught his eye again. The little girl was approaching his ex-wife and trying to slip beneath her arm, the uncertainty in her eyes telegraphing her need for reassurance.

Instead, Renee physically recoiled, glaring at the tiny child. "I told you to stay over there," she said, gesturing emphatically toward the spot where Lilly had been standing. "Get away from him now. You've already done enough."

Christina swiped her ID card, then hurried through an automatic door and into the heart of the emergency department. With its blues, greens, and natural wood tones, the modern layout was designed to calm civilians rudely thrust into the space. But Christina's pulse picked up as she spotted Harris off to one side of the nurses' station, in the consult area, with one of her fellow physicians.

In one strong arm, Harris was holding Lilly. Though Christina's daughter looked comfortable enough, leaning her head against his shoulder, the tall cop's stiff posture betrayed a tension she could feel from across the open space.

Cy Goldstein, an emergency-department veteran respected for his thoroughness and gentle manner, was explaining something to Harris. The dark eyes behind Goldstein's silver wire-framed glasses were wells of calm sincerity.

"Sorry to interrupt," she said as she approached them. Reaching for her daughter, she added, "Just let me take her off your hands, and I'll get out of your—"

"Mommy!" Lilly wriggled to get to her.

Harris passed her to Christina, the pain in his expression making him look a decade older than when she'd last seen him and somehow more vulnerable, dressed in off-duty jeans and a gray sweatshirt with the leather jacket he'd worn last night. "There you go," he said. "The doc here was just telling me they're taking Jacob for a CT scan. He's still—he hasn't said a single word or even tried to lift his head since . . ."

Suppressing an impulse to give Harris a hug, Christina asked her colleague about Jacob's Glasgow Coma Score and a rundown on his vitals.

A balding man with a round face, Goldstein looked to Harris, his raised brows clearly questioning whether she was here in a professional or personal capacity.

"Tell her everything." Harris's voice was rough as old burlap.

With a solemn nod, Goldstein shared the GSC, which was concerning but not dire. No deterioration of the vitals, pupils equal and reactive. But her colleague's tone told her what he wouldn't say in front of any worried father.

If Jacob's unconsciousness was the result of a serious brain bleed, it could kill the three-year-old before they could do anything about it. The CT scan and the other tests Goldstein had outlined would give them more information—and buy time until the neurologist Christina had arranged could get here. If surgery was indicated, a chopper would rush Jacob to the nearest Level I pediatric trauma center. Christina prayed it wouldn't come to that, but both training and experience had her forming a mental flowchart detailing every possibility.

Including those with the most heartbreaking of outcomes.

"Mommy, I hafta go," Lilly said, looking distressed as she struggled to escape Christina's grip.

"It's okay, honey," she said, doing her best not to sound exasperated by her daughter's timing. "Just a minute."

"Go now," Lilly whined, just as Christina caught sight of Renee on the opposite side of the nurses' station. Standing outside one of the urgent-care treatment areas, she was supporting herself with one hand braced against a column, her head bowed and her wavy, reddish-blonde waves obscuring her face.

In the course of her work, Christina had seen so many patients' family members in the grip of unimaginable pain, but her heart stumbled at the sight of her oldest friend so clearly devastated.

Rushing toward her, Christina struggled to keep hold of Lilly, who was whining, "Mommy, no. No want," and trying even harder to get down.

"Be still, please, just a minute," Christina said, wincing as her daughter stiffened and cried out.

Renee's head jerked in their direction, her face wet and blotchy, her eyes and nose red.

"Oh, Renee," Christina said, reaching out to hug her in spite of Lilly's fussing. "I'm so sorry about Jacob. What a terrible—"

Renee's eyes were locked on Lilly, a look that froze Christina and had her daughter dissolving into tears.

"She *pushed* him," Renee hissed, fury twisting her face into a stranger's. "On *purpose*, when he tried to bring her back down for me."

"She's *two*," Christina said as she turned her body away, clutching Lilly to her. Her daughter pressed her face to her chest, hiding from Renee's wrath and heaving choking sobs. And she was wet now,

Christina realized. Scared by a grown woman into losing control. "Just twenty-eight months. She couldn't possibly have meant to—"

"*She* pushed through a gap in the netting she'd been told twice to stay away from, hoisted herself up on top," Renee said.

A wave of dizziness engulfed Christina, and selfishly, she thought, *It could be my baby, right now in the CT tube. My Lilly, as lost to me as Doug.*

But Renee wasn't finished. "While I was telling her to stay still and calling for a manager to bring a ladder to get her down safely, Jacob climbed through after her, just trying to help, and he—" Renee stopped a moment before gearing up to shriek, "She *pushed* him, and he tumbled backward. Get that child away from me. Get her out of here, *now*!"

Harris came running, thrusting in front of her to grasp Renee's raised wrists as she lunged forward. While Christina froze in horror, too shocked to react to the physical threat, he peered into Renee's face.

"Calm down right this minute," he warned. "Do you want to be here for Jacob? Because if you can't settle yourself, you'll be escorted out."

"You don't even care," she wailed, fighting to get away while Harris struggled to contain her. "You've never cared about us. Don't pretend you—"

"Please don't do this," he said. "Jacob needs you. He needs *us*."

As a nurse and a hospital security officer approached, Christina fled with her daughter to a small restroom designated *Family.* Grateful to find it unoccupied, she locked the door behind them and went to her knees.

"Miss Renee doesn't mean it," Christina swore before kissing her daughter's damp and overheated temple as Lilly's sobs echoed off the tile. "I know she didn't, baby. She's just worried about Jacob, that's all."

At the mention of Jacob, the crying wound down.

"Jacob hurt," Lilly said. Exhausted by her weeping, she felt boneless in Christina's arms—and looked so vulnerable, with tear trails glistening like snails' tracks across her winter-chapped pink cheeks.

"How?" Christina asked, her heart pounding so hard, she felt the pulsing in her teeth as she thought of Renee's accusation. And whether it was remotely possible that a little girl scarcely out of diapers was capable of deliberate malice. "How did Jacob fall down? What happened?" *Did you really push him?*

Rather than giving her an answer, Lilly looked up, clearly miserable. "Wet, Mommy. I cold."

"Of course you are." Pulling herself together, Christina started digging through the big purse she'd grabbed on the way out the door earlier. Bypassing her wallet, bagged Cheerios, and lip balm, she whisper-shouted, "Yes!" when she came up with training pants and a change of clothes—probably from last Sunday, when she'd taken Lilly to visit her grandmother before the trip to Europe. There was a small pack of disposable wipes, too, thank heavens.

As she worked to clean and change her daughter, Lilly sobbed quietly, seemingly in a world of her own. "No, Jacob," she murmured to herself. "*No* come down now. No grab!"

A wave of nausea hit Christina as she wondered whether that really was all this boiled down to—Jacob grabbing Lilly to pull her back toward the gap when she refused to come down with him? And Lilly, who could be stubborn as the dickens, pushing him away? Not out of a desire to hurt him—Christina doubted any child her age could comprehend the consequences—but from an impulsive, purely toddlerlike frustration at having her will thwarted.

Horrible, yes, she thought as she wrung cool water from a couple of paper towels. But the act had been no more *deliberate* than the injury to a young mother she'd recently treated, whose toddler had broken her nose with a well-placed kick during a bedtime tantrum, or another injury that had occurred when a man with dementia had scalded his elderly wife by knocking a pot of boiling water from the stove.

As Christina wiped her daughter's face, she felt a flare of anger. As upset as Renee had been, she'd had no right to lash out, to raise her fists to strike as she had. Didn't she realize how terrifying this must all have been for Lilly, too? How her daughter could be scarred?

Emotionally scarred, but alive and physically whole. Christina's stomach turned with the thought. But a protective instinct overwhelmed all else, as primitive as it was fierce. She knew then that she'd do anything—fight or even kill—to keep her own child safe.

And if that meant stepping back from her duties as a friend and a physician right now, that was what she would do, without hesitation. She'd call Annie to come take them home or arrange for a cab—whatever it took to get Lilly out of here.

Decision made, Christina glanced down at Lilly, only to find the toddler's clear, blue gaze holding hers with an intensity that made her breath catch.

"Hurt Jacob," Lilly said, as plainly as if she were talking about a dropped egg or a worn-out toy. But did she mean it as a statement of fact or a confession?

"He—he *fell*," Christina corrected, pushing the words past the hard knot in her throat. "But everyone here is working very hard to make him better."

"All gone," the child said without the slightest emotion, her high voice echoing like an angel's in the confined space. "Like Katie-Mommy. Broken."

The green tile whirled around Christina, though somehow she remained on her feet, gaping. Had her daughter really said what she'd heard, and what had she meant by it? But with nausea flapping great bats' wings in her stomach, Christina couldn't remember how to speak, much less form the one question overwhelming all the others.

How do you know about Katie? How could you possibly know?

CHAPTER SEVEN

Harris's day passed in a hellish blur, much of it spent waiting for test results and consultations with a pediatrician and the neurologist Christina had arranged for. Waiting for his son to sit up, ready to play or to annihilate his favorite fries and chicken nuggets, instead of lying so unnaturally still beneath a sterile sheet with machines monitoring his vitals.

Intent on keeping her from plunging off the deep end again, Harris stuck close to his ex-wife, a woman he found himself once more bound to, out of fear this time, rather than what they'd both once foolishly believed could pass for love.

Others came and went. Renee's mom, who'd hugged him without a moment's hesitation and then wept against his chest until Renee, incapable of handling so much raw emotion, had called her aunt to take her mother home. Nearly all the men and women of his department also stopped by to meet him in the hallway, there to show that whatever stresses and strains the job brought, they would always support a brother in blue. There were friends as well, including some from the veterans' group he now led, guys assuring him they'd be there for anything he needed, anything he could bring himself to ask.

He hadn't been surprised, though, when he'd spotted Christina, quietly slipping out with Lilly and a slightly younger woman whose wheat-blonde, waist-length hair was pulled back in a clip. He'd crossed paths with Annie Wallace on calls a few times, a flashier version of her sister, with her full lips, eyes as clear and blue as Lilly's, and a set of curves that had sparked more than one fight at the Shell Pile, where she tended bar during the tourist season.

When he'd stepped in to cover for one of his officers during a short-handed shift last summer, he'd quickly realized that the thirty-year-old didn't deliberately instigate these brawls. A smile here, a kind word there, a few of those half-insightful, half-flaky philosophies of hers, and before she knew what was happening, she was once more inciting mayhem among the bar's well-lubricated crowd.

If she were half as perceptive as her sister, she'd figure it out and tone down the wattage a bit. But as Fiorelli had once put it, "With all the attention that girl's getting, ain't never gonna happen."

As if feeling the weight of his stare, Christina had stopped short of the exit. She'd turned to look back to where he stood just outside the exam room, an apology in her warm brown eyes. Breathtaking eyes—or maybe it was just him, the old attraction stirring before he remembered to crush it.

She was holding Lilly's hand, looking nervously past him as if she feared Renee would burst out from behind him and charge the two of them. Harris still couldn't believe that whatever had happened at the Kid Zone had been intentional, but he couldn't bring himself to go to talk to them, to tear himself from his duty to his own child.

After gently explaining to one of Renee's friends that his ex didn't wish to be disturbed now, Harris started back to check on Jacob when a familiar voice behind him froze him in his tracks.

"Chief Bowers, you missed our meeting."

Hearing the disdain in the man's voice, the thinnest veneer of civility—though he knew the forty-five-year-old could lay it on thick when talking to investors for the waterfront development he was angling to build on a protected wetland—Harris counted slowly to five before he dared to turn around. And willed himself not to let City Councilman Reginald Edgewood provoke him into flattening his hawklike nose.

But face-to-face with an expensive suit, silver-tipped high-dollar haircut, and oddly patrician features for a man who'd grown up in the same rough neighborhood as he had, Harris couldn't keep the sarcasm from his voice. "As much as I'd love to spend two hours justifying my every bowel movement since this vandalism started, you may have heard my son's had a serious accident."

"There's no need to be coarse," said Edgewood, his mouth twisting as if he'd bitten into something rancid. Probably bad caviar on the silver spoon he liked to pretend he'd been born with. But Harris had seen another side of him, a side reeking of whiskey and stumbling through a field-sobriety test. A night that Reg Edge would forever hate him for witnessing, not to mention holding him to account for. "Naturally, I'm sorry about the boy. Jacob? Isn't that his name?"

Jaws clenched, Harris stared down the smaller man. *Don't you dare pretend you feel compassion, not when you've been doing everything you can this past year to make it impossible for me to do my job.*

"I just thought you might've called my office, that's all, to let my secretary know that you've been—"

"I hope to hell you never have to see your own son lying helpless when there's not a damned thing you can do. Because I wouldn't wish that on *anybody*." Not even a man angling to get his brother-in-law, Frank Fiorelli, appointed chief in Harris's place so he could twist the laws to his own benefit.

"Understandable you're upset. A terrible thing," Edgewood murmured. "Have you considered—if you want, we could name an interim chief for the time being. To take the burden off you, just until your boy's feeling better."

Harris had never been so tempted to pistol-whip anyone into a grease spot, not even the vilest lowlife. But he knew that others on the council, at least a couple of them, saw right through Edgewood's sudden need to *turn my life around and give back to the community that has given me so much.* Besides, Fiorelli might be a good cop when the mood struck, but given his special talent for offending everyone he came in contact with, the mayor and veteran council members had to know that Edge's brother-in-law would be a huge liability as chief.

Reminding himself that assaulting Edgewood would only play into his hands, Harris said, "Thanks, but that's not necessary. I promise, though, you'll be the first to know if anything changes. I'll be in touch, okay?"

Without waiting for a reply, Harris turned and headed back to the four-bed pediatric ICU where Jacob was currently the only patient. As his ex-wife stood sentry, watching every breath their son took, Harris claimed a spot near the window, where he focused his gaze on the sun as it dipped beneath a distant, low ridge covered by a mix of dark-green pines and bare-limbed oaks.

He wasn't sure how long he'd been staring before he heard a woman speak behind him. "How are you holding up?"

Turning, he saw the neurologist they'd spoken to earlier. A large woman with thin, reddish braids pulled into a twisted updo, Dr. Marshall's bright smile and white lab coat stood out against her warm brown skin.

"Still standing so far," he answered, though he felt as likely to tumble as the skeletal remains of a bombed-out structure. "But like I keep asking everyone who'll listen, shouldn't he have opened his eyes by now? I mean, you told us before, the scans looked encouraging, and he was—you said he might—"

"Let's take a look, shall we?" she asked gently as she approached the spot where Renee was rooted. "May I?"

Nodding mutely, his ex stepped out of the doctor's way, looking so pale and shaky that Harris reflexively reached for her hand. Avoiding his touch, Renee stepped away from him and crossed her arms over her chest, watching Dr. Marshall's every move.

Though the neurologist explained what she was doing, it was tough to watch her peeling back his son's eyes, shining a flashlight into each pupil. Tougher still when Jacob squirmed and tried to push her hand away as she checked his pain responses.

When he began to whine and fuss, Renee burst out, "Stop it, can't you? Stop tormenting him."

"I'll only be a few more minutes," said Dr. Marshall gently. "If you could step back, please, Mrs. Bowers."

"We're not married," Renee blurted. "I only kept the name for my child's sake. I thought—"

Jacob cried out.

"Leave him be!"

"Renee," warned Harris, his hand barely touching her arm before she jerked away.

"Don't you *Renee* me. Don't you dare, after everything you've—"

"Mama?"

Barely louder than a whisper, the voice froze all three adults in their places.

Dr. Marshall, the first to recover, said, "Your mother's right here, Jacob. Can you open your eyes for her?"

Harris stood frozen, his heart crashing like a wrecking ball through his chest.

Jacob's eyelids twitched, cracking open slightly.

"Daddy," he murmured, a single word that nearly drove Harris to his knees.

Except that afterward, Jacob said nothing, lapsing back into a deeper sleep.

"It's often like this," Dr. Marshall assured them. "Different than you might see on TV or in a movie. People don't just pop out of comas, with all the lights flipped back on. It's usually more gradual, like a big house with one or two bulbs being screwed back in at a time."

"But this is a good sign, right?" Harris scarcely recognized his own voice, the quiet, desperate hope clashing with a crushing fear. "A sign that he'll recover fully."

"An excellent sign, yes, and children in his age group can be surprisingly resilient. But as for a full recovery, we won't know for some time yet. There may need to be some therapy, and—"

"He's going to get better," Renee insisted. "He'll be my sweet boy again, just like always."

Dr. Marshall nodded pleasantly before completing her examination. And in her silence, Harris understood that his ex's hope-fueled vision of their son's future wasn't necessarily the one they had in store.

Once she'd left, Harris said to Renee, "We should head down to the cafeteria for a quick meal. The nurse told me they close at seven, and I know you haven't eaten anything all day."

"I'm not leaving him," Renee insisted. "But if you're hungry, go on."

"Let me bring you something."

"Do whatever makes you happy. You always do," she said in a voice that told him she would probably pitch anything he bought into the trash out of spite.

He should have walked then, gotten out while he could, but something made him say, "Renee, you have to stop this."

"Stop what?"

"Lashing out at everyone who wants to help. Pushing away your family and Christina, treating a toddler like some kind of agent of evil—"

"So you're defending her now," she said, her face hardening, "after what that child did to our son? I should sue the woman."

"Christina, you mean?" he asked. "Your *friend*?"

"Who knows what all of this is going to cost?" Renee gestured around the room. "And she's got money, plenty of it. Besides, if she were raising that child of hers better—"

"Can't you hear yourself?" he asked, wishing her mother or her aunt would come back and talk some sense into her. Earlier, she'd made similar statements about suing the Kid Zone for not having a secure play area, no matter how many times he'd assured her he would deal with whatever the insurance didn't cover later. "I told you, forget about who's to blame. At least for right now, let's stay focused on getting Jacob better."

"What do you even care?" she started, prompting him to throw his hands up. "You've never cared. You've always wished I'd never gotten pregnant."

The fact that she'd conceived, only two months after they'd started dating and despite his use of protection, had certainly not been in their plans. But from the moment he'd first heard his unborn son's heartbeat, he had made his choice—one he had never once regretted.

"Fine," he said, knowing better than to argue. "If you need to make me out to be the bad guy to get through this, go ahead and do it." He, at least, was better equipped than a two-year-old to deal with her wrath. For one thing, he'd had a hell of a lot more practice. "But right now, I'm heading downstairs. And I *will* bring you back something, whether or not you choose to eat it."

He walked out, his appetite gone, though his pounding head and churning gut reminded him that he needed fuel to get him through this. On his way to the cafeteria, he ran into the one department cop he hadn't yet seen—Fiorelli, in uniform for the shift that would be starting in less than an hour. He wore his usual scowl, but his brown eyes were sympathetic as he offered Harris his hand.

"Chief," he said. "A hell of a thing. The poor kid. Anything I can do?"

"Thanks for coming, Frank." Harris returned the man's firm grip, reminding himself not to hold Edgewood's earlier behavior against the councilman's in-law. "It means a lot, you showing up here." It did mean a lot, with Harris knowing how little use his most senior officer had for him.

"Would've made it over sooner, but I was late hittin' the rack this morning and never saw any of the messages till the wife woke me up an hour ago."

"At least one of us is rested." After leaving Christina's this morning, Harris had grabbed a few hours' sleep before the call came, but at this point, he was running on a heady mix of frayed nerves and bad coffee.

"If you don't mind my saying, you look like hammered shit."

Harris snorted. "See how you look hanging out all day at your kid's bedside with the woman you divorced nine months ago."

Fiorelli winced. "That's a real ballbuster."

"New definition of hell," Harris affirmed. He was collecting them. Put this one on the list, right after getting blown to pieces five years back.

They talked briefly about Jacob's condition, and Fiorelli surprised him by saying, "I made a couple calls. Got everybody in the parish prayin' for him, for you and Renee, and her family."

"Thanks, man." Harris was surprised to hear that Fiorelli was religious. But when the chips were down, most cops were, especially when it came to family. "That means a whole lot to me. Just like you being here. But if I want to make the cafeteria before it closes . . ."

"Okay if I walk with you?"

"Sure thing," said Harris, realizing that Fiorelli had another reason for coming here before his shift. Maybe something his brother-in-law Edge had put him up to. "You hungry?"

"For hospital food? Hell, no, but . . ."

"Spit it out, Frank. What's up?" His temper rising, Harris braced himself to hear Fiorelli, too, suggest appointing him interim chief for the duration.

"It's that case from last night," Fiorelli said instead. "It can wait, though, if you need to—"

"You got something on our vandal?" Harris asked, forcing himself to switch his focus to what had happened at Christina's. "Tell me we've got video."

"Get this. They were dummy cameras. Not hooked to a damned thing. Alarm company said there's been some issue with the working units, and these ones were just in place till the replacements could be installed."

Had someone who knew about the camera problem decided to seize on the opportunity? "So this alarm company, they local?"

"Ocean City," Fiorelli said, naming a larger shore town about a half hour to the north. "And I've got a call in to OCPD, checking out their techs already."

"Good work," Harris told him, impressed to see him taking the lead for once, instead of dragging his heels or outright hiding from anything that smelled like work. "We'll want to check and see if any of our last few B&Es and trashed houses used the same security company, too."

"Already on it, and Alphabetty got the hot doc's prints late this afternoon, too."

"Christina Paxton's, you mean?" All the sensitivity training sessions in the world would never scratch the surface of this man's political incorrectness.

"Yeah, caught her at home a little while ago so Del could exclude her prints and run the others through the system." Del—Marco Del Vecchio—was a day-patrol guy who'd been cross-trained as a CSI. Because they didn't have the budget for anybody full-time. "But you know we won't get squat, just like with the burglaries."

"More than likely, you're right." Harris stepped aside for a white-haired woman clutching a small handbag, then continued, "Unless somebody got sloppy, or the thing with the car was really personal."

Fiorelli grunted something about not liking their odds.

"So, assuming we get a goose egg on the prints, what do you have?" Harris asked him.

"A big, fat zero. That's what I figured, just like the other cases." But then Fiorelli puffed up a little, sticking his chest out like a banty rooster. "Or at least that's what I figured until I started digging into the hot doc's background."

"Christina's? What did you find?" Regardless of how upset she'd gotten with him last night under questioning, Harris couldn't imagine that she was somehow involved in trashing her own Mercedes. "She's a respected physician, a single mom. I can't imagine she's got time to get herself into some sort of—"

"Whoa, whoa. What the hell? That's not what I'm saying. I'm tellin' you I found a motive, that's all. A damned good reason someone might want to give your sainted lady doctor a rough time. And maybe more than that."

Harris shook his head. "What do you mean?"

"I mean I've seen people, plenty of them, outright killed for less."

~

The following morning, Annie stopped by the house on Cape Street with a bag of doughnuts and a huge smile, her hair hanging like a beautiful blonde veil behind her. "Got your favorite. Cinnamon. Even though *everybody* knows that honey-glazed rule."

"You didn't get my voice mail?" asked Christina, who'd pulled on a pair of comfortable jeans and a dark-green cashmere sweater. She would have still been in bed, except Lilly was up early, and Max was eager to go out. "Sorry, but I don't need you to watch Lilly. I'm taking a personal day." Between the need to get the house's alarm system and phone line repaired and her bone-deep dread of running into Renee again at the hospital, Christina had been forced to concede to necessity.

As Annie slipped out of her jacket, annoyance quirked one corner of her mouth. "No, I didn't get your voice mail. Who even listens to those things, anyway?"

"I sent a text, too." *Because I knew you'd say that.*

"No, you didn't." Annie dug her phone from her purse and groaned down at the screen. "I could've slept in."

"But then there wouldn't be fresh doughnuts." Christina snatched the bag from her and opened its top, the faint warmth and sweet, yeasty aroma easily overpowering her recent resolution to eat healthier.

"Doughnuts!" Lilly came running in from the family room, her blue eyes alight at the rare treat.

Christina's stomach lurched at the sight of the toy in her daughter's hand—the same green plastic T. Rex with which Jacob had playfully pretended to menace her. Since coming home from the hospital yesterday, Lilly had been playing happily with the toys he'd left behind. There had been no more mention of the accident, and Christina was afraid to bring it up. Afraid Lilly would say something even more alarming than she had on several occasions already.

A few minutes later, she had Lilly in her booster seat, where she was blissfully singing to herself while working on the powdered-sugar doughnut from the bag and a sippy cup of milk. Rather than sitting at the table, the sisters were standing, eating their doughnuts with coffee, in Christina's case, and hot brewed tea in Annie's, while leaning up against the counter. *Grazing like animals,* their mother would have put it, having tried and finally given up on breaking them of the habit of eating on their feet as teens.

Missing her mom's voice—even her occasional scolding—Christina hoped she was having a great time with her friends. Her thoughts quickly soured as they veered from adoptive to birth mother, or the stranger who'd called Annie, claiming to be the woman. And acting as if she had some right to ask forgiveness, a concept that turned the bite of doughnut into an unappetizing lump in Christina's mouth.

Swallowing, she wiped her fingers on a napkin. "I forgot to ask, with everything that's happened: Did you ever check your phone's call log for that number? You know, from that woman who—"

"I know which woman," Annie said, setting her half-eaten second doughnut on the counter.

Looming hopefully nearby, Max raised his black nose like a periscope.

"Go lie down, boy," Christina ordered, knowing from experience that the big dog would get sick if he gobbled down anything so greasy. "Outta here."

Lowering his ears, the greyhound gave her his most tragic look before trudging over to lie near Lilly's chair. In the hope of falling crumbs, no doubt.

"The phone just said 'Private Number.'"

Christina bit back a curse. "But no more calls since then, right?"

"No, thank God."

"Good." Christina hadn't heard any more mysterious voices last night, either. But with the monitor unplugged, the home line disconnected, and her cell set to automatically reject anonymous calls, harassing her from afar would be much harder.

Unless this woman decides to come again in person. Chills erupted at the thought. Though Christina had no proof that the voice she and Annie had both heard was related to the vandalism, the suspicion floated, like the fragile tentacles of a jellyfish, just beneath the surface.

As if she'd read her sister's mind, Annie asked, "Have you heard any more about what happened with your car?"

After Christina had called Annie for a ride yesterday, she'd ended up telling her sister about the damage. But not about the woman on the baby monitor—not yet. She couldn't bear to admit to the things that she'd been hearing, since Annie knew about her issues of two years before.

Besides, Christina was supposed to be the one who had her life together, in spite of how so much of it had recently imploded. *And the crazy things you've heard your daughter saying.*

Her stomach quivering, Christina glanced at Lilly, who was chattering at the green T. Rex as she attempted to feed it chunks of doughnut.

Reassured that she wasn't listening, Christina lowered her voice to answer Annie. "I suspect the investigation's on hold, with Harris tied up with Jacob right now."

"I imagine so." Annie winced. "Have you been following the paper lately?"

"I have." Christina remembered reading the editorial in the local weekly suggesting that Seaside Creek's reputation and economy were at risk unless the *grossly undermanned* police department was beefed up and the vandalism stopped. The following week, a slew of outraged letters had followed, decrying the thought of higher taxes to benefit a bunch of *rich, big-city snobs*—one of the more polite descriptions of the absentee homeowners whose property had been damaged. Several had suggested that if Police Chief Bowers couldn't find a way to get his job done on the budget he'd been given, they ought to find someone who could. "Maybe people'll lighten up on him once word gets around about Jacob."

Annie snorted. "For about ten minutes, maybe. But after that, Harris had better get somebody behind bars fast, or he could go from hero to zero in no time flat. If what I'm hearing is true, I might even run into him at the unemployment office."

"What you're hearing from whom?"

Her sister shrugged. "Around town, that's all. What's it matter?"

Christina sighed, suspecting she was right.

Annie hesitated, chewing at her lower lip. "I hate to bring this up," she said, "but with Renee in this situation, I'm thinking it could be a long time before she's available for child care."

"Renee's never watching Lilly again." Christina thought of her daughter's terrified sobs echoing off the tile of the hospital restroom. "Not after the way she acted yesterday."

"You know I've never been Renee's biggest fan, but she had to've been out of her mind, with poor Jacob in a coma."

"I understand that. I do," Christina whispered. "And I feel terrible, absolutely sick, about what happened. But I'm not taking any chances, so I'll be looking for someone new. Someone I can trust with Lilly."

"It happens I'm available," Annie ventured, "and I'd absolutely love to help out on more than just a fill-in basis."

"What about your temp job?"

"That's over." She shrugged and waved it off. "I mean, you can't believe how boring—but me and my best girl, Lilly? We always have a blast together."

It was true, Christina thought. Annie doted on her only niece, loving it when people, fooled by their similar coloring, mistook Lilly for her own child when the two of them were out together. And Lilly adored her aunt, too, but why wouldn't she? Annie was all things fun, wrapped in a pretty package. Never too tired or sad or harried to get down on the floor and play.

Yet Christina still had reservations. "I thought you were tied up moving this week."

Annie had been telling everyone that the landlord was jacking up her rent again, but the truth, Christina knew, was that their mom had finally had enough of bailing out her younger daughter on the first of every month. Telling Christina that Annie would never "grow up and get a real profession" if they didn't both stop enabling her carefree lifestyle, their mother had adopted a strict tough-love policy. No more financial help.

Annie made a face. "Oh, that. Well, you try finding a decent place around here on a budget. I've even looked at renting a single room in a house, but the ones I can afford are total—hey, I know." Her expression brightened. "What if I stayed here? You've got like *tons* of room. What are there? Five bedrooms—or six—in this place?"

She said this as if she had just thought of it, but Christina recognized the telltale signs that she'd been planning this: Annie shifting her weight from one foot to the other, her gaze slipping off to the right. She'd been waiting for this chance—the chance to live rent-free, with her sister picking up the tab for food and utilities. But was it really enabling Annie if Christina needed her, too?

To stall for time before she had to answer, she stuffed her mouth with another bite of doughnut.

"Come on, Christina. I could be a real help," Annie pressed. "I'll keep the place picked up and feed her balanced meals. No more doughnuts or any junk food without your approval. And when you come home late, I'll have something ready for us. It'll be fun—like having a 1950s wife of your own."

Christina couldn't help but laugh at that. "I can just picture you in heels and one of those ruffled aprons."

Though another sister might have resented the thought of serving as her more successful sister's domestic help, Annie was grinning. "I can think of a few old boyfriends who would've paid big bucks to see that."

"What about the latest?" Christina asked, trying to sound casual. But if she decided to use her sister for more than a stopgap substitute, she needed to assure herself that Annie wouldn't be having any of her sometimes questionable choices around Lilly.

Annie looked her in the eye. "I'm taking a break from men right now, trying to focus on my course work."

"You're taking classes again?"

"Didn't I tell you? Yeah." She shrugged. "I've decided to switch majors and get my degree in business. Even Mom thinks it's a good idea."

"That's great, Annie," Christina said, wondering whether her sister's commitment to completing school would hold steady this time. "But keep in mind, your moving in would only be a temporary solution. In a month or two, I'll be looking for my own place—a condo or a small house." She emphasized *small*, having neither the time nor the inclination for a lot of upkeep—or a permanent roommate.

"Or you'll be moving in with Mom, if she has her way." Annie wrinkled her nose.

"I told her before she started renovations that I'm sure we'll all be happier long-term if Lilly, Max, and I have our own space." As much as their mother loved spending time with Lilly, she'd never had a high tolerance for messes. Or the idea of a large dog living in the house.

"But for now it would be okay? My coming here?"

"I'll have to ask the homeowners' permission," Christina said, figuring she could always blame them if she decided this was a terrible idea.

Annie flashed a perfect smile, her blue eyes reminding Christina of Lilly's when she'd first heard there were doughnuts. "You'll really ask them? Today? Because I'm already packed up."

Before she could answer, Christina noticed what her daughter was up to. "Don't give him that, Lilly! He'll get sick," she warned, but it was too late. Max had already scarfed down the half doughnut Lilly had offered.

His strong whip of a tail drummed a happy rhythm against the table leg.

Fifteen minutes later, Christina was cleaning up vomit from the family room—of course Max had picked the one carpeted area on the entire ground floor—when there was a knock at the front door.

As Annie hurried to answer, Christina warned, "Check the peephole."

"It's Harris." Annie hurried to undo the dead bolt. "How's your little boy? We've been so worried about him."

Harris came in with a puff of cool air and the fresh smell of the sea.

"He's better this morning than he was. Even talked a little more," he said as Max wagged his way over and pushed his long snout beneath the lawman's hand. "He's got a ways to go, but the doctors are saying things look hopeful."

Annie clapped her hands together. "That's fantastic."

"I'm so glad." Christina wadded up the towel and stood. Though she had earlier called the floor nurse for an update on Jacob's condition, she sighed to hear the relief in Harris's voice.

Reflexively, she glanced at Lilly, who didn't look up from the area rug where she was playing with the plush pony her grandma had given her. Christina's eyes widened as her daughter made the pony kick the green T. Rex, a blow that sent the dinosaur tumbling from the coffee table to land—in slow motion, thanks to her hand—on its head. Horrified to realize what she was acting out, Christina's first instinct was to snatch the toys away.

Instead, she left her daughter as she was, afraid Lilly might throw a tantrum—or blurt out something even more disturbing than what she'd said yesterday.

All gone. Like Katie-Mommy. Broken.

"I've been—I've been thanking God myself," said Harris, either not noticing or pretending not to notice Lilly's play. He'd changed into fresh jeans and a sweater, which he wore beneath a lighter jacket. If he'd slept, though, it hadn't been for long, judging from the dark stubble on his jawline and the tired look around his eyes. "And thanks to you, too, for getting Dr. Marshall for us. She seems to really know her stuff."

"The nurses think she walks on water." Christina ducked into the laundry room off the kitchen, where she left the soiled towel and carpet cleaner. As she returned, she added, "Far as I'm concerned, that's the best way to figure out who you'd want working on your family."

"Good strategy."

She flashed what she hoped passed for a smile. What was he doing here? "How 'bout some more of that ill-gotten coffee?"

"I'm good for now, thanks. But I was wondering, think we could talk?" Shifting his gaze to Annie, he asked, "Would you mind if I spoke to your sister privately?"

"Of course not," Annie said before looking to Christina. "Should I take Lilly upstairs and get her dressed?"

Christina couldn't get a word out. Was he about to tell her that Renee planned to try to file some kind of complaint about Lilly? Surely, no law would hold a toddler culpable. Or did he know something about the damage to her car or the woman on the monitor?

"How 'bout we go for a short walk?" Harris suggested. "I could use a little of this sunshine." When she hesitated, he said, "C'mon, Christina. Humor me. It's nice out, close to fifty. Better enjoy a little milder weather while we've got it."

She, too, had heard another winter-storm advisory for later in the week. They'd be on the edge of it, which might mean only a few inches. Or it could jog the other way, dumping a foot or more of snow.

"Go ahead," Annie told her. "Lilly and I will be fine."

"Okay," Christina said, anxiety prickling at the back of her neck. "Just let me grab my jacket."

She ended up leashing Max as well, hoping the fresh air would help settle his stomach. Or maybe she really wanted the big dog as a buffer between Harris and whatever news—or questions—he'd brought.

The three of them headed for the beach, where the churning gray-blue surf rumbled, scrubbing the sand and polishing the clear quartz pebbles known locally as Cape May diamonds. Coming in off the water, the wind was chillier than she'd expected, ruffling the white feathers of a few of the heartier gulls.

"Hard to believe there's a storm brewing out there somewhere. Doesn't seem possible, on a day like this one," Harris told her as he climbed onto the jetty. Made of piled rock, it extended some fifty yards offshore, providing protection from the worst waves, and serving as a popular platform for fishermen in the warmer months.

"I can't take Max up there," she said, raising her voice to be heard. She knew that greyhounds' long, thin legs could be fragile, and the algae that grew in patches could be dangerously slick.

"That's okay." He craned his neck, looking across the water toward the south. "I'm just trying to see—there it is."

"What's that?"

"The Willet's Point lighthouse. The light's long since been replaced by that flashing buoy the coast guard put nearby. Foghorn's gone, too, but on a clear day, you can still just make out the silhouette."

She smiled at a memory of the first time she'd seen the lighthouse up close. "When I was around twelve, my parents took Annie and me inside once and gave us a tour. Renee, too, come to think of it. We were inseparable back then."

"I thought it had always been locked up tight," he said. "Don't tell me the whole bunch of you walked out there over those rocks."

"No way would my parents take a chance like that, especially not with three kids in tow." She shivered at the thought of navigating the treacherous path carved into the jagged rocks arranged like vertebrae along the point's spine. Submerged probably twenty hours a day, the rocks' weathered surfaces would be even more slippery than the jetty. "We took Dad's little fishing boat and tied it up by the ladder."

She remembering how seasick she'd been with their boat bobbing at the base, and how terrified she'd been to climb up the rusted rungs to the lower gallery platform and the lighthouse's heavy double doors. If she hadn't known her spider monkey of a nine-year-old sister, who'd clambered up with ease and then turned and stuck her tongue out, would've lorded it over her forever, she never would have risked the twenty-foot fall into the sea. Or maybe she'd been more afraid of Renee, who'd followed, telling everyone at school what a baby she was. Maybe telling Christina that she didn't want to be friends with such a loser anymore.

"You remember that scheme to make it into a tourist stop after the place was decommissioned?" she asked.

"It wasn't exactly on my radar." Harris shrugged, a reminder that his family would have been more focused on day-to-day survival.

"My dad was involved with the historical society back then," Christina said, not mentioning that her father had been the group's president, "so he had the keys—this was all before the fire, of course. After that, the plan was off."

She frowned, thinking what a shame it was that an electrical blaze had so heavily damaged the interior, including the living quarters once used by shifts of coast guard light keepers. "We might've been the last people to see it from the inside. It was cool as can be, with real bedrooms and a kitchen, like a little house beneath the top level where the light was."

"Then you have to check it out. Just give Max a bit of slack and step on up here. I won't let you slip." Reaching down, he offered her his right hand. There were scars visible in the webbing between his thumb and index finger, another sign of the high price he'd paid for stopping a disturbed soldier with mass murder on his mind.

"It's all right," he assured her when she hesitated. "You can trust me."

Her eyes locked with his. "So you really don't . . . blame Lilly for what happened? Renee was—"

"The divorce has been hard on her," he said. "And losing her teaching job. If she lost Jacob, too, I'm not sure how she—hell, who am I kidding? I have no idea how either of us would survive it."

"Lilly doesn't understand what she did," Christina said, needing him to understand. "She was only trying to make him let go of her arm so he wouldn't pull her where she didn't want to go."

"Of course it was something like that. Little kids fight sometimes, and Jacob can get pretty bossy when he plays with other children. I know she never meant to hurt him. At that age, they don't even understand the concept." He smiled at her. "When Jacob started speaking, you know what was the first thing he asked us? If he—if he could go and play at Lilly's."

Christina's vision swam until she blinked away the gathering tears. "They remind me of two siblings, at each other's throats one minute and hugging the next."

"Come on, Christina." Harris reached down. "Take my hand. Step up here."

She slipped her hand into his, letting the coiled end of Max's leash run through her fingers as Harris helped her onto the big, flat rock where he was standing. Gently turning her to face the peninsula, he pointed out the faint silhouette of a red-and-black conical figure in the distance. As they stood together, looking, she felt the past lapping at her ankles, receding into a present where things were even less clear.

Despite the warmth of the callused fingers wrapped around hers, she shivered. If he meant to make her feel secure up here, the effect was offset by her own long-dormant regrets, along with a pleasant tingle reminding her of how very welcome his touch had once been . . . and how long it had been since she'd been—

She sucked in a ragged breath. She was still grieving for Doug, or she should be, no matter what challenges they'd faced in their marriage. And no matter how much he'd begun to seem part of a different woman's life, one receding in her memory's rearview as quickly as her years in Dallas.

But some things couldn't be denied, as she looked up at the handsome face, the hazel eyes that studied her with such obvious concern. "You're not the same man, are you? You're different now. We both are."

"I was no man back then," Harris admitted, "just a stupid punk, bent on getting even for something out of your control. Never thought I'd get the chance to tell you how sorry I am about it."

"You're sorry," she repeated, trying to understand what she made of an apology so many years belated. Would it have made some difference if he'd told her long before, before Doug? Did it make any difference to her now?

"I do forgive you," she said, hoping at least that getting it out in the open would make dealing with him easier. But that didn't mean she was about to let him make a fool of her again. Pulling her hand free, she asked, "But that's not why you came this morning, is it?"

"No. It's not. I'm afraid I'm here on official business."

Her heart accelerated. "You found something? Or someone?"

"Just a question, that's all," he said, "about why you lied to me."

CHAPTER EIGHT

In the few seconds that passed before she turned and hopped back down to the packed sand, Harris watched Christina's shock turn to fury. But as much as he hated to undo whatever scant trust he'd built, he couldn't lose this chance to startle her into giving him the information he needed.

"You're still the same con artist," she accused him as he followed in her wake. "Only now you're hiding it behind a badge—"

"Why didn't you tell me you were being sued," he pressed, "to the tune of 3.2 million dollars?"

When Fiorelli had filled him in on it last night, Harris's first reaction had been anger. He'd asked her directly about inheritance issues, and she had lied to his damn face. Since then he'd cooled down, reminding himself that she had every reason to be wary of sharing personal information with him. But he swore he was going to get some answers, if only to determine whether she was in real physical danger.

"Because I'm not," she snapped back at him. "Not anymore. It's all been worked out. Doug's son and daughter—"

"Your stepchildren."

"Believe me," she said bitterly as he pulled even with her, "we've never thought of one another as related. Never once, thanks to the previous administration."

"Previous administration?"

Her sigh was followed by a pained smile. "Doug's first wife. Evelyn had a lot of issues with his remarriage. The age gap, the *trophy-wife* thing." She sketched out air quotes with her fingers. "You name the objection, even though they'd been divorced for years before he met me. I tried to head things off by signing a prenup. Everything Doug owned or inherited before the wedding passed directly to his kids."

"*All* the kids?" he asked, imagining how little the ex-wife would like seeing her own children's portions reduced by a Lilly-Come-Lately.

"All three of them," Christina confirmed, "which created hard feelings, as you might imagine, especially since I'll be trustee for Lilly's share until she comes of age. So they came after me for everything: the house, Doug's percentage of the new practice he established, even the life-insurance policy he'd taken out especially so I would be provided for."

"Provided for how well?"

She crossed her arms and looked at him, her mouth pursed.

"People always hate talking about money," he said. "They'll spill their guts on every other subject—adultery, past abuse, you name it—but you start asking for figures, and they clam up every time. But you don't have to worry. Whatever you tell me about your bank account stays with me. I swear it."

After a moment's hesitation, she blew out a breath and answered, "It was for a million, because he knew I couldn't keep up the house on just an ER doctor's salary."

Must've been some house, then. "So was it the ex or the kids themselves who sued?"

"I'm sure Evelyn was the instigator, but the suit was in the kids' names. Legally, they're not children anymore. DJ—that's what everybody calls Doug Junior—is twenty-three now, and Ashley's nineteen."

"College kids, then?" he guessed.

"DJ's just started med school at Johns Hopkins."

"Sounds pricey." And extremely time-consuming. *But the kid could drive up here from Baltimore in less than three hours if he took it in his head to screw with his late dad's second wife.*

"Very expensive, yes, but there'd be nothing for him to gain at this point."

Unless all he wants is the chance to shake up the woman whose kid cost him a fatter piece of the pie. "And what about the daughter? She tied up in school, too?"

"Maybe community college or some kind of job-training program." Doubt threaded through Christina's voice. "You'd never know it to talk to her, but Ashley has a learning disability. Enough of one that her mom really had her work cut out for her getting Ashley through high school—and fending off the boys."

"Pretty girl?"

"Extremely. And so sweet—we got along famously at first, until her mother convinced her that *consorting with the enemy* was an act of treason."

Harris imagined that protecting a daughter like that from those who might seek to take advantage would get to be a habit. Which moved Mama Bear higher on his list of suspects. "So where's home for this family? They in Dallas, where you and your husband lived?"

Christina shook her head. "No. They're back in Pittsburgh, where Doug started out."

Pittsburgh was a longer drive—maybe twice the distance the boy would need to cover from Baltimore—but still doable, especially if the *previous administration* was sufficiently unhinged. "But you said it's all been settled?"

In the bright morning sunshine, Christina's blush was easy to see. "Yes. I just wanted it over before I moved back home, so I caved on everything except the car and that one life-insurance policy I mentioned—a drop in the bucket compared to what they were getting. And

Lilly's share, of course, though if I have anything to say about it, she'll be through school and have her own career established before she even hears about the money."

"Smart," he said before returning to the point. "So First Wife's kids ended up with more than the will stipulated, but not everything. And I take it this Evelyn had already gotten some kind of settlement at the time of their divorce."

Christina nodded. "They were satisfied, the lawyer said. And why not? They have more than enough money to go to school, to travel, to do just about anything if they don't get too crazy. What more could they ask for?"

Harris snorted, thinking of all the trust-fund brats who flooded these shore communities every summer. Entitled and obnoxious, ripping through town on their expensive wheels, then throwing fits when he ticketed them or had their fancy rides towed. Privileged young jerks walking out on restaurant bills or stiffing some poor local server after running up a huge bar tab. Using their daddies' high-priced lawyers to weasel out of charges for everything from DWIs and public lewdness to sexual assault. "I know that type. I arrest them—or kids like them—way too often. And for everything they have, what they've been handed without lifting one damn finger, all they want is *more*."

She shook her head, distress gleaming in her eyes. "I can't believe that they would—"

"And what they can't get, they'll destroy, like a toddler stomping a cookie when he's told to share it," Harris said, needing her to face what she clearly didn't wish to. "Or scratching the hell out of their father's car when it doesn't come their way."

She went quiet after that, clearly struggling with the concept that the vandalism had been personal. It must be easier, he thought, to assume the vandals were simply misguided individuals who'd mistaken her for someone she considered *really* rich.

They left the beach to walk along the street front, passing more grand historic houses painted a variety of colors, many sporting turrets and ornate, contrasting trim. Too fussy, and nearly impossible to keep up all that old woodwork in this beachfront climate, but he had to admit, the Old Town area kept a hell of a lot of area painters and contractors and their families in groceries.

And, yeah, the homes were nice to look at, landmarks he took an odd and complicated pride in. They'd be even prettier come summer, with their shutters open and colorful flags and awnings out, but he liked this time of year best. Liked driving empty streets and keeping watch over empty houses. Liked having more time to spend with Jacob as they collected shells on empty beaches and then went inside to make hot chocolate and grilled-cheese sandwiches with cups of canned tomato soup.

The thought of his son sent a fresh pang slicing through him, one Harris fought to compartmentalize as they made their way back to the big white Victorian on Cape Street. Breaking the silence, he asked Christina to repeat the ex-wife's and her kids' full names and locations, which he recorded on his smartphone. Apparently still lost in thought, she volunteered nothing else.

"Is that all?" she asked as they stood on the front porch.

He nodded. "I have to head over to the station for a bit. Then back to the hospital."

"Coffee for the road?" she offered. "I'm sure I have a spare travel mug—and frankly, you look like you could use the caffeine."

"Well, if that's your professional opinion."

She offered a weak smile, her cheeks pink with the cool air and the walk, her eyes bright with a quiet intelligence that had always drawn his eye. Though she had never been the prettiest or most popular girl in high school, she'd outworked and outstudied the loudmouthed guys always trying to dazzle their advanced classes with their brilliance. She'd outscored all of them from her perch below the radar—including one Swamp's End smart-ass who'd been so sure he had a lock on the scholarship he'd counted on to take him far from Seaside Creek. Outscored him by 2 percent on the test that would've kept him from having to enlist.

After letting him inside, she went straight to the kitchen to pour coffee. Before he could follow her, however, Lilly wandered into his path, looking up at him with a serious expression.

"Jacob daddy?" she asked, her hands full of the stuffed horse and toy dinosaur—one of his son's—she'd been playing with before.

Harris heard Christina's sharply indrawn breath before she called, "Annie, could you please come get Lilly?"

"She's fine," said Harris, squatting down despite the bum right knee that would make rising painful. "Yep, I'm Jacob's daddy. He misses you, princess."

He heard the quickness of Christina's footsteps, felt her hovering behind him, his cop-honed senses picking up on her anxiety. What the hell was she afraid of? Did she really think he was about to Mirandize the tiny girl?

"Just a minute," Annie called faintly from another room. A bathroom, more than likely, since he heard the sound of water running.

"For Jacob," Lilly said, thrusting both the dinosaur and her own toy horse into his hands. "Jacob come back?"

"I hope soon, sweetie," he said.

Lilly hugged him, so surprising and so earnest that he amended yesterday's odd assessment of her almost unnerving calm. She was a toddler, that was all, a tiny two-year-old probably in shock from seeing her closest playmate silent and unmoving, not to mention dealing with the fury of a caregiver she'd come to trust.

Harris hugged her back. "I'll take them to him," he said of the toys he still held. "And they'll help make him better."

"All better," Lilly echoed solemnly before looking to her mother. "No like Kaydee-Mommy. Kaydee-Mommy got dead."

He turned his head, confused enough by what she'd said to check out Christina's reaction. In her wide-eyed pallor, he saw what he'd missed a moment earlier.

Christina *hadn't* been afraid of anything he might do to her child. Instead, she'd been fearful of what Lilly might've—and had—told him.

But what the hell did it mean? And how could he get an answer without causing Christina to panic?

"L-let me get that coffee so you can be on your way," Christina said, willing her voice to remain steady. But the way Harris's gaze slid from Lilly to her made her feel as if she stood before him naked, her entire history exposed. Weighed and measured. Judged, not so much for the accident of birth that had led to her and Annie's abandonment and subsequent adoption, but the way her history had come back to haunt her two years before.

Once he dug deep enough—and she had no doubt he was clever and determined enough to find some way around medical privacy laws—to find out about her diagnosis, would he suspect she'd been the one filling her child's head with wild stories? The one, perhaps, who'd vandalized her own car and maybe even disguised her voice to call her sister?

Would he set Child Protective Services on her, fearing she might prove to be a danger to her own daughter?

Panic clawed at her throat. She couldn't lose Lilly. Couldn't risk the only thing that made her get up every morning.

While Lilly headed back toward the crate of toys kept in the family room, anxiety ripped through Christina. Moving back into the kitchen, she spilled coffee as she poured.

"Sorry," she said as she reached for the roll of paper towels. "You wouldn't think someone trained to sew up wounds with the tiniest of stitches would be such a complete klutz in the kitchen."

Harris looked at her with an unreadable expression. "You seem kind of rattled. Is there something more you want to tell me?"

She shook her head. "Of course not. I'm just—it's upsetting, everything that's happened. First, with the car and that voice I heard, and now, with Jacob. I don't know how you're standing there so calmly when he's back at the hospital."

"He's going to be all right. I know it."

"I'll look in on him," she offered, needing to see for himself whether Harris's optimism was well founded, "if it's okay with you and Renee. When I head back to work tomorrow."

"I appreciate that," he said as he accepted the mug. He took a sip and closed his eyes a moment, his fleeting look of pleasure reminding her sharply of a time she wished she could forget. "This stuff is worse than crack," he told her.

"I know." She was addicted to it herself. And she was as jittery as if she'd already downed two pots' worth, waiting for him to hurry up and clear out. Still, some perverse part of her had her offering, "Could you use a sandwich, too? Have you had anything?"

"I appreciate the offer," he said, "but I need to be on my way. Before I leave, though, one more thing."

She nodded. "Sure."

"You want to go ahead and tell me what that was all about, with Lilly?"

Christina's shoulders went rigid. "You mean . . . ?"

"Who's this Kaydee that she mentioned? The Kaydee with the dead mom? The one you clearly didn't want her telling me about?"

"I was embarrassed, that's all. I never should've let her watch that stupid movie." The story rattled out so quickly, she didn't have a moment to think about it. "But I was so tired that night, and the TV was keeping her occupied while I put together dinner. I didn't even notice how inappropriate it was until she started talking about this dead woman nonstop. And then there were the nightmares . . ."

Harris stared at her, his silence weighed down with expectation. Not far behind him, Annie, who had reappeared, tilted her head.

Christina flicked a look her way, mentally begging her not to contradict the story.

Her sister blinked hard, clearly confused, but for once in her life, she thought, instead of popping off with whatever came to mind. Or mentioning the call she'd received from the woman who claimed to have once known Christina by that same name.

"What movie was this?" Harris asked.

"I'm not sure. Just something on cable I had on for background noise." Christina shrugged. "Sometimes it can get a little spooky out here. I'm more used to hearing traffic, neighbors barbecuing by their pool. The quiet here's been—it reminds me of the things I've lost."

There was a momentary grimace, an acknowledgment in his nod. As if he'd sensed the truth in that part of the lie that she was spinning. "Well, rest assured my deputies are passing by more often," he said, "and I've asked them to do their computer logs parked nearby so they can keep an eye on things. Until we figure out what's going on and put a stop to it."

"Thanks, Harris. And I hope you'll let Renee know we're keeping Jacob—keeping all of you—in our thoughts."

He nodded before telling her he'd be in touch as soon as he had more news for her. At the front door, though, he turned and added, "And please don't hesitate to call me if you think of anything, no matter how small, that could help with the investigation. Anything you might've . . . forgotten to tell me today."

A chill detonated at her center, but she did her best to hide it, letting him leave without further comment.

It took less than half a minute for her sister to ask, "What's going on, Christina? What is it you're hiding from him?"

As Harris filled up his Tahoe on the way back to his office, he couldn't stop thinking about the girl whose memory was choked with regret. In his mind, his sweet Christina had been so many things: smart, pretty, funny once you got to know her, with a blushing, awkward innocence that had left him hot and hard and wanting far more than some nobody like him had any right to expect.

Thing was, he realized as he replaced the gas cap, the Christina he'd recently encountered had been scarred by the passing years, just as he had. Not on the outside, maybe, but she was clearly not the person he'd once known so well.

Doctor. Mother. Widow. Liar, too. Of that part he was certain, convinced that the *Kaydee* her daughter had spoken of had nothing to do with any movie.

He'd seen it in her sister's dropped jaw, in the startled blue eyes that so quickly sought Christina's face. Annie had recovered swiftly, but it was clear that the name had meant something to her. Something that Christina didn't want discussed.

Was it related to her husband's death? Though she'd answered his questions when confronted about the recent lawsuit, Harris suspected she never would have volunteered the information if he hadn't pressed for it. Maybe she honestly believed she'd worked things out with her husband's other heirs. Or maybe her reticence had more to do with wishful thinking, the desperate hope that she could put the unpleasantness of the lawsuit behind her and move on with her life.

Whichever was the case, Harris wondered as he climbed back into his vehicle what else he might find if he kept picking at the scab of Christina's recent past. His money was on a *Kaydee*—or perhaps *Katie* was the correct pronunciation. Find this person, whether she turned out to be a professional rival, her husband's lover, or maybe even a long-lost relative who felt left out of the inheritance, and Harris's instincts told him he was sure to come up with some answers.

But as he pulled back out onto State Street, it occurred to him that maybe it wasn't really answers he was after so much as an antidote to the ache he felt whenever he spent any time around Christina Wallace

Paxton. Feelings he had no business allowing to resurface, not with his son in the hospital, his ex-wife at his throat, and the city council growing increasingly impatient with his lack of progress on the recent break-ins.

That was when it hit him: the return of his libido was more than just nostalgia for a time when they'd both been young, with the whole summer—their whole lives—spread out before them, wide and deep as the Atlantic. This was karma instead, payback for the harm he'd done, making him want her now, all these years later, when she was farther out of reach than she had ever been before.

The irony hit him so hard that it dislodged a bark of laughter. Grimacing, he clamped his jaw shut, glad no one was around to hear him. Or to take note of the pain and longing that had echoed with the sound.

He didn't have time to wallow in it, though, not if he meant to put this case—and with any luck, his foolish attraction—behind him. Grimacing at the thought, he picked up the radio and asked the dispatcher to have Officer Del Vecchio meet him at the station as soon as possible.

Some forty minutes later, Harris was working at his desk, the door closed, as he did battle with the city council's most recent request for him to tighten the budget's belt another notch. He knew Seaside Creek had financial issues, but no department had been asked to sacrifice as much as his. Especially since the election of Reginald Edgewood just over a year before.

It had been his own damn fault, Harris told himself. When he'd slapped the cuffs on Edge the night he'd come across the one-car accident, the businessman had tried everything he could think of, from intimidation to threats, to convince him to overlook the mishap—since his BMW had only taken out a fire hydrant and not, say, a troop of Girl Scouts. *Then what about a contribution to your next campaign for reelection?* Edge had finally sputtered.

Irritated with his attempted bribery, Harris had told him, "I don't need your money—or your vote. I serve at the pleasure of Mayor Bradford and the city council," before hauling his entitled ass straight to jail.

After serving sixty days—the judge had been no more impressed than Harris—the businessman had immediately filed to run for an open council seat.

"Screw him," Harris mumbled. He wasn't trying to win any popularity contests with drunk drivers, and if pushing back on this budget pissed off some small-time politician with a bug up his ass, he wasn't losing any sleep over that, either, not while he had the backing of Mayor Bradford and at least half the council. For now, anyway, though he knew their confidence was waning with every day that he failed to make an arrest in the recent rash of break-ins.

A tap at his door, and Marco Del Vecchio leaned inside. He was an athletic-looking guy with thick, dark hair that was nearly always too long for regulation. Harris didn't care so much about that, but recently, he'd caught Del's big, dark eyes checking out Aleksandra Zarzycki often enough that he'd pulled the younger officer aside to give him the standard *Don't shit where you eat* lecture. "And, anyway," he'd added, "in case you haven't noticed, the rookie's got at least two inches on you. Maybe three."

"Some things in this life," the lean six-footer had fired back with that cocky grin he flashed so often, "are well worth reaching up for, my friend—um, Chief, sir."

"You need me to wait out here?" Del Vecchio asked now. "You look a little"—he waved vaguely in the direction of Harris's budget printouts—"distracted."

"Trust me, you're not interrupting anything I wouldn't pay good money to get out of. Come on in."

"Sorry it took me a while to make it over," Del Vecchio explained. "I was tied up with Mrs. Mosley. Again." He rolled his eyes before those straight white teeth made another appearance.

"I've been telling you, you've gotta stop responding. Yeah, it's sad, a woman in her eighties outliving all her family, but we've got a whole community to serve, not just one little old lady who thinks nothing of calling 911 so"—Harris pitched his voice to creaking heights—"*that handsome young Italian policeman can help me find my Mr. Whiskers.* Or did she need you to move her sofa back from where she had you put it last week?"

"I can't help myself." Del Vecchio shrugged. "She makes the best zeppole you've ever tasted."

"A doughnut by any other name," said Harris, who'd heard every cop-and-doughnut crack imaginable once too often but couldn't resist needling his subordinate.

"An *Italian* doughnut," Del Vecchio corrected. "Did you know her maiden name was Bartolossi?"

"Well, I'm afraid you won't be available to cater to Mama Zeppole for a couple days, Del. I need to send you out of town to do a little actual police work."

"Out of town?" Del Vecchio looked skeptical. "Tell me it's a prisoner transport from Florida. I hear it's nice down there this time of—"

"Get your head out of Disney World, Marco. This is serious. I'm going to need you to drive down to Baltimore and then out to Pittsburgh." Harris gave him details on where to find Evelyn Paxton and her two kids, and the kinds of questions he needed answered. "I especially want you to get a bead on their feelings about Doug Paxton's second wife, Christina. Figure out whether somebody's nurturing a big enough grudge to harass her—or hire a third party to do it for 'em."

Quickly catching on, Del Vecchio took down the pertinent information, impressing Harris, at least until he dropped one final question like an afterthought.

"You think I should have a partner working with me? Maybe someone to assist with the note taking and all the driving?"

"Fiorelli, maybe?" Harris asked, just to mess with the kid.

"Actually, I was thinking this might be good experience for the rookie, a chance for me to teach her how to—"

"Nice try, but Zarzycki's not coming along for you to flirt with and treat like some kind of personal secretary." Not that Harris imagined she'd put up with either for five minutes. Since he'd hired her last summer, she'd taken to the work like a pro, but she'd unfailingly rebuffed her fellow officers' questions about her personal life, along with friendly invitations to join them for a beer or coffee after her shift. Excluded from such gatherings by his rank, Harris didn't care, but he had definitely taken notice. Especially in light of the inconsistencies between her résumé and his impressions of her.

"I'd never—" came Del's protest, along with a look of offended innocence.

"Save it, and go on home, pack yourself an overnight bag, and get going. Let me know as soon as you've made contact. I may have some further inquiries for you to follow up on."

"You've got it, Chief," Del Vecchio said breezily as he started for the door.

"And one more thing," Harris added. "If anybody asks, you're going to Camden to brush up on new state mandates as part of your CSI training. Make sure to moan about it a little, too, so they don't get suspicious."

The younger officer did a double take. "You aren't worried this could be connected to someone in the department, are you?"

Harris shook his head. "I don't have any reason to suspect it, but people talk. It's human nature. So let's not take any chances of compromising our investigation, okay?"

But as Del Vecchio gave his assurances and left the office, Harris knew he wasn't only concerned about word getting back to whoever had frightened Christina so badly that she'd run out into the freezing cold wielding a golf club as a weapon. He was more worried about how she'd react if she found out he was having his officer asking around about somebody named Katie.

CHAPTER NINE

The following day Christina reported to work, working her monthly shift at a satellite clinic in the underserved community of Bridgeport, about twenty miles to the northwest. If she'd thought her own ER was busy, the hectic pace of the clinic was enough to leave her breathless. All day long, a steady stream of mostly indigent patients crammed the tiny waiting room for their chance to have babies vaccinated, coughs addressed, and infected wounds cleaned out and repacked. By the time they made it to her, most were impatient from the long waits, their frustration compounded by the fact that a large percentage didn't speak English or lacked the basic skills to fill out—or even read—the paperwork they'd been given.

She was yelled at several times, greeted with tears several more, and threatened at least once—if she'd correctly understood the large Hispanic man who appeared drunk but was actually having a diabetic emergency. Once he was transported to the hospital and the rest of the patients had been finally dealt with—an hour after the posted closing time—her neck and shoulders ached, and she was totally spent.

"I'm dead on my feet," said Gina, the RN who'd been working with her, as she pulled her purse out of the drawer she'd just unlocked. "I don't know how you do the ER day in and day out. Give me my usual geriatric patients any day. This place was insane."

Christina commiserated for a minute, but she didn't mind a shift like this one now and then. She could see the good that she was doing, even when the patients didn't, and the time passed quickly. Blink, and it was dark already and time to head home to her daughter.

As dusk gave way to a scattering of stars, Christina climbed into the loaner vehicle she'd picked up that morning and headed through the small town, which she'd come through on numerous occasions as a kid. It had changed, she noticed, with many of the original redbrick buildings now shuttered since the town's longtime main employer, a glass plant that had stood more than a century, had closed, taking most of the town's jobs with it. But some of the oldest buildings at one end, she noticed, signaled an attempt at revitalization. Along with an antique store and a boutique, she spotted an arts-and-crafts co-op. And a number of vehicles were parked in front of a brightly lit place called the Sweet Shop, where she spotted a bakery counter and a collection of vintage ice cream parlor–style table-and-chair sets.

Charmed, she swung the small SUV into an empty space, thinking she would bring home cupcakes for her daughter and Annie, who'd been watching Lilly all day. And maybe a cookie to nibble for the ride home. The clinic had been so busy that Christina had worked straight through lunchtime.

After locking the Mercedes, she headed for the Sweet Shop's front door, only to stop abruptly when her gaze was drawn to a couple sitting in the farthest corner, or rather, to the familiar wavy, reddish-blonde hair that fell down the petite woman's back. Unable to see the woman's face, Christina told herself it couldn't possibly be Renee. Not here, so far from Seaside Creek, with her son in the hospital after a serious injury.

Christina told herself to go inside, that her instinct had to be wrong. For one thing, she didn't see Renee's Jeep parked anywhere along the street, where its bright-yellow paint job would make it impossible to miss.

Besides, she couldn't avoid her friend forever. If *friend* was still the right word, after what had happened between Renee's son and her daughter.

The woman seated at the table tipped her head as she spoke to the man with her—a tilt that made Christina zip her jacket to ward off a sudden chill. She knew that mannerism, remembered it from all the way back in junior high school, when Renee went into puppy-dog-cute mode every time she flirted with a guy.

But it couldn't possibly be Renee, not here, and not flirting with *this* guy. The shaggy, dark-haired specimen looked easily ten years younger—early twenties, she thought. His handsome face visible in profile, he tucked a thick strand of shiny hair beneath one ear and flashed a wry smile, as if the woman he was with had just said something witty.

Christina stood rooted a few feet shy of the door. Despite the thumping in her chest, she did her best to tell herself she should go inside as planned.

As she hesitated, the young man looked around the shop before leaning down to pull a large manila envelope from a backpack sitting on the floor beside him. With a few words, he passed it to the woman, whose head moved, sending a warning jolt up Christina's spine.

Turn just a bit more my way. You have to. Because she was almost certain it was Renee, with that hair, that build—even the jacket she was wearing looked familiar. But Christina had spotted something even more unnerving: the way she quickly tucked away something the young man had slipped her beneath the level of the envelope. Something she pushed down into her pocket quickly, clearly meaning to keep it hidden from view.

Had the young man given her money? Or had it been drugs that passed between them, along with whatever was in the envelope she slid into her tote?

Have I been leaving my daughter with an addict, a woman I only thought I knew? Because Christina really didn't know her, did she? Not after fifteen years punctuated only by a few phone calls before she'd gotten too busy, and the time or two she'd run in to her old friend at the grocery store when Christina had been in town visiting her family. Even those occasions had felt uncomfortable, awkward—both of them seeming to realize how little their adult selves had in common, other than the past.

"Excuse me," a female voice said behind her, causing Christina to jump.

"Sorry, dear. I didn't mean to scare you," said a white-haired woman in a hot-pink ski cap with a pom-pom. Her nose was pink, too, from the early evening's chill. "But are you going in, or could I get past? My George is like a little boy, waiting by the door at home for me to come back with his treat."

In answer to the crinkling at the corner of the woman's kind eyes, Christina stepped aside. "Of course. I was just leaving."

"Are you—are you all right, miss?" the older woman ventured. "Forgive me for saying this, but you're very pale."

"I'm—I'll be—I'm fine," Christina lied, turning away and breaking into a run as she headed for the loaner. The suspicions twisting inside her made her feel as if she'd come down with a stomach virus.

Once in the SUV, she circled the block, checking side streets for the yellow Jeep. When she didn't spot it, she told herself that she'd been wrong. The day had been both long and grueling, that's all, causing her brain to assign meaning to a random interaction between a pair of strangers, one of them a woman whose hair color could've been bought at any drugstore.

But as she turned onto the state highway that would take her back to Seaside Creek, Christina wiped her eyes, reminding herself that hallucinations came in other than auditory forms.

That night in bed, she dreamed she was inside one of the painted, white rooms of the lighthouse living quarters, looking out through the salt-filmed window at the sea. Every fifteen seconds, the foghorn—though part of her knew that it had long ago gone silent—gave a mournful blast, and the steel-gray lightened to silver with each pulse of the light above.

Only this time, her father wasn't there, explaining how coast guard crews had manned this lonely station for years. Her mother, too, was nowhere nearby, and she couldn't find Annie anywhere.

Christina ran from empty room to empty room, calling their names with a child's desperation, though she sensed she was grown now. As she raced for the staircase that would lead her to the beacon, she paused at another of the windows.

Looking down into the water outside, she saw a woman floating facedown—long, strawberry-blonde hair spread out on the waves that lapped around her.

With Jacob still in the hospital, Renee wasn't happy about Harris leaving town first thing the next morning.

"I'm just heading up to Philly," he told her when she met him outside their son's room. "Call or text me if there's anything you need, and I can be back in an hour and a half."

"Philadelphia?" She frowned. "Why would you want to go there?"

"I don't," Harris told her truthfully, "but try to think about it this way. I'll have a better chance of covering all these insurance co-pays if I'm still employed."

He smiled, trying to make light of the comment. Except that his ex-wife didn't smile back.

"I guess you'd better go, then," she said. "Is Jacob—how is he this morning?"

Harris's smile widened. "He woke up asking for dino-pancakes. Whatever the heck those are."

"Just something I make with batter, blueberry eyes, and a little imagination." Her eyes shining, she added, "I can't wait to get him home to make him some again."

"I know," Harris said, wanting to reach out and offer her the hug she clearly needed. Despite the relief provided by her mom, who was sitting with Jacob as much as she could manage, and his own overnight stint, Renee looked as stressed and exhausted as she had the last time he'd seen her. Knowing that his touch would be unwelcome, he instead asked, "You hanging in there? Eating? Sleeping?"

"Trying. It's just—I kept waking up last night, thinking I was hearing him crying from a nightmare. I jumped out of bed and ran into his room to check on him two different times before I remembered he wasn't there."

"He'll be home soon. I'm sure of it."

Her mouth tightened, her eyes avoiding his.

"What, Renee? What is it?"

"It doesn't matter."

"It clearly does," he said.

"It's only—Mom got a letter from her community association. You know, it's supposed to be fifty-five and older to live there, with absolutely no kids under eighteen. They've given us thirty days to move out. Can they even do that?"

Harris nodded. "They're legally within their rights."

"That's what I was afraid of. And with me still laid off, there's no way I can even think of—"

"You need another loan?" he asked, knowing she wouldn't accept it if he called it a gift. He paid child support and plenty of it, but he understood it wouldn't be enough to keep her out of a dicey neighborhood like Creekbend. And he'd be damned if his son would grow up there, no matter what the cost.

She shook her head. "No. I'm going to fix this, Harris. I'm fixing it myself."

So he wouldn't have to deal with any jurisdictional niceties, he was driving his personal vehicle, a blue Charger. He pulled onto the Garden State Parkway, still wondering how Renee thought she was going to manage. After she'd been laid off, she'd talked about finding a new job within commuting distance, but as far as Harris knew, she hadn't had an interview since the new school year had started. She was hoping, she kept saying, that the strapped school district would get the federal grant it needed to rehire her. And after what had happened at The Kid Zone, he didn't see working for Christina Paxton as an option for her any longer.

He shelved the worry for another time and allowed his mind to wander to last night's conversation with Del Vecchio, who'd called from Baltimore after tracking down Christina's sort-of stepson, DJ Paxton. Del had learned that the med-school student's mother had taken leave from her bank job in Pittsburgh to care for her widowed mother as she lived out her final days in hospice. The nineteen-year-old sister had gone with her, in part to put some distance between her and her latest loser of a boyfriend.

After giving him the address—in a Philadelphia neighborhood just over the river from New Jersey—Del Vecchio had told him he'd head over first thing in the morning.

"Tell me about Doug Junior first," Harris said. "Did you get the idea he might've decided to take a road trip to Seaside Creek to harass his dad's second wife?"

"I don't see it," said Del Vecchio. "Vibe I get from this kid, Christina Paxton and his little half sister aren't even on his radar. Looks to me like he's frantically paddling, trying to stay afloat with his course work and dealing with his mother's meltdowns over the grandmother dying and his younger sister's boyfriend drama of the week."

Something in Del Vecchio's words, a note of dismissal in the younger cop's tone, had made Harris reel him back in so he could conduct the interview himself. Because to him, it sounded like Del had already ruled out the first wife as a suspect, judging her too overwhelmed by responsibility—or maybe just too middle-aged and female—to do something as nutty as carving an offensive word into her former husband's car.

But in Harris's experience, people who were pushed beyond their capacity to cope—whether they were struggling med-school students or stressed-out mothers sandwiched between the needs of their parents and children—were likely to do the damnedest things. Things like taking out their frustrations on another woman via a baby monitor and paint damage.

After crossing the Ben Franklin Bridge an hour later, Harris pulled up at the address his officer had given him in front of a tan-brick row house in the middle of the block in an older working-class neighborhood. Judging from the number of Flyers pennants, Italian flags, and Christmas lights still hanging in the windows, he suspected the tall and skinny attached homes were packed to the rafters with the kind of old guys who wore black socks with their sandals in the summer and unzipped parkas with white wife-beaters in the winter months. The old women would be hockey fans, too, the kind who asked their visiting children, *Are youse stayin' for dinna? I could take out a lasagna from the freezer, or we could maybe pick up cheesesteaks.*

Or maybe he'd spent too many years policing shoebies at the shore.

But regardless of the stereotypes, he knew one thing for certain: Doug Paxton's first wife, Evelyn, had come a long way since leaving this narrow street. When he'd looked up her home address in Pittsburgh, he'd seen that the divorcée was living in an attractive, brick two-story in a decidedly upscale East Side neighborhood. A quick check of the *Post-Gazette*'s online archives told him she'd remained active on the social scene, too—her fashionably thin, impeccably dressed figure photographed at galas benefiting special-needs kids.

Shutting the Charger's door behind him, Harris hit the alarm button and headed for the front door. As he started up the concrete steps, a brown-eyed woman whose smooth face belied her age opened the front door and stood watching through the glass storm door, her arms folded over her chest. Her sweater, boots, and leggings all looked expensive, but the stress in her eyes shone through her flawless makeup.

He spread out his badge wallet, letting her see his identification.

Opening the storm door, she said, "Wait. That's a New Jersey ID, isn't it?"

"Yes, ma'am. I'm Chief of Police Harris Bowers, Seaside Creek, New Jersey. Are you Evelyn Davis?" he asked, wanting to gauge her reaction to his use of her maiden name.

"It's Paxton." She flipped back her chic, highlighted hair, sounding more confused than irritated as she claimed her married name. Her face, however, barely moved at all, frozen in place by some cosmetic treatment. "Is this—is this about my daughter? Has she been—"

When she cut herself off, he cocked his head. "Go on. You were going to ask me something?"

She bit her lower lip, scraping off her lipstick. "Please come in. We're letting out the heat. My mother would—she was always scolding me about it."

She ushered him in past a stairway and then hurried him through a room containing an empty hospital bed—stripped of linens—a storage buffet, and a long table pushed to one side. On both the buffet top and the table, there were baskets containing prescription medication bottles of all sizes, along with various personal items, from lip balm and tissues to what looked like a well-worn Bible.

"I'm sorry to have to take you through here," she said. "This house's layout is—this is normally the dining room, but—but—" Pausing in one of a pair of doorways, she covered her mouth with a hand, her eyes filling with tears.

Reaching for a nearby box of tissues, he offered them to her. "I was sorry to hear about your mother's illness. Has she . . . ?"

She nodded, her eyes expressing her sorrow despite her weirdly still face. "Last night, yes. It was a blessing, really. Or so I keep telling myself."

"I'm sorry," he said, meaning it, because whatever grudge this woman might hold against Christina, losing a parent was never easy.

She nodded. "But there are so many things to be done. The medical-equipment people are already—they insisted on coming for the bed and her oxygen this morning. And I have to go—I have an appointment at the funeral home a little later. I need to choose her clothes and—I thought I was prepared for this. I thought—"

"Is someone with you?" he asked, remembering what Christina had told him about the pretty nineteen-year-old daughter. The one who couldn't be left on her own in Pittsburgh. "Is Ashley here?"

She blinked when he said the name. "Actually, I'm not—let me get her. Why don't you have a seat in here."

As she darted through a door leading into a small linoleum-floored kitchen, he headed where she'd indicated, into a dark, paneled living room with plush, green carpeting and a seventies-style sofa set that he imagined would be donated to charity any day now. He remained standing, checking his phone for messages, until she returned a short time later, a smile stretched too thin over her face. "I should've known. She was out cold on the pullout in the basement. She'll be up in a few minutes."

"But you weren't sure of it, were you?" he asked, feeling bad about pressing the woman on a day like this, but needing to get to the point quickly. "You thought she might've been out, and over on my side of the bridge, maybe? She been borrowing the car lately, maybe heading over to visit her stepmother?"

Evelyn Paxton stiffened. "Stepmother? What on earth? You don't mean that woman, do you? My husband's—"

"Your ex-husband's second wife, Christina."

"She's hardly their stepmother. She barely knows the children, probably wouldn't recognize them if she tripped over them by now. My husband almost always flew to Pittsburgh to make his visitations. I insisted on it, for our Ashley's sake. She doesn't handle change well. The divorce was a terrible blow to her."

Harris wondered whether that was true. Or whether the woman who'd never remarried, who continued to use her ex's name and had now twice referred to him as her husband was the person who had the issue with change. Deciding to throw a little more fuel on the fire, he added, "Maybe your daughter was hoping to get to know her little sister."

Bristling, Evelyn clenched her hands until the knuckles whitened. "*That child* is not my children's sister, and whatever that woman's saying to get you to harass my boy and distract him from his studies—he told me all about it last night when I called about his grandmother."

"I don't believe anyone's harassing your family, ma'am. We're just attempting to nail down a few details so we can put our investigation to bed."

Again, she stiffened, a glimmer of fear flashing over her face before she locked down her expression. "What kind of investigation?"

"Just a little vandalism." He tried out a dismissive snort, thinking she might be more forthcoming if she imagined he was just going through the motions. "Well, that and some harmless prank with the baby monitor in her kid's room."

"But you said *Chief* Bowers, didn't you? Your department sends the police chief for some minor little nothing?"

He dredged up a sheepish smile. "You haven't been to Seaside Creek, ma'am, have you? Little shore town, practically deserted this time of year, so we don't have much else to worry over—especially when some rich lady doctor starts squawking." Laying on another *aw shucks* shrug, he added, "You know how that type can be, ordering us around like we work for her."

She rolled her eyes. "I can well imagine. And probably crying over how my family *stuck it to her* after Doug's death, when she only had herself to blame."

"Herself to blame?" asked Harris, his sympathy for the woman shrinking by the second. "I'm not sure I follow you."

"If she'd watched his diet and kept up with his medical appointments the way I did, he could have lived a long life."

"So you're thinking—you're saying you believe Dr. Paxton's responsible for her husband's heart attack?"

"Not responsible. Of course not. But the woman *is* supposedly a doctor. And she knew his family history. If she hadn't stressed him by insisting on having a child of her own—"

"Who cut into your own son's and daughter's inheritance, I imagine?"

Her pointed chin rose and her nostrils flared, her body shaking as she spat out, "She was never the maternal type. Anyone could see it. She only had that child to give her a way to get her hooks into that money until the girl comes of age."

"So what about your kids? Do they handle their own inheritance? Or do you help with—"

"Of course they don't. None of the three will see a dime until they're thirty, according to my husband's will."

"Working in a trust department, I guess you'd know a lot more than I would about such matters." Such as how to work things so she'd earn a sizable chunk of change each year she spent managing what he suspected would be millions.

"So you're implying, what? That I would indulge in some sort of low-rent harassment to get back at a woman I haven't spared a thought to in months? Because it's *over*. She's already signed the paperwork, and the estate will settle in a few weeks. She gave in."

"Gave in to your demands, you mean?" Harris asked, wondering whether it was possible that the damage to the Mercedes and the voice on the monitor weren't the first acts of intimidation that had been directed toward Christina. *But why wouldn't she admit it, if there've been previous incidents? Is she that afraid?*

"She folded because she *knows*," Evelyn said, whatever control she'd managed crashing down around her as tears streamed down her frozen face. "She absolutely knows that *I* should've been the one by his side until the end. And he should've been right here with me now, seeing me through last night, through all of this, the way I saw him through when first his mother and then his dad—when they—"

"Mom?" came a soft voice from behind him. "Are you all right?"

Turning, Harris saw a young woman hurrying toward them, a bare knee poking through a pair of artfully—expensively—worn jeans that fit her like a glove. Unlike her mother, she looked as if she'd just awakened, her tousled dark-brown hair highlighted with hot-pink and electric-blue streaks, and her wide-set eyes devoid of makeup. Despite the rumpled look, with one naked shoulder jutting from the oversize sweatshirt she wore, the combination of a fresh face and nubile body confirmed Christina's claim that her mom had to beat back the boys with a stick just to get her through high school. Especially if the girl's learning problems made her especially vulnerable to such attention.

While her mother dropped, weeping, to the sofa, he turned his attention to the young woman now standing beside her, flashing his badge briefly. "Your mother was just worried. Worried about you. I gather you went out last night."

"Aw, yeah. I—" Ashley said, her attention flitting between Harris and her sobbing mother. Stretching out her hand, she rubbed the older woman's back, her bright-blue nails chipped. "I didn't mean to scare her. I just borrowed Mom's car, like I do all the time—"

"To meet up with yet another horrible boy, I imagine," her mother cut in, her voice an angry shriek, "while I was left here to deal with all this." She flung a gesture in the direction of the room containing the empty hospital bed.

"I was seeing *my friends* from the coffee place, that's all," Ashley corrected her, with an air of patience suggesting she routinely dealt with such overwrought outbursts. So routinely that she'd learned not to fuel the fire by getting emotional herself.

Jerking away from her daughter's hand, Evelyn hunched forward to hide her face as she wept.

"I had to. It was—last night was so intense, you know?" Lowering her voice to a whisper, Ashley confided to Harris, "I've never seen anybody dead like that. Especially my own grandma."

He reminded himself that Christina had mentioned the girl having learning issues, though to him, Ashley sounded no different from any of a thousand teenagers he'd dealt with. "So who was it you went to see?" he asked.

"Listen," she said, "I'm sorry if my mom called to report me missing. She kind of overreacts sometimes, especially when she's upset. But if she'd bothered to check just down the street"—Ashley hooked a thumb in that general direction—"or look down in the basement, she'd have seen that I've been back since, gosh, I guess it would've been around twelve thirty."

"Twelve thirty?" he repeated, not correcting the girl's misapprehension about the purpose of his visit.

She shrugged. "Okay, maybe more like two. There's this twenty-four-hour Dunkins where we all go after our regular Starbucks closes."

That must be one caffeinated bunch, he thought, but he'd rather see nineteen-year-olds hanging around cafés than sneaking into bars like he had around that age. "So you've made some new friends, just since you've been in Philadelphia?"

"Sure," she told him. "It's—I know this hospice stuff might sound, like, superdramatic. But a lot of it involves waiting around while someone else makes gross smells and noises in her sleep. And it took *forever*."

Her mother's head jerked up, her red-rimmed eyes wounded. "I'm sorry if my mother's *dying* inconvenienced you."

"Mom, I didn't mean it like that. Sorry," the girl said, but it was too late. Her mother blasted to her feet and rushed out of the room.

Ashley sighed. "Sorry about that. She's not normally so—you know."

"Except about your father's widow, you mean?"

Ashley stilled, her pretty face freezing in a way that looked more like her mother's. "Christina?" she said. "Wait—I thought you were here because my mom reported me gone."

"You might not've noticed on my ID, but I'm from Seaside Creek, New Jersey. I'm the chief of police there."

She shook her head. "Wait. That's where—Christina's living there now, isn't she? But why would she—"

"There's been some harassment. Vandalism, stuff like that. We're looking to see if there could be some connection to—"

"You aren't thinking that my *mom* would—oh my God. Don't be ridiculous. She might sue somebody, but she'd never stoop to anything illegal."

"But it is true, isn't it, that your mother doesn't like Christina?"

"Well, yeah. But it's not like she's ever spent more than five minutes with her, face-to-face—and she hasn't mentioned her in, like, months."

"But she can't accept it, can she," he asked, "that your father was able to move on when she couldn't? That he's really gone now, and she'll never get another chance to make things right with him?"

Ashley shrugged. "Everybody has their weak points, I guess. Maybe my mom's is holding too tight on to the people that she loves."

"That could be," Harris said, thinking it was possible that the opposite might be true. That Evelyn Davis Paxton's greatest issue might be holding too firmly not to love, but to hate . . . hate for the woman who'd replaced her . . . the woman she blamed for her ex-husband's death.

CHAPTER TEN

Initially, he'd planned to wrap the knife in burlap and dump it off one of the half dozen or so bridges around the community. Maybe some warm day next summer, the thing would come up in a crab trap, but by then it would be so eaten up with rust from the briny water, no one would think a thing about it.

Then it came to him that that was stupid. It wasn't like a gun, where some cop could use ballistics to match it to the carvings he'd done. Maybe if he'd jammed it into the bitch's back instead, then they'd match the blade's length to the depth of the wound during the autopsy, or they'd find some tiny trace of blood he'd missed, no matter how well he thought he'd cleaned it.

The longer he considered it, the more he convinced himself that the risk of being spotted ditching the knife was too great. Besides, he'd really come to like the sturdy weapon, the way the haft felt when he wrapped his hand around it.

What he liked even better, though, was the thrill that shot straight to his groin every time he returned to the fantasy of sheathing that blade inside warm flesh. Of clapping his free hand over her mouth and plunging the weapon deep inside her, again and again.

Though the original plan had been simply to scare her, to teach the bitch a lesson, wouldn't getting rid of her solve so many problems?

Again he pictured himself taking her, his cock painfully hard as he imagined ramming the knife in to the hilt. Like a cold steel fucking, only this kind, with a little care, would leave no DNA behind.

Eager to ensure it, he pulled on his gloves—the heavy, cut-resistant pair he'd worn in her garage, since, careful as he was, there was always a chance he could nick himself and leave his blood for the cops to find.

As dusk deepened, his heart pounded with mounting anticipation. Pulling up the black hood of the sweatshirt he wore beneath his gray ski jacket, he slumped down behind the wheel, only a row away from the silver vehicle—another Mercedes—that he'd watched her park this morning.

There was nothing more to do now but wait. Wait and pray that she would head out across the lot alone.

It was dark by the time Christina hurried across the half-empty employee parking lot as she left work Monday evening. Dark and swiftly getting darker, thanks to the heavy clouds bearing down on them. Already the temperature was dropping. Her lungs ached with each indrawn breath, and her exhalations emerged in white plumes.

She slipped on a patch of ice and gasped as she caught herself barely in time to keep from falling. But it was the swift approach of footsteps from behind that had her whipping around, her entire body tensing. Seeing the petite Renee approaching, Christina forced herself to remain where she stood, close to a security light, rather than running for her loaner vehicle.

By the time Renee drew near enough for Christina to make out the angry furrow beneath her brows, it was too late to make a break for it. Too late to do anything but try to defuse the explosion Christina felt coming.

"Sorry I didn't make it back upstairs," she said, guilt needling her with the memory of the three texts she'd received asking her to stop by Jacob's room in Pediatrics, where he'd been moved once his condition was upgraded. "I did pop in before my shift started. Jacob was sleeping, though, and you weren't—"

"I'd just stepped out for a few minutes. But you knew that," Renee said, her hair frizzy and her ski jacket hanging open. Devoid of makeup, she was paler than ever, her light freckling standing out, and her eyes shadowed by fatigue. "You've been deliberately avoiding me. If I hadn't been watching out the window—"

"I'm not avoiding you," Christina lied. "I just—I need to stop by my mom's place before this storm hits, make sure everything's battened down. And Annie texted to say she has dinner in the oven."

Renee stared a hole in her, shutting down the excuses. Riding a breath of icy wind, the first few flurries spiraled down between them.

"I did talk to Dr. Marshall," Christina said. "I was so relieved when she said Jacob's completely conscious and responsive, and she expects a full recovery. That's amazing news."

Renee nodded, her eyes gleaming. "We're hoping he'll come home tomorrow. And I—I'm praying everything can just go back to normal, and he'll be playing with Lilly again before we know it. He's been asking for her."

"She's been wanting him, too, and believe me, I've been praying for him. You have no idea how hard. But I have to tell you, I have Annie watching Lilly for me now—"

"Hear me out, please." Renee shoved away a thick lock that the wind had blown across her face. "All I wanted was to tell you in person that I—I didn't mean what I said to Lilly."

"And I'm very sorry for what she did, everything that contributed to Jacob's fall. I've tried to talk to her about it, but I'm not sure she gets the concept."

"I know she doesn't understand," Renee conceded, her flushing face a reminder of how difficult it had always been for her to admit that she'd been wrong. "And I was—it was my emotions talking. I *love* your daughter. You must know that."

"It's been a stressful time. I can't imagine how terrified you must have been. There's no need to explain," Christina said, but she couldn't stop thinking of her daughter, shaking so hard before her bladder had let loose.

"There is," Renee insisted as more flurries alighted on her hair and jacket, "to you and especially to Lilly. I just want to take it all back, make it like none of this ever happened."

"I understand. I do." It wasn't as if Christina didn't have regrets of her own, hadn't said things that no apology could ever entirely erase. But Renee hadn't apologized exactly, had she? Instead, she'd only explained why she'd acted the way she had, while Christina had been the one to say how sorry she was. It reminded her sharply of junior high school, when her own lack of confidence had allowed her friend to call the shots.

"Is she—is Lilly all right?" Renee asked.

Christina nodded, telling herself that slights she'd suffered at thirteen didn't matter; only the present mattered. And her child. "She's happy enough. Or at least distracted, with Annie turning herself inside out to entertain her."

But last night, her daughter had come to her crying at about two a.m., climbing into Christina's bed claiming she was scared the bad lady would come smash her head in, too. Which was why she couldn't back down, no matter how much the teenager inside her wished to.

"Harris—Harris brought the dinosaur. And Lilly's stuffed pony, too. That was so sweet of her."

"Jacob's been like a brother to her." Christina's throat tightened at the thought of how close the two had become in the short time since she'd brought Lilly home to Seaside Creek.

"Then don't keep her away from him. Or me. I want to watch her for you again. I want—listen, Christina," Renee said, closing her eyes as she forced out the admission, "the truth is, it's been hard for me to find work. Harris pays support, of course, but decent child care's so expensive, if you can even get a slot, and with my mom still working . . . . This job, with you and Lilly—it's been a godsend. I can bring him along and still—"

Christina forced herself to interrupt. "I think you need to concentrate on Jacob's health for the time being. There'll be additional appointments, follow-ups for tests, and maybe therapy to work on any lingering deficits while the injury's still fresh—"

"I'm so much more reliable than Annie." The pleading tone had given way to something harder. Something Christina remembered from other times when her friend hadn't gotten her way. "She'll just leave you in the lurch when you need her most, and we both know it."

"My sister's living with us. We're working around her class schedule at the college."

"College, my ass. She's had the exact same advantages you did—and a heck of a lot more chances—but everybody knows she's a career barmaid who hangs out with sleazebags and slackers."

Christina stiffened, ignoring the biting cold and the snowflakes that were now coming down in earnest. Snowflakes so like the ones that had sifted through the darkness as she'd held her infant sister in her arms.

"You and I have been friends for a lot of years," Christina said, understanding that it had cost Renee—cost her dearly—to admit how badly she needed the job, "and I hope we can be friends still. As long as you don't imagine that friendship gives you permission to talk trash about my family."

A few spaces beyond them in the lot, she heard the sound of an engine turning over. Considering the building rage on Renee's face, the way she was glaring, Christina felt grateful that there was a witness nearby.

At least until Renee spoke. "You used to think—you were grateful when I took you under my wing. Grateful I would have a little dweeb like you for a friend. But now you believe you're better than me, don't you," she demanded, her voice rising, "with your fancy car and your big house?"

"My mom's *client's* house. My *husband's* car," Christina reflexively corrected before remembering the ugly word that had been carved into the glossy black paint. Ugliness directed at her and her alone.

"Well, it's all yours now, right? Maybe not the house, but everybody knows it *could* be. And we're all supposed to kiss your ass and call you *Dr.* Paxton."

"I've never once asked you to call me that, Renee. You know that."

"No, but you might as well, while you're treating me like the help. Somebody you can dismiss on a whim."

"Oh, come on." Christina's annoyance ratcheted higher. Whatever the local rumor mill was saying, she had neither the money nor the inclination to buy some beachfront showplace. Plus, she was freezing standing out here, her gloveless fingers tingling. "I've told you at least a dozen times how grateful I've been to find someone I know and trust with Lilly." She'd paid Renee generously as well. Possibly excessively, in the hope of ensuring a stable child-care situation for a daughter who'd experienced far too many changes lately.

"But you don't trust me anymore." Renee's chin rose with the accusation.

"I don't. I can't," Christina admitted, "because I've seen firsthand—on more than one occasion—that you have . . . you have anger issues."

"Anger issues? *Really?*" Renee's sarcasm sliced the frigid air like a hot blade. "I can't imagine why."

Christina shook her head, anxiety a burning coal in her throat. Because she didn't want to think what she was thinking, to imagine that her old friend, out of jealousy or resentment or heaven only knew what, could have anything to do with the vandalism—or the voice Christina had heard. *She can't know about my birth mother, can she?* Or could the rumor mill have somehow gotten hold of the whole horrific story? Despite their adoptive parents' repeated warnings that the real details were best kept to themselves, had Annie told some loose-lipped friend that there was far more to their adoption than her mom and dad's vague assertions that they'd privately arranged to take in the daughters of a distant cousin who'd died?

Forcing the suspicion from her mind, Christina said, "I'm sorry for you, Renee. Sorry about you and Harris, sorry about your job, and deeply, deeply sorry that Jacob was hurt. But right now, I have my own issues to deal with. There's no way I can handle yours, too. And no way I'll risk my child's well-being, not for you or anyone."

"This isn't right. You can't just—"

"If you'd like," Christina said, her voice softening as she saw the tears gleaming on her friend's cheek, "I can get you a referral. There's a county program. They have counselors at no charge, to help with life transitions."

Vibrating with outrage, Renee shrieked, "You think I need a shrink now? You think—"

"I've considered seeing someone myself. I just thought you might—"

Renee's hard stare shut her down.

Realizing she was only making things worse, Christina pulled a key out of her coat pocket and clicked the Mercedes's fob. A short distance away, the silver SUV's lights flashed as the alarm system chirped its recognition.

"Good night, Renee," she said, not knowing how else to end the conversation. She started walking toward the rental, forcing herself not to break into a run.

And stumbling, her heart freezing with her onetime friend's parting shot.

"You know what, Christina? You're not only freaking crazy, you really are a cunt."

CHAPTER ELEVEN

With the dark sea churning at his back and wind-whipped snowflakes swirling all around him, Harris knocked at the blue door of the Victorian on Cape Street. No one answered, so he tried again, assuming from the dented red Kia parked out front that there was definitely someone at home. Someone in need of new tires and an up-to-date inspection sticker. But he wasn't here to hassle Christina's sister about the condition of her hatchback.

"Come on, Annie. Answer," he muttered.

Moments later, he heard the dead bolt disengage, and she peeked through a narrow gap, with Max's big, tan head poking out a couple of feet below hers. The moment he set eyes on Harris, the greyhound grinned up at him as if he were a long-lost friend, his shoulders pushing the door wider.

"That's some watchdog you've got there."

"Christina's running a little late," Annie told him, "but you can come in and wait if you'd like. Well, if you don't mind hanging with one of Lilly's kid flicks. I've just finished bathing her, and we're winding down for—"

"Actually, I came to see you," he said, hoping he could be in and out before her sister showed up.

"Me?" Annie visibly tensed. "Listen, if this is about those parking tickets, I'll be in to settle up as soon as—"

"I'd rather you use the money making sure that car of yours doesn't go skating off the road," he said. "But that's not why I'm here, either."

"Um, sure." She motioned for him to come inside. Fidgeting a little, she rolled down the sleeves of the form-fitting Henley shirt she wore over dark leggings.

Enveloped by the warmth and the rich, beefy aroma of roasting meat, he spotted Lilly sprawled on the sectional, wearing fuzzy pink pajamas and clutching a threadbare blanket as she stared at one of Jacob's favorite movies. The one where cars spoke in funny voices that Harris sometimes imitated just to crack the kid up.

A wave of longing hit him, an ache to hang out with his own son, building pillow forts at his place while the storm did its thing outside.

Maybe it showed on his face, for Annie quickly asked, "How's Jacob?"

"Bouncing back like—he's great." His throat tightened, and he couldn't go on. Couldn't describe the raw fear, the desperate prayers, the relief that had roared through him when his kid had started chattering away this afternoon as if nothing had happened. "You'll tell Lilly for me later?"

"That's fantastic news," Annie said, "and sure I'll tell her. Hey, do you mind?" She hooked a thumb in the direction of the kitchen. "I want to pop these rolls in the oven to go with dinner."

Nodding, he followed her, the greyhound at his heels. "Whatever you're making smells fantastic." Since Renee had left the house they'd shared—a house purchased and renovated by enthusiastic volunteers when he'd first come home to recover—there'd been precious little in the way of cooking, unless you counted frozen pizzas.

"Just a pot roast. Seemed like the weather for it," she said, hesitating a moment before adding, "There's plenty, if you'd like to stay. Lilly had her dinner earlier."

"Thanks, but I'm heading back to the hospital to give Renee and her mom a break for the evening." Absently, he stroked Max's sleek head. "Nurses are great up there, but we don't like to leave the little guy alone."

"You're a good dad," Annie assured him.

Not good enough, not soon enough, he thought. But this was no confessional, and no damn shrink's couch, either, so he claimed a stool by the counter and waited for Annie to slide a tray of doughy, pale globs into the lower unit of the double oven.

When she turned back toward him, he got down to business. "Since I was here a couple days ago, I've been wondering about this *Kaydee* business—what Lilly said the other day."

Annie picked up a kitchen towel and wiped her hands repeatedly, though as far as Harris could see, they were neither damp nor dirty. "My sister—don't you remember what she said about the movie?"

He nodded. "But listen," he said. "Before I was a cop, I was an MP."

"Yeah, sure." She shook her head impatiently. Everyone in town had heard the story. Undoubtedly, it had been chewed over plenty in the bar where she worked each summer—how a guy from a dicey family like his had ended up the so-called hero who headed their police force.

"My point is," he added as the dog wandered toward the family room, "I've spent half my life being lied to. So I know bullshi—BS—when I hear it."

He glanced toward Lilly to assure himself he hadn't corrupted any more innocent ears, but she was clearly in the thrall of the characters rolling, roaring, and honking their way around the big screen.

When he looked back, Annie was glaring at him across the counter. "So somebody trashes my sister's car and cuts the phone line, and the best you can do is make her out to be a liar? Or do you figure she's a criminal, too?"

"People avoid the truth for a lot of reasons," he said carefully, "not all of them against the law. What I'm trying to figure out is why somebody might want to harass her, maybe hurt her next time. Have you thought of that?"

Fussing with her sleeves again, Annie darted a glance toward Lilly. The greyhound stepped up onto the cushion beside the clearly sleepy toddler, settling his long body carefully against hers.

"Your niece could be at risk, too," Harris continued, sensing that Annie was weakening. "And maybe you as well, since you're here at the house, too."

"I—I shouldn't talk about it. Not without discussing it first with Christina."

"Then maybe we ought to have a different conversation," he said. "Down at the station, as soon as Christina gets home. About the bench warrant I found on you, for not showing up for your last court date—"

"For a couple of *parking* tickets?" Annie asked, her eyes shooting wide with disbelief. "You can't—you wouldn't—come on, Harris. This is stupid."

"It sure is," he agreed, knowing it would be more paperwork than it was worth and stir up a whole lot of hard feelings. Plus, he'd never been one of those cops who'd relished throwing his weight around, not with someone as inherently harmless as he judged Christina's sister to be. "But you don't have to be. C'mon, Annie. Work with me. Because you and I both know what happened here the other night was more than simple vandalism. It's personal. I know it."

It frustrated him no end, but he'd found no mention online or in any of the law-enforcement databases he had access to of any *Katie* in association with Christina Wallace Paxton. He'd tried various spellings, a dozen or more increasingly far-fetched permutations, and he couldn't come up with one damn thing.

Before leaving Philadelphia, he'd asked Ashley Paxton about it, but the nineteen-year-old, who didn't seem to have lying in her makeup, had said the name meant nothing to her. She'd also made it clear that despite her mother's issues, she personally remembered Christina as a *supernice person, even if she did seem a little young for Dad.*

Christina's hospital coworkers, whom he'd discreetly questioned earlier, had been no more helpful. Though she'd been working in the ER only a little over a month, Christina appeared to be both well liked and respected by everyone he'd talked to. The head of the department had told him she was doing amazingly well, considering her circumstances.

Circumstances? Harris had pressed, after which the man had murmured something about her recent loss and excused himself to get back to his patient.

"Tell me about this *Katie*, Annie," he pressed, seeing how her eyes were filling, their red rims near to overflowing. She was ready to spill, he knew—unless Christina showed up and shut things down. "Who the hell's this *Kaydee-Mommy*, and how did she *get dead*?"

"Okay, you win," Annie said, her shoulders slumping. "Only you can't tell my sister. She'd kill me if she knew."

"You've hardly touched your dinner," Annie said as she and Christina sat together at the kitchen table that evening.

Christina had claimed the spot from which she could see Lilly dozing on the sectional, both toddler and greyhound half-asleep in front of a video turned down to low volume. Not far beyond them, the gas fireplace was burning, its flickering glow a contrast with the light snow sifting past the window.

"Tell me the truth," Annie said, her fork shaking a little as she laid it down. "Is the roast dry?"

"Are you cold?" Christina asked, her gazing settling on her sister's hand.

"Cold? No. Just a little worried. I don't have a lot of practice making dinners like this."

"Well, it's all delicious," Christina rushed to assure her. "The veggies came out great, too, just the way Mom makes them." Who would have guessed her sister would be the one, of the two of them, to learn to cook?

"And you know this, how?" Annie asked, folding her arms. "Because I swear I haven't seen more than two bites actually make it to your mouth."

Christina grimaced and set down the glass of red wine her sister had poured for her as she'd recounted what had happened in the parking lot after work. Christina had barely touched it, either, her stomach as unsettled as her nerves. "It's not the food. It's just—Renee and I have been friends since junior high school, and now—"

"You've been gone a long time." Annie's blue eyes were sympathetic. "People change. In this case, you."

"What do you mean, me?" Christina felt the sting of indignation. "I've never for one second snubbed her. You know I'm not like that."

"I didn't mean it that way. I mean . . . well, to tell you the truth, Renee's always been kind of a—you know, a *bitch*." With a cautious glance in Lilly's direction, Annie whispered the last word before offering an apologetic grimace. "I'm sorry, but your so-called friend is only happy when she's ordering everyone around and passing off her opinions like they're some kind of hot gospel."

Christina remembered how desperately Annie, three years younger and a little clingy at the time, had wanted to hang out with them. But Renee had been ruthlessly adamant: junior high girls couldn't be seen with elementary school *babies*.

"You're right," Christina admitted. "She could be like that, but she was fun, too. And when I hung out with her, I felt . . . she always knew which activities we should be in, what I should wear, how not to be a giant geek."

Annie waved a hand. "News flash, Christina. Anybody who spends as much time as you do blabbing about arterial bleeds and tropically acquired parasites is still a giant geek."

Christina snatched a roll from the basket and lobbed it at her sister's head. When Annie neatly ducked it, Max was off the sofa in a flash, gobbling the missile in a burst of speed that did credit to his racing heritage.

Christina only hoped she wouldn't end up mopping up more dog puke later.

"Anyway," Annie continued, "back then, you were, like, under Renee's *spell* or something. She had to go *everywhere* with us, even on that one trip to the lighthouse." Judging from her sour expression, Annie still resented having been forced to share that special occasion with the girl who'd driven herself like a wedge between them.

"I only wanted to fit in for once, and Renee seemed to know how."

"And look how well that's worked out for her," Annie said with a shake of her golden head and a snort that reminded Christina how, in tiny Seaside Creek, all the year-round locals knew one another's business. "Honestly, it's a wonder she and Harris lasted as long as they did before he finally—"

"There's never an excuse for cheating." Christina heard the sharpness in her own voice, despite the sympathy she felt whenever she remembered how affected he had clearly been by his son's injury. Or maybe she was compensating for the guilt chewing its way through her whenever she remembered how she'd held on to Harris's hand after he'd helped her step up onto the jetty . . . and the flush of pleasure that had whispered over her skin like a ghost of that lost summer.

She swallowed hard, reminded that it was Doug's touch she should be missing, not the man who'd betrayed her. To say nothing of how Harris had hurt her friend. Or ex-friend. But with her brain spinning, the distinction hardly mattered.

"You're right," said Annie. "There's not, but that's not—wait a minute. I thought you had a thing for Harris."

"What? How could you—"

"A long time ago, I saw you two together. It was on the boardwalk."

Christina stared. "You were—you were *spying* on us?"

"Please." Annie waved off the accusation. "I was hanging out with my own friends, that's all. But it's not exactly like you were subtle about it, sucking face outside the Kohr Brothers stand like you meant to melt the frozen custard."

Cheeks burning, Christina wished she could slide beneath the table. Because if Annie knew, who else might? "So why didn't you *say* something? Warn me that he'd only end up—"

Annie laughed. "Are you kidding? I figured he was just what you needed, a hot fling you could forget when you set off for college. My gosh, I don't think you ever even went out on a date all the way through high school."

Her face on fire by now, Christina grimaced, wishing she could have been so free and easy about it all. Maybe then she could've have been the one to do the hurting instead of getting hurt.

"Well, thanks for not saying anything to Mom and Dad about it," she said. "Dad would've lost his mind." Their adoptive father, who'd done everything he could to help direct her thoughts toward higher education, had insisted the road to failure was lined with bad choices, bad boys foremost among them. And Creekside boys would no doubt have merited a category all their own.

"Do I look like some kind of narc?" Pushing back her chair, Annie grabbed the platter to put away the leftovers. "Especially with all the stuff you had on me."

True enough. Unable to compete with her older sister academically and all too conscious of their parents' disappointment, Annie had started sneaking out at night at a young age.

"It doesn't really matter," Christina told her. "It was all such a long time ago." Noticing her sister's plate, she asked, "You weren't hungry, either?"

"Not really," Annie said absently before changing the subject. "Renee doesn't know, does she? You know, that you and Harris were together back then?"

Christina got up and scraped her nearly full plate into the sink disposal, remembering that Renee had been away that summer visiting family in Maine. "I can't imagine she does. Or something tells me she wouldn't have missed the chance to throw it in my face."

From the kitchen, she heard her sister's ringtone. After detaching the phone from the charger where she'd had it plugged in, Annie grinned and answered, "Hey there, gorgeous!"

Had to be Kym or Haley, or another of her sister's fun-loving but flaky friends. Or it could be one of the good-time guys they all hung out with, though occasionally two of them would pair off and date for a while, or even move in together. But their romances, like Annie's winter temp jobs, tended to be as short-lived as they were fluid.

After Christina waved off her help with the dishes, Annie wandered into the book-lined study and closed the door behind her to continue her conversation.

As Christina washed up, she wondered whether she should tell Harris what had happened between her and his ex-wife. Renee had known about the word carved onto the car, had been there when it was discreetly covered with a tarp and loaded onto a flatbed by two men from the dealership. She knew how it had upset Christina, had commiserated with her, yet the hatred in her eyes when she'd thrown it back in Christina's face had been undeniable. And frightening. Yet running to Renee's ex-husband, possibly causing her more problems, still somehow felt disloyal.

Christina's mind wandered to what she'd seen—or thought she had—in Bridgeport at the Sweet Shop. She thought about that furtive exchange, fear forking through her like summer lightning.

What if she hadn't imagined it? If Renee was part of some conspiracy meant to—*impossible.* Christina couldn't allow stress to give way to paranoia.

"Sorry to duck out on the cleanup," Annie said as she returned, "but I have to head out for a while. Kym's picked up some stomach bug and needs me to finish out her shift over at the Shell Pile."

"She's probably got food poisoning if she's been eating off that dive's bar menu." Though Christina knew her sister worked the club during the tourist season, she'd had no idea how rough the place was before she began stitching up participants in the almost weekly closing-time brawls . . . and treating more than one recent case of explosive digestive issues.

"Yeah, well," Annie said with an offhand shrug. "She's already told Larry I'll be pinch-hitting for her."

"But what about the weather? It's supposed to be getting worse."

"It'll be fine," Annie said, her stock answer to every practical consideration. "I should be home a little after midnight. Larry says he's closing then, or maybe earlier if it's really slow."

"I don't like it, Annie. That car of yours . . ." A mental picture formed of her sister's hatchback careening off the road and sinking into the marshy creek on the way to the little bar.

Her sister gave her a one-armed hug and kissed her on the cheek. "Don't wait up for me."

Christina felt a pang of disappointment. After the argument with Renee, she didn't want to be alone. But Annie's eyes were bright, and she was bouncing on the balls of her feet, a reminder that as beautiful a home as the Victorian was, her lively sister would find it a prison if she were forced to stay cooped up for days on end. Christina thought about Renee insisting, *She'll just leave you in the lurch when you need her most, and we both know it.*

Maybe some time flirting with the Shell Pile's shady clientele would keep her sister content. Still, the image of Annie's car sinking into freezing water had Christina thinking of the crushing moment she'd been informed that a body had been pulled from the lake where Doug's car had been found parked.

"Take the Mercedes," she blurted out, hurrying toward the purse she'd dropped onto the counter when she'd arrived home. "It's got all-wheel drive and heaven knows how many airbags."

"And heated seats, too, I'll bet," Annie said happily. "Are you sure?"

Not really, thought Christina, knowing that if the loaner vehicle were damaged with her sister behind the wheel, she'd end up paying for any repairs out of pocket. But she'd rather take a chance on that than sit around all evening mentally replaying the most hellish ordeal of her life.

"I'm positive," she said, shoving the key into her sister's hand. "Just be careful with it. And no drinking, or you call me."

"No drinking when I tend bar," Annie vowed, raising her right hand as if she were swearing on a stack of Bibles. "Too many empty calories, for one thing."

Christina nodded. "That's great," she said, "but if you slip, no judgment. Promise. Just let me know so there won't be any trouble."

Annie stared at her a moment, a spasm of unreadable emotion passing over her face. "I—you're too good to me, Christina. Way too good."

Frowning in confusion, Christina shook her head. "Is there something wrong?"

"Of course not. It's just, Mom's been on my back so much lately, she's had me feeling like nothing but a loser. For you to trust me, to let me help you out—it makes me feel . . ."

"I love you, Annie, and right now, I swear, I don't know what I'd do without you." Maybe this was what her sister had needed all along. Not to be carried for life, like the helpless infant she'd once been, but to be trusted to do some of her own heavy lifting.

A few minutes later, she was gone, leaving Christina to turn on the outdoor lights for her, along with the alarm system, which had been repaired with the phone line the day before. After shutting off the fireplace and TV, she scooped up Lilly and took her upstairs.

"Story, Mommy?" her daughter asked sleepily.

After some negotiation involving the brushing of teeth and the successful completion of her business with the potty, Christina happily complied, grateful when Lilly fell asleep again by the end of *Goodnight, Moon*. Switching the light off, Christina gave her daughter one last kiss before heading to her own room to dive in to a novel one of the lab techs had recommended. But with her brain rehashing every moment of this evening's showdown with Renee, Christina couldn't focus on the story, and she was tired, anyway, from a long day on her feet.

Giving up on the book, she shut off the bedside lamp and stroked Max, who'd turned up his nose at his own bed and claimed the spot beside her. As she lay watching the snow blow past the window, the security lights reflected off the white streaks passing before a sea of endless darkness. Though the Victorian was well insulated, the low moan of the wind's voice reached her, along with the pounding of the waves against the shore. There were sounds inside the house, too, creaks of complaint from the 140-year-old timbers, the hiss and rumble of the heating system, and a gurgle from the plumbing.

Somehow, all these elements wove themselves into something soothing and familiar, and she found herself drifting on a raft of warmth, dreaming of sun-soaked sand and the warm lap of gentle waters. Dreaming of looking up into a hazel gaze.

Christina had no idea how long she'd been sleeping when some new sound—could that be a thunderclap, with the snow?—startled her awake. Shivering with cold, she reached to pull up her missing comforter, silently cursing the thieving greyhound, who must have pawed it away to make a cozy nest.

But the big dog had left the bed, she realized, and when she looked up, she saw the window standing open, the snowflakes blowing in . . .

And a human figure silhouetted by the outside lights. A man-size presence, real and solid, standing in her room.

"Leave now," it told her firmly, in a voice she knew too well.

CHAPTER TWELVE

In a darkened alley behind Cape Street, Officer Frank Fiorelli sat in the department's only unmarked vehicle. With its peeling gray paint, drooping headliner, and wheezing carburetor, the geriatric sedan wasn't about to run down any perpetrators, unless they were on foot. But when it came to powers of invisibility for stakeouts, Old Reliable was tough to beat, and the heater was fan-fucking-tastic, allowing him to rest his ass in comfort as a cold wind off the nearby water misted the air with icy droplets.

Glancing down at his phone, Frank grinned, seeing he had enough of an Internet connection to check his e-mails and maybe later surf some porno where he wouldn't have to worry about the little woman popping in at the wrong moment and deflating the soufflé. All while on the clock and following orders, as long as he looked up now and then to check things out—especially the backyard of the Victorian a couple of houses down.

Not that he expected to see a thing. Despite his earlier suspicions that he'd stumbled onto a plot to intimidate the hot doc out of her dead husband's money, it seemed the case had been settled in such a manner that the plaintiffs would have nothing to gain—and a shitload to lose—if they were caught hassling the not-so-merry widow.

Plus, he was certain he'd put a stop to the rash of vandalism last night. If the culprits—a bunch of teenage stoners so freaking stupid it was a wonder one of them had thought of wearing latex gloves—didn't want a boot up the ass and a brass-plated *Go to Jail* card, they'd find some other way to get their kicks. Maybe join a bowling league or something that wouldn't trash their futures and cost their parents more in legal fees than any of them were worth.

As the wind sent swirls of snowflakes spiraling between the mostly empty houses, Frank sat back, imagining his name on the front page of the paper. There'd be a photo, too, of Chief Bowers giving him a commendation for ending the crime spree the chief himself had been powerless to stop. Privately, Bowers would finally admit that, just as Frank's councilman brother-in-law was always saying, Frank was the one who ought to be chief, the one who'd put in the years and sweat to merit the position.

But those fantasies, Frank knew, were never going to happen. If he were dumb enough to claim credit for breaking this case, his reward, he knew, would be his own swift dismissal. Plus, the dumb punks he'd spared would end up facing charges, including the one kid he gave a damn about.

Shifting in his seat, he took out his lunch—not the rabbit-food combo his wife had shoved into his hands before he'd left the house, reminding him of what the doc had said about his expanding waistline, but the giant Italian hoagie he'd picked up from his cousin's deli before closing because, well, he was a Fiorelli, and Fiorellis didn't run on carrot sticks and fucking hummus.

He was halfway through the sandwich, the delicious prosciutto, hard salami, provolone, and raw onions singing on his taste buds, when out of the corner of his eye, he caught a blur of movement. He cursed as a tomato-and-shredded-lettuce wad dropped into his lap, splattering him with enough oil and oregano for his wife to smell a mile away.

Shoving the trash into his bag, he leaned forward, squinting into the darkness and noticing that the Victorian's back gate was swinging in the breeze. Was that the movement he'd spotted, or could it have been an intruder, slipping inside the fenced backyard while he'd been distracted?

An uneasy feeling gurgled through his gut, a rumbling that had him recalling Alphabetty's theory about some rejected lover taking out his anger on the hot doc's high-priced Mercedes. Though Bowers himself had told Frank only yesterday that his investigation hadn't turned up anybody like that, he couldn't help remembering the vandal he'd confronted, who'd sworn he and his crew had nothing to do with what had happened at this address.

Fiorelli had figured it for another lie, one of about a hundred the desperate kid had spouted when backed into a corner. But even a busted clock's right twice a day, so it was possible that particular statement might've been a true one. Which meant the real culprit could've come back with something more than vandalism in mind.

He reached for the radio, thinking, *Better safe than sorry*. Before he could request backup, though, the radio blatted out a call for Zarzycki, yet another domestic at an address both of them knew well. She was likely to be hung up there for a while, he knew, since with these particular frequent flyers, it was always difficult to figure who'd been whaling on who *this* time.

"Have fun, Alphabetty," he said, mentally congratulating himself for getting out of what could easily turn out to be another all-night goat screw.

Then he spotted a four-legged creature, its tail tucked as it skulked near a couple of scruffy-looking pine trees along the alley's edge. Stray dog. This area was crawling with poor mutts assholes dumped once they grew inconvenient. It pissed him off, imagining his Newfoundland, a shaggy black mountain of love and trust and slobber, lost and scared on her own.

But as the thin, light-colored dog lifted its head, Fiorelli recognized the hot doc's greyhound, shivering like crazy in the cold.

"How'd you get loose, Skinny?" Had the animal gone out through a doggy door to do his business, then found that the back gate had blown open?

When he turned on the car's headlights to see better, the greyhound startled, tucked his thin tail even tighter, and trotted off down the alley.

"No, buddy. Don't run off now," Fiorelli said as climbed out and followed, feeling the icy kiss of snowflakes as they melted against his face. "You ain't got hair enough on you to line a pair of kiddie mittens."

Thinking only of how happy the doc would be to get her dog back—maybe happy enough to brew him some of that special rich-people coffee she had—he jogged past the scruffy pine trees . . .

Never noticing one slim shadow separating itself from the others. Never noticing until the cold steel took its first bite, deep and cruel.

Harris stood in the darkened hospital room, watching over his son's gentle breathing. He should be sleeping himself, reclining in the chair he'd sprawled in more than once since Jacob had been here, and making up for all the long hours he'd put in the last few days.

But there was no way he could sleep now, not with the story Annie Wallace had told him chewing at his brain. The story of two girls he had once thought of as privileged, who'd had a hellish start.

"For years and years, she had these awful nightmares," Annie had said, considering herself fortunate not to remember the events that had provoked them. "She'd wake up the whole house with bloodcurdling screams like you would not believe. And always afterward, once our parents calmed her down, she would have to be brought into my bedroom to see I was still breathing and touch my skin to make sure I was warm."

Harris's heart twisted at the image of Christina, as small and vulnerable as Lilly, on another night, raw and cold as the one now taking shape outside. Picturing her huddled with her arms around an infant, both of them abandoned to the elements, totally alone.

He'd thought his own childhood harrowing, with a father who drank too much, and a mother, God rest her soul, who'd cowered each time the old man raised his voice. Though she couldn't find the strength to stand up for herself, at least she'd kept him safe, had even been willing to shield him with her body until he'd grown big enough to stand up for them both.

During the times he wasn't drinking, though, Harris's dad had been a decent man. A man who'd struggled as hard to provide as he struggled for sobriety. Who'd loved them both in his harsh way, the best way he knew how.

Flawed as his parents were, Harris knew both would have been appalled by what their biological mother had done to Annie and Christina. Or *Katie*, as her name had apparently been in the first years of her life.

"My sister hates it with a passion, but at least she knows her real name," Annie had said. "I never knew mine at all. And the birthdays we both celebrate are guesswork—hers, especially, might be off a little because of malnutrition."

Harris cursed under his breath, wishing like hell he could forget what he'd heard.

"The question is," he'd asked with a pear-size lump in his throat, "how would Lilly know her mother's birth name? Would someone in the family have told her?"

"Gosh, no. No one's brought it up in years, and as far as I know, Mom and Dad never told anybody the real story about how they came to adopt us. They never even mentioned it to us, if they could help it. I still remember when they finally told me. I was nine then and starting to ask a lot of questions about why my sister was in therapy and who the heck was Katie. I'd heard her scream that name before, but when I asked her about it later, she just slapped me."

Holy hell, thought Harris, his stomach turning as it often did when he was drawn into the investigation of crimes involving children. The idea that Christina had for so many years carried the burden of that early memory explained so much about her, from her seriousness about her grades to the deep sense of responsibility she felt for her younger sister.

Though he'd thought he'd let go of his animosity years before, he felt any lingering resentment slide off his shoulders. He was freaking glad she'd won that scholarship, a scholarship she had worked for and deserved.

"So how do you think Lilly got hold of the name Katie?" he'd asked, taking one last run at it from a slightly different angle.

Annie had dropped her gaze, avoiding his stare, and murmured, "You—you might think this sounds crazy."

"What sounds crazy?" he'd prompted. "C'mon, Annie. Believe me, there's nothing you can say that's gonna shock me."

But he'd been wrong about that. Dead wrong. What Annie told him next had sure as hell surprised him. Surprised and kept him awake until he stepped out of his son's hospital room about twenty minutes after midnight to answer his vibrating phone.

"What the hell? You're sure?" he asked after Maya, the night dispatcher, gave him the address for the automatic alarm.

"127 Cape Street," she confirmed, the excitement in her youthful voice unmistakable. "And the resident hasn't responded to the monitoring company's attempts to reach her, either on the landline or her cell."

His heart hammered as he dug for his keys. "Where the hell's Fiorelli? I told him to take the unmarked car and stick close to that area." He'd been going to send Zarzycki, but Frank had whined so much, he'd let himself be talked into switching their assignments. *If he's off on another bender, I don't care who his brother-in-law is, I swear I'll can his ass.*

"Sorry, but I couldn't raise him on the radio or on his cell phone, either." Clearly as frustrated as he was about it, Maya huffed, "*Again.* And Alphabetty's finishing up with a domestic. The Lewises are at it again."

"That could take some time," he said, having given prior orders that the next time Karl and Vicki got into a drunken slugfest, they both needed locking up. "And, anyway, I'm heading over."

As much as he hated to leave Jacob, Harris told himself he would be back before his son woke in the morning, and he let the duty nurse know to keep a careful eye out as well.

"I'll keep trying Fiorelli," Maya promised.

"And if I call in and tell you I need backup, I don't care what you have to do—have Zarzycki handcuff both those idiots to opposite ends of that trailer of theirs, wake up the entire day shift, or call in mutual aid, if that's what it takes," he said, referring to the agreement Seaside Creek had with its nearest neighbors in case of emergency.

"You asked me to remind you about the budget," she said, sounding apologetic. "Overtime's already maxed out for the quarter, and it's only—"

"Council can take it out of my hide later," he said through gritted teeth, "or have my badge if Edgewood's convinced them that's what they really want."

Christina's scream was loud enough to shred her throat. Loud enough to wake her.

The reality she'd been so certain of rained down like shattered glass, leaving her alone in the dark bedroom, heart kicking like a mule.

Night terror—Doug's not in this room. She stared at the closed window. *There's no one here with me, but—*

She felt around for the greyhound, who'd been curled up beside her, only to find that that part of the dream was true. Max was neither next to her nor in his own bed in the corner.

From down the hall, she heard the sound of Lilly crying, undoubtedly frightened by her mother's shriek. As Christina tossed aside the comforter, she felt the sear of shame, the memory of all those nights she'd upset her family during her childhood.

She thought she'd outgrown the disturbances, at least until they'd come roaring back two years ago, around the time of her father's death.

Stress can be a powerful trigger, a med-school friend who'd gone into psychiatry had advised her once. *Just like hormonal changes,* she'd added, referring to another, even more shameful issue Christina had confided in her. *Don't be too hard on yourself. You'll be fine again in time.*

Shoving her arms into a warm robe, she slipped her feet into a pair of scuffs and hurried down the hall toward Lilly.

"I'm coming, sweetie. It's fine," she said, wondering whether her daughter could have been fussing for a long time, unheard, since Christina hadn't yet replaced the monitor she would never again trust.

From downstairs, she heard something—footsteps or a cabinet closing. Her sister, coming home from the Shell Pile. Christina called, "Don't worry about Lilly. I've got it covered."

As she hurried down the hallway, Christina realized the crying had stopped. *But I didn't dream it. I was definitely awake then.*

With the night-light in her daughter's room to guide her, she raced through the doorway. And stared down in confusion at her child's empty bed.

Telling herself there was no need to panic, Christina groped for an explanation. "Lilly? Are you in the potty?" Yes, that had to be it. She'd had to go, and decided, for the first time in the nighttime, to try it on her own.

But Lilly wasn't in the nearby hall bath and not in the master bathroom, either. Christina fought to keep her panic tamped down.

Back in the hallway above the stairs, she called down, "Annie? Do you have Lilly with you?"

No answer rose in the dark stairwell, nothing but a strong and pungent odor.

Gasoline, she thought. *But how, here in the house?*

"Annie," she repeated, the stairwell echoing with her fear. "Annie, Lilly! Max, where are you!"

A new sound came, a whoosh that drowned out the wind's voice outside the old house.

A flickering light made shadows dance along the walls of the long hallway. A dance that spoke of death and stank of smoke and ash.

The alarm system started shrieking, an earsplitting racket that almost, but didn't quite, obscure Christina's daughter's terrified screams.

CHAPTER THIRTEEN

Harris pulled out of the skid as his Tahoe fishtailed around the corner of a mostly residential street just outside the historic district. A rear tire spun on ice before the back bumper caught a hydrant. Hard enough to leave a dent, but he didn't give a damn about that. Nor did he take the time to worry about the condition of the plug.

Right now, all he cared about was getting to Christina before whoever'd carved that obscenity on her car found a way to make good on the implied threat.

Yet her sister's voice kept running through his head for some reason, along with her crazy theory about how Lilly might have heard the name her mother had been born with.

"I've seen these shows on TV, these interviews with parents. About little kids, like Lilly's age, who've all of a sudden, out of nowhere, started talking about their old lives, about how they were killed."

"What kind of down-the-dial cable crap have you been watching?" he'd asked, wondering whether she also bought into those so-called documentaries about secret weather-control experiments, conspiracies surrounding 9/11, and real-life mermaids washed up on beaches.

"It's not like that." Annie's face had gone red. "There've been books about this kind of stuff, expert studies, even an article in my mom's *Reader's Digest*. These kids come up with things they have no business knowing. Some of them say they've lived before, that they were these people."

"So you're thinking Lilly's one of these kids, that she's reincarnated or something like that?" Harris was mostly thinking that Lilly's aunt was even flakier than he'd suspected. Except that he remembered the strange look on the toddler's face from the day Jacob had been injured. A look that had gotten him thinking of old souls in young children.

Maybe he was the crazy one.

"I don't know what to think," said Annie, "except that something's going on around here. Something bigger and uglier than vandalism."

A blurred movement in front of his headlights had Harris pumping his brakes. Despite the icy road, the Tahoe jerked to a stop, and something that looked like a small deer or maybe one of the stray dogs that had become such an issue lately disappeared into the darkness somewhere to his left.

If it was a stray, it was in for a rough night out here, with the chill factor down in the teens. But Harris pushed the thought aside, caring only about getting to Christina safely.

He was a block away from her place when he caught sight of the aging Toyota Camry he'd sent Fiorelli out in, all its lights off. The unmarked sedan was parked a few houses down the alley behind the Victorian at 127 Cape, close to where Harris had kept watch before Jacob's accident. As waves slammed the beachfront in front of the houses, spray misted the air, sheeting the vehicle with a layer of ice that glittered as his headlights reached it.

Harris's gut dropped when he spotted the driver's-side door standing open to the falling snow—and no Fiorelli in sight.

Rather than off slacking somewhere, was his officer in trouble?

Pulling up behind the vehicle, Harris forced himself to stay inside the Tahoe long enough to radio dispatch. "10–48," he said. *Officer needs assistance.* "I want everybody you've got out here. Fire and paramedics, too."

If his instincts were wrong, and there was some innocuous reason Fiorelli wasn't answering his radio or cell phone, Harris knew he'd hear about it. But he'd gladly risk Edgewood's bitching about his squandering resources before he'd take a chance on leaving one of his guys down or dead . . .

And he couldn't forget that Christina and her sister weren't responding to calls, either, and that Lilly was inside, too.

Harris bailed out of the Tahoe, a flashlight in his right hand. The wail of the Victorian's alarm had his blood rushing in his ears, its roar competing with the howling wind and crashing surf.

That was when the realization hit him. *This is going to be bad.* Far beyond the brand of bad he'd need to justify his actions.

An image flashed through his brain: the bomber, Private Cody Yardley, with a dead-eyed look, his hand reaching beneath his jacket at the same moment Harris himself went for his sidearm. The fiery eruption of a shock wave that struck him as the blast burst his right eardrum.

Shoving back the memory, Harris made a quick circuit of Fiorelli's cruiser, his gun in a left hand that would never be as dexterous as his damaged right had been. Seeing no sign of Fiorelli in or near the vehicle, he followed the partly filled tracks in the snow. A single set, they led straight toward Christina's place . . .

A house whose lower windows pulsed with an eerie yellow-orange light as dark smoke forced its way through crevices between aged timbers.

He needed to get the hell out before he hit another complication. But the explosion of flame held him spellbound as it burned through the fuel he'd poured and fed hungrily on rugs and furnishings, cabinetry, and the walls leading up the staircase. With a folded hand towel he'd grabbed from the kitchen covering his nose and mouth, he listened as the bitch's frightened calls for her family turned to panicked shrieks as the growing fire set off the alarm he'd thought he had once again disabled.

The alarm was one more in a string of unwelcome surprises, which had begun when a woman he recognized had followed his target to the parking lot. Only this hitch, the damn alarm, could well mean he would very soon have company—company he couldn't risk catching him anywhere nearby, reeking of ash and covered in someone else's blood.

Still, he stuck around as long as he could in case the bitch decided to charge through the flames to reach the ground-floor exits. But with as much gas as he'd poured on those steps, the fire was hottest in that area—hot enough to assure him there was no way she was getting down alive.

And no way he could risk remaining any longer, sweltering in the heat and choking on the thick smoke. Since he could no longer make out any screaming, it didn't matter, anyway.

It would seem his work was done.

This is no nightmare. The house is burning.

With the flames leaping up the stairwell, Christina fought back her panic, ordering herself to function logically, efficiently, as she would when dealing with a medical emergency.

But it was no use, not when the frantic cries she'd heard down the hallway behind her were her daughter's, not some stranger's, and her own adrenaline-soaked maternal instincts had her shrieking even louder.

"Lilly, where are you?" she called as she ran back to her child's room. "Come out! We have to leave now."

As she stared at the bed—still vacant—the room's night-light flickered. She switched on the elephant lamp at her right. Soft illumination flooded the room, enough for her to see the layers of dark smoke hovering beneath the ceiling and Lilly's hooded purple jacket draped across a chair.

Grabbing the jacket, Christina heard a bang from downstairs, and both lamp and night-light went out, casting her into darkness, broken only by the faint light seeping through the shaded window.

Power's out. Somewhere below, the wiring must have burned through. The smoke alarm, still blaring, must be running on a backup battery.

She raced back to the master bedroom for her forgotten cell phone—it would give her at least a little light, light she desperately needed to find Lilly. Coughing as she ran, she tried to tell herself the smoke up here wasn't bad yet. And fought to keep believing that her daughter's voice really had come from somewhere upstairs with her and not the blazing first floor.

Snatching her cell phone off the nightstand, she called Lilly's name once more, and once more got no reply. What if the cries she heard had really been from downstairs? If her daughter had been down there with Annie, as Christina had first thought, wouldn't her sister have grabbed her and hurried out to safety, probably with the dog in tow?

She pictured her sister, with Lilly in her arms, phoning 911. Pictured Annie comforting the toddler, then putting her in the Mercedes, where they'd be warm and dry.

Unless it wasn't Annie I heard moving around down there.

Terror fell on her like an ax blow as she remembered the pungent smell of gasoline. An odor that only made sense if someone had deliberately set the blaze.

What if whoever did this has her? What if she's taken Lilly? Choking on the thickening smoke, Christina thought of the voice on the monitor, the voice she'd initially feared was in her daughter's room.

Except that when Christina turned around, Lilly was standing in her bedroom doorway, weeping as she held her ears to muffle the alarm's noise. Not knowing whether to be horrified that Lilly was there or relieved that she'd come out from wherever she'd been hiding, Christina cried out her daughter's name and scooped her up in her arms.

CHAPTER FOURTEEN

Already smelling wood smoke, Harris was thirty feet shy of the back gate when something sent him sprawling. Something that grunted as the tip of his boot caught a low hump, camouflaged by a thin, snowy layer.

His momentum pitching him forward, Harris smacked the ground like a bag of wet concrete. Scrambling to recover, he turned both his light and gun to see Fiorelli lying on his side and staring at him, his brown eyes fixed and open, and his face unnaturally white beneath a flap of coal-black hair. Despite the blue lips, Harris put down his weapon to shake him repeatedly.

"Frank!" he shouted over the wind. "Fiorelli, wake up!"

But there was no reply, not even when Harris shook him and said, "Come on, man. You can't do this."

Only after he failed to find a carotid pulse did he accept that he was looking at a dead man. At a corpse who'd only grunted because his own kick to the man's ribs had forced air from his lungs past vocal cords that would never speak again.

His gorge rising with regret, Harris cursed and rolled Fiorelli onto his back. Finding that rigor hadn't set in, Harris pounded the man's chest, praying for a miracle—or at least a chance. But the skin had already gone waxy, the flesh as cold as meat from a refrigerator case. And when he brushed away the snow around the body, he came across a red-brown puddle leaking from beneath the body, already freezing around its edges. Blood from a wound or wounds either hidden by Fiorelli's jacket or on his back.

His gun was missing, too, Harris realized, almost assuredly taken by his killer.

"I'm sorry, Frank. I'm sorry," Harris told him as he rose, knowing that as horrifying as the loss of an officer was, his own first duty was to the living. To getting Christina and her family out of the burning house—and as far as possible from the armed cop killer who had most likely set the fire.

If this son of a bitch didn't murder them before trying to cover the evidence with arson. Pain twisted in his gut, but there was no time for doubt or grieving, no time to do anything but barrel forward.

Scarcely able to keep his eyes from closing against the stinging wind and snow, Harris quickly realized that in weather like this, with the cover of the thickening smoke and darkness and the alarm drowning out the sounds of movement, an assailant could come at him out of nowhere.

There were other sounds as well: the shattering of window glass along one side of the ground floor, the crackling of flames strengthened by fresh oxygen, licking the Victorian's exterior. Garish color flared up, yellows and oranges reflecting off white paint stained with soot.

With so much old wood and the howling wind, Harris knew the house would go fast, the moisture from the snowfall no match for the head start the flames had gotten.

He gritted his teeth, telling himself the suspect would be operating with the same challenges he faced. But before he even stepped up onto the back porch, the heat presented a new issue, one that had him coughing up air bitter with soot, his skin feeling like it was melting before he could get near the door.

As another window splintered, Harris realized that he was never going to get in this way. Jumping off the porch, he started running toward the front of the house, desperate to find some way to get inside—hoping to discover that the ocean side of the house wasn't yet ablaze.

As he rounded the front, he spotted a silver SUV pulling up. Recognizing the Mercedes emblem on the hood, he stopped in his tracks, relief flooding his system. It had to be Christina, returning from somewhere with her daughter safely strapped into the car seat.

He hurried toward them, eager to keep her from driving too close to the danger.

The SUV slammed to a stop, and a wide-eyed woman jumped out to stare openmouthed at the flames.

"Christina!" It was Annie, staring at the fire with huge eyes. "Oh my—Christina! Lilly! Where are they, Harris?" She was looking at him now, her face a mask of terror and disbelief. "Are they *in that*?"

He stared at her, shock rolling through him in waves icier than anything the weather could dish out. And the realization hitting him that he'd wanted—*needed*—so badly to believe they were safe inside the vehicle that he'd leaped on the possibility, wasting valuable time.

"Fire department's on the way," he managed. "Tell them—tell them I'm going in. And I swear to you, I'm not coming back without Christina and Lilly."

The gash ran from wrist to elbow, a deep slice up Christina's left arm. She'd gotten it after using a chair from Lilly's bedroom to smash the glass out of a window that must have been painted shut. After zipping Lilly into her jacket to protect her from the shards, Christina had ducked to carry her out onto the steeply pitched porch roof just below it. One fang of glass from the frame's edge must have caught her, though she hadn't felt it—at least not until she realized that the sleeve of her robe was dripping with blood, and knew the glass must have nicked the ulnar artery.

After frantically checking Lilly for any similar wounds, she stood there holding tightly to her weeping daughter, coughing in the smoke-filled air and shaking with adrenaline. Worried about sliding off the steep, icy porch roof, she kept her back to the exterior wall and closed her eyes against the rush of pain that finally shot up from her arm. But they couldn't rest there, not with the fire soon to come after them. For all she knew, the roof might already be burning from beneath.

Lilly's sobs gave way to chatter, words Christina could barely make out with her daughter's head so close to hers.

"Mur-mur-murder Mommy," Lilly kept repeating, a mantra that coincided with a blast of wind that started Christina shivering. "Kill me."

"Stop that! Stop, please!" she said, her own tears burning like acid as they rolled down her cold face. "Mommy has to—has to call the firemen."

While maintaining her grip on Lilly with her right arm, she used her left hand—ignoring the blood soaking through her sleeve—to pull her cell phone from the pocket of her robe. With the movement, the deep gash sent fresh pain spiking through her, and everything went black for a moment, save for the spangles of bright color that splashed across her field of vision.

You can't pass out. Her heart pounded even harder. *You'll drop her.*

Christina sucked in a freezing lungful of choking air, but when her eyes flashed open, it wasn't Lilly, but her cell phone that she saw skidding toward the roof's edge, picking up speed with every inch it gained.

With their lifeline vanishing, Christina screamed in wordless protest—and saw the phone's progress halted, as though by her order, against a weathered shingle halfway down. She pushed Lilly's back against the outer wall beside the window. "Stay right here! Don't move," she ordered before scooting in the direction of the cell.

But when she glanced back, Lilly was crying again, reaching for her, calling, "No, Mommy. No leave babies."

Babies, she'd said, the plural sending Christina's mind spinning backward in time, to the snowy night she'd been abandoned. Horrified, she cried out, "I'm not leaving, sweetie. I won't. But I have to get—" Rocked by another wave of dizziness, she paused to catch her breath. "Have to get the phone."

Once more she edged forward, still in a seated position, and shivered as wind-driven snow assailed her. But smoke came with it, too—a thick, black cloud that started her coughing again—and left her terrified that the fire was closer than she'd imagined.

When another gust cleared the air, she saw that the phone had vanished, undoubtedly continuing its downward skid and sailing off the edge into the darkness.

"Damn it!" she cried, realizing that her last chance to phone for help had gone with it. Panicking, she shouted, "Help! Please help us!" until a coughing fit forced her to stop.

As she fought to recover her breath, she accepted that all the yelling in this world wasn't going to do either of them any good. If she was going to get her daughter and climb down to safety, she'd have to do it on her own.

Gritting her teeth against the pain, she tried crawling back to where she'd left her daughter. But for every inch she progressed, she slipped downward two inches on the ice glazing the shingles, which forced her to take things slower.

Smoke billowed once again, and from somewhere not far away, a crackling sound competed with the cacophony of storm noises and—were those sirens coming her way?

Hope leaping inside her, she told Lilly, "Someone's coming!"

Except that when the smoke cleared, Lilly was no longer where Christina had left her, but instead, was sliding past her, her eyes rounded in terror and her mouth wide in a voiceless scream.

"No!" Christina spun onto her belly and launched herself after her daughter, shooting down the pitched roof so swiftly that she had no idea how she'd stop them both from falling.

Harris took off at a dead run but stopped in his tracks along the house's side. With only one good ear to process all the noise around him, he couldn't be sure whether the woman's scream he'd just heard had come from inside, or whether it had been Annie, crying out behind him.

Or even whether the sound had definitely been human, rather than the smoke alarm in its death throes or the shriek of nails as they were pulled from burning wood.

Desperately, he scanned the side porch, where more flames were emerging from a broken ground-floor window. Though this portion of the house didn't seem as heavily involved as the back, the wooden exterior was already catching, the fire climbing higher by the second.

Then he caught sight of a lit screen on the icy ground—the cracked screen of a still-functional cell phone. Scooping it up, he instantly recognized the background photo on the home screen—a shot of Christina's adoptive mother smiling, Lilly in her arms.

As he opened his mouth to shout Christina's name, he heard a woman's scream.

When he looked up, his pounding heart squeezed into his throat, for right there, dangling about ten feet above him, he spotted a small child's legs kicking. Lilly, he soon saw, was dangling, suspended by the hood of her jacket and the hand holding it in a death grip.

"Christina, I'm here, underneath you!" he shouted, though he couldn't see her from this angle. "You're going to have to let go of her."

"No!" Christina cried. "I can't let her fall."

As he holstered his weapon, something warm dripped onto his face, and he saw that Lilly's intensifying struggle was threatening to send her slipping from the jacket.

"She can't breathe—she's strangling," he yelled back, realized that was why the child was silent. "You're gonna have to trust me. I promise you, I'll catch—"

Before he understood what was happening, Lilly plummeted into his arms. Above him, Christina shrieked, still clutching the jacket her child had slipped out of.

"I've got her. I've got her!" Harris shouted up at her, scarcely believing it himself. "There, you're okay, Lilly."

Lilly's wails assured him she was breathing.

"It's all right. You're safe," he told her before spotting Lilly's jacket fluttering downward. "Christina?"

Directly above him, Christina's hand dangled limply, and another drip of warm fluid spattered on Harris's face.

Blood, he realized. *Her blood.* Had the same bastard who'd murdered his officer mortally wounded Christina, too? Blindsided by the thought, he swore to himself that no matter what it took, he wasn't going to allow her to die. He'd climb up there somehow and find a way to get her down.

As he struggled to figure out how, he tried to help Lilly into her jacket. Screaming as only a hysterical two-year-old can, she cried, "No! No want," until Harris was relieved to see Annie rushing toward them.

"Take her," he said, handing off the frightened toddler and her jacket to her aunt. "Get her to the car *now*. There could be a shooter nearby."

Annie looked around them, clearly as frightened as she was conflicted. "But Christina. We can't leave my sister—"

"She'd want Lilly safe. You know that. And I swear to you I'm going to get her down."

Tears streaming down her face, Annie nodded, then carried the wailing toddler back toward the SUV.

Harris backed up, staring at the unmoving woman lying prone on the porch roof's edge and wondering how the hell he could get to her. With the roof overhanging the columns supporting it by at least ten feet, he couldn't climb up that way. And he spotted the interior staircase through one of the unbroken windows and saw it fully engulfed in flames.

Still, he refused to give up, though he had no idea how he'd manage. And no idea whether the woman he'd once felt far more for than he could allow himself to admit was still breathing . . .

Or whether he'd find her stare as cold and blank as Fiorelli's.

CHAPTER FIFTEEN

The first thing Christina was aware of was the quality of Lilly's weeping. No longer panicked, but hopeless and exhausted, as if she'd been left alone to cry for hours.

"Bad lady," she cried. "Bad lady kill Katie."

Desperate to reassure her daughter that she would always be there to care for her, Christina fought to open her eyes. But her lids were so damn heavy, and she couldn't move a muscle.

"Mommy's only sleeping," someone whispered. Annie, warm and gentle as a summer breeze.

Lilly abruptly stopped crying, then, in a knowing voice, insisted, "Mommy dead."

Gasping as she jerked awake, Christina fought to sit up. To break free of this nightmare. But someone was pressing down on her right shoulder with a hand so large and strong she couldn't—

"Don't fight, Christina. You'll hurt yourself."

She went still. There was something familiar in the male voice. Something that triggered a memory.

"You're gonna have to trust me."

Shards of the recent past spun back together. The fire, the ice, the weight of her daughter hanging from her own injured, outstretched arm.

"It's morning now—almost noon," Harris told her. "You're safe at the hospital."

Her eyes shot open. "I—I dropped her. I dropped Lilly," she said despite the painful tightness in her throat. "Where is she? Where's my daughter?" With her head pounding, and the room—so bright she raised a hand to shield her eyes—whirling around her, Christina had no idea whether the voices she'd heard earlier had been real.

Her skin prickled as her daughter's words reverberated in the small room. *Mommy dead.*

What if, instead, Lilly had been the one lost forever? If Lilly was stranded in the next life with a father who'd scarcely made time for her before his own death?

"Easy there," Harris said, his voice as ragged as her own. From the smoke, she remembered. Those billowing black clouds that had melted off the snow before it reached them. "They had to do a little surgery to stitch up that gash on your arm."

His warning came too late. As she moved, a slicing pain brought tears to her eyes.

"Be still," Harris said. Unnecessarily, this time. She couldn't have moved if she'd wanted to, couldn't do anything but clench her teeth as she waited for the worst to pass.

"Lilly's going to be fine," he told her as his thumb rhythmically stroked her shoulder. She held on to those tiny movements, used them to tether herself to consciousness.

"You dropped her to me, to safety. Remember?" Harris asked her. "She's been checked out and admitted for observation, but just as a precaution."

When she could speak again, she said, "But I heard her talking. She was in here with me. With Annie."

He moved to adjust the shades so the impossible white glare of the snow outside wouldn't force her to squint. "You might've heard her in the ambulance. Lilly was so hysterical to be with you, the EMTs made an exception and let you ride together, with your sister to help keep her calm."

"But they were . . . right here, just a minute ago." Christina's protest died as she became aware of the bandages on her left arm, the IV in her right.

"Nurse said it's just some kind of saline solution to rehydrate you," he explained, as if she wouldn't recognize Ringer's solution when she saw it. "I think they've given you something for the pain, too. Something pretty strong, from the sounds of things."

She winced, irritated that he thought her whacked out of her mind on pain meds. And annoyed because he was most likely right. "Why did they admit Lilly? Tell me everything."

"She was coughing quite a bit, so I understand they're monitoring her lungs for swelling. But your sister hasn't left. She said to tell you Lilly's doing great, that you don't need to worry about anything else—"

"Anything *else*? The house is gone, right? Burned because someone—someone tried to kill me." It hit her that the owners would be devastated by the loss. Her mother, too, when she found out what had happened. But the idea of how close her own daughter—both of them—had been to dying came hard on the heels of the first thought, along with so many unanswerable questions. *Who would do this? Why? What could I have done to make someone so angry?*

"Did you see the bastard?" Harris asked.

Now that her eyes had adjusted, she saw that the jeans he wore were smudged with ash, the sweatshirt smeared with what she suspected was her blood. His face needed both a shave and washing, dirt lining the creases in his forehead. And his hazel eyes were somber, carrying a weight that she sensed ran far deeper than physical fatigue.

She shook her head in answer to his question. "I heard someone moving downstairs. At first, I figured it was Annie coming home. Then the smoke alarms went off, and I smelled gasoline. I couldn't find Lilly. She was hiding somewhere."

"Little kids'll do that in fires," he said.

Blinking back tears, Christina said, "By the time she finally came out, the place was black with smoke, the stairs were completely engulfed. There was no way out, nowhere but that icy roof."

"I'm glad you thought to go there," he said, his gaze meeting hers as he took her uninjured right hand and squeezed it gently before releasing it.

She found herself wishing that he hadn't let go. "I can't—I can't tell you how grateful I am that you found us, Harris."

"I only wish I could've done more." He raked dark hair off his face, a flush reddening his skin beneath the grime. "I ran to the garage for a ladder, thinking I could get you down. But it took forever to even break down the damn door, and with this freaking hand of mine—"

"Well, I clearly got down somehow," she said. "I sure don't remember climbing."

"The firefighters showed up a couple of minutes later. But as a cop, I damn well should be capable of—"

Reaching toward him, she grasped his hand and turned it over, then carefully examined the web of scarring on it. Though some might find it unattractive, she marveled at the surgical skill that had clearly gone into its reconstruction . . . and at the strength he'd found, whether or not all of his old dexterity remained.

"This hand caught my daughter, Harris. *Caught* her, when she might've been killed by that fall." As she squeezed his fingers, she couldn't imagine anyone, no matter how fit, moving an unconscious person down a household ladder alone. He most likely would've broken both their necks in the attempt—because she absolutely knew he wouldn't have let the fire take her. "That's no small consolation. It's everything to me."

"I was at the right place at the right time. For her, at least," he said brusquely as he withdrew his damaged hand from hers.

"What do you mean?" she asked, sensing there was more to the story.

"We lost an officer there last night." His voice went bitter as he added, "*I* lost one."

"Oh no. What happened?"

"It's not official yet, but the ME's saying it looks like knife wounds to the back. I'd asked—I ordered my guy to keep a close eye on your place. Appears he was attacked after getting out of his car, possibly to investigate something he hadn't figured was serious enough to call in."

"I—I never heard a thing from outside, not with the storm," she said, scarcely able to comprehend that someone had died attempting to keep her safe. What kind of monster was this killer? "I'm so sorry. Who was the officer who died?"

"Frank Fiorelli," Harris said. "You met him at your house a few nights back."

"I remember," she said, recalling the dyed black hair and bulging gut. There had been some kind of tension between him and Harris, she remembered, but the look on Harris's face told her that wasn't making this one bit easier.

"I had to tell his—his wife this morning."

"That must have been terrible."

"That's one word for it," he said. "No kids, but they're real close to their nephews. And they were going to Hawaii. They'd been saving up for years."

Christina nodded, understanding his need to recite the awful litany. She'd done far too many death notifications, in waiting rooms and exam rooms, crowded corridors, and even speaking to distant relatives by phone. But as hard as it was to lose a patient, how much worse would it be if she'd been responsible for putting that person into harm's way? *In this case, though, you were, weren't you, if this arsonist was really out to kill you?*

As impossible, as unthinkable, as it was, she couldn't deny the reality of it any longer. *Someone wants me dead.*

"If I'd had any idea that the person who damaged the car would do something like this, I would've—" She shook her head, horror mingling with frustration. "I still have no idea why anyone would come after me. Before, I hoped it was a random thing, like you thought at first. Just some vandal confusing me for the homeowner."

"It must be tough to face," Harris acknowledged. "But if there's anything you can think of that might help us bring this asshole to justice, we need it. Any possibility, no matter how slight. I've looked into your husband's first wife and the kids, called in other agencies to check their alibis. But all three were at Evelyn Paxton's mother's viewing last night, plenty of witnesses to vouch."

"I told you, it's not them," she said.

"Let's say you're right," he allowed. "Which may leave us with some coworker who seems a bit off, a former neighbor who gave you a bad feeling, an especially aggressive or fixated patient, one who's sexually aggressive or inappropriate—"

"You're thinking it's a man, then?" The idea seemed off somehow. But whether it was pain meds or exhaustion, she couldn't pin down the reason.

"I can't rule out anyone for certain," Harris said. "Statistically speaking, though, a male's a lot more likely to physically engage in close quarters—and coming up behind an armed cop? I don't see a lot of women doing that."

"I see your point." She'd seen drugs produce incredibly violent behavior in people of either sex. But this killer had taken out an officer and set her house ablaze, then escaped without detection, none of which sounded like someone blasted out of his or her skull on PCP or bath salts.

"I want you to really think about this, Christina. Help me stop this killer before he comes back for another try."

He again. Even more troubled by the assumption, Christina allowed her gaze to drift. When it reached the window, her mind shot back to the parking lot outside it. To last night's argument with Renee, who'd called her the same name that had been emblazoned on her car. To Renee, who might be in league with the young man she'd seen at the little bakery . . . if she had really been there.

Christina shivered as Lilly's voice echoed through her memory. *Bad lady hurt Katie.*

Harris was staring, studying her eyes intently. "What are you holding back, Christina?"

She shook her head, alarmed to realize the hallucinations had clearly returned. Lilly hadn't been speaking to her in this room before.

"I was just thinking of what happened on that rooftop," she lied, fighting back tears. "How my daughter slipped from my hands . . ." *And how she could again, if I lose sight of what's real and what isn't.*

"But you weren't alone," he reassured her, pulling tissues from the box on the bedside tray. When he leaned close to blot the moisture gathering beneath her eyes, there was something so intimate in the gesture that she held her breath. "And you aren't now, Christina, or you don't have to be."

She looked up into his green-flecked eyes, understanding that once again, he was asking her to trust him. To trust the boy who'd used her and then sneered at her pain.

But there was no derision in the look Harris slanted down at her, not a trace of mockery. Instead, she read the swift play of emotion, regret warring with anguish.

A muscle in his jaw twitched, and she saw something else, too: an aching loneliness, a longing for something that had almost lived before he'd destroyed it. Drawn in by the intensity of his expression, she said nothing as he moved in even closer. When she caught his ashy scent, her pulse bumped at her throat, her dizziness returning as she understood he was about to kiss her.

I need to stop this. Right now. I have to remember.

For a single moment—which left her half-relieved, half-disappointed—she thought he would stop or give her a chaste peck on the forehead as if she were a small child. But since that summer so long ago, there had been nothing chaste or childish between them. Nothing but an artifact of old attraction, one she'd never imagined still capable of reigniting.

Then his mouth found hers, and the hunger of their eighteenth summer flared again between them, a pull so searing that it burned away the memory of the intervening years, the miles they'd traveled, the vows each of them had made to love and honor another partner. Dismissing the commitment to reason that had guided her life, Christina gave in to simple impulse, to the need to reach up, slide her hand over a strong jaw rough with stubble, to slip her palm along his neck, then let it glide beneath his collar.

Lost in sensation, she was breathing hard; they both were when she heard a footstep and a woman's gasp. "Oh! So sorry—I'll come back for vitals later."

Senses flooding back at last, Christina jerked away, grimacing as she jostled her injured arm. Harris stepped back just as quickly, his face reddening as he shook his head. The doorway was empty.

"Damn it, that was so wrong. I'm sorry, Christina. I never should've—"

"I didn't stop you."

"No, but I—you're barely out of surgery."

"You're not yourself, either. You've lost an officer," she managed, her skin clammy and her stomach roiling as she fought back the waves of pain, along with the worry that this—this lapse would be all over the hospital in no time. "And I needed—I'm so scared now, Harris. Terrified and confused and—" It had been so damn long since she'd lost herself in a man's touch like that. In something as simple as a kiss.

You're fooling yourself if you think anything about that kiss was simple.

"You're in no condition to know what you need. Or want. If it had been Renee who walked through that door—"

"That would've—it would've been bad," she said, certain Renee would have gone nuclear, regardless of how clear she'd made it that she was completely finished with her ex. "Especially after—I should've told you before."

"Told me what?" he asked.

Too shaken to hold back any longer, she said, "The two of us had a huge argument last night. Right outside the hospital as I was leaving work."

"A fight about what?" he asked, mouth tightening in a look of annoyance. "I thought she was done with blaming Lilly, especially now that Jacob's so much better."

"She did apologize for scaring her," Christina told him. "And she asked to come back to work for me. I gather she could really use the money."

Harris nodded.

"But I told her I've asked my sister to watch Lilly. Or more to the point, that I couldn't hire her back again, not after what I saw." Christina related the rest of the conversation, giving him every difficult detail until her face was burning.

But in the back of her mind, she knew she was using the subject to fill the empty space between them. Hard as it was to talk about Renee, it was still easier than coming to grips with how she felt about what had just happened. And how she ached for him to pull her into his arms and kiss away the doubt and terror that were eating her alive.

Harris had a hell of a lot to answer for in his life, but reaching for a woman drugged on pain meds, kissing her when it was obvious she was still reeling with the shock of an attempt on her life, ranked right up there, especially when the town he'd sworn to safeguard had a killer on the loose.

The killer of the first police officer Seaside Creek had lost in its long history.

As the person who knew Christina best, it had made sense for him to question her as a potential witness—or it would have if he could have made himself ignore the way he felt whenever he was with her. Forget the way he'd begun obsessing over past mistakes and speculating about how different things might've turned out if he'd followed the instincts that kept telling him how right they were together.

But he couldn't forget, no more than he could roll back time to change things. And he couldn't risk blurring the line between the personal and the professional again. Not unless he wanted to lose what little respect he had for himself. Or complicate an already difficult relationship with another woman, with whom he'd share custody of his son for years to come.

"For what it's worth," he told Christina, "I think you're right about Renee needing some help coping. I thought it was just me she's been so pissed at, but I see now, her anger's spilling over."

"Will you talk to her about it?" Christina asked. "The counseling, I mean."

"I'll do my best," he promised, "for Jacob's sake. I don't want her frustrations slopping over onto him, too."

"You can't think she'd hurt him. She loves Jacob."

"I've never thought it for a second." His ex certainly hated and blamed Harris for her problems and poor choices, but he'd never seen her be anything but loving and protective of their son.

"And I really can't imagine her being violent," Christina said. "Certainly not the kind of violent that could involve attacking Officer Fiorelli or setting a house on fire with Lilly and me inside."

He tried to think about it logically, to distance himself from the anger, frustration, and regret he felt toward Renee.

"You're right," he said. "For one thing, she called me earlier, said she'd heard about the fire and Fiorelli's murder. I didn't have much time to talk, but she seemed genuinely relieved to hear that you and Lilly had escaped and that the doctors were saying you'd be all right. And even if she was faking her concern, she'd never risk losing custody of Jacob. Especially not now, with him just out of the hospital."

Christina studied him, her brown eyes thoughtful. And beautiful, in spite of all the nicks and bruises she had picked up and the ash that dulled her hair. "Do you still love her?" she asked.

If anyone else had asked, he would have ducked the question or snarled and told her it was none of her damn business. Instead, he admitted, "I don't know that I ever really loved her. I tried to very hard, figuring that if I went through the right motions, did the right things, the rest would come."

"Why?" she asked. "I mean, why get involved with Renee in the first place? The two of you—I mean, she's always been very pretty, but her personality and yours—"

Harris snorted, remembering how he'd been warned off by more than one friend about the sharpness of Renee's tongue and the swiftness of her judgments. "By the time I'd finished with the surgeries, the rehab, and the award ceremonies they insisted on, all I wanted was to get back home, back to normal. The people here, God love 'em, gave me a hero's welcome, a job, even this great old house they took up a collection for and renovated themselves, but I didn't have a home, not really. And with my family all gone, I guess I just set out to sink down whatever roots I could to keep me from flying off the edge."

She nodded, a pained look tightening the flesh around her eyes. "I wanted—wanted to tell you how very sorry I was to hear about your parents after their accident. And how—how relieved I was to find out you weren't with them when it happened."

"Thanks, but I should go now," he said, his words suddenly hard as chips of flint. He couldn't bear her sympathy, especially when the emptiness he'd felt without her had been the reason he'd enlisted. The reason he hadn't been there when his mother had most needed him, to stop his father from insisting on driving to his own dying brother's bedside, despite having a blood alcohol three times the legal limit. Harris had carried the weight of that guilt for fifteen years now, blaming himself, and sometimes, at his lowest points, Christina.

Do your job now. That's all. And whatever the hell you do, don't make the mistake of touching her again.

"I've gotta get back to the station," he explained. "I have an investigation to get back to. In the meantime, I've got the staff here keeping a close eye on any visitors, and I'll send an officer over to watch your room as soon as I can spare one."

"I imagine they'll cut me loose with a prescription this afternoon—Lilly, too, if everything checks out all right. Then I can get back and—"

She blinked hard, her eyes stricken.

"What is it?" he couldn't help but ask.

"Max. My dog. Did he—did the firefighters find him?"

He shook his head, an unwelcome pang of sympathy hitting hard. "Not that I've heard. But it's possible—maybe somehow he found his way out. Animals sometimes—"

"I didn't even want him. He was Doug's idea. Doug's dog. But I ended up being the one who fed him, the one who sneaked him treats and made time for him—and pretty soon, he was mine, heart and soul."

Harris thought back to the flash he'd seen just before he'd spotted Fiorelli's car. A flash that could've been a greyhound.

He considered telling Christina but remembered how cold and wet it had been that night, how often patrols found animals on the road killed by passing traffic. He'd tell his guys to keep an eye out just in case, he decided, but as for offering her false hope, somehow it seemed too cruel.

"I'm sorry, Christina. I've got a soft spot for big dogs, too."

She nodded in answer, looking so miserable that he quickly changed the subject.

"Will you go to your mom's place?" he asked.

She nodded. "It's kind of a mess right now, with the renovation stuff, but she's got that on hold anyway until she's back home to supervise the contractors."

"Can't blame her there."

"Me neither, not after all the issues she's had," Christina said, "but the old place is still home, and after what we've been through, home's what we all need."

"So Annie will be coming with you?"

"Under the circumstances, I'm sure my mother won't mind." Christina's mouth puckered as she thought about it. "Well, maybe she will a little, considering how long it took her to get Annie to move out in the first place."

Harris snorted, but the comment reminded him of a question he had for Christina. "What was your sister doing in your rental car last night?"

"She said she'd cover a sick friend's shift at the Shell Pile last night, and I didn't want her going out in that little beater of hers."

He stared at Christina, trying to figure out whether she was lying to him. Or whether she'd been lied to. "You sure she said the Shell Pile?"

"Definitely the Shell Pile. She said they were trying to stay open till midnight if the weather held. Why?"

"Because the board of health shut the place down last week. They can't reopen until they get everything back up to code. Owner told me it'll be June at least, if he can score the credit he'll need for the upgrades."

"But—I must be confused," Christina said, color flaming in her cheeks. "Maybe from the anesthesia. Or the—"

"Or maybe because your sister deliberately misled you about where she went."

Christina blinked hard, then shook her head. "I'm sure it's a mistake, that's all. Or at worst a white lie. She could be seeing someone, maybe someone she's worried I won't think is good enough. But then, who could be? She's my baby sister."

She smiled, clearly trying to make out like it was no big deal. But if Christina was trusting her sister with her child, there were things she ought to know.

"You know that bar's got a reputation, don't you?" he asked before carefully stepping into what he knew would be a minefield. "You know your sister does, too?"

"What?" she demanded, her eyes blazing. "First you're accusing her of lying, and now what? You're saying she's—she's—"

"Not drugs or solicitation or anything like that—"

"*Solicitation?* Annie's no prostitute."

"I told you I'm *not* saying that. But there's been a lot of flirting. Stirring up fights. And hanging out with men with less-than-stellar reputations. Including Reginald Edgewood." Harris scowled at the mention of his least favorite city council member.

"Who?"

"You might not remember him. He was older than us by ten, twelve years, but he was a legend, always talking himself out of trouble, wheeling and dealing his way to the right side of every pissant trade or hustle."

"Wait a minute," Christina said. "I think I met him a few weeks ago at this hospital fund-raiser that the head of my department twisted my arm to go to. While Mrs. Edgewood was giving this emotional talk about living with heart problems, he was trolling the edges of the room, trying to chat up all the doctors about investing in some new harbor development he's building."

"That's him." That was Reg Edge's biggest deal yet, a large resort marina, which would supposedly include luxury homes and a yacht basin. "You don't want to do that. Trust me. Federal permit problems out the wazoo."

"Don't worry. He already struck out by asking to meet with the financial decision maker in my family." She rolled her eyes.

Harris shook his head. Definitely Reg.

"But this guy was way too old for Annie. And she wouldn't want anything to do with a married man—"

"I'm afraid that when it comes to men, your sister doesn't always make the wisest choices."

Christina's face had gone an angry red. "Apparently, it's a weakness that runs in the family."

Her tone left no doubt whose choice in men she was referring to. Or that she had any intention of repeating her mistake, despite her earlier lapse.

Though he'd come to the same conclusion, it still pissed him off enough that he fired back. "So, you figure that you got that from your adoptive mother or the one who left you . . . *Katie*?"

"What the hell?" she exploded. "Who told you that? Oh, never mind. I don't want to hear it. Just get out. Leave now."

Realizing he'd let his pride talk, that he'd blindsided her with something so personal, it should have been handled with asbestos gloves, he said, "Shit, Christina. That was—"

When she grabbed the call button and stabbed at it repeatedly with a finger, he knew that he was only making things worse.

"Okay, I'm leaving. And I'm sorry. That was a low blow, and I didn't—"

"Don't you dare tell me you didn't mean it. Just go. And don't come back."

CHAPTER SIXTEEN

After everything he'd done for her, everything he'd dared, the bitch only cried when he told her. Cried and shouted at him, "I never wanted this! It has to stop and stop now."

Beneath the level of the café's table, he balled his fist, the unfairness of it making him want to pound her pretty face in. Her soft face, all pink and wet and splotchy, with no trace left of the coldness when she'd first said, "Hell, *yes*, I'd like to kill her."

"You *told* me," he reminded her, keeping his voice low so the other diners wouldn't stare. Not that he gave a damn about what they thought, but he couldn't afford the risk that one of them would reach for a phone. "You said you wished you had the guts."

"But I didn't mean for you to—you never understand me," she cried, her voice sharp enough to cut glass. "Never have and never will. I think—I need this to be over."

"Okay. No more," he said quickly, just to get her to shut up. Because some things, once put into motion, took on a life of their own. A life no weak-willed woman could ever understand. He unfolded his right hand and slipped it inside the pocket of the jacket, fingering the hilt of a weapon he couldn't seem to make himself give up, the way he had the gun. There was power in a cop's blood, a raw-edged rush he'd never felt in his life, and he imagined that it lingered on the knife, no matter how he'd scrubbed it in bleach water.

The little bitch must have seen it, too, for her eyes were wet and bulging. Scared, he thought. Or maybe . . . was she angry instead? He'd never been that great at reading faces. All he knew was that this particular expression usually meant noise.

"I don't mean just that," she said, smearing her mascara badly in an attempt to blot her eyes with a napkin. "I mean—I mean us. We have to end this. It was fun at first, but now this—" She cut herself off and sat up straight, reared back from him a little. "You're happy about it, aren't you? Proud of what you've done?"

"What *we've* done," he protested, though he was secretly pleased she had seen it. Understood what he was capable of. Once she had the money, he'd need her to remember. Need her to leave control of it to him.

"No." As she pushed back from the table, the chair legs made a scraping sound that turned heads and drew their waitress's eye. "I didn't. This was your choice. It's one thing, playing tricks on her, making her wish she'd never—but you've gone way too far. As always. That's why this time I'm done with you. We're finished."

"You're done with me?" He slapped the tabletop with both hands, making the silver next to his plate jump. Forgetting that they were in public, he exploded. "You're fucking backing out on this *now*?"

"Don't make a scene," she whispered, raising shaking hands. "I didn't mean it."

But it was already too late, for he recognized the brisk stride of the manager heading his way. He'd seen that same determined walk many times before. To save face, he pretended not to see and instead pulled out his wallet. Plucking loose a couple of twenties, he dropped them on the table, then said loudly, "Let's find ourselves another spot. Food's crap here, anyway."

Knowing what was good for her, she followed along meekly. Understanding that she didn't get to say when this was over. She'd already long since crossed that bridge. There could be no turning back.

~

"Here she is," crooned Annie as she carried Lilly into Christina's hospital room the following afternoon, once the pediatrician and the doctor overseeing Christina's treatment had both decided they were ready to be released. "With her hair all clean and shiny, and her beautiful new clothes."

Christina smiled, knowing the adorable tunic and striped leggings had been chosen from among the hand-me-downs brought in by one of the nurses, whose own daughter had outgrown them. But as much as Christina appreciated all the help her coworkers had offered, she couldn't help being reminded of the days she and Annie had spent in a Philadelphia hospital three decades before. Days when donated clothing, stuffed animals, and offers of adoption had come pouring in, in response to media coverage featuring the "lost girls" photos.

She still remembered how the nurses had vied to see who could brush her hair—as blonde as Lilly's back then—or sneak her a homemade cookie and carry her to see her baby sister in the nursery, the way Annie carried Lilly now. Christina remembered how, with more adult attention than she'd ever known, she'd been giddy with excitement those first days after their rescue, as happily distracted as her daughter looked now as she wriggled her way down from her aunt's embrace.

"Mommy, look!" Lilly cried, excitedly pointing out the sparkly cartoon princesses adorning the tops of both her hands. "I got stickers!"

Squatting beside the bed, Christina clutched Lilly in a one-armed embrace, so happy to see her daughter whole and smiling that hot tears leaked from her own eyes.

"I love you, baby. Thank God," she said, careful to keep her bandaged left arm, now in a sling, from being squashed between them. "Thank God." *And thanks to Harris,* she thought, cringing at the memory of how she'd ordered him from her room after he'd called her Katie.

"Why you crying, Mommy? Where your stickers?"

"They don't give them out to grown-ups," Christina managed as she wiped her eyes.

"I share." Lilly solemnly peeled off a Pocahontas and pressed it onto Christina's top, right over her heart.

"Thank you so much," Christina told her, kissing the crown of Lilly's head before carefully tucking the paper princess, who had lost most of her sticky backing, safely inside the sling.

Annie pulled Lilly's jacket out of a shopping bag and said, "This stank like smoke, but the housekeeping department washed it for us."

"Everyone's been wonderful. I hope you thanked them for me," Christina said, grateful that she wouldn't have to scramble to buy Lilly another one immediately. And grateful for her sister's help, too, though she was dying to get the chance to question her in private.

"I did," said Annie, who wore the same clothing she'd had on the night of the fire. The same night she'd lied about her whereabouts. Fresh and clean as the outfit looked, someone must have washed it for her as well. "So, are you ready?"

"Just waiting for the nurse to print out a prescription with my discharge instructions."

But it was a different nurse who came in—the short, plump Sheila Handy, who sometimes picked up extra shifts in the ER.

"So this is your little darling. Isn't she precious?" she said, her silvery ringlets and broad hips so grandmotherly that rather than shrinking away, as she sometimes did with strangers, Lilly immediately warmed to her, showing off the stickers the other nurses gave her.

Blue eyes beaming up at Sheila, she asked, "You have stickers, too? For kids?"

"Of course I do," said Sheila, clearly not caring that she was being played. "Would you like to come see my collection at the desk? I think I might have a couple of kitties. And a puppy sticker, too."

"I have a puppy! Maxie!" Lilly blurted out, prompting Christina to exchange a stricken look with Annie, with whom she'd shared the news about Max when she'd stopped by the room last night.

"Okay if I borrow this little peanut for a minute, Mama?" Sheila asked.

"Sure thing. Just don't go too far, please," said Christina, who had on the clean yoga pants, long-sleeved T, and athletic shoes she'd kept stashed in a gym bag in her locker in the naive hope she would find the time to head over to the nearby YMCA after her shifts.

Once Sheila left with Lilly, Christina asked her sister, "So, you haven't told her about—about the dog?"

Annie shook her head. "Of course not. I figured—I thought it would be best coming from you . . . once we know for sure."

Christina prayed that whatever death had come to their sweet big boy had come without fear or pain. And that she could find some way to break the news of yet another loss to Lilly.

Not wanting to dwell on the heartbreak, Christina changed the subject. "So did you call and ask Mom's neighbor whether she still has a spare key to the house?"

"Oh, I didn't need to. I—um—I found my old key in my purse," Annie said, a flush coloring her fair face. "But I won't be staying. After I drop off you and Lilly over there, I'll head over to Kym's apartment."

"What? Why?"

Annie shrugged, avoiding her gaze. "She says I can crash on her couch. She'll let me use some of her clothes, too. We're almost exactly the same size, right down to our shoes. Isn't that crazy? We could almost be sisters."

"You know what's crazy?" asked Christina, oddly miffed by the comment. "You're bailing on your real sister when I need you the most." *Just like Renee warned me.*

"I'm not bailing," Annie said, looking tired and close to tears. "It's just—I swore I was never sleeping in that house again. I can't go crawling back now."

"I know you and Mom have had your issues, but don't be ridiculous. All your things were burned, for heaven's sake. And I really do need your help with Lilly, especially until I'm able to lift with my left arm again."

Annie hesitated, her gaze darting to the cell phone she was holding. "I've tried to call her three times," she said, her mind still clearly on their mother. "I figured someone had to let her know you and Lilly were in the hospital, and her client's house is toast."

Christina grimaced before she picked up on Annie's phrasing. "*Tried* to call her, you said?"

"It went straight to voice mail. I left a message one time, but I don't know if it went through. Or if she'd bother listening if she saw my number."

"Phone systems can be different overseas. Her cell's not working, that's all."

"You don't think maybe Mom's got me blocked?"

"Don't be ridiculous." That didn't sound like their mother at all.

"She said it was for my own good, that she was cutting off my rent because she really loves me."

"Mom does love you, Annie. More than you can ever know." Maybe it took motherhood, whether by biology or a binding contract, truly to comprehend the willingness to do the hard things, from holding a screaming toddler for a vaccination to cutting off a daughter financially when her adolescence had long since passed its expiration date.

"She said she's determined to make me a responsible, contributing member of society," Annie recited. "Like you."

Christina winced, hearing the pain in her sister's voice.

"We all contribute in our own way," she assured Annie before adding, "and I know you have a lot to offer. Too much to let yourself get sidelined by the wrong man."

Annie looked up, her blue eyes stricken. "Wrong *man*? What?"

"I know you weren't at the Shell Pile the other night," Christina said, "so I figured you must've been with someone—someone you didn't want me judging—"

"I—no." Annie shook her head rapidly. "You have it all wrong. I told you I was covering for—"

"Don't dig yourself in any deeper. Please." *Can't you see how badly I need to forgive you?* "Just tell me why."

Looking at her with pained eyes, Annie laid a hand on her own chest. "So now you're saying I'm a liar, too? I thought—I figured you were the one person I could always count on. The one human on the planet who would always take my side."

"Oh, save it," Christina said, realizing that she was being manipulated, with no more finesse than Lilly was using to coax more stickers from a nurse eager to fuss over her. Only Annie was no two-year-old, and Christina was no willing participant in the game. Or was no longer. "I know for a fact the Shell Pile's closed for repairs."

"Did I say I was going to the Shell Pile? Are you sure? Because I meant to say Harpoon Hattie's. That's where Kym's been working these last few months. They get a lot more local traffic in the winter."

Clamping her jaw, Christina looked away, not buying her story for a moment. And shaking with fear that Annie's lie could somehow be linked to the fire that had taken place only a few hours after she'd left the house. Had Harris questioned her yet? Or was he about to?

"Please don't be mad, Christina. I'll tell you everything—I promise."

But at that moment, the nurse returned with Lilly and Christina's discharge instructions and prescription. So for now at least, Annie's *everything* would have to wait.

Dread had a weight to it, Harris decided as he turned into the fifty-five-and-older subdivision where his former mother-in-law lived. With several inches of snow still on the ground, the well-kept cottage-style homes looked cheerful in the silvery afternoon light. But the lead in his gut warned that this visit would be anything but pleasant.

As he turned onto Sandpiper Street, his mind kept wandering back to the ME's preliminary report, which had told him that someone had come up behind Fiorelli and plunged a sharp instrument—a knife, most likely—into his lower back six times.

Lazy as Frank could be, he had well-developed cop instincts. So what could have gotten him out of the car in the snow to let someone sneak up on him?

Harris had no answers, might never have them, though he swore he'd never quit until he found the killer or killers. The more he thought about it, though, the more sense the idea of at least two perpetrators made. One to lure Fiorelli from the car, and a second to slip up behind him. But that scenario played out best if the lure was someone his officer would have been more inclined to view as an innocent in need of help. Someone very young, very old, or maybe a petite, fragile-looking female, such as the one who'd shouted an obscenity at Christina in the hospital parking lot the other night.

He pulled up in front of his mother-in-law's small, white one-story, every atom in his body assuring him this visit was not going to go well. As he approached the front door, it opened before he could knock, and Renee's mother, Kathleen, greeted him with a welcoming smile.

"Just wait until you see him, Harris," she said, looking as happy now as she'd been miserable after her only grandchild's accident. And as glad to see Harris as ever. "Our little guy's back in fine form!"

Harris kissed her cheek in greeting, relieved and grateful that she'd forgiven him after the long, cold war that he and Renee had called a marriage had spiraled to its inevitable conclusion. Whether she'd only remained cordial for her grandson's sake or really still thought of him as the son she'd never had, as she'd claimed, her attitude served as a welcome counterbalance to his ex's vitriol.

Inviting him inside, Kathleen, who still wore her fading red hair in a braid and maintained a pixielike figure that belied her age, walked him to the kitchen table. Waving an arm, she said, "Ta-da!" and gestured toward Jacob, who looked up from the phonics worksheet he'd been coloring.

His son bent over his sheet again. "B makes *buh*," he said, reading, "Busy Bee, Bad Bull." Or maybe he'd just memorized the page his grandmother was helping him with.

Either way, Harris was so relieved to see his kiddo bright, alert, and obviously healthy that he lifted him up and pulled him into a bear hug.

"Daddy, you're squishing me!" Jacob said, laughing.

"All right, all right, boy genius." Harris put his son down, so proud to think his kid was already reading—maybe just a little—that he ruffled the boy's golden-brown curls.

"Ow!" Jacob said, raising his hand when Harris came too close to his sore spot.

"Careful with him, Harris," Renee scolded, slipping into the room with a brush in hand. Dressed in her heels and black slacks, she pushed her reddish-blonde waves behind her shoulders. She wore more makeup than usual, her eye shadow picking up hints of the sweater's emerald hue. Beautiful, by nearly anybody's standards—or at least she would have been if not for the sour expression on her face.

"I'm okay," Jacob said, so quickly that it pained Harris to see his son taking on the role of peacemaker. "It didn't hurt, really."

"Sorry, champ," Harris said before turning his attention to Renee. "You look nice. You heading out somewhere?"

"If I were," she said, "I'm not sure what business it would be of yours."

Unless you're meeting up with trouble.

"Renee has a job interview this afternoon," her mother piped up. "At the Happy Hands Day Care."

"Happy Hands?" Harris echoed, noticing the way Renee avoided Kathleen's eyes. Lying, maybe? Or just annoyed that her mother had shared the information. "I know the guy whose wife owns that place." He let that tidbit settle before adding, "If you want, I'll make a call, put in a good word—"

"I don't need your help," Renee said, the color in her face making her freckles vanish.

"You're right. You won't need me," he said. "With your experience, they'll be lucky to have you." *And I'll count myself a hell of a lot luckier if I don't have to explain to our kid why his mom's in trouble. Because you're lying to me, aren't you? Who are you really meeting with?*

"Thanks," she managed.

"You have time to talk a couple of minutes?" he asked. "I promise, I'll be quick."

She glanced at the seashell-shaped clock hanging on the wall, ticking away the days she had left before she had to leave this house. "I guess so," she said before tensing abruptly. "Why? Is it Christina? Has something happened to her?"

"What makes you think that?"

"Don't use your cop voice on me. For heaven's sake. Someone's clearly out to get her."

"That poor girl," Renee's mother said. "She's been through so much lately."

"Christina's fine," he told them before gesturing to a doorway leading to a living room saturated with more of Kathleen's beach-themed decorative touches.

"You go ahead, Renee," her mom said. "I'll just fix the sandwiches. Jacob, could you help me make the tuna salad?"

Harris suppressed a shudder. Thanks to a nasty case of food poisoning back in high school, even the smell of tuna got to him, giving him one more reason to want to escape the house as soon as possible.

Renee ushered him out of the room and closed the door behind them. Rather than inviting him to take a seat, she folded her arms in front of her chest and stared at him expectantly. "Well?"

Cutting right to it, he said, "I was a little surprised by your concern for Christina's well-being. Especially since I understand you two had an altercation the other night in the parking lot at Shoreline."

Renee froze. "Did she tell you that?"

"Is it true?"

"Whether it is or not, I can tell that you believe her. But, then again, of course you would."

"What the hell's that supposed to mean?"

She gave him a sly smile he'd once mistaken for a sign of wit. "Maybe it means I'm tired of pretending that I never knew. That I had no idea how hot you were to get into her pants that summer after high school."

He winced. "Christina tell you that?"

"Are you kidding? Dr. Ice Queen? But my friends all knew about it. I remember them laughing at how you slipped it to her and then couldn't drop her fast enough."

His first impulse was to deny it, but he knew she wouldn't buy it. "Listen, Renee. That's not anything I've ever talked about. Or anything I'm proud of. I was a selfish kid, that's all, pissed off about some scholarship that she had every right to."

Renee snorted, the meanness in her coming out full force. And making him wonder again what the hell he'd ever seen in her. "Serves her right, as far as I'm concerned. Did she tell you that she had the nerve to fire me, after everything I've done for her?"

"And this surprises you, after you did everything but call her kid a demon seed?"

"For heaven's sake, I took it back. And after everything I've been through, everything I've suffered, that stuck-up bitch stood right there and told me I have anger issues."

Again, casting herself as the victim. "So you called her a—you know what you said. I have to tell you it hit Christina pretty hard, too, seeing as how she'd just found that very same word carved on the side of her Mercedes."

"Yeah. I know that." She shrugged. " But she'd made me mad, really angry. I mean, after what her daughter did to our son, she freaking *owes* me the benefit of the doubt."

"I think she might've had a point about you, Renee. You've been under some huge stress this past year—"

"I'm looking at the main one."

"Maybe you oughta try looking in the mirror instead."

"You're the one who filed for divorce," she shot back, her eyes filling with tears. "The one who left me high and dry—no job, no money."

"You weren't unemployed when I filed. And you and I both know the marriage died a long time before we ever pulled the plug."

"You should know. You killed it, from the moment you—"

"We both know the story. The beginning *and* the end."

He was letting her get to him. Taking a deep breath, he reminded himself he had a duty here, one that had no bearing on Renee's convenient dismissal of so many crucial facts. Reminded himself that he needed to be a better man, the kind of role model he hoped to God his son would grow up to do one better.

"The thing is," he went on, keeping his voice as calm as possible, "what you said, only hours before Christina Paxton's house burned almost to the damned ground, forces me to ask certain questions."

As his meaning began to sink in, Renee's eyes widened, and her jaw dropped a little lower. She shook her head slowly.

But it didn't stop him from continuing, no more than the heaviness that lined his stomach. "It forces me to check on your whereabouts and your associates," he said, "including where you're really going today."

She went dead white before a flush rose like a tide.

"So now you're, what, accusing me?" she asked, hair swinging in a wide arc as she shook her head. "You think I burned those people's house down? Or you're trying to get even with me—get our son away from me by pinning—you're talking about murder!"

"I don't think you're a killer." Although that sharp tongue of hers should have been registered as a lethal weapon. "And I don't think you're an arsonist. I'm doing the job I'm paid to do, following up leads—"

"Because you're jealous I have someone in my life now."

"You're dating again?" he asked, blindsided.

Her eyes narrowed dangerously. "You sound surprised that anybody'd want me."

"Not at all," he said, risking a half smile. "I just figured that after a prince like me, you'd be ruined for any other guy."

Instead of biting his head off as he more than half expected, she gave an unexpected chirp of laughter, reminding him of better times.

"So who's the lucky man?" he asked, trying to sound casual.

Waving it off, she said, "Nobody you'd know. And it's only been a few dates."

But that wasn't what she'd said at first. *I have someone in my life now,* she'd said. "This isn't someone you've met on the Internet, is it?" He'd heard a lot of stories in the course of his job. None of them with happy endings.

"Not the Net, no. Actually, Mom had me drive for like an hour one day to pick up this special detergent that doesn't make her break out in a rash. I spotted him just standing in the aisle, looking so confused by all the different brands of—"

"So this guy's basically some stranger you picked up at a store?"

She rolled her eyes. "Don't make it sound so sleazy, Harris. We just got to talking—Jacob wasn't with me—and he asked me if I'd like a coffee."

"At least let me check out this guy's background before you decide to let him hang around my son. You need to be careful."

"You're absolutely right," she said, her voice sharp with annoyance. "I wouldn't want to get stuck with somebody who works all hours and wakes up shouting and swinging with flashbacks."

"Renee . . ." He winced, but the time for apologies was over. He'd gotten the help he'd needed to put the worst of his PTSD behind him, for her sake and Jacob's. Help that had come far too late to save her trust—and their marriage.

"I'm sorry," she said quickly, the words almost startlingly rare in his experience with her. "But I need you to stay out of my business. And I really need to go now."

He had more questions but sensed he'd gotten as much from her as he could for now.

Stalking from the room, she called, "I'm running late, Mom, thanks to Top Cop here. I'll pick up something on the way home." With that, she headed for the mudroom, grabbed her coat and purse, and slammed her way out the back door.

Returning to the kitchen to say good-bye, Harris breathed through his mouth, though it was little help against the fishy odor.

"That sounded like it went well," Renee's mother said lightly. "But while you're here, I thought you might as well have lunch, at least. And don't tell me you've eaten, because I know you well enough to be sure you haven't taken the time, with everything that's happened . . ." Her eyes softened. "I was terribly sorry to hear about Officer Fiorelli."

"Thanks so much," he said, wondering, not for the first time, how his ex had turned out so volatile when she had such a sweet mother. "I really should be on my way, though."

Jacob walked up to him, proudly offering a plate. "But, Daddy, look. I made your sandwich special."

Harris looked down at the chips; raw, cut veggies; and two slices of whole wheat oozing glops of—God help him—tuna salad soaked in mayo out the sides.

"Please," said Jacob.

"Well, in that case," he said, forcing a smile because—hey, the kid would only be three and a half once, and Harris had survived worse. Much worse, and very recently, he thought, a chill ripping through him with the memory of his son lying so still and so small in the pediatric ICU. "I guess I'd better stay, then."

Some twenty minutes later, he was on his way back to the station, trying to convince himself the roiling in his stomach was all in his head, when he spotted movement out of the corner of one eye. With no traffic behind him, he braked hard, sliding several inches before the Tahoe's tires gripped the icy road. He then reversed a few yards, uncertain what he'd seen but trusting the instinct that insisted it was worth investigating.

Staring down the narrow alleyway between the backyards of two rows of historic homes, he studied an assortment of trash receptacles, damaged doors, stripped siding and other detritus left over from some construction project, and back fences—often in poorer repair than anything found along the street fronts.

A long, brownish head poked out from a gap in one such fence, prompting Harris to grin. "Well, I'll be damned."

At the same moment, the tan flash he'd seen on the dark road the night of the fire sprang back to mind again.

"The dog," he muttered to himself. "It must've been the greyhound he saw."

It made sense that Fiorelli might've spotted the loose dog after the arsonist let it outside. On a night as raw as that one, the cop, who was known to like canines better than he did most people, could've gotten out of his car and whistled for the animal, meaning to collect Max and then return him to Christina.

Except the arsonist had heard or seen him and recognized that he was a cop. Realizing his plan was in danger, he'd used the distraction to slip up behind Fiorelli while he wasn't paying attention.

Harris knew that he could be way off, but the scenario explained a lot. Including why he might've been wrong in theorizing earlier that there had to have been more than one arsonist.

Not wanting to spook the dog, Harris put the SUV in park and walked down the alley, his unhurried pace belying his eagerness to return to Christina this living, breathing embodiment of good news, one he hoped like hell might prove the key to regaining her trust.

"C'mon, Max. Come here," Harris called, thoughts of the kiss he'd shared with Christina filtering back into his mind. Thoughts of how damned good it had felt, holding her all these years later. Feeling the same attraction, wild as storm-driven surf.

Scowling at himself for letting his mind wander, he tried whistling, which prompted the shivering greyhound to appear, bonier than ever—and far more pitiful, with his thin, damp coat and his big, brown eyes looking so uncertain.

"How 'bout a truck ride, big boy?" Harris coaxed as he moved closer. "We'll even stop for a hamburger. I promise," he said, figuring the animal must be starving by now.

Clearly unnerved by his ordeal, Max slunk away at Harris's approach.

"Come on, Max. Let's go see Christina," he urged, creeping up more slowly than before. Nodding toward the Tahoe, he said, "I've got blankets back there. Heat, too. Sort of."

Gritting his teeth with frustration when the dog melted away from his outstretched hand, Harris wondered if the bastard who'd killed Fiorelli had hurt Max that night, too, or merely scared him so badly that he was unwilling to trust anyone other than his owner.

"Just a few more inches," he said as he made another, even more careful approach. "That's a good boy. Let's *go*."

At the last word, Harris lunged forward, grabbing for the collar around the dog's thick, muscular neck.

Panicking, the greyhound somehow slipped free of the blue band, leaving it dangling empty in Harris's outstretched hand.

"Shit! No!" he said as the greyhound wheeled around and sprinted down the alley, moving with a speed no other breed of dog could match . . .

And racing off in a direction that Harris knew would lead him straight out onto Seaside Creek's most heavily trafficked street, where he prayed to God he wouldn't find the animal Christina loved so dearly . . . flattened.

Annie hung a right to cut over onto Columbus Avenue, heading toward the two-story where she and Christina had been raised. Christina didn't love the idea of her sister behind the wheel of the rental SUV before she had a chance to call and square things away with the dealership, but with her own left arm in a sling and her driver's license missing in the burned Victorian, she was running low on options.

Five blocks from the pricey beachfront, the old, gray-shingled Cape Cod sat on the more modestly priced edge of the historic district, where it had been in their adoptive father's family for generations. The moment the house, sheltered by the bare arms of a pair of maples, came into view, Lilly drummed her heels against the bottom of her car seat and squealed, "Gramma!"

"Not today," Christina said, glancing back over her shoulder. "Grandma won't be back for four more sleeps." She held up the appropriate number of fingers to show her daughter.

"I take naps. *Then* Gramma!"

Christina laughed at the miracle of toddler logic. "Sorry, kiddo. Doesn't work that way."

"But I *want* her."

"Me, too, " Christina said, though she was supposed to be the grown-up in this outfit.

"And me three—especially if she was pulling a pan of that homemade mac and cheese of hers out of the oven," Annie chimed in, her smile giving Christina hope that she would stick around long enough to say why she had lied about her whereabouts on the night of the fire, instead of skipping out on her promise to explain things.

"Mac 'n' cheese!" Lilly echoed, taking up the call as they pulled into the driveway.

"No mac and cheese today," Christina said firmly, knowing that if she didn't lower expectations, she'd be hearing the refrain all afternoon. "Remember what I told you. We won't be able to cook at all at Grandma's."

Her father had firmly resisted any changes to the house he'd grown up in, claiming that its dated quirkiness was what gave it character. But two years after his death, their mother had finally waded into the updates she'd been longing for, one project at a time.

As they climbed out of the car, Christina shivered in the freezing air, the used but clean ski jacket a coworker had given her draped over her shoulders. Though she was glad to see that someone, probably the neighbors who'd been collecting the mail, had shoveled the front walk and driveway to keep the place looking lived in, she frowned at the sight of several plastic-wrapped newspapers on the front porch.

"That's odd," she said. "Mom told me she was going to stop the paper."

Annie picked them up. "Maybe it slipped her mind. Or the newspaper people are related to the kitchen contractors."

Christina nodded, irritated on her mother's behalf about the drama involving a botched cabinet order and countertops cut to the wrong size, which had resulted in the need to reorder and a frustrating delay.

"Guess that's what I get for putting it ahead of getting that darned basement refinished first, like your father would've wanted," her mother had grumbled while piling sweaters, slacks, and more shoes than she needed into the suitcase she was taking on her trip.

"Forget the basement," Christina had advised her, wrinkling her nose at the thought of the glorified hole in the ground, with its dank chill and musty odors. "You shouldn't be going down there, anyway, with those steep steps and your knees. You could fall—"

"And break my neck before I ever got to cook in my fabulous new kitchen!" Her mom had laughed when she'd said it, the sparkle in her eyes hinting that she was finally ready to put the past, along with her husband's long decline, behind her and embrace this new phase of her life.

Christina wondered how long, if ever, it might take her to reach the same point. To put aside the grief that stole up on her at unexpected moments, the what-ifs that appeared out of nowhere, leaving her with so many regrets about things she had or hadn't done.

Annie unlocked the door and let them in, and Christina was flooded with gratitude to be back in a place she'd always equated with love and warmth and safety. Lilly ran straight for the staircase, pausing to ask, "Go play now? Go up?" clearly remembering that her grandmother, worried about the construction mess, had moved the wooden box where she kept an assortment of Christina and Annie's old toys to one of the two guest rooms.

"Sure, sweetie. No jumping on the bed, though. You hear me?"

But Lilly was already clomping up the stairs, happiness bubbling in her wake as she made for the treasure trove of dolls, stuffed toys, and stacking rings.

Considerably less enthused, Annie let out a sigh as she looked around the first floor. "What a mess."

Christina conceded that the place looked a little sad—with thick plastic sheeting taped over various gouged-out sections of the demolished kitchen, and dust, probably still settling from the tear-out, covering the living room's chairs, TV, and even the framed paintings of various lighthouses that her parents had collected. But at least it wasn't freezing. Had her mom forgotten to turn down the thermostat? Or maybe she'd just left it on a timer.

"Smells a little funky in here, too," Christina said, wrinkling her nose at an unpleasant odor. "You don't think she left something in the freezer before they unplugged it?"

"Our mom? Are you kidding?" But Annie sniffed and made a face.

Christina checked the side-by-side fridge and found it empty and spotless, though the old appliances were due to be donated.

Annie crossed her arms. "Mom would be insulted that we doubted her housekeeping."

"I won't tell if you don't. Maybe there's a dead mouse somewhere?"

"Or maybe the place just needs a little airing out. But let's worry about that later. First, we need to make a shopping list. What do you want me to pick up for dinner?"

As they headed for the family room, Christina said, "I don't really care, as long as you grab some of those baby carrots Lilly likes, and maybe some fruit we can cut up for her. Milk and cereal for the morning. Mom still has that old fridge in the basement, right?"

"Yeah," Annie said, tapping out the list on the smartphone. "Anything else?"

While Christina thought about it, she plucked off the sheets covering the sofa so they could use it, only to sneeze at the dust she'd sent whirling through the air.

"Bless you," Annie said, sliding a finger along the thin layer coating the top of the old mahogany piano, a pensive look on her face, though she had never learned to play anything much beyond "Chopsticks."

"We'll clean up a little before Mom comes home," said Christina, who had dutifully slogged through years of lessons yet hadn't touched the instrument in years. "She'll appreciate that."

Annie slipped her phone into her small purse and then sighed. "She'll appreciate it a lot more if I'm not in it when she gets back."

"Seriously, Annie? I thought we'd established that this is an emergency, and I really need—"

"I want to be with Kym."

Something hummed in the back of Christina's brain, like one of those forks the piano tuner had struck on those rare occasions when he'd come to the house. But whatever the vibration meant, she couldn't allow herself to grasp it, so instead she shook her head. "Back at the hospital, you promised you'd tell me where you were that night—that you'd tell me everything."

"I—Christina, don't you see?" Tears gleamed in Annie's blue eyes. "I'm *trying*."

"I have no idea what you're saying," Christina fired back, her fists clenching until pain shot up her injured arm. "All I know is you're leaving me high and dry after I fired Renee. Is that what you want to prove to everyone? That you're still the same old irresponsible Annie who can't be expected to follow through on one damn thing?"

Annie stared at her, apparently too hurt to speak. And Christina felt a twinge of guilt. The same old guilt she'd always succumbed to whenever her sister was involved.

You take care of her and wait here just a minute, the long-forgotten voice whispered through her memory. *Mama'll be right back.*

But Christina was no longer that three-year-old, nor her sister a helpless infant—no more than the woman who'd left them there had any right to call herself their mother . . .

Mother. Christina's skin prickled as she remembered Annie's panicked call the morning Jacob had had his fall. Remembered her sister's claims that a woman had called spouting some lunacy about not meaning to have left them, saying she'd been taken.

Understandably upset, Annie had disconnected, Christina recalled. But long before, there had been another Annie. An Annie who, after she'd learned the true story as a child, had fantasized, making up wild tales about how their *real* mother would someday come back to reclaim them.

"She's called back again, hasn't she?" Christina demanded. "That woman who says she's our birth mother."

"I—I'm not—" Annie's face reddened as she shook her head, but she couldn't even spit out a full denial.

"Tell me you didn't buy into whatever bullshit she was selling. You didn't go to meet this whack job that night, did you?"

Anne darted a desperate look toward the entryway, as if she might make a break for it.

Christina stepped in front of the opening. "Just tell me, and you can go. Tell me where you really were when Lilly and I were trapped in that burning house."

"I don't—I don't want you to be mad."

"You always say that," Christina reminded her, "and yet you're standing here royally pissing me off right now."

A tear rolled down her sister's beautiful face—a face so much prettier than her own that Christina had often suspected they'd had different fathers. But before she could answer, a light rap on the side door behind Christina made both women jump.

Sucking in a deep breath, Christina turned and stood on her toes to peer through the door's small windows. "Harris."

Annie was backing away, saying, "Damn it. I was going to call him."

But Christina was already opening the door to let him in.

"Christina," he greeted her, his expression sharpening as he looked over her shoulder to fix her sister with a hawklike gaze. "And Annie

Wallace, I thought we'd *never* get the chance to catch up. You've been dodging my calls."

"I was—I was just about to head out." Growing pale, Annie dug the key to the rental car from her pocket. "To the grocery store to pick up dinner."

"And miss the big surprise?" asked Harris, sliding a wry grin Christina's way. A grin that had warmth blossoming low in her belly with the memory of his lips on hers.

Annie was stammering something else, but it was lost as Harris turned his head and nodded to a uniformed officer—the tall, dark-haired young woman with the impossible last name. She was smiling, too, holding a strap of some sort in her hands, which was attached to a wriggling, wagging Max, who yelped and pulled away the moment he caught sight of Christina.

"Maxie! Oh my gosh!" Christina pushed halfway through the door and dropped to her knees as the greyhound bounded up the concrete steps. Surging past Harris, eighty pounds of what had once been track-hardened muscle bowled her over onto her butt. But she only squealed and hugged him with her good arm and let him lick the side of her face.

"That's one lucky boy," Harris said in a low voice that snapped Christina's gaze to his eyes. "Damn lucky he finally let Officer Zarzycki and me corral him before he ended up getting run over."

"Thank you! Thank you both so much," Christina said, allowing Harris to help her to her feet, and laughing as she realized her dog was wearing a navy sweatshirt with *SCPD* in white block letters across the back. "What's he got on? Is that yours?"

Harris shrugged. "He was shivering so hard. And starving. Wolfed down a couple of plain hamburger patties I had 'em grill him at the drive-through like they were nothing."

Knowing Max, he might well bring them both up later on the carpet, but Christina was too relieved that he was alive to care. "Thank you again. Thank you both."

As the dog ran, wagging his tail, to greet Annie, Christina invited both officers inside.

"You're more than welcome, Dr. Paxton," Officer Zarzycki called. "I was really glad Chief found him. But I need to head back over to the station now."

"Thanks again for your help," Harris told her with a nod. A moment later, he shut the door behind him, sending a look toward Annie that made it clear he had no intention of letting her escape.

CHAPTER SEVENTEEN

Harris heard movement on the second floor, followed by the sound of Lilly's laughter. Turning toward the sound, the greyhound wagged his strong tail so hard that Annie said, "Ow, dog," as she fended off a whipping from it.

Max bounded for the staircase, looking faintly ridiculous in the sweatshirt. Judging from the happy squeals Harris heard moments later, Lilly was as excited to see her dog again as Max was to see her.

"I'd better go check on those two," Christina said as a series of thumps and squeaks followed. "Promise or no promise, I hear Lilly jumping on the bed."

"Why don't you let me?" asked Annie, looking all too eager to escape.

"You stay here," Christina said, giving her sister a look that said she meant business. "I'll be right back, and then we'll all talk."

Jaw set, Annie flipped her wheat-blonde hair over one shoulder in a gesture Harris read as defiance, maybe even resentment that Christina had played the big-sister card. Gesturing toward the ivory sofa and two coral-colored wingback chairs that made up the living-room seating area, he suggested, "Why don't we sit in here?"

"Whatever," Annie said, clearly in the mood to play the part of thirty-year-old teenager in all her petulant glory.

A faint smell caught his attention, and he surreptitiously sniffed. Apparently, he wasn't quite as subtle as he'd figured.

"Dead mouse, we think, or maybe one of the contractors accidentally left behind his lunch," Annie explained as she pulled out the piano bench, which was nearer to the escape routes of the stairway and the outside door. She perched on its edge, then folded her arms beneath her full breasts in a way that lifted them into view.

Keeping his gaze above her neckline, Harris turned one of the chairs to face her. "So, you gonna tell your sister, or would you rather we talk about it back at the station?"

The question was part guesswork, part bluff, but from the deer-in-the-headlights stare she gave him, it was clear she didn't know that.

"Yeah," he said, answering the question she seemed unable to find the courage to ask him. "I figured it out. Like anybody else could, if they asked the right questions."

Thanks to a few tips from Annie's ex-boss, Harris had gotten his first inkling that the Wallace sister whom longtime residents still referred to as *the fun one* might be hiding an issue that was definitely no laughing matter.

He saw he must be right about it, for Annie's face went ashen, and her right foot jerked to life, tapping out a nervous rhythm.

"How much is it, Annie?" he asked. "How much are you into Reg Edgewood for?" He stared hard, feeling a muscle in his jaw tighten. Because he'd love another excuse to arrest the man, to get him removed from the city council for his shady dealings.

She shook her head. "What are you talking about?"

"He's loaned you money, hasn't he?"

She shrugged a shoulder. "He's helped me out a few times. You know, a fill-up for my car when I was running on fumes, and he paid the vet bill for me after my old cat got out and a car hit him."

She sighed and shook her head before continuing. "I was a wreck that night at the bar when I found out poor Smokey hadn't made it. When Reg heard what'd happened, he went by the office, without a word to me about it, and paid off my vet bill—all twelve hundred dollars of it."

"That was nice of him," Harris said. Except that Edgewood didn't do nice. The guy wouldn't loan his grandmother a postage stamp without expecting to be repaid with compound interest. "So what did he want in return?"

"He wouldn't take a dime, if that's what you're thinking. He *did* ask me to go out to dinner when his wife was in the hospital recovering from some heart procedure, and he was missing her home cooking."

"You went?"

"Just the once," she admitted. "But I told him it would have to be just dinner. I don't do married men. Not ever."

"So how did he take that?"

"If he was disappointed, he did a fantastic job of hiding it. We've talked a few times since then. That's all."

"And just how much of that talking has been flirting?" Harris asked, though it wasn't a fair question. From what he'd heard and seen of her behavior, teasing, joking, and provocative behavior came to her as naturally as chomping down on a hunk of raw meat did for a shark like Edgewood. Only when he deigned to share his dinner, you could be sure there was a buried hook.

Annie rolled her eyes. "I'm friendly with him, that's all. *Pleasant,* like everybody is who counts on tips to pay the bills. But he's given me some good advice about going back to school and all that—I reenrolled part-time and switched over to a business major."

"You pay for that yourself?" he asked, already knowing there was no way, not on the seasonal unemployment she drew this time of year.

She shrugged off the suggestion. "I couldn't score financial aid, and my mom's cut me off, not that I can blame her after I quit showing up for classes last time. Back when I was still wasting my time pretending I was ever going to make it through the nursing program. The anatomy class alone—" She sighed. "I've never had Christina's head for all that gobbledygook."

"So you took a loan out for the business classes?" *Let me guess.* "From Reg Edge?" The high school dropout and *selfless* mentor of big-breasted blonde bartenders. While his poor wife was in the hospital, no less.

Dropping her gaze, she tightened her jaw.

"Sorry that took so long," Christina told them as she trotted down the stairs, "but I've got Lilly started with a movie on Mom's iPad upstairs, and poor Max is out cold on the bed beside her. I'll take your sweatshirt off him and wash it—"

Reaching the bottom of the staircase, she stopped and looked back and forth between her sister and Harris. "What's going on here?"

"Your sister was just telling me how she got the money for tuition this semester."

Christina gave him a fierce look. "I thought we were waiting until I came back down to talk."

"*You* might've thought that," he said, "but your sister's an adult. And I have a murder investigation to get on with."

Christina's cheeks went red. "Annie has nothing to do with Officer Fiorelli's death."

"If I thought she did, believe me, she'd already have the cuffs on," he said, wishing Christina had stayed upstairs so he could get this out of the way without her running interference.

"Well, anyway, our mom paid her tuition. Didn't she, Annie? Tell him."

When she said nothing, Harris rose to face Christina. "Thing is, she's told me already. It wasn't your mother at all. Turns out your sister's gotten chummy with—"

Annie shot up from the piano bench. "There was nothing, nothing at all wrong with that loan. We have a written contract, and the interest rate he's charging me is cheaper than I could get from anywhere else. *If* I could convince any bank to lend me money."

"Wait a minute," Christina said. "The interest *who's* charging you?"

"It was Reg, Reg Edgewood. He's just a friend, that's all."

Christina flicked an anxious look toward Harris, clearly recalling his warning about the man. "Why wouldn't you have asked me? I would've gladly helped out."

"You were just moving in and talking to Mom every day when I had to pay it. So I just assumed she'd told you all about her plan to make me straighten up and fly right."

From Christina's grimace, Harris suspected Annie had that right. It was clear, too, that her sister was conflicted, caught between two family members who were clearly at odds.

"Anyway," Annie continued, "the loan from Reg is no big deal."

"Sure, it isn't," Harris put in, "until you miss a payment. Is that where you went Tuesday night? To settle up your interest?"

"Wait a minute," Christina said. "I thought you were meeting the woman from the—"

"I went over to a friend's. That's all," Annie admitted. "I just needed some time for myself. Was that too much to ask after taking care of Lilly all day?"

"What friend?" Harris asked. "I'm going to need a name and address."

"Then why lie to me about it?" Christina demanded of her sister. "It's not like I was keeping you chained up, Cinderella."

"I—I thought it would sound better to tell you I was working for a sick friend instead of just saying I wanted to go by Kym's place, maybe have a drink or two."

"This is Kym Meador?" Harris asked, remembering one of the waitresses whose witness statement he'd taken after that fight at the Shell

Pile. An attractive young woman with straight black hair, thick eyeliner, and a silver nose ring, she'd loudly insisted that the behavior of female employees was in no way responsible for the offending men's behavior.

She'd only simmered down after he'd pointed out that the men had been the ones arrested—and her boss had finally told her to *put a sock in it, why don'tcha?*

Annie smiled. "Yeah, that's her. We've been best friends forever. You go and ask her, and she'll tell you. She'll tell you I was there."

Harris had no doubt Kym Meador would tell him anything she figured would help Annie. Whether or not it happened to be true.

Christina frowned at her sister. "I thought you weren't drinking, so you could focus on your classes. And you told me Kym was sick. I guess those were lies, too?"

"Come on, Christina. Cut me some slack. It's been a tough week."

Her sister lifted her left arm, still in its sling, toward Annie. "Tell me about it."

"I mean, I adore Lilly. Don't get me wrong, but you've even said yourself that she can be a handful."

"If you didn't want the job, you shouldn't have insisted."

"I *did* want it. I still do. And it wasn't just Lilly, anyway. I had my course work and those weird calls from—" Annie darted a look toward Harris and abruptly shut down.

"Go on," he urged. "Who called you?" Though he still didn't believe she could be the killer behind Fiorelli's death, it occurred to him that Annie could be something else entirely: the intended victim of the fire that destroyed the house that she, too, had moved into.

Could the previous vandalism of Christina's car have been a message meant for Annie? Or was he reaching, aching to attribute these crimes to Reg Edge solely because he wanted the bastard to be guilty? Especially since he couldn't imagine Edgewood going to such extremes when it sounded a lot more like he was angling to maneuver Annie into his bed with his checkbook.

"You might as well tell him about the calls, too," Christina told her sister. "After all, it was you who told him about *Katie*, wasn't it?"

When Annie dropped her gaze, Christina pressed, "Oh, come on. Who else could it have been?"

"I couldn't help it," her sister blurted. "He said I'd go to jail for some stupid parking tickets if I didn't—"

Christina zeroed in on Harris, her gaze as sharp as broken glass. "You *threatened* my sister?"

"If you ever sit down for a hand of poker with me," Harris said, trying to break the tension with a half smile, "consider yourself forewarned. I play a mean bluff."

"No surprise there," she said, reminding him she'd already pegged him for a cad and a liar. Or at least she wanted to believe it—when she wasn't kissing him back or trusting him to catch her child.

But that wasn't fair, was it? Reading anything into actions she'd taken while desperate or drugged. Telling himself not to be pathetic, he shoved the memories aside . . . or tried to.

Instead, he remembered holding her hand up on the jetty while pointing out the stony hulk of the abandoned lighthouse on Willet's Point. Hearing her ask, "You're not the same man, are you?"

I sure as hell don't want to be. It was a thought that left him aching. Left him realizing he not only wanted her safe, but just plain *wanted* her, God help him.

And there was not a damn thing he could do about it.

Drawing a deep breath, Christina told herself her that coming clean with Harris—as much as she dared, anyway—was the right thing. Still, her voice shook as she asked, "You know how I told you I heard a female voice, back on that first night when the garage was broken into and the alarm disabled?"

"Sure," he said, "the one we've been thinking must have come through the hacked baby monitor."

"Well, Annie got an anonymous call on her cell a few days back from some woman claiming she's our mother."

"So you really want me to tell him everything?" her sister asked, uncertainty in her eyes.

Nodding, Christina fought to steady her voice, to radiate a confidence she wasn't feeling, as well as the faith that they could trust him. "My daughter could've died in that fire. An officer *did* die, and for all we know, it's related to this woman somehow."

"Why don't we all sit down?" Harris waved them toward the sofa.

Annie meekly went to one end while Christina claimed the other. Harris took one of the two upholstered chairs, which he angled to face them.

Looking at her sister, he asked, "So, what was it this woman wanted?"

"Sh-she started out saying how it wasn't her fault, and she never meant to leave us."

"What did she say next?" Harris asked. "What did she want from you?"

"She said we had to come and find her. She needed to talk to us."

"It's what she said to me, too, that night on the monitor," Christina admitted. "She told me if we didn't find her, we'd both stay lost forever."

Harris frowned at her and shook his head. "You didn't mention that before."

"I was shaken. I forgot that detail."

He held her gaze long enough for her to understand he didn't buy it, but he let it go and asked both of them, "Did she give you any idea where to look?"

"I didn't give her a chance," said Annie. "I hung up. You have to understand. I almost died that night. Because of what she did."

"I thought you had," Christina said, the gooseflesh prickling along her upper arms. "If those sanitation workers hadn't come along and found us when they did . . ." She remembered the monstrous truck rumbling like a beast so high above her, two big men rushing toward them, and how she'd been too numb to scream. It was another detail she'd forgotten—or was stress causing her mind to manufacture false memories? How would she know?

"So what about you?" Harris asked her. "She tell you anything that might help you find her? Like her name, for starters."

Christina shook her head. "No, but then . . . I don't think this woman really wants us to come find her. I think she's out instead to scare us. Or maybe to string us along, to make us desperate enough that we'll buy into whatever her scheme is."

"And what do you imagine that might be?"

Christina shrugged. "I suspect it will come down to money."

"Why's that?"

"A couple of years ago, I hired a PI to take one last crack at finding her. I needed some medical history, that's all."

"You never told me," Annie said.

"I would've if we'd found anything. But there was no trace. I'm afraid, though, that it's possible the inquiries could've led someone to us here. Some opportunist."

"So you don't believe she's who she says she is?" asked Harris.

"If she were the real deal, would she be carving up my car or burning down the house where I was staying?"

"She would never have done those things," Annie argued. "At least, that wasn't the vibe I got from our conversations."

Something went cold inside Christina when she heard her sister use the plural. "I thought you only spoke with her the one time?"

Annie hugged herself. "She, um, she called again earlier the other day, before you came home from work."

And before the house caught fire. "You never said a word to me," Christina blurted out. "Why not?"

"I had no idea what to do. What to believe. That's the real reason I went to Kym's that evening. After I broke down and told her, I was such a hot mess she poured me a drink so I could calm down."

"What was it this woman said that upset you so much?" Harris's tone was calm and understanding. For the moment, anyway.

"She convinced me she was our real birth mother."

"She changed your mind, then?" Harris asked. "About Lilly, I mean?"

Annie looked down into her lap, picking at a jagged thumbnail.

"What about Lilly?" Christina asked, instantly on guard.

After a longing glance at the door, Annie answered, her voice barely above a whisper. "I just thought that maybe Lilly could be one of those children. Those toddlers that you read about, channeling the dead."

"Channeling the *what*?" Christina sputtered, a wave of lightheadedness dimming her vision. She might have blamed the medications she was taking if she hadn't heard her daughter's voice running through her brain. *Kill me. No leave babies.*

At the sound of footsteps on the staircase, all three of them looked that way. But instead of Lilly, it was only Max, heading back down toward the sofa.

"She doesn't think that now, though," Harris answered for her sister. "Isn't that right, Annie? Not unless the dead have suddenly started using phones."

"I—I guess that's true." She tried to laugh, but it came out sounding strangled.

Christina patted the vacant center cushion, too confused by this exchange to care that her mother would have had a fit about her letting Max on the furniture.

"So what did this woman say to change your thinking?" Harris asked her.

Annie scooted farther over to make room as the dog slipped up between them and laid his head and neck across Christina's lap. "At first, she gave me some crazy story about some man jumping into her car when she stopped at an ATM, then forcing her to ditch us. When I called her on it, she admitted it was drugs."

Finding her voice again, Christina asked, "And that's when you decided you believed her?"

Annie nodded. "If you only could've heard her crying. I—I knew in my heart then that she's not just some nut pretending to try to take us for a ride. I could sense it, Christina—you would have, too. This was a woman coming clean about something she hadn't ever admitted, even to herself."

It didn't shock Christina that her sister would accept some stranger's claims. It seemed that Annie's childhood dream, common enough among adopted kids, of being reunited with a birth mother who'd all along been tragically misunderstood had never really died.

But Annie didn't remember the terrifying ordeal her older sister did.

Christina's own childhood fantasies had involved angry confrontations, at least until she'd finally accepted, with the help of the therapist she'd been taken to see about the nightmares, that holding on to hurt and rage was only hurting her. *Forgetting is the best revenge*, her *real* parents had often told her. And for years, she'd almost managed it, or at least managed to pretend she had.

Harris prompted Annie, "So your biological mother—"

"We don't know that," Christina insisted.

"All right, then. This *woman* claimed she was in the neighborhood that night to make a drug buy?"

Annie nodded. "Only she knew there was no way this biker dealer she did business with was going to sell her a hit if she showed up at his place with a couple of babies in tow. She started crying into the phone then, swearing she'd gotten treatment and that she's been clean for years now. But at the time, she was so strung out, she couldn't think of anything but scoring her next hit."

Her sister's look was thoughtful, her tone maddeningly sympathetic as she continued. "She was a lost soul before she got help. The drugs were running her life."

Once more, Christina saw those disappearing taillights. Red lights that somehow in her mind became two shrinking flecks in Lilly's eyes. Shaken, Christina said, "She drove off and left us. How can you buy into her—"

"She claimed they wouldn't let her leave, that they held her."

"For *months*?" Christina snorted in disbelief, knowing the police had spent at least that long looking for the woman. "Probably started partying and forgot she even had kids. Or she was whoring herself to score her next hit."

She knew how harsh she sounded but couldn't bring herself to care. Why should she, when that woman—on the off chance she was the person she claimed to be—had nearly cost them their lives? When she might very well be involved in the fire that could have taken Lilly from her if Harris hadn't come in time?

"If it's true," Harris said gently, "you should count yourselves lucky that you escaped that lifestyle. I've seen what it does to kids, having a parent caught up in addiction. Never seems to end well for anyone involved."

Christina swallowed past a painful lump, knowing he was right. She'd seen too much of it herself, in emergency departments from the East Coast to Texas.

"So what else did this woman say?" Harris asked her sister. "Name, location, anything that could help?"

Annie shook her head. "She was crying so hard by that point, and then she disconnected. Just like the first call, there was no number showing on my cell, so I couldn't call her back. And she hasn't called me again since the fire."

Christina said, "That alone should tell you something. Don't be so naive."

"I'm not a child, Christina." Her sister jumped up from the sofa, her voice vibrating with frustration, and her eyes shimmering with tears. "So you can stop treating me like one. Finally."

"I'd be happy to do that, Annie—if every single time I did, you didn't find some new way to disappoint me."

"Come on, you two," Harris said, gesturing for peace with raised palms.

But it was too late, with Annie shouting, "That's it. I'm out of here. I'm going to Kym's now, like I told you."

"Please don't leave." Pushing Max's head from her lap, Christina came to her feet, too, panic roaring through her, along with the certainty that she couldn't have said anything more crushing to her sister if she'd plotted it for months. "I didn't mean it. I'm so sorry. I'm just—"

"You're finally saying what you *really* think, and we both know it. What you've been too polite, too busy being the *perfect* daughter, to let out of your mouth before."

"I love you, Annie," Christina said, too desperate to care about the show they were putting on for Harris, or even poor Max, who was whining and pressing close to her legs, clearly upset by the shouting. "I need you—and not just to take care of Lilly. You're the only sister I have."

Jaw tightening, Annie dug the keys to the Mercedes from her handbag and picked up the jacket she'd thrown over the back of the unoccupied chair. "I'll have Kym drop me by and bring the car back later."

"We have to talk," Christina pleaded as Annie went for the door.

"You've already said enough for one day, don't you think?"

Knowing the only way to deescalate this situation was to give the sisters time apart, Harris was up and after Christina in one fluid movement, grasping her uninjured elbow before she could reach the door that Annie had just slammed behind her.

Looking down into her tear-streaked face, he said, "Let her go for right now."

Christina shook her head, her hair swinging out around her shoulders. "I have to make her understand I didn't mean it."

"She knows that," he said gently, feeling her shaking beneath his grip. "Or she will, once she has time to calm down. And you, too, Christina. You've been through a hell of a lot."

"I can't believe I said that. I'm such an idiot."

"You're not an idiot. You're human. A human who'd just been socked with a lot of upsetting information, including a couple of huge secrets your sister's been keeping from you."

The tension in her body eased a little, but the pain in her eyes burned like a bed of hot coals. "First Renee, now Annie," she said. "I've driven away everyone I care about. Everyone who's ever cared for me."

"Not everyone," he said, meaning to add that there was a little girl for whom she meant everything upstairs now, a mother who'd be home again to see her and support her soon. But somehow, he didn't finish, his pulse picking up as he mentally dared her to make of his statement what she would.

To his astonishment, she moved a step nearer and leaned her head against his chest. Slowly, he pulled her even closer, his intention—or so he told himself—merely to offer comfort.

What he hadn't guessed was how much of it he would draw from her, how the warmth of her body, the way she fit so perfectly against him and the syncing of her breaths to his, could drain away so much of the stress and confusion he was feeling.

He stood there, rocking her slightly, rubbing his palm over her back, not daring to speak, or risk saying anything that would shatter whatever was happening between them. Anyway, wasn't it words that always went wrong for him, words that made a mockery of what he was feeling?

"What are we doing here?" she finally whispered. "What are you—"

He ducked his head to press his lips to her temple. "Trying desperately not to open my mouth and fuck things up again . . . Oh hell. There I go. Sorry about the language—"

Instead of taking offense, she laughed—a rich, warm sound that he wanted to drink in like water. Amusement lit her face, making her more beautiful than her younger sister. More beautiful than any woman he had ever known.

That was when he realized he was in even more trouble than he'd imagined. His hand slipped along her rib cage, over the sweet curve between her waist and hip on its way back to his side.

"You've saved my daughter and got me rescued off that rooftop," she told him, "and brought my dog back from the dead, too. So I think we'll let it slide this once. And, anyway, what are a few *fucks* between good friends?"

No sooner had the words escaped than she was pulling away, flushing furiously. "I—I didn't mean that the way it came out. I only meant to—"

It was his turn to laugh this time, so hard that she finally smacked his arm, her face redder than ever.

"Stop it!" she blurted out.

"Don't mind me," he told her, getting himself back under control. "I'm just so damn relieved *I* wasn't the one to put my foot in my mouth. This time."

"I'm so happy one of us, at least, is entertained," she said dryly. But there was a spark or something in her eyes that told him her pulse was racing just as his was, that she felt the wild energy arcing between them, brighter and hotter with every time they came into contact.

That it was a good thing, a damn good thing, that they'd found some way to break the growing tension other than the one he couldn't stop himself from picturing in excruciating detail.

He couldn't risk touching her again, he told himself, getting any more involved with a woman who was at the center of a critical investigation. But not even that would stop him if he didn't get the hell out of this house soon.

And the way she was looking up at him, her lips slightly parted and her eyes glazed with awareness, assured him she had the same need pulling at her, the way the moon called to the tides.

"I—I'd better go now," he said, though he had more to discuss with her.

"That would—that would probably be best. Before I—" Closing her eyes, she shook her head. "I have a lot to think about."

"Since your—since your sister took off, how 'bout if I run to the store for you. Pick up dinner. And you'll need dog food, too, right?"

She nodded. "I'd appreciate that so much. I'll have to pay you back, though, if that's okay. I'm sure it'll take me a few days, at least, to get a new bank card and ID."

"Don't worry about it," he said. "Just tell me what you'll need. And don't be shy about it, either."

"You're a godsend. Thanks," she said before giving him a brief list. "I'm afraid you'll need to stop by the vet's office—Dr. Olsen's clinic—to pick up Max's food. I'll call ahead and make sure they have it ready for you."

"I know where that is, sure, but that reminds me, I forgot to give this to you earlier." Slipping his hand into the inner pocket of his jacket, he came up with her cell phone. "I found it the night of the fire, underneath the porch roof. The light helped me to find you."

"It's still working?" she asked as she reached to take it from him.

"Corner of the screen's cracked, but it'll do you," he said before handing her a wound-up white cord. "I found an extra charger lying around the station, too, so I plugged it in awhile for you."

In the interests of his investigation, he might have done more than simply charge her cell phone, but he'd been unable to figure out

Christina's passcode. He'd been almost relieved she'd secured her private data, since the idea of going through her texts and e-mails without permission had bothered him a lot more than it should have.

If he was thinking straight, it wouldn't have, especially now that he knew she'd been withholding more information from him. What more was she hiding? And how could he break down her barriers without losing his fragile grip on his own self-control?

CHAPTER EIGHTEEN

As Harris left, Christina stood inside the entryway. With her hand splayed against the front door's cool wood, she catalogued her symptoms—the dry mouth and palpitating heart—but couldn't quite come up with a diagnosis.

Relief, she told herself. That had to be it, because she had no doubt, none at all, how close the two of them had come to using sex as a release valve for the pressure they were both under.

Would it really be so terrible, countered that portion of her brain still throbbing with frustration, *if I trusted him for a short while, with my body, not my heart?*

Shock rippled through her at the idea. The very *dangerous* idea, she quickly realized, knowing that if she and Harris ever came together, there could be nothing casual about it. For one thing, she wasn't wired that way. She'd learned that lesson years before. Learned it from the boy who'd left her wary of men for years.

But that boy had grown to manhood, into a loving father, a shift she'd witnessed with her own eyes, despite Renee's aspersions.

There was more to it than that, though. He was a shrewd investigator as well, one Christina knew would stop at nothing to find the person who'd murdered Officer Fiorelli and burned a piece of Seaside Creek's cherished history almost to the ground.

She wanted this person caught as well and would not be able to rest easy until he or she was behind bars. But her stomach knotted with the worry that in uncovering this criminal, Harris might publicly expose her sister's relationship with this local loan shark, a man that Christina intended to pay off herself as soon as possible.

Leaving Max behind to snore on the sofa, she headed to the second floor to look in on Lilly.

"Hey there, button," she said as she walked into the small bedroom she'd slept in as a child. At her adult height—five seven—Christina had to duck a little in order not to bump her head on the inward-sloping upper walls. Somehow, rather than seeming confining, the room felt like a cozy refuge. Or maybe it was the familiar furnishings, which her mother had recently repainted in a crisp white that looked great against the sea-green walls, and the handmade quilt on the single bed that comforted her, along with the knowledge that Annie's nearly identical bedroom lay just across the hall.

Picking her way among the toys to reach the slightly rumpled bed, Christina shut off the movie playing on her mother's iPad and knelt down by her daughter, who sat with legs crossed on an oval braided rug on the warm golden maple floor. There, Lilly had spread the contents of the box of toys around her, where she was happily organizing them into groupings based on some criteria Christina couldn't decipher.

"Mommy play?" Lilly pleaded, picking up the scattered pieces of a simple plastic toy set known as Tiny Family and raising them like offerings.

"Okay," Christina said, folding herself into the awkward space. "But only if I don't have to be the mommy."

Lilly laughed at this outrageous suggestion, thrusting the mother figure toward her, with its yellow plastic hair and benign, painted smile.

"This the mommy," she insisted, smiling with two pearl-like rows of tiny teeth. "Kaydee-Mommy."

Of course it is. Nausea churning in her stomach, Christina stared, unable to accept the figure. And terrified of whatever her daughter might say next.

"Who told you that?" she asked, assuring herself that someone must have. There could be no other explanation—certainly not the one that Annie had floated for Harris. It was just one of those offbeat ideas her sister got in her head sometimes, probably from Kym or one of her other New Agey friends.

"Kaydee-Mommy tell me," Lilly answered, picking up a child figure with the other hand and showing her how *Kaydee-Mommy* whispered into the little girl's ear.

Christina tried to ignore the cold waves that swept over her. "Can Katie's mommy—can she talk to me, too?"

Lilly looked up at her, her eyes as blue and guileless as the strip of January sky peeping between the curtains. But in her mind's eye, Christina saw points of red reflecting in the pupils, then shrinking down to nothing.

Raising the mother toy, Lilly moved it, clearly pretending it was speaking, "They kill me, Katie."

Right hand shaking uncontrollably, Christina picked up a dark-haired daughter figure and had it enter into the conversation. "Who did?"

"Bad people," Lilly said through the mother toy. "Why they do that, baby? I only want to see"—she crawled nearer and came up on her knees before pushing an index finger into Christina's chest—"you."

Christina felt the thumping of her heart beneath that tiny finger. Felt the tears in her eyes, hot and stinging, and wished to God she'd gotten the medical history that she was after. Because this couldn't be real.

But mental illness certainly was. Hadn't she seen the evidence pass through her ER countless times? Hadn't she experienced it for herself, a situation that she'd been warned might put her at risk for more hallucinations under the wrong conditions?

Yet on she went with the charade, as if she were living in the world of Annie's fairy tales instead of the real one, where an educated woman, a woman who had always put her faith in science and learning, considered the possibility that her daughter really could be speaking to, or for, her dead grandmother. *Channeling* her, as Annie had so sheepishly suggested. "Where are—where are you now?"

"Silly Mommy," Lilly said, crawling into her lap and snuggling against her. "I here now, with you. Here with you forever."

~

As Harris left the historic district, he turned onto the main route tourists used to reach the shore. Instead, he headed inland, along a plowed but nearly empty road, so often bumper-to-bumper during the summers. He passed business after business shuttered for the season: pizza joints, bars, frozen-custard stands, bicycle-rental outfits, "seaside chic" boutiques, and half a dozen gift shops. A few concerns, like the tattoo parlor, a deli, and a small convenience store with gas pumps remained open, each of them run by one or two employees.

Turning onto a heavily wooded county road, Harris headed for Christina's vet's office. As the Tahoe jounced over the rutted surface—torn up from years of road salting and last winter's freezing temperatures—he crossed a small bridge spanning Seaside Creek and the tidal marsh that flanked it, its tall, gold-brown winter grasses mashed down in places by the snow.

As the land began to rise again, the marsh gave way to stunted trees that obscured many of the older cottages and aging singlewides that made up his old stomping ground. Despite Creekbend's grinding poverty and sporadic violence, and the painful childhood memories he would never completely shake, Harris couldn't help but appreciate how beautiful the area looked with the snow covering the rooftops and rusting cars—many of which hadn't been on the road in years—and clinging to the north side of every straight, gray tree trunk. He spotted a bright-red cardinal, swooping among the low branches of a holly, and a trio of whitetail deer pawing icy clumps to browse whatever they could find beneath the surface.

Or maybe it was only beautiful because the snow had hidden the ruins of the broken-down bungalow where he'd lived as a kid. Had blanketed the painful history that had shaped him.

Another mile down the road a short time later, he was just leaving the veterinary clinic when his phone buzzed with a call from the station.

"Bowers here. What d'you got?"

"Finally figured out Fiorelli's e-mail password," said Zarzycki, who'd clocked in early to work on the old desktop computer the patrol officers sometimes used to write reports or look up information. Though most of the younger officers used mobile devices, Fiorelli had preferred hanging around the station, sucking down coffee and dragging out his paperwork. "Should've figured it would've ended up being something gross."

"I'm trying to rise above the temptation to ask."

With a snort, she told him, "Bimbo69."

Harris sighed and shook his head.

"Turns out Bimbo's his dog's name," she elaborated. "Found it written on the back of a picture he had pinned up on the bulletin board, a shot of the two of 'em riding around in that old convertible of his. A '69 Camaro."

It bothered Harris more than he would've thought that he would never again see that familiar sight around town. Never again give the asshole a halfhearted wave, only to have Fiorelli flip him off, then tip back his head and howl with laughter, affectionately rubbing the giant Newfoundland's thick, black scruff as they passed.

"Good work putting it together," said Harris before changing the subject. "So what about those e-mails? You find anything of interest?"

"Actually, I did. There's a couple of messages from the owners of area security companies. A list of current and recently departed technicians working for them."

"Yeah. Frank was investigating the vandalism cases, looking to find any possible link between the security techs and the homes that were hit."

"And he didn't mention that he'd found one?"

"He did?" asked Harris.

"The message was already open when I checked it. He had to have seen it."

"When was that?"

"It was sent two days before—before he died."

"And this link?" asked Harris.

"An ex-employee of First-Rate Security who'd gone to work for the competition. And his employment dates correspond to client incidents."

"Any info on why he left the first company?"

"Not in the e-mail, but when I called First Rate's owner, he told me this guy was a newer employee, and he was let go after two of their clients had their houses broken into and trashed not long after this kid had worked on their systems. Owner figured he was just incompetent, but now he says he wonders if it was more than that. Especially when I told him the kid had gone to work for Secure-Shore, the company used by the owners of some of the other damaged houses, including the old guy who was assaulted."

"Mr. Gunderson," he corrected her. The poor man, now too scared to live alone, deserved the dignity of his name.

"Right. Walt Gunderson," she said, as if it had only slipped her mind for a moment.

"So what's this employee's name? We got an address on him?"

"It's Eric Edgewood, at 49 South Bluefish—"

"Oh, for—the city councilman's son?" Harris choked back a curse, Reg Edge's sneer springing to mind.

"Which would make him—"

"Fiorelli's nephew, yeah," Harris said, picturing a handsome twenty-something with thick, black hair and an ever-changing cast of girlfriends. High school wrestling champ and homecoming king a few years back, when Frank had shown off pictures and boasted about how clearly the kid owed his good looks to his favorite uncle. But the bragging had stopped abruptly around the time that Eric unexpectedly left college amid rumors of a cheating scandal and moved back home to run deliveries for a family member's deli.

"And he still lives at home."

"With my biggest fan, yeah." Harris sighed, thinking of how, since Frank's death, Edgewood had lost no time blaming his family's tragedy on Harris's failure to get a handle on the vandalism problem. Next week, there was going to be an emergency council meeting to discuss what was being termed "the current crisis."

Harris had only heard about it when a still-friendly council member had forwarded him a text about it, noting how odd it was that the current police chief hadn't been invited to attend.

"So . . . you want me to go pick Eric up?" Zarzycki asked. "Take a little of the heat off you?"

"Thanks, but no thanks, Aleksandra. Good rookies are too hard to find for me to let you paint a target on your back, too." Not that he bought that she was really a rookie. The more he saw of her work, he'd be willing to bet money that the three-year gap in the work experience on her résumé had nothing to do with a period of postmilitary unemployment, as she'd claimed. And the less he cared about whatever secret he sensed lurking in her background, as long as he could keep her on the Seaside Creek force. "I'll track down Eric myself a little later."

"They're sure to think it's some kind of retaliation. The city council, I mean."

Harris winced, remembering that day at the hospital right after Jacob had been injured, how he'd told Edgewood, *I hope to hell you never have to see your son lying helpless when there's not a damn thing you can do.* "They can think whatever they want to. But I intend to do the questioning myself."

Keeping his job might matter to him, but only if he didn't have to do it hamstrung. Because his real responsibilities, to his officers and his community, mattered a hell of a lot more than any paycheck.

By the time he made it back to the Cape Cod about an hour later, the silvery winter sky had faded to a dusky gloom. Soon, it would be fully dark, but Christina had turned on the front porch light, which bathed the snow-covered front yard in a welcoming glow.

When she answered his knock, he could see that her eyes were damp, and she was holding something, a book maybe, tucked beneath her left arm in its sling. But with a thirty-pound bag of dog food over one shoulder and three plastic grocery sacks hooked over his bad arm, he held off on any questions as she waved him inside.

"Sorry I took so long."

"That—that's fine. Thank you so much." She opened a hall closet containing coats, jackets, and assorted winter gear, her movements jittery. Using a foot, she pushed aside a pair of boots to make more floor space. "You can drop the dog food right here."

"When I went to pay, the woman working the desk at the vet's office wouldn't take my money," he said as he lowered the sack of what had to be pricey prescription pellets. Max, he noticed, was nowhere in evidence. Probably somewhere sleeping off his big adventure.

Closing the closet door, she said, "I called them after you left. Told them to put it on my bill."

"The woman said you had, but she wanted me to let you know the dog food's on the house—and they were so sorry to hear about the fire and everything."

Christina stiffened, looking mortified. "You told her?"

"Didn't have to. This isn't Dallas. It's usually so quiet here, especially in the dead of winter. When something happens, people talk, especially when it involves one of our own."

"Of course. It's just been so long." She turned and stalked into a formal dining room, but not before he glimpsed her using the back of her hand to wipe her eyes. "But I don't want anybody's pity or their charity. I just want this nightmare to be over. Is that too much to ask?"

He'd struggled with the same embarrassment, the same confused mix of gratitude and frustration after returning from the naval hospital to continue his recovery from the graft surgeries he'd endured. Returning to a hero's welcome while still stinging from what had felt more like a failure. But he sensed there was more to Christina's outburst.

"What's going on?" he asked as he transferred the grocery bags to the gleaming, oval surface of a dark wood table. "You're upset."

"And why wouldn't I be, Harris? I thought I was doing the right thing, coming back here to be closer to my family. And now . . ." Her eyes filled once again, her throat bobbing as she fought to keep herself under control. "Now it seems like someone wants to kill me. Someone who's not particular about who else gets hurt."

"Come here," he said, taking the item she'd been holding—which turned out to be not a book, but a computer tablet in a leather case—and placing it on the table next to the bag holding a still-warm rotisserie chicken in its plastic shell.

As he moved in to wrap her in his arms, her stiffness melted away. He stood rubbing her back and rocking her, trying to focus on the framed painting of a lighthouse weathering a storm—he recognized the familiar red-and-black of the Willet's Point light—hanging near a china cabinet. He didn't dare speak for fear he'd blurt out a suggestion that he had no damn business making.

But it was impossible to ignore the warmth of her body, the yielding softness of her breasts against his chest. Desperate to distract himself before she felt exactly how her nearness was affecting him, he looked down at the iPad and saw a search-engine results page with a list of links. The purple ones, he realized, were those she'd clicked and read, sites such as Children Who See Dead People, Psychic Kids, and Does Your Child Talk to Angels?

What the hell? He'd expect that her sister's searches were overrun with such links, but it was hard to believe that down-to-earth Christina would be swayed by Annie's flaky theories.

He must have tensed because Christina pulled back, then sucked in a breath when she followed his gaze down to the tablet.

As she quickly flipped the cover closed, she said, "You'll stay for dinner, won't you? It's getting late, and I'm sure you haven't had a thing all—"

"What's your daughter said now?" he asked. Seeing the denial taking shape on her face, he added, "Don't bother lying to me. You'd never make a poker player, not with that blush."

She hesitated, her gaze darting from the doorway they'd just entered to the one leading to the kitchen, which had been sealed off with heavy plastic sheeting.

"You aren't thinking of making a break for it, are you?" he asked.

"Of course not. I was just thinking we should eat now, before the food gets cold." Turning her back to him, she went to a glass-front china cabinet, which contained a display of deep-blue-and-white plates, along with a collection of crystal glasses his own mother would have been in awe of. "We'll use the good china, since Mom's everyday stuff is all packed up."

"Dinner can wait a few more minutes," he said as Christina opened up the door.

She struggled to get out plates one-handed until he said, "Let me get that before you pop your stitches."

Backing away to let him in, she said, "Grab one of the smaller plates for Lilly, will you? She was exhausted from the hospital—fell asleep right where she was playing, leaning against Max—but she could wake up hungry any minute."

He did as she asked, turning to see her pulling a chair with a booster seat from the corner. "Come on, Christina. Don't make me drag it out of you. What else has Lilly said?"

She went back to the cabinet and opened a drawer containing silverware. As she reached for the forks, he saw her hand trembling like the last autumn leaf barely clinging to a branch.

"There has to be a rational explanation," she insisted.

"There always is," he told her, thinking of the many investigations he'd seen, both as a marine and as a civilian. Thinking of how often a situation made no sense until one piece put it all into perspective. A missing piece such as the discovery Zarzycki had just offered that proved to be the key. "It's just a matter of whether we can find it. Tell me what happened, and I'll help you."

She turned to face him, her eyes shining. "Lilly—Lilly showed me with her toys. Showed me how Katie's mommy whispers in her ear. And then she pretended she was the doll, telling me how the bad men killed her. How she'd only wanted to see her babies . . . and it all seemed so damned *real*."

Maybe it was the hushed quality of Christina's voice or a draft from the room's curtained windows, but a chill swept over him, as slowly and gently as one of those slow-breaking, half-frozen waves that rolled in on a bitterly cold day.

"How could she know, Harris? How could she know more than anybody unless—"

"So you've bought into Annie's theory?"

"Channeling? Reincarnation? I guess those aren't any crazier than imagining Lilly's been in touch with the dead. I swear, I must be losing it. I've never for a single moment believed in any of this woo-woo stuff. I can't, but . . ."

Harris saw her struggle for some rational explanation. Something that followed the rules of the world she lived in and belonged to.

Throwing her a lifeline, he asked, "What if this same woman who called Annie has found a way to get to Lilly? Have you had her out somewhere? Maybe at the library at story time, or the church's Mother's Day Out program?"

"I haven't had the chance, working days the way I have been. But I think Renee's taken her to the church with Jacob a few times so she could run some errands. I told her I didn't mind, but should I have checked it out first? Is there any reason to believe someone there might be involved?"

"I'd have to look into it, but then there's also that baby monitor you were using. What if the same person who hacked in to speak to you was able to use it to talk to Lilly?"

Christina frowned, her gaze unfocused, before shaking her head. "I don't think the monitor works that way. Isn't her end microphone only?"

"There's a speaker," he said, warming to the theory as he spoke. "I took down the model number and found the instruction manual on the Internet. It's made so you can reassure your child from the handheld unit, or the one you were keeping in the master bedroom."

"I'm embarrassed to say I never knew that. The system was a shower gift, and I never got through the booklet that came with it. There was—I had a lot going on right then."

"I understand," he said, noticing the way her gaze avoided his. "Life gets hectic, and babies are a real adjustment."

"For some of us more than others," she said quietly, still not meeting his eyes.

There was something there, he realized, some hidden guilt he ought to root out. But his cop instincts were trampled by a deeper and more basic impulse, the need to make her understand that whatever inadequacies she was feeling, she was not alone.

"Don't be so hard on yourself," he said. "Sometimes even good parents cut a few corners, while flawed novices like me blunder through the best we can."

He caught the scent of cooling chicken, its once-tantalizing aroma morphing into something rancid. Or maybe it was the memories making him sick, memories he'd tried and failed to block.

She looked up again, insisting, "You're great with Jacob. And not only with him, but with kids in general."

"I've worked at it. A lot," he admitted. "As I have no doubt Renee has told you, I didn't exactly start out a shining example of a dad or husband. In fact, I—"

"You never really cheated." She shook her head, a glimmer of what he dared to interpret as hope written on her face. "Did you?"

"Is that what Renee said?"

"Not in so many words, but she led me to believe it."

He grimaced. "Makes me wonder why she didn't just come out and let you—let the whole world know—what I really did. Maybe she thought that was worse, admitting that she'd stayed after—after I . . ."

"You what?"

"I never committed adultery. Not once, Christina, but I did worse. I—I hurt my wife. Bad enough that she didn't leave the house afterward for weeks."

Christina stared at him in disbelief, hearing the surge of blood in her ears. He'd hit Renee? Tiny Renee? She pictured them arguing, their faces red as they shouted at each other. For some reason, the scene she imagined had no sound, and why would it? The cause of the disagreement didn't matter.

What did was the moment she imagined him drawing back his arm, raising a fist like a small boulder. The moment he smashed it into the woman he'd vowed to honor and protect. The woman who'd given him a son he claimed to love.

Seeing the remorse, the shame in Harris's face, Christina's eyes filled with tears. And in that moment, whatever fantasies she'd been entertaining died, fantasies that had lapped like warm, summer surf around her ankles, tricking her into thinking—at least on some unconscious level—that maybe somehow they could find a way back to what they'd almost had. A way to get it right, this time with the man who'd sprung from the wreckage of the thoughtless boy who'd hurt her.

Except he was still hurting women, only physically, just like the wife-beating father who'd raised him.

"It was an accident. I swear it," he said.

She'd heard the same excuse in the ER, from so many men, whose wives and girlfriends *accidentally* walked into an open door to blacken their eyes or slipped and fell and cracked a cheekbone, along with a rib or three.

He grimaced. "After—after the explosion, the doctors at the naval hospital spent a lot of energy putting my body back together. A lot of surgeries. A lot of treatment—hyperbaric chamber, water therapy, you name it."

"Looks like they did a good job of it," she said, though she suspected that, in places hidden beneath his clothing, he bore scars that would be hard to look at, especially for someone who'd never been around burn patients. But his face remained heartbreakingly handsome and clouded with regret.

"They did what they could, and believe me, if you'd seen what I looked like in those first months—the first year or two, to tell the truth." He pulled out a chair and sank down into it, as if the admission had drained him. "But the thing is, with everything I had to go through to get physically functional again, I never took the other side seriously—the emotional fallout of getting myself blown up and finding out four people hadn't made it."

Claiming a chair a seat away from his, she nodded, telling herself that no matter what he'd done, he deserved the same compassion as any of the patients she saw. Patients who had included, on more than a few occasions, men and sometimes women suffering from PTSD as a result of past military service.

But as much as she sympathized with everything they'd been through, she'd seen the other victims, the spouses sporting fractured mandibles and petechiae—broken blood vessels beneath the skin and the whites of the eyes—from strangulation; the children, so traumatized they'd lost the capacity for speech. Had Jacob been there when Harris had hit Renee? Had that innocent, sweet-natured boy absorbed that response to frustration into his developing psyche?

"I kept saying I was handling it," Harris said, his eyes distant, "kept resisting every effort to get me to open up about what I'd been through."

She swallowed hard, relating in spite of her intentions. Hadn't she responded with the same denial when Doug had first suggested that something was amiss? Hadn't it had equally disastrous results?

At least you never did anything that endangered your husband or your child.

No sooner had the thought risen than a buzzing built in her ears, punctuated by the drumbeat of her own heart. Because she knew, deep down, that left untreated, she could have done just that. Could have eventually been tricked into the unforgivable by the voices she'd been hearing.

But Harris was still talking, his explanation cutting through the clamor. She sucked in a deep breath and forced herself to focus on what he was saying, not herself.

". . . figured a real man didn't sit around and talk things through. He sucked up everything and got on with his duty, the way men did in those old flicks my mother used to watch. She might've stayed married to my father, but her heart belonged to John Wayne."

"My—my mom loves those old movies, too." She frowned, though, as she wondered how many souls—how many families—had shattered on the rocks of those old-school expectations. Men, taught to bury all their feelings. Women, raised to sympathize, to serve, and demur to the primary wage earner, no matter how much abuse he dished out. "But I don't think they're meant to be taken literally."

"Trust me when I say that even at his worst, the Duke was a better role model than my dad when it came to how to treat a woman. Dad's the reason why I don't drink, why I never should've gotten married."

"He was drinking, wasn't he? On the night of the rollover?"

Harris nodded. "His brother had had a heart attack. He was racing to try to be there in time—and God forbid he'd ever let my mom take the keys, or that she'd insist he did."

"I'm so sorry," she said uselessly, her gaze drifting across the family photos hanging on either side of an antique oval mirror. How lucky she and Annie had been to be raised in this loving household. Hers wasn't a perfect family by any means, hadn't been and never would be. But at least addiction and abuse had never had a seat at the table. "I know you had a lot of—you lost your entire family in one fell swoop."

"I'm answering your questions, not making damned excuses," said Harris, the bitterness in his voice unmistakable. "And I sure as hell don't want your pity."

"I pity Renee, not you. She's the one who got hurt." She spat the words, answering his anger with her own. Maybe because she didn't want to ache for him, too. Didn't want to be another patsy who imagined she could fix a broken man. "How many times?" she asked him. "How often did you hit her?"

"I didn't hit her, not exactly—or at least not the way you're thinking. And it was just that once, as she shook me awake when I was—I was caught up in a nightmare. Trying to get to Yardley, stop him. Stop him before he detonated, this time, so I could save the others."

"Wait a minute. You weren't even conscious?" From her own childhood experiences, she knew the flashbacks triggered by posttraumatic stress disorder could seem incredibly real, the resulting night terrors far more vivid than a normal dream.

"I flailed out with an arm. Knocked my pregnant wife right off her feet. She hit the nightstand face-first. I'll never forget the blood."

"In your *sleep*?" Christina repeated.

"I hit her. Hard enough to—her nose was broken."

"She's never said a word about it."

"She was embarrassed by the black eyes and, I think, even more embarrassed about staying." He raked his fingers through his short hair, looking as if he meant to pull it out. "When I was the one who should've been ashamed."

Her gaze latched onto his. "But you were *dreaming*. And you clearly got help afterward."

He stood again and started pacing. "I damn well did. I saw a doctor afterward, went to counseling religiously. Joined a veteran's group to talk things through, to figure out what I'd been trying so hard not to feel that it kept cropping up in my sleep. Slept in the guest room, just in case—except I never went back, even when she asked me."

"Back to where? You mean Renee's bed?"

"I couldn't take the chance again. I couldn't risk—she doesn't weigh a hundred pounds. I could've killed my child's mother."

"So you're saying that all this time, you haven't—? Not since she was pregnant?" Knowing she had no right to ask the question, but unable to resist it. Just as she was unable to resist her own upwelling of compassion for a man who had clearly punished himself for years. Punished himself for something out of his conscious control.

"We tried to make things work, for Jacob's sake, tried for a lot longer than we probably should have. But Renee—she might've been able to get past what happened, but what she took as my rejection was another story."

"You said you went to counseling. Did you ever try together?"

"She didn't feel the need, she always said, not when it was all my problem."

That sounded like Renee, like her wounded pride and anger talking.

Christina rose from her seat, mostly because his pacing was making her neck ache.

"And then she found someone else," Harris admitted. "Someone who reminded her she was still a young, attractive woman, for a little while, at least."

"*She* had the affair?"

"It wasn't her fault."

"But you didn't?" Christina asked, still trying to wrap her head around it. "Even after the two of you were finished? Find some other woman?"

He snorted. "What? And ruin her life, too? Turn her furious and bitter? I have enough to do with my son and my job, my work with the VA on the weekends. I'm a peer-support volunteer. It helps—helping others. Helps to take my mind off things I was never meant to have."

"You don't mean that," she said as she followed behind him. "You can't. And *please*, will you quit pacing so we can have this conversation?"

He stopped, then wheeled around to face her, so close that she could feel the anger rolling off him in waves. "I damn well don't need your advice on this. Don't want it."

Only inches from his face, she thrust her chin high to look into his eyes and threw down the question like a gauntlet. "Then what is it you do need from me, Harris Bowers? Because after the way you—the way you look at me, the way you touched me earlier, I can tell you, you didn't come here just for dinner."

CHAPTER NINETEEN

Harris stared down into her deep-brown eyes, the ground beneath him shifting as her pupils dilated. He felt himself falling into their expanding darkness, swallowed by the need and loneliness he saw reflected in them.

Still, he didn't make a move, the long habit of self-denial holding him back, though his body was shaking with temptation.

Shaking as it hit him that she knew the worst about him. Knew what a wreck he'd been, knew his most shameful secrets. Knew, too, that he'd kept celibate for more than four years now. Four long years, while he'd told himself that some men were better off alone.

His thoughts arced back to his father's sadness, to his shame and self-loathing each time he'd sobered up and left the family. Harris thought, too, of his mother, who'd invariably beg the man who hurt her to come home, neither one of them knowing how to live without the other.

And God forgive him, he couldn't live without this, either. Couldn't hold off another moment before Christina was in his arms, his mouth claiming hers with a kiss that left no doubt about what it was he wanted.

Her lips parted, their kiss deepening in an instant, a contact that burned what remained of his self-control to ash. And if he'd thought it was good then, at eighteen, with the heady mix of lust and vengeance in his veins, he'd been mistaken. For the sounds she made in her throat, the murmurs of encouragement and the way she wriggled as he pulled her tight against his body made him want to push her back, to take her here and now, atop this table.

With her murmur pitching higher, she turned her shoulders slightly. Realizing her injured arm was pinned between them, he came up for air.

"I—sorry. Didn't mean to hurt you. I could—I could stop," he offered. "We could—maybe we should think this over, before things go any—"

"I'm going upstairs to check on Lilly. You should—I think you should put the food away in the refrigerator in the basement. I'm not feeling very hungry."

"I am." He slid one hand lower, until he'd cupped her ass, and his whiskers, in need of a shave this time of evening, lightly scraped her neck. "So I'll be praying she's a damn sound sleeper."

Christina pulled away to look up at him, her eyes huge as she gave a shaky exhalation. "This is—this is crazy. I'm heading up."

Turning on her heel, she made a break for it. He followed for a few steps, enjoying the hell out of the sight of her heading up the stairs. And drawing in a deep breath, trying to suck in enough oxygen to bring himself back to sanity. Which might prove a challenge, since so little of his blood flow was going to his head.

With a grimace, he distracted himself by finding the door to the basement and heading down a steep and narrow flight of stairs with the groceries, as she'd suggested. Stashing the food quickly, he turned to head back up, only to fall victim to a hitch in his bad knee, which caused him to catch his foot on the lip of one crooked stair and pitch forward. Gut clenching, he recovered barely in time to keep from falling and reminded himself to watch his step . . .

Including the one he was about to take. The one that could cost him both his job and the self-respect he'd spent years rebuilding.

And what about the cost to Christina? Would he hurt her, too, when he was forced to pull back to focus on the investigation? To follow it wherever it led—even if that meant closer scrutiny of her sister's relationship with Reginald Edgewood and the man's possibly criminal son? The son that Harris knew he should be picking up right now so the kid could be questioned about his involvement with the burglars who had, at the very least, ransacked house after house and assaulted an old man.

Christina had it right. This was crazy, and Harris had better put a stop to it right now, before any more damage was done . . .

The rightness of the decision settled over him, along with the certainty that Christina would come downstairs anyway with a fussy toddler in her arms.

Taking a deep breath, he walked past the piano and into the house's living room. As he tried to make out what to say, how to tell her he thought he really needed to get going, he squatted in front of the fireplace, needing to do something with his hands.

Happy to find that at some point it had been converted to gas, he opened the damper and lit a cheery blaze. When he turned back around, he saw Christina standing alone, wearing a thick, wine-colored robe that fell past her knees. She'd taken off her sling, he realized, and like her feet, her lower legs, so close to his eye level, were bare.

"Lilly's fast asleep. Out cold for the night, I believe. But I—um—I was thinking," she said, sounding nervous as her fingers clutched the collar's overlap, "of all the reasons I should send you home right now."

He stared up at her, needing to know what lay beneath that robe more than he needed to draw his next breath. Aching to touch, to taste, to have his fill of her for whatever span of time the two of them could manage.

"I've been thinking along those same lines," he admitted as he came to his feet. "But right this minute, I can't think of anything but you."

A few short hours later, Christina woke shivering, her nude body bathed in flickering light and shadows. Though the afghan had slid to the floor, the fire was still burning, and Harris's arm was wrapped around her, cradling her in a protective embrace.

He was sleeping, his face peaceful, and utterly unself-conscious about the scarring that marred the perfection of his tight, toned body. Scarring she saw as a badge of honor, proof that he'd learned to put the needs of others first.

Heaven only knew, he'd put *her* needs first. Several times, using his clever fingers and his mouth until her doubts morphed into a white-hot ball of pleasure. With his pupils dilated and his erection impossibly hard against her, he'd been shaking with need by then, yet she'd sensed that with a word, she could have stopped him even then, could have paid back the deception of his youth with her own cruel brand of interest.

Instead, she'd whispered, "Now I want you. All of you. No holding back. No regrets. No promises beyond this."

And when their bodies joined at last, it had been better than she remembered. So right, so good, it banished all the loneliness she'd felt, not only since Doug's death, but before it—the loneliness that came with a marriage, not of equals, but with a man who'd come to think of her more as a patient to be managed than a partner or a wife.

The thought touched off a wave of guilt. How could she blame her husband, her poor husband, after what she'd done?

And how could she ever expect another man to really love her? Because Harris was certain to find out the rest, with all his digging.

Certain to discover that the scars she bore were no less serious than his, no matter how deep she kept them hidden.

But he hadn't asked for love. Hadn't asked for anything more than the temporary harbor each of them had offered.

She'd do well to remember that, she thought as she reached for the fallen afghan to cover him and then found the robe she'd borrowed from her mother's closet. As she dressed, she heard a noise from upstairs, whimpers and the sounds of scratching—claws scraping against woodwork.

Christina tensed, her thoughts flying back to that night in the Victorian, when she'd imagined she'd heard footsteps in the hallway. She didn't remember closing the dog in the bedroom with Lilly. Come to think of it, she knew she'd left the door ajar because she'd wanted to be able to hear her daughter if she began to stir. Wanted Max to be able to find his way downstairs without waking Lilly if he was hungry or thirsty or needed to go out.

Stomach fluttering a warning, Christina glanced at Harris, wondering whether she should wake him, ask him to check things out. An instant later, good sense came flooding back. How could she ask him to check on her own dog and child, especially here, in the house where she'd grown up, the house that sprang to mind whenever anyone mentioned *home*? Was she really going to let Max, who wasn't exactly known for his brilliance, scare her by accidentally pushing a door closed, or let the act of making love with Harris make her dependent?

There was another whine, this one clearly canine, and the clawing noise grew more insistent. Insistent enough that she thought of how upset her mom would be if she came home to find the door to the newly repainted bedroom scratched and scored by greyhound toenails.

"Hang on, Max," she murmured as she shoved her feet inside her shoes. But at the base of the stairs, the flutter in her stomach intensified, and the darkness of the open space above seemed to spiral in on her.

In that moment, the rush of the waves filled her ears, though she knew it was impossible to hear the ocean from this distance. The woman's voice came next, words that echoed through her memory as winter's breath. "If you don't come, baby, you'll both stay lost forever."

And whether it was fear, ongoing stress, or pure imagination fueling it, a white-hot jolt of pure energy shot through her. Along with the instinctive comprehension that this time, there was no mistake, no room for doubt or hesitation. Springing up the staircase, she ran straight for the bedroom where she'd left her sleeping child.

CHAPTER TWENTY

Harris started awake, disoriented and uncomfortable, his neck cramped from the angle of his head against a sofa cushion. Rubbing away the ache, he looked around to get his bearings.

The fire and the furnishings around him brought everything rushing back. What he'd done. What they'd done together.

But how long had he been sleeping, in a house awash with darkness? And what sound was it that had wakened him—the closing of a door? Something being dropped?

Something's wrong, his instincts told him, his stomach tightening and his breathing coming faster. His pulse thrumming at his throat, he wondered whether this disturbance he was sensing was a figment of his imagination. Or just guilt washing over him for breaking every vow he'd made since first seeing Christina again?

Stay professional. Stay focused. Don't risk hurting her again.

And above all, no matter what, don't dare fall in love.

But, remembering the feel of her in his arms, her sweet sigh of satisfaction before her body had melted into sleep, he couldn't make himself regret being with her. He'd felt such contentment washing over him, a peace that he'd never guessed existed. A rush of warmth that he realized came from hope.

So where's she gone? And what the hell was that noise?

Needing to check things out, he dressed quickly, warning himself not to be too quick to imagine the worst. Not when, likely as not, she'd only gone to check on Lilly or use the bathroom upstairs.

Once dressed, he reached for the nearby chair where he'd laid the concealed-carry gun he wore off duty, along with its under-waistband holster. Reached for it and felt a shock that traveled, balls to skull, when he found it missing.

"Shit!" He reached around, fumbling for a lamp. Before he found a switch, a high, small voice came from the staircase.

"Where my mommy? Mommy gone."

"Lilly?" Jesus. He lunged toward her, every short hair behind his neck rising, and his heart crashing as he spotted the tiny silhouette behind the stairwell banister posts. Had she gotten his gun in its holster? Could she have possibly figured out on her own how to release the safety?

Going for the shortest distance, he reached through the posts and grabbed at her. With a cry of alarm, she flattened herself against the opposite wall—out of his arm's reach.

Pulling back so he could come around the banister and climb the stairs to meet her, he said in the calmest voice he could manage, "Stay right there. It's all right. I just need to—"

She tried to scramble upward to escape him, but she was crying so hard—wailing now—that he was easily able to grab the struggling child and check to make sure she wasn't holding anything, least of all a loaded semiautomatic.

Breath coming in gulps, he thanked God. "It's all right. It's okay, Lilly. I didn't want you to hurt yourself, that's all."

But what if she has already? If the sound that woke him was the crack of gunfire? If the reason Christina hadn't responded to the sound of her child wailing was that she was lying somewhere, somewhere nearby, her staring eyes already sightless as blood pooled around her head?

As he struggled to contain the wriggling toddler, he felt for the light switch. "Christina! Christina, where are you?"

No answer, or at least not any that could be heard over Lilly's protests.

"Want Mommy! My mommy!" she cried as she fought to escape.

Finding the switch, he flipped it, flooding the stairwell and entryway with light . . .

And solving at least one mystery as he spotted his gun, still in its holster, lying on the living-room floor beneath the chair where he'd put it. It had to have been knocked down somehow or kicked aside as Christina went wherever she'd gone.

But there was no damn way, no way in hell, she would have left her daughter behind.

"Shh, honey," he told Lilly. "Let me put you down a minute, and we'll find your mother."

The little girl stopped crying, her fine, blonde hair a fuzzy halo around her head. "Find Mommy?"

"I promise. Absolutely." He came back down off the stairs, where he set her down before retrieving and strapping on the Sig Sauer.

"What that?" Lilly asked.

"It's for some grown-ups only," he explained, as he'd explained to Jacob whenever he locked the weapon in his gun safe at home. "I'm the police. We keep you safe from bad guys."

"Bad people like kill Katie-Mommy?"

"Like them, yeah," he said, once more wondering where the hell she'd heard such a thing and what it really meant.

With his gun secure, he reached for her again, but Lilly ghosted out of reach, heading toward the kitchen and calling for her mother.

“Don’t go in there,” he warned, thinking that all the heavy plastic might be covering up the island and the torn-out counters, but there were likely to be nails and splinters, all kinds of hazards for a fast-moving toddler to get into. He thought, too, of that off smell, the faint odor of decomposition. If an unlucky rodent had gotten caught among the folds and suffocated, it stood to reason that all that plastic could prove dangerous to a child as well.

Stopping short of the kitchen, Lilly instead scaled a bar stool, one of three that stood against a pass-through countertop that looked into the space. Pushing aside more plastic and a dusty piece of cardboard, she smacked at something with a flashing green light. Something he didn’t recognize until the answering machine began to play a message.

“Oh, dear, Liz—this is Nelda. I was so awfully sorry when I got your message. So disappointed and sad to hear you’re too ill to come with us on the trip.”

Harris froze, his brain spinning at what the woman was implying. Because surely Christina would have known had her mother canceled her trip to Europe.

“I’ve had food poisoning myself before,” continued Nelda. “Terrible, and you’re absolutely right. There’s absolutely no way you could get on a plane in that state. So you just concentrate on feeling better, sweetheart, and be glad we all bought trip insurance. Call that doctor daughter of yours now and get her to fix you up. And after we get back, we’ll bore you with all our pictures and start planning our next trip.”

“Grandma,” Lilly said. “That Gramma? She come home?”

Harris only stood there, his heart belting out a breakneck rhythm. Because how could Christina’s mother, Elizabeth Wallace, come home from her vacation when it seemed she’d never left?

Without answering her question, he scooped up Lilly and started upstairs with her, praying Christina had only gone back to her own bed, taking the dog with her. And praying that the subtle odor his nose had caught, the smell of flesh corrupted, was really no more than a mouse trapped somewhere, rotting.

He'd made it only up the first two steps when he heard the unmistakable sound of a key sliding into the front door.

He turned, relief crowding into his throat. "Christina?" Where on earth could she have been, without a car at her disposal?

Instead, Annie came in, her blonde hair pulled back and her blue eyes confused when she spotted Harris holding Lilly.

"What's going on?" she asked. "Where's Christina?"

"Auntie Annie!" Lilly cried happily, wriggling until he put her down.

"I'm not sure," Harris answered as Lilly wrapped her arms around Annie's legs. "I fell asleep, and when I woke up—I was just going up to check. But I thought you were gone for the—"

"Hey, sweetie." Annie ruffled Lilly's hair before returning her attention to Harris. "I realized she was right. I was being a selfish jerk leaving her alone here." As she looked him over, she gave him a knowing look. "But she wasn't quite as alone as I thought, was she?"

"Somebody had to pick up groceries."

Annie rolled her eyes. "Your shirt's untucked and buttoned up wrong, Harris. And I know it's not from—" She cut herself off, blinking hard, her body stiffening. "What the hell was *that*?"

A moment later, Harris heard it, too, an anguished cry from the rear of the house that had him drawing his weapon from its holster. Adrenaline surging through his system, he nodded toward the child and ordered, "Take her upstairs. Lock yourself in the bedroom. *Now.*"

Face draining of color, Annie didn't argue. Grabbing Lilly, she started upstairs, the child crying as she wailed, "Bad people. Hurt Mommy!"

As Harris headed for the kitchen, he hoped to hell Lilly was wrong. Prayed that Christina had only slipped on the ice taking the dog out, since he realized that with all the commotion, the greyhound would have most likely come downstairs to investigate.

As he pushed through plastic sheets toward the back of the kitchen, the smell of death grew stronger, along with what sounded like a woman sobbing as though her heart had been ripped to shreds.

As he found the back door left ajar, dread filled his chest, as cold and wet and heavy as fresh-poured concrete. He had a premonition, even before he flung it open, of what he would find out on the house's back porch, of what would pull those wrenching sobs from the woman he'd been holding in his arms such a short time earlier.

"Christina, are you hurt?" he asked, seeing her at the bottom of the steps down to the backyard. The greyhound was pacing and whining behind where she knelt, still in her bathrobe, leaning over what could only be a body.

The porch light streaming down highlighted her face as she looked up at him, her face raw with anguish.

"A-all this time," she said, "I didn't want to call her on her trip because I didn't want to spoil her vacation. And she—she's been right here, lying—lying under the steps. Max found her when I let him out. He came down here and wouldn't—wouldn't leave this spot. I—"

Recognizing that Christina was in shock—and probably half-frozen—Harris rushed to her and pulled her to her feet and into his arms. "God, Christina, I'm so—I'm so sorry."

Though it lay mostly in the shadow of the back porch, however, his first glance told him the person whose body he was looking at hadn't died of natural causes. Despite the freezing and exposure, the signs of violence and head trauma were unmistakable . . .

And horrifyingly similar to those he'd first seen on eighty-three-year-old Walt Gunderson after his assault.

Shivering racked Christina's body, tremors so violent she felt as if her flesh would tear from her bones. For Lilly's sake, and Annie's, too, she fought to pull herself together, to draw on those same reserves that allowed her to keep her emotions in check while she did what needed to be done.

But it was no use. She was far too cold, inside and out, to offer any comfort. Even when Annie began to scream once he'd told her, fighting to get past Harris, who refused to let her near the back door—near the *crime scene*.

Not understanding anything except her mother's and her aunt's tears, Lilly wailed in sympathy, in a scene more nightmarish than anything Christina could remember. The ringing in her ears that had started when she'd dragged the body—*not the body, Mom*—from beneath the steps intensified, drowning out the noise just as the tears in her eyes blurred her vision.

Her thoughts detached like balloons, bobbing untethered beneath the ceiling as Harris scooped her up and said something she couldn't understand to Annie and Lilly. He carried her upstairs, Annie showing him to her old bedroom, where Lilly had earlier played and slept. Grunting as he stooped, he laid her in the double bed and pulled the covers up to her chin.

Max stood quivering near the bedside with his tail tucked to his belly and his brown eyes bulging. Like her sister and her daughter, the sensitive greyhound clearly needed reassurance. Reassurance that Christina was too shattered to give them.

Harris hugged her hard, and she focused on his moving lips, struggling to make his words come into focus. "I know you won't believe this right now. I know that I can't fix this. But I swear to you, I'll see you through it. And I will do right by her."

Christina tried to answer, but there was a lump in her throat, too hard and sharp for speech.

And in his face, those gold-flecked hazel eyes she knew so well, she saw that he knew. He understood, and he meant every word he was saying.

"Help is on the way," he said. "All you have to do is breathe. Breathe for me. Nothing else right now. Okay?"

Her shaking eased a fraction, enough to let her nod in answer. He smoothed the hair from her face and then turned to her sister. She was holding Lilly, who'd gone quiet, clinging as she sucked her thumb and stared with wet blue eyes.

"I need you to stay in this room, all of you," he said. "Warm her up if you can. She's freezing cold, and I have no idea how long she's been out there."

Wiping away tears, Annie said, "I—I can run a warm bath for her."

"That's a good idea, but I need you to wait for now. I'll let you know as soon as my deputies and I can clear the house."

"Clear the—what—what happened to our mother?" Annie asked, her voice hitching every few words. "Do you—please, just tell me. Tell me what you think."

Harris shook his head. "Too soon to say. I only know there was a message saying she'd canceled her trip due to illness."

"But she—I don't understand this. It's impossible. It can't be real. I need—I need my—"

From downstairs, Christina heard knocking—at the front door, from the sounds of it.

"I have to go," he told them. And then to Annie, "Please don't call anyone just yet."

Striding out, he closed the door behind them. Closed all four inside a bedroom in a house of desecrated memories . . . a house that could never again feel anything like home.

CHAPTER TWENTY-ONE

Around three a.m., Harris went to tell Annie they'd cleared the upstairs in case she still wanted to run that bath to help warm up Christina. Instead, he found the sisters and Lilly, all three nestled with their arms interlaced, as if they'd been comforting one another until they'd succumbed to exhaustion—and their desperate need to escape the unthinkable in the only way possible.

With a bar of light from the hallway slanting across Christina's face, he saw her eyes jerking back and forth beneath the lids and her mouth twitching downward. Suspecting she was caught up in a nightmare, he ached to go to her, to pull her close enough to remind her and himself of what they'd shared—had it been only hours ago?

But Harris didn't move. He couldn't, unable to bear the thought of waking her to face an even uglier reality. A reality that he knew from his own struggles with traumatic memories would spin up bad dreams like waterspouts for years to come.

He knew, too, that it was possible she'd associate this shock and horror, her unbearable pain, with the pleasure they'd found together earlier. That every time she looked at him, she would taste bile and feel the cold of her mother's frozen flesh beneath her hands. That she would see the ice-filmed eyes, the face so cruelly distorted—

He swore under his breath, wishing to hell that he could gift Christina with amnesia, even if it meant her forgetting him forever. He'd give her up, would give up any chance of happiness forever, if he could only make this right for her, could make it right for all of them.

He sighed, partly from fatigue and partly from the knowledge that there was nothing he could do to return Elizabeth Wallace to her family. And nothing that could make up for his failure to have stopped these crimes in time to save her.

The greyhound rose yawning from the braided rug where he'd been curled and walked over to lick Harris's hand. Taking the hint, he scratched Max behind the ears and whispered, "You keep an eye on them, big boy. Keep her safe and warm as long as you can." *For me.*

Closing the door softly behind him, Harris left the four where they were, knowing that the morning would come all too soon, along with the news that Annie and Christina's mother had apparently been killed in the house's kitchen. Murdered, though someone had clearly done his best to wipe down every surface and cover any lingering grout stains with some of the contractor's plastic sheeting. But the killer or killers hadn't done the job well enough to escape Marco Del Vecchio's sharp eye for stray spatter, or the reagents he'd brought in his CSI kit.

"Can you move that light a little to the left?" Del Vecchio pointed out the side of a dark cabinet to Zarzycki, whom he'd asked—big surprise there—to help him with the evidence collection.

When she'd complied, Del Vecchio continued, gesturing to the line of fine spray at eye level that Harris could now make out. "I'm thinking this could be cast off from whatever blunt object was used to beat her. Killer focused on cleaning up the blood from her wounds and didn't think to check anything at this height."

"Good work," Harris told them, wondering why the killer or killers would have stuck around to clean up anything instead of leaving the scene as it was, and why, indeed, the body had been wrapped in a piece of plastic sheeting and hidden under the back steps. Clearly, Harris thought, the killing hadn't been intended to send another message to Christina. Instead, it seemed more similar to Walt Gunderson's brutal assault after he'd stumbled onto an ill-timed break-in.

Had the same thing happened here? Only in this case, the victim had died, causing the person or persons who'd inflicted the injuries to panic and flee without taking anything—that he knew of—from the house. Maybe they'd figured that the more time that elapsed before the discovery of the body, the less forensic evidence would be left behind.

Unfortunately for the killers, though, the cold had kept the body well preserved—assuming Elizabeth Wallace had died on or around the date Harris had found marked on the desk calendar he'd found in the nook she'd used for an office. A day she'd clearly long looked forward to, marked as it was with the underlined word *Europe* and three fat exclamation points.

Without disturbing the body, he could clearly see that she'd been bludgeoned with some heavy object, just as Gunderson had been. Repeatedly, from the looks of the numerous deep contusions, including defensive wounds on the upper arms, and at least one visible depression in the skull. There might well be other injuries he couldn't see, but Harris and his officers had been careful not to touch her, leaving the team from the regional medical examiner's office to their grim but essential work.

After leaving his most senior officer in charge and two others to help Del Vecchio with the evidence collection, Harris pulled Zarzycki aside. Keeping his voice low, he told her, "We need to round up Eric Edgewood right now, before word leaks out and any evidence he might have kept around goes missing. Or *he* does."

One of her sleek, dark brows rose. "I haven't mentioned seeing his name in that e-mail to Fiorelli. Not to anybody, I swear."

"Good," he said, zipping his jacket as they headed out the front door. "My Tahoe. We'll ride together."

He didn't say another word until they were safely inside his SUV, the engine sputtering a moment before it rumbled to life. "You know," he said then, "just because you didn't let the word out doesn't mean Fiorelli didn't. He could've clued his nephew in, given him a come-to-Jesus talk or maybe even told his daddy on him, thinking to scare the kid straight. Before Frank ended up dead."

She jerked a stricken look in his direction. "You aren't thinking Eric might've killed his own uncle? Over a few burglaries and some property damage?"

"Kid's failed at college, a couple jobs—he's a long way from his glory days in high school. And here he is, back in his hometown, every person he grew up with seeing him screw up once again. Could be, he couldn't stomach the thought of doing jail time."

"Or one of his buddies might've done the killing," she suggested, her seat belt latching as he took off. "No telling what kind of thugs he's gotten tangled up with. Because he didn't break in to all those houses on his own. Not with all that damage and the heavy stuff pulled out. For all we know, he may have kept his hands clean, just passing on the info on which houses were unprotected."

"I'm sure that's what his attorney's going to tell us."

"How quick you think he'll lawyer up?"

"Twenty bucks says Daddy Edge'll be calling his guy before we leave the house. Especially when he figures out I'm trying to link him with this body . . . and maybe Fiorelli's, too."

It wasn't a lawyer Reg Edge called first, but the mayor, to scream about Harris's *obvious vendetta* against his family. Wearing a heavy, steel-gray robe, with his mussed hair revealing a normally hidden bald spot, he stood in a high, domed entryway, his anger echoing off the marble as a long-haired orange cat arched its back and rubbed against his legs.

"He told me he just wanted to ask my son a few questions," Edgewood went on as Harris and Zarzycki walked his struggling son between them, "and next thing I know, they're handcuffing Eric for no reason, frog-marching him to the door like a couple of goddamn storm troopers."

Unimpressed, the cat looked up at him and meowed plaintively. *For food,* thought Harris, amused by how unimpressed the animal, which didn't look like it missed many meals, seemed by any other household concerns.

"My poor boy," Edgewood's wife, Molly, cried out, the pink silk of her own robe flapping around thick ankles. She was a dark-haired woman in her mid-forties, attractive enough, apart from the swelling, that it was hard to believe she was Frank Fiorelli's sister. "Please," she implored them. "This is all a misunderstanding. It has to be."

"You got this?" Harris asked Zarzycki. He wanted to have a word with both of the parents before they headed to the station with their son.

"Yup," she said, despite her left eye, which was already swelling closed after the struggle put up by Edgewood's sainted son. "You're going to behave for me now, aren't you, Eric? Because if not, I've got this shiny new stun gun on my belt I've been dying to try out."

One look at the expression on her face, and the kid—if one could call a heavily tattooed, shirtless twenty-three-year-old a kid—stopped struggling. "I'm okay," he said, his shoulder-length black hair swinging as he looked to his distraught mother. "I'll be fine, Mom. Please don't cry. They only startled me. I thought they'd broken in."

"Not another word," his father bellowed, holding the phone away from his mouth. "Not one until you've spoken to our lawyer."

The cat meowed at him once more, turning up the volume.

"Please," said the boy's mother, looking from Zarzycki to Harris. "Just let me grab his slippers and a shirt. It's cold out there, and he—he's always had a weak chest—"

"You do that, ma'am," said Harris, not wanting to upset the woman any more than necessary.

Rather than attempting to comfort his wife, Edgewood shoved aside the cat with his foot when it yowled at him again. "Move it, you pain in the ass. Not you, ma'am," he said into the phone. "The damn cat." He then continued his complaints to the mayor about Harris's *gestapo tactics*, speaking so loudly that he didn't hear his son's next, quiet words.

"Thanks for humoring my mom," Eric told them both. A handsome young man with dark eyes, he favored her, rather than his father. "She hasn't been well. Her heart."

Harris nodded. "So I've heard. And by the way, I'm sorry about your uncle. We're very close to making an arrest." He kept his voice carefully neutral as he said it, not wanting to tip his hand that Eric himself had moved into the suspects' column. That he was, at present, at the top of the list.

"That's great," Eric said, sounding as if he meant it. "Uncle Frank might've been kind of a crank, but he sure as hell didn't deserve what happened. My mom's sick about it."

Harris nodded. "You know he'd kick your ass if he was here, assaulting an officer when we just wanted to ask you a few questions."

With a stricken look, Eric turned and looked up at Zarzycki's darkening eye. "I really didn't mean it. I—I've done some dumb shit in my life, as my father reminds me on a daily basis. But I've never hit a woman. Never would have if I hadn't been startled out of a dead sleep."

"Eric, I told you. Shut your damn mouth," Edgewood ordered, the cat flattening its ears and growling at him when he took a step nearer. "You have the right to remain silent. Have brains enough to use it."

Eric glared at his father before telling Zarzycki, "I'm really sorry, Officer. I hope it doesn't hurt much."

"I'll be okay," she said. "But don't think that's going to keep me from giving that Taser a little extra juice if you decide to throw another elbow. Got it?"

Eric nodded as Molly Edgewood reappeared, her arms full of a sweatshirt and jacket to cover her son's bare chest, and a pair of hard-soled slippers for his feet.

"I'm going to unlock the cuffs so you can get dressed," Harris told him, having already searched Eric to make sure the kid wasn't hiding any weapons. "Don't make either one of us regret it."

"You don't have to put them on him, do you?" Eric's mother asked Harris when her son finished and then put his hands back behind him to be recuffed. "He'll behave now, won't you Eric? And the neighbors—if any of them are awake and looking out their windows . . ."

"I'm sorry, Mrs. Edgewood," Harris said as he snapped the cuffs once more. "It's protocol, for everybody's safety."

"It's all right, Mom," said Eric. "I'll be fine. I'll see you in a few hours, as soon as Dad bails me out."

"Who says I'm gonna bail you out?" his father asked.

"The same son who picked you up after your last drunk-driving arrest."

Reg Edge's face turned redder than a sunburned tourist.

When she nodded, Eric went quietly with Zarzycki, looking nothing like the kind of man who might well have recently beaten to death someone else's mother, let alone stabbed a blood relation. Harris had noticed, too, that Eric Edgewood, for all his arm and back ink—designs including Vikings, swords, and a dragon skull vomiting out flames—had no scars on his knuckles or any signs of recent injuries.

Had he used a weapon to bludgeon Christina's mother? Or had a more violent conspirator done the actual dirty work?

"Mayor Bradford wants to speak to you," crowed Reg Edge. Covering the mouthpiece, he added, "And she *doesn't* sound happy."

Harris took the phone and turned his back to him.

"Stella," Harris said by way of greeting, "sorry you've had a second rude awakening tonight." Earlier, he'd called her to report the murder of Christina's mother, knowing the mayor took serious crimes in what she called *her city* personally—as well she might, after four consecutive terms.

"Never mind that," she said, fatigue making her sound older than her sixty-plus years. "Just explain to me why I've had that insufferable jackass yelling in my ear at this hour. Tell me his son's not a suspect in either of our murders."

"That's what I'm here to find out, ma'am. We have some questions for him. Unfortunately, he displayed some poor decision making after his mother showed us to his room. Hit one of my officers in the face."

"Is he all right? The officer, I mean," she asked, the concern in her voice sounding genuine. But then, she'd just spoken at Frank Fiorelli's funeral, a reminder to all of them how dangerous the work of law enforcement could be.

"She'll have a shiner, I'm sure, but she's a pretty tough one," Harris assured her.

"And you'll treat this young man with kid gloves?" Stella asked him. "Everything by the book? Because the council's already impatient to get this crime wave behind us. If *Reg Edge*"—she pronounced the nickname with all the affection usually reserved for wads of phlegm—"convinces the rest of them you're targeting his son because of some personal grudge, I won't be able to protect you any longer. Do you hear me, Harris?"

"Loud and clear, ma'am," said Harris, turning so his suspect's parents could hear what he was saying. "I'll be certain to show Mr. Edgewood and his family every courtesy. But I also promise you, I'm going to get some answers to what's been happening around here. And I'm going to put a stop to it, wherever my investigation leads."

~

Back at the station, Harris left Eric Edgewood cuffed to a table in the interview room and then encouraged Zarzycki to get herself a bag of ice for her eye. "Unless you'd rather go to the ER, get yourself checked out for fractures or a concussion."

She made a scoffing sound. "I can write my report any way you want, but truth is, the little weenie only caught me with an elbow while he was trying to escape."

Harris nodded. "I saw that, too. *And* that he feels bad about it." Something he wasn't above using to get answers. "So why don't you bring your ice pack into the interview room while he's being questioned?"

She ducked a nod, and he grabbed a cup of coffee that tasted old enough to vote. But he slugged down a few swallows, sludge or not, before deciding it wasn't worth the effort.

Like interview rooms in every station he'd been in, Seaside Creek's was decorated as if the object was to bore the suspect into a confession. Always on the cold side, with cinder-block walls painted a grimy-looking beige and a few uncomfortable chairs around a table bolted to the floor, it also contained a camera with audio capabilities.

Once Zarzycki settled herself, he asked Eric's permission to record their discussion digitally. "Unless you want to do like Daddy says and wait for his lawyer to tell you what to say."

"Or we could just clear things up now," Zarzycki said, lowering the ice enough to peer through the slit of her left eye at the young man slumped onto his elbows. "Let you explain what really happened."

Well played, thought Harris.

After a moment's hesitation, the kid said, "I never meant for this—for anyone to get hurt."

Taking it as permission, Harris switched on the equipment and Mirandized Eric before asking him to repeat what he'd said before.

His eyes red and his hands shaking as he looked at Zarzycki, he said, "I wasn't thinking, just freaked out. All I wanted was to get away. Sorry you got hurt."

"I know you didn't mean it," she said quietly, adding a little shrug. "We all make mistakes, don't we? Things we'd give anything to take back."

Now certain that she was no stranger to an interview room, Harris teased out the thread. "You didn't mean for anybody else to get hurt, either, did you? But things—sometimes they spin out of your control."

A tear slid down the kid's face. "That poor old man," he said. "That address I gave them—I reversed two of the numbers in the text. I swear to you—I *swear* it—I'd done my part. My job was to make sure nobody was home, and I did it. I just screwed it up. Big-time."

As was so often the case after a person had held the truth back for so long, he seemed relieved to tell his story, even though he had to know it would mean jail time. The more facts that came out, the straighter Eric sat in his seat. "I only meant to do it once." He explained that it had all started as a favor for a friend, who'd promised to reward him with whatever drugs they could score. At first, it gave Eric a rush, thinking of assholes like his old man coming home to find their crap gone. He'd figured they'd get newer, better versions of things, anyway, once their insurance companies coughed up. So he'd taken part again and again, he and his buddies laughing about it as they got high together later. It had made him feel like some kind of genius, the guy who kept his hands clean but still got to enjoy the after-parties and what seemed like harmless fun.

Harmless fun that Harris was more than half-convinced had led to the deaths of not just one but two people, and to heartbreak for so many more. An image slipped up on him, of Christina's shock when he'd found her, her bewilderment and confusion. How she'd gone limp in his arms, as if something vital inside her had irreparably shattered.

And yet this kid, this tattooed loser of a mama's boy, sat here making excuses.

"After listening to my dad chew my ass every single night, it felt great," he told them. "And when you're buzzed enough, the idea of smashing out a few walls and plugging up some drains and turning all the taps on sounds hilarious."

"Some of those places," Harris told him, "ended up with over a hundred thousand dollars' worth of damage. Damage you and you alone will be financially liable for—and I don't mean your daddy—unless you share these friends' names."

"They're my—they're my crew. My buddies."

Harris slapped his hand on the table, making the kid jump. "They're goddamned arsonists and killers, Eric."

"No! They wouldn't kill anybody. They're not like that."

"Tell that to that old man they beat half to death. You've already admitted you know they did that—"

"Only because he came downstairs with a freaking baseball bat in his hands, so they just took it away from him and . . . things got out of hand."

"Like they got out of hand the night they burned that big Victorian on Cape Street?" Zarzycki said, allowing a feminine softness, like Edgewood's mother's, to creep into her voice. "The night they killed your uncle after he confronted you?"

"It wasn't them! They were never there. They swore they were finished with the kid stuff—we all were, after Uncle Frank ripped us a new one when he figured it out."

At the confirmation that Frank not only had known the vandals' identities but had taken it upon himself to let them off, Zarzycki sent a loaded glance toward Harris.

"Then let them swear it to me," he yelled, no longer just playing the Bad Cop but well and truly pissed. Because it was all too much, the memory of Frank's widow at the funeral, the sad-eyed relatives—this lying loser among them. And Christina, who'd cried herself to sleep with her sister and her daughter, and all so a bunch of numbnuts could get cheap kicks and buy dope. "Or screw it—I'm just going ahead and charging you with the murder of Officer Frank Fiorelli. My officer. Your own blood. You think his death has hit your mom hard? How the hell do you think your being named his killer will—"

"You can't!"

"I can, and I will," Harris said, standing up and pacing the room. "You know what? Your uncle didn't like me, and I didn't always care for the man, either. But he was a cop—one of *my* crew—and I took it as my personal responsibility to always look out for him, to always make sure he went home to his wife."

The kid was crying now, choking on his own sobs. But Harris was beyond caring.

"And that wasn't your pals' first murder, either, was it? Your friends decided they had to kill your uncle to cover up what had happened when somebody finally found that poor woman on Columbus Street."

"W-what woman? What are you talking about? *Columbus* Street? I never—I swear I never gave the guys any addresses over there."

Gritting his teeth until his jaws ached, Harris kicked a chair and sent it clattering to the floor.

Someone, probably the night clerk, knocked at the door, but breathing hard, Harris didn't answer. He was too busy running through an exercise he'd learned—and taught others—in counseling, one designed to help him regain control so he didn't tear this little shit apart.

Zarzycki put down her ice pack and said, "Maybe you should step out, Chief. Take a break for a few minutes while I help Eric put together his list. I have the phone I took from you right here in my pocket," she said to the kid. "We can get this sorted out tonight. Who knows, maybe we can even get you before the judge so you can bail out and get home first thing in the morning."

Wildly optimistic as her suggestion was, a light came on in Eric's frightened eyes. A glimmer of hope as he sensed the possibility of freedom.

"I'll be back in ten," Harris said with a nod. But there was another knock at the door, this one more insistent. When he opened it, Harris found his wheelchair-bound night clerk/dispatcher. When he looked past her, Harris saw the reason for the apology in her brown eyes. A rumpled-looking little man with a patch of fuzzy fair hair crowning an otherwise bald head.

Adams, a defense attorney who did a good business making the problems of the sons and daughters of the area's wealthy go away, immediately lit into Harris for speaking to his client without him present. Clearly trying to intimidate the boy, judging from the shouting and banging of furniture he'd heard from outside the room.

"You and I both know that *boy's* long past legal age now," Harris said as he blew past him, not caring that word of this was sure to get back to Reg Edge, the mayor, and the rest of the city council in record time, "so you can kiss my ass."

CHAPTER TWENTY-TWO

Harris was still kicking him himself for losing his temper when someone knocked at his office door. Figuring it would be Zarzycki, he called for her to come in.

Instead, the night clerk wheeled in, wearing the wireless headset she used to handle dispatch. Normally the soul of confidence, the former marathoner and current Paralympic hopeful looked flustered, her light-olive skin a shade paler than normal. "I'm really sorry, Chief. I tried to tell him to wait up front, but he wasn't listening for anything."

"Next time Adams tries that," Harris told her drily, "you have my permission to roll over his toes."

She flipped her shiny black bangs out of her eyes, mischief in her smile. "How 'bout you lend me your gun instead?"

"For the last time, Maya, no guns for civilian employees." He sighed. "And the lawyer, he's basically all right. Just doing his job like the rest of us."

Even if Reg Edgewood had sent him. And even if Adams ended up talking Eric out of cooperating further.

"So you aren't worried the suspect you were questioning will clam up about his buddies?" Maya asked, which was no surprise to Harris, since he'd long suspected that the clerk, who often complained of being bored stiff by slow off-season night shifts, had developed eavesdropping superpowers.

"Not really. Adams is no fool. As soon as he gets up to speed, he'll realize that his client's best shot at avoiding a long prison sentence is to cough up the names and disavow all knowledge of the murders. Otherwise, one of the friends will roll on his buddies after I bring 'em in."

Maya beamed, her young face full of admiration. "So you've got it solved, then? Everything? The vandalism and both killings?"

"We're still a hell of a long way from celebrating." *If I ever feel like celebrating anything again.* "And, anyway, if these leads do eventually pan out, it'll be because of Frank Fiorelli's police work"—even if he'd completely, perhaps fatally, screwed up by attempting to keep the nephew he loved out of trouble—"and Officer Zarzycki's investigative skills."

"In the online management classes I'm taking," Maya said, "they tell you the best supervisors deflect credit to their subordinates."

Harris snorted but said nothing, knowing that if she'd wanted someone to emulate, Maya could've chosen a whole lot better. But he knew, too, that young people like his night clerk, who was the same age as Eric Edgewood, needed their role models. Even gods with feet of clay like his.

"Speaking of Zarzycki," he said, "is she still in the interview room?"

Maya shook her head. "Nope. Came out a few minutes ago and went to her locker for some aspirin for her eye."

"Ask her to stop by my office when you see her again, will you?"

"You bet."

Thanking her as she left, Harris opened his laptop, meaning to check the department's manpower situation for the next few shifts. But he couldn't focus on his officers' work schedules, his brain repeatedly circling back to Christina's suffering.

Or how she'd been made to suffer, with the damage to her car, the burning of her temporary residence, and finally—or more likely, first of all—with the murder of her beloved mother. There was also that other bit of strangeness: the odd things Lilly had been repeating. Statements regarding the death—the killing—of someone the two-year-old called *Katie-Mommy*.

It was almost as if whoever had been pumping the toddler full of stories *knew*. Had known all along that Christina's—the former Katie's—adoptive mother had been murdered.

No matter how hard Harris tried, he couldn't make those pieces fit with the neat scenario he'd suggested in the interview room earlier. Sure, there were often weak spots in any cop's or prosecutor's theory, inexplicable gaps that would forever remain mysteries. But in this case, the holes were big enough to drive a bus through. Enough to have him doubting that Eric Edgewood's friends truly had been involved in Elizabeth Wallace's murder. Or Frank Fiorelli's, either, since it was possible he'd been killed not because he'd discovered what his nephew had been up to, but instead because he'd gotten too close to the person out to burn Christina and her child alive.

The same child who would inherit a third of her father's family money. Harris remembered something that had slipped out when he'd spoken to Doug Paxton's *previous administration*. Something about the estate finally settling very soon.

If Lilly died before its distribution, wouldn't that give a larger share to Evelyn Paxton's two grown children? Or, more to the point, keep any of the money from ending up in the hands of Christina, whose very existence was clearly hateful to the first wife?

It sure as hell sounded like a valid motive to him, one that reminded him to check his e-mail. There—thank God for small favors—he found a message from someone from Delaware River Port Authority, which policed the same Ben Franklin Bridge that had so recently taken him to Philadelphia.

Though tolls were currently collected in only one direction, license plates were digitally recorded going both ways. Including the license plate of an Audi registered to Mrs. Evelyn Paxton of Pittsburgh.

The car, it appeared, had crossed over into South Jersey on several recent occasions, including the evening before the damage to Christina's vehicle and phone line had taken place. His next move would be to contact the New Jersey State Police to check the vehicle's movement on the Garden State Parkway, which offered the most direct route to Seaside Creek. But that info, he decided, would better wait till morning, when he could call a trooper friend to get his request expedited. Also, he'd want to see whether he could get a CCTV grab from either agency, where he fully expected to find photos of Evelyn Paxton herself behind the wheel.

"Did you come another night, too, you vindictive bitch?" he asked his computer screen, remembering the day circled on poor Elizabeth Wallace's calendar. But try as he might, that scenario refused to gel fully in his head, either. Christina and Annie's adoptive mother had been repeatedly bludgeoned, her head and upper body covered in wound after wound. Could a thin woman in her late forties, maybe early fifties, have dealt out that kind of punishment? Even if Evelyn Paxton's rage had been sufficient to fuel an attack on Christina, could she have worked herself up to the point of going after Christina's mother?

He closed his eyes, trying to focus. Did Evelyn Paxton want Christina, the woman her obsessive mind cast as husband-thief and killer, to know the pain she was experiencing, facing her own mother's imminent death?

Another knock snapped him out of his reverie.

"C'mon in," he called. It was Zarzycki, ice pack still in hand. "How's the eye?"

"Feels better than it looks. And before you ask, no, I'm not going to the ER. I'm not missing one minute of this. I want to be here when we get the son of a bitch who knifed Fiorelli in the back and beat that poor woman to death."

"Gotcha," he said, not sharing his uncertainties with her because he knew she'd harness the energy of her hope—and anger—to see her through this night. And it was still possible that the alternate theory he'd come up with would turn out to be a bust, that they would instead get a confession out of Eric.

"So how 'bout that lawyer," he asked, changing the subject. "You clue him in on what we had already?"

She nodded. "In the hall outside, yeah. He mumbled something about dumb shits who can't wait to spill their guts, then pulled out a pad of paper and went back in."

There was another rapid-fire knock at the door, but this time, Maya didn't wait for an invitation before wheeling back inside.

"I don't know where this came from or how long it's been here, I swear." The words gushed out of her as she rolled toward his desk. "It was sitting on top of the file cabinet, and all I could see from my chair was one corner sticking out."

As Zarzycki stepped out of the way, Maya reached toward him, offering a large manila envelope. In large, blue-ink block letters, someone had hand-printed FOR CHIEF BOWERS ONLY! across the center. Below, in the same hand, with the words triple underlined, came the second and final line.

URGENT!

There was no return address, no postage, no indication whatsoever of where it might've come from.

"Lay it on the desk, please," Harris told her. Though it made little sense to think that anyone would risk being spotted hand-delivering a rigged package to a police station, someone who knew this office well might realize there were no security cameras. And with the station so understaffed this time of year, especially at night, it wouldn't be difficult to walk in and drop the envelope on top of the file cabinet while Maya was outside her office assisting an officer, relaying a message, or visiting the restroom.

"You might want to leave the room," Zarzycki told Maya.

Maya rolled back a few feet, out of the way, but lingered in the doorway. "It didn't feel weird," she said, sounding more worried about being left out than she was of getting hurt or poisoned. "It's not heavy or lumpy or anything like that."

Harris lowered his head to eyeball the envelope from desktop level and saw that it was perfectly flat. He was no handwriting analyst, but the printing, he thought, looked feminine, the humped *M*'s and rounded *R*'s somehow familiar, though he couldn't place them.

"It's probably nothing," he declared, opening a lower desk drawer and pulling out a pair of thin nitrile gloves, "but just to be safe, both of you step out and shut that door behind you."

Once they had complied, he pulled on the gloves and used a letter opener to slit one end of the envelope, careful to keep it turned away from his face. When no dust or powder puffed out, he gently spun the open end to him and noted that the contents consisted only of several sheets of what appeared to be ordinary printer paper.

His pulse accelerated in anticipation as he pulled out the three pages.

Pages that had him recoiling as he read an allegation as explosive as any letter bomb.

CHAPTER TWENTY-THREE

Though her rest was light and often broken, Christina mostly slept as the police went about their business. At one point around dawn, she climbed out of bed to check the window, praying it would all be over. That they would have disappeared and left her to wake up from this awful nightmare. To pretend, for as long as she could, that her mother was still coming home.

Only four more sleeps, she heard herself telling Lilly. Except the voice was in her head, and Lilly was out cold, curled against Annie.

Outside, she saw SUVs and cruisers, at least three of them, bearing the markings of the Seaside Creek Police Department. And a single white van, the kind with solid side panels rather than windows for the cargo area. A man shut the back doors, revealing the words *South Jersey Regional Medical Examiner.*

Christina's stomach spasmed, and she tasted bile. *They've put her in there. Inside that cold van, in a body bag, her corpse a block of ice.*

Except it hadn't been really, had it? More like half-frozen meat.

Running for the bathroom, Christina made it barely in time. Long past the point when her stomach had been emptied, she stood there, fighting off the impulse . . . and the images of a stranger's face—

That's it. It's someone else. Some poor woman Mom asked to house-sit, some poor soul whose features were so battered that even her own family, whoever they are, will scarcely recognize her.

The rational side of Christina's brain understood what she was doing. But the wounded child in her clung to the lie long enough for her to escape into a deeper sleep.

By the time she woke alone, the window showed that it was daylight. She spotted a sliver of a blue sky with those high, wispy clouds she associated with the coldest days of winter.

But the eaves were dripping, and as she watched, a small icicle lost its grip and plummeted to earth. As she made her way back to the window, she saw it was a true thaw. Snow remained, but only patches, and the police and ME's vehicles had melted away, too.

There were strangers' cars outside, though. Two that she could make out. Hearing voices from below, she hastily dressed in the same clothes from yesterday, raked her fingers through her tangled hair, and went to check on Lilly.

She found her daughter in the dining room, eating a bowl of cereal. Dressed in a fresh outfit, she looked up at Christina, her innocent blue eyes shining. Someone had combed her silky blonde hair and tied it in short pigtails. "Gramma house," she said.

"Yes, sweetie, we're at Gran—at Grandma's house," Christina affirmed, fighting her way past a spasm of grief. Over the past two years or so, she'd had far too much practice acting normal, after her illness and her father's death, and then Doug's—but this? How would she survive it, even for her child's and her sister's sakes?

"Annie?" she called, thinking her sister must be nearby, since surely the two-year-old hadn't gotten her own cereal or trekked down to the basement fridge for milk.

But Lilly was pointing at the framed painting hanging opposite the family photos. The painting of the abandoned lighthouse out on Willet's Point, standing tall and proud against the storm-whipped waves.

"Gramma's house," she repeated, sending chills rippling through Christina.

From behind her, an unfamiliar female voice said gently, "Hey there, Christina. Annie called and asked me to come over."

Turning, Christina recognized her sister's longtime friend and coworker, Kym Meador, a slender woman with a long, black ponytail and a tiny silver nose ring. Even at this hour, her eyeliner was thick and dark—possibly tattooed on. Reinforcing this opinion, the colorful, inked plumage of some exotic bird peeped out of the scoop-neck sweater she wore with knee-high boots and jeans as tight as leggings.

"Of course," Christina said, relieved her sister hadn't asked a stranger. "Hello, Kym. And thanks for coming at this hour."

"Well, first of all, it's like eleven thirty, but it doesn't matter. Annie can always count on me, any time of day or night," Kym said, stepping close to hug her fiercely. "I can't tell you how very sorry . . ."

When she choked up, overcome, Christina nodded. "I know," she said, fresh tears blurring her vision as she stepped back out of range of any more well-meant hugs. "I can't believe—it doesn't feel real. Where's my sister?"

Kym glanced down at Lilly, who was chewing a mouthful of cereal while intently studying the painting of the lighthouse. *Gramma house.*

Shaking her head, Kym said, "She took Max out for a walk. She said she needed some space, but she'll be back soon."

"How is she doing?"

Kym shook her head. "It's hard, so very—first your dad's cancer and now this. It isn't right. It isn't. Your mom—she was this amazing person, running her own business, taking in two babies who'd been—"

Christina looked away, a rushing noise in her ears drowning out the rest. Of course Annie would've confided to her closest friend about their background. It's what people did; they shared intimacies. Well, most people, anyway. Christina herself had never wanted her girlfriends' pity.

Or maybe she'd sensed, even in the days when she and Renee had been practically joined at the hip, that the queen bee might one day turn against her, then wield her secret as a weapon. But what did it matter anymore? What did anything matter, with their *real* parents both gone, leaving her, and Annie, too, utterly alone?

"There's coffee," Kym said. "I brought a thermos. Or if you'd rather, I'll get you some cereal, or I think I saw some—"

"I don't want anything," Christina said reflexively before her head pounded out a message of caffeine deprivation. "Or maybe just the coffee, thanks. Black would be fine."

"Sure thing," Kym said, leaving through the doorway that would take her to the living room. The living room where Christina and Harris had made love what now seemed like a century before.

Remembering, she felt sick. Sicker still when she glanced at the room's second doorway, to the kitchen, which was now blocked by a yellow *X* of crime-scene tape. As the door at the back of it, the one leading to the house's rear porch, would surely be, too.

Shifting her gaze, she looked to Lilly, who stared at her with solemn eyes, her mouth turned downward and the tip of her nose red. "Mommy sad," she said, the sorrow in her voice a reminder that whatever they were told by the adults around them, children of her age soaked in ambient emotions the way green houseplants absorb toxic chemicals.

I want my mother, Christina ached to say. *Need her.* But instead, because she *was* a mother, she explained, "It's okay to miss people sometimes, even when they live in heaven."

Brightening, Lilly said, "My daddy in heaven."

"And now Grandma is there with him, and he's showing her around, helping her to—"

"No!" Her daughter shook her head, her small face turning stormy. "We go find Gramma. Get her. Bring her home."

Late that afternoon, Christina sat on the edge of her mother's bed, fighting to control her breathing. Freshly showered, she'd rummaged through the closet until she'd come up with a faded pair of jeans and a Philadelphia Eagles sweatshirt from her mom's slimmer days. But slipping into the clothing had nearly overwhelmed her, with the faint traces of her mother's lightly floral perfume permeating the fabric, along with memories that could never be erased.

At least she'd have clothes of her own when Annie came back. Unable to bear being in the house, her sister had volunteered to take Lilly to the closest shopping mall, forty minutes away. There, she'd promised to purchase necessities for all three of them, using the freshly activated emergency replacement credit card Christina had had delivered to the house.

And why shouldn't I pay? It's my fault, every bit of it. If I hadn't come back, we'd still have a mother . . .

The officer she'd spoken to earlier had tried to reassure her, telling Christina she shouldn't jump to conclusions so early in the investigation. But what else could she think, with nothing missing from the house? *This was meant to punish me, to destroy me completely. To shatter any hope of rebuilding my life in Seaside Creek.*

"Well, you've won, whoever you are," she said aloud, pulling out her phone and going through the contacts until she found the name she wanted. Throat tightening, she thought of what she would be giving up, what she would once more have to go through, if she went ahead and did this. But nothing compared to the image her mind conjured, of Annie or even Lilly left the way she'd found her mother. Christina couldn't bear to think it.

"Thank you so much, Dr. Chambers," she was saying a short time later. "I—I can't tell you what this means to me."

"Thank *you*, Christina," her former supervisor answered, his West Texas twang as familiar as it was reassuring. "You just let us know when you're back home, and we'll get you in to sign the paperwork with HR."

Back home. As she ended the call, the words were like a wasp's sting, the pain radiating from her heart. Because whatever it was to her, Dallas would never be home, with its own set of bad memories. But it was a known quantity, at least, the last place she'd felt safe.

And so very alone . . .

Someone tapped at the closed bedroom door.

"Is that you, Kym? C'mon in," she called, tucking the cell phone into her back pocket and opening the door.

"Chief Bowers is here to see you," Kym said as Max pushed past her, prancing and wagging with happiness to see his mistress. "Can you come downstairs? He called earlier, but when I told him you were showering, he just said he was on his way."

"Did he—did he mention what he wanted?"

"No, but he's brought pizza, and don't tell me you aren't starved by now. You have to be."

Christina sighed, but realized her aching head and shakiness meant her sister's friend was right. She needed to make herself eat something, and right now a cheesy slice sounded like less effort than any other option.

"All right," she said, "and thanks, Kym. Thanks for giving up your day. You've been—you've been a godsend."

"I really haven't done all that much. Cleaned up a bit, answered the phone."

"I've heard it ringing off and on all day."

"Word's gotten out. Your mother's friends—they're all in shock, of course, and wanting to know what they can do. I've made a list for you downstairs."

"I couldn't bear it, talking to them all, so thank you."

"I'm glad to be here. Anything for An—" Cutting herself off, Kym shook her head. "Never mind. That's not important. What's important is this isn't just pizza. It's Pennisi's." She smiled enticingly, naming a little hole-in-the-wall dive many of the locals swore by.

In the back of Christina's mind, something clicked into place. Something that made sense of her sister's recent behavior, but this was no time to have that conversation.

Downstairs, they found Harris waiting in the living room, staring at the unlit fireplace. Was he thinking about last night, too, wondering what he'd gotten himself into—and how to extricate himself from their personal relationship while still doing his job?

She couldn't help wondering how to tell him she was packing up her daughter and turning tail to run south the moment she could. Or maybe she was wrong about Dallas, where trouble could find her again all too easily. She had money enough to buy a name change, erase her tracks, and find a new life for her and Lilly somewhere the person out to destroy her would never think to look.

Looking up, his eyes found hers, the compassion in them hitting her with such force, she had to look away. Oh, how she was going to miss him—miss ever again having anyone who would look at her that way.

"How are you?" he asked, the familiar rumble of his voice resonating in her bones.

Unable to speak, she merely shook her head, wishing he would come hold her yet somehow relieved when he kept his distance.

"Pizza in the dining room?" asked Kym. "She hasn't had a bite all day," she said to Harris, "so whatever you've got to say, that has to come first."

Nodding in answer, Harris said, "That works for me. I got half plain cheese, half Italian sausage and green peppers. Hope that covers everybody."

"Sounds great. Thanks," Kym said as she led the charge.

"There are paper plates in the bag. I brought some iced tea, too."

Christina's stomach squirmed, but once she started eating, her body took over the operation, chewing without tasting. They ate in utter silence, Kym sitting while both Harris and Christina stood by the table.

Halfway through a second slice, Christina's gaze strayed to the painting, her mind replaying her daughter's troubling words. As she stared, her vision swimming, the image came to life, waves beating against the lighthouse and the wind whistling past the column. A female silhouette moved past one of the windows.

Gramma house.

She caught Harris studying her, his forehead furrowed with concern. Taking a deep breath, she put down the half-eaten slice and drained her cup in the hope that the caffeine and calorie infusion would kick her brain back into gear. And that the shock she'd suffered last night hadn't tipped her into a form of madness from which there would be no coming back.

"If everybody's finished, I'll put away the rest," Kym said as she gathered up the trash. "Then I really need to run home for a little while. My little dog'll need to go out."

"Go ahead," Christina told her. "I've got the cleanup. And thanks again, for everything."

Kym hesitated, shook her head. "It's nothing, really."

"It's a huge thing, your staying with me." Christina wiped her fingers on a napkin before reaching out to squeeze her hand. "I want you to know I get why you're doing it—and believe me, it's the least of my worries, if that's what's been holding you two back."

Kym nodded, her lips pressed together as her dark eyes studied Christina's face and then filled with tears. After giving her a quick hug, she found her purse and said, her voice roughened by emotion, "I'll check in with Annie later, but meanwhile, if there's anything you need, you have my number."

Once she'd gone, Harris gave Christina a look. "I get the feeling I've missed something."

Christina nodded. "She loves Annie. I mean, as in, they're a couple. I should've realized earlier. Annie tried to tell me, but I wasn't ready to hear it at the time."

She recalled her younger sister's face, remembered the moment she'd said so pointedly, *I want to be with Kym.*

"And you're okay with it, I guess?"

"*Okay*'s not really a word in my vocabulary right now," she said, "but as for my sister and her—her girlfriend, I'm a little surprised, that's all. Now that I think about it, though, I see it. See that maybe all these fleeting relationships with men, this unsettledness about her, had been masking something else. Something she felt too scared to admit out in the open."

He nodded. "She'll especially need your support now, after what's happened."

"Just as I'll need hers," Christina said, guilt seeping in at the thought that she wouldn't be around, either to give or receive it. And Annie would never come with her; she already knew that. Maybe without Christina here to paint a target on her back, her sister would be safe. Or was that just her struggling to convince herself? "And I think Kym will—she'll be good for her."

Christina found herself relieved to think that their relationship, at least, would make her sister less vulnerable to the married—and probably predatory—Reg Edgewood. And she would be certain, before she left town, to make good on any debts.

"Let me wrap up this leftover pizza and take it downstairs," she said. "I think I saw some foil in the—"

"Don't do that yet," Harris suggested. "Annie and Lilly are on their way. They may want some, too."

Christina's gaze jerked toward him, her heart kicking in alarm. "What? How would you know—is something wrong?"

He held up his scarred hand. "It's fine. It's only, when I couldn't reach you earlier, I called her to let her know I need to talk to both of you about an imminent arrest. She was just about to check out, so I asked her to—"

"An arrest?" Christina's pulse thumped in her ears.

"Several arrests, actually," he corrected himself. "Come on in here. Let's sit down and—"

She shook her head. "I've spent the whole day being coddled, told to lie down. To rest, to take a shower, to eat, and I'll feel better. But I don't feel better. I can't, and I won't until I understand. Am I—am I the reason my mother's dead?"

His mouth stretched in a grimace. "I take it, then, you don't to wait for Annie?"

She locked eyes with him, letting her scowl do the talking.

"Okay," he said, turning toward the doorway. "You may not want to sit, but I'm dead on my feet here. It's been a hell of a long day. Or days. I've lost track."

She followed, vibrating with impatience, then took a seat on one end of the sofa while he claimed the nearest armchair. Only then did she notice how bloodshot his eyes were and how pale he was.

Feeling a twinge of guilt, she said, "You weren't kidding, were you, Harris? Have you gotten any rest at all?"

He shrugged. "I finally delegated enough to grab a few hours this afternoon. Enough to hold me."

Hold me. His words echoed through her mind, made her body ache for him to do just that and to let her hold him back. But, just as after the first time they'd been together, he said nothing now, *did* nothing to acknowledge that anything had changed between them.

And this time, she swore she wouldn't be foolish enough to tell him she'd fallen for him all over again. What could it do but hurt him, since she didn't mean to stick around?

Unless . . . "So what is it? Do you know who did this to my mother?"

"I have a pretty good idea," he admitted as Max strode into the room and stretched out in front of the hearth. "But there's something I have to clear up first."

"Just tell me, Harris. Tell me everything. I need to—I've been torturing myself over it." Her poor mother must have been so terrified. "What did I do that cost my mom her—"

"No, Christina, no." As the words came, she sensed whatever wall he'd erected inside himself crumbling. In two steps, he crossed the distance to sit down beside her on the sofa and wrap her in a hug. Tangling his fingers in her hair, he squeezed her tight against him. "You can't ever blame yourself."

"Then it was the vandals?" *Nothing to do with me at all.* She prayed it would be true. "It was just another break-in?"

"It's possible," he allowed. "The—the injuries we saw last night were consistent with the type of injuries sustained by the man I told you about before—and we've confirmed that your mother called her home-security company to inform them of the dates she would be gone."

From there, he recounted the arrest of security-company employee Eric Edgewood, who had eventually given up his criminally minded friends, a group of local males between the ages of seventeen and twenty-five. "We acted fast, rounding up all four of them before somebody could tip them off, and they ran. When I woke the judge to get the arrest warrants, he signed search warrants, too."

"And you found something?"

He nodded. "Evidence in the room of the ringleader. Items stolen out of beachfront houses, glassines of white powder—they were doing it for drugs and kicks. Idiots claimed they never meant for anybody to get hurt."

Covering her mouth with her hand, she looked away. How could she have imagined that learning that her mother's death was a result of something senseless, and very nearly random, would make her feel one bit better?

"There was—should I stop here?" he asked gently.

She shook her head, her voice hoarse as she forced the words out, "All of it. Please."

"There was a bat, too—a wooden baseball bat found in the trunk of the beater this asshole was driving. A bat taken from Walt Gunderson when he heard noises in the house and came down the stairs with it. It still had blood on it."

"His blood, or my—?" She couldn't get the word out.

"That'll be for the forensics team from the medical examiner's office to determine. But, Christina, I'm not sure we'll find your mother's DNA on that bat. Or any link to Frank Fiorelli among their belongings, either."

"Why not?"

"Because I've questioned these guys separately, before they got the chance to get their stories straight. In every case, I made sure they knew their buddies couldn't wait to rat them out and cut some kind of deal with the DA." He shook his head. "These aren't sophisticated criminals, just young delinquents who like to think they're tough. They broke fast, every damn one of them."

She braced herself, heart pounding, to hear whatever came next.

"The thing is," Harris went on, "they've admitted the robberies, the vandalism, even to beating Mr. Gunderson after he surprised them. But not a one would cop to the damage done to your car. You see, they'd been tipped off that someone was living in the big Victorian on Cape Street. And one of them had spotted me watching the place. They knew it wasn't worth the risk."

She narrowed her eyes, considering. "So you don't believe they torched the house, then? Or stabbed Fiorelli?"

"If they were a brighter bunch, I might think they were denying hitting that house or this one for fear of implicating themselves in either murder. But they seemed genuinely surprised to find out that a woman was found dead here, surprised and worried I was just trying to pin my unsolved cases on them."

"So what's been ha—what's happened to me and to my mother—you think it's something separate?"

"Most likely, yes."

"Why?" She swallowed back her fear, then forced herself to face it.

Pushing a hand down into the cushion, he rose from the sofa and crossed to the piano. From its top, he picked up a large manila envelope. The sight of it filled her with a sense of déjà vu, quickly followed by a wave of nausea.

"Renee brought that to you, didn't she?" she asked, anxiety needling the tender flesh behind her neck as she remembered the meeting between Renee and that young guy she'd witnessed at the Sweet Shop.

He frowned. "This was left for me in my office, no signature, and no one around to see who did it. But it could have been her, I suppose. She knows her way around, and she'd feel comfortable enough with our routine to—you're sure?"

Leaning forward, she dropped her head to her hands and drew in a deep breath. "I am."

In fits and starts, she told him about that evening she'd passed through Bridgeport, explaining what she'd seen through the window of the Sweet Shop—and how she'd talked herself out of believing it could be Renee.

"You've talked yourself out of telling me a lot of things, haven't you?" he asked gently. "Because you weren't sure you could believe what you were seeing, hearing. You don't trust your own senses—or maybe I should say, your mind."

At the slither of papers being pulled from the envelope, she shuddered, guessing even before her first glance what he held in his hands. Her personal medical records, her records from that time two years before.

"I should've—should have known," she said, voice breaking as it hit her. *He knows everything. All of it.* "Should've realized she had this on me. The other evening in the parking lot, the night she called me—called me—"

"Let's just go with the c-word," he suggested, sitting back down next to her.

She shook her head. "Thing was, though, that wasn't the only c-word, or even the worst." The conversation spun back through her mind, including the moment so branded in her memory so painfully that she repeated it verbatim.

"'You know what, Christina? You're not only freaking crazy, you really are a cunt.'"

"You're sure?" He stared at her, his expression clearly troubled.

"Maybe I am still a little crazy," Christina said, thinking of the living image of the lighthouse in its frame, "but there's not a damn thing wrong with my memory. Still, it's hard to imagine. Could she really be vindictive enough to gaslight me over the baby monitors and fill my daughter's head with whatever gossip she'd picked up?"

If Annie had told one person the circumstances of their adoption, it stood to reason that others might've heard the story. Heard it and repeated it until it reached Renee's ears. "Why would she do this? I don't get it. Jealousy? Resentment?"

"Maybe a little of both," he said, "but I'm betting that wasn't her only motivation."

"Why else, then? Why bring you my patient records?"

With a shaking hand she reached for them, hoping that, by some miracle, they would prove to be fakes. Instead, her mouth dried in an instant as the damning phrases jumped out at her. *Patient presented with severe psychomotor agitation . . . paranoid delusions . . . involuntary commitment recommended.*

Tears blurring the page, she looked up at him and tried to explain. "I—I—during the move here, someone broke into the Mercedes in a hotel parking lot. They didn't get much—I know better than to leave anything of value. And who would care about a box of paperwork, anyway?"

"So that's how your records got out. From there, they could've been sold online—identity frauds do a brisk trade on anything with birth dates and Social Security numbers on them. Or maybe that's what this thief was after in the first place."

Heart racing, she struggled to explain. To erase the disappointment she imagined she saw in his eyes. "You have to understand. It was a bad time, when I—Lilly was about two months old. I'd taken some time off, and I really thought that I was coping. But it was so much harder than I imagined, handling almost everything on my own. Doug was busy with work, and, to be perfectly honest, he left everything to me. He really—he loved Lilly in his way, but I could tell he was only humoring my wish to have a family. He'd already raised two kids, and he was older, old enough that what he really wanted was to focus on his interests during the little time he could take off."

"You didn't have anyone to help?"

She shook her head. "I could've—should've hired someone. That was Doug's suggestion when he saw how fried I was getting. But I was stubborn enough to think I could handle it on my own. I mean, all those other mothers—a lot of them single and with far fewer resources seem to manage, and I had taken three whole months off . . . but Lilly was a fussy baby. She cried all the time. She spit up milk—she wouldn't take the breast at all. It felt like the ultimate rejection."

"Babies can be tough. Even with Renee and me working together, I can remember a few nights—"

But Christina barely heard him. "She never seemed to sleep, and I got so worked up, so worried I was failing her—damaging her—just like my biological mother failed me. It didn't help a bit that I wasn't really eating or sleeping, either." She remembered random compliments from her Dallas friends and neighbors, some of whom had asked her secret for taking off all the baby weight so quickly. As her hair grew dull and her eyes sunken, the praise stopped—and she began to imagine them whispering behind her back.

"What about your family? Couldn't you reach out to them?"

"No way, not then. My father—the cancer was in his bones by then, his brain, too. It took my mother and my sister both to see him through those last few months."

"And you couldn't be here. That must have been upsetting for you."

She nodded. "For the first time in my life, I was really failing. Failing my child and my husband—*both* my families. And then the voices started, when I was alone." Her throat closed, but she had to go on. He had to hear all of it. "Voices telling me I should've known I couldn't do this. That for all my training and my education, my marriage to a man from a long line of achievers, I was only going to end up one of those crazy women you hear of, hurting their own children. That I was every bit as messed up as the woman who left Annie and me out by that dumpster."

She was shaking now, shaking so hard she felt as if she'd fly apart. It was all in the records, how Doug had eventually caught on as she'd grown increasingly paranoid and manic. How he'd first taken off some time, then finally made the tough call to have Christina hospitalized after she'd started talking about how much happier and better off everyone would be without her. Talking about going to live out on the streets, the way she'd been born to, or ending her pain—everyone's—by flinging herself off the High Five Interchange into rush-hour traffic.

Though her eyes remained dry, she felt herself crumbling inside as she confessed how her mom and Annie had had to be told the reason she wasn't able to return home for her father's funeral. Even after she'd been sent home with Doug following five days of treatment, she would need close supervision, and in-home help with Lilly for the next few months to make sure she didn't relapse.

"And after I self-reported before my return to work, there was this humiliating meeting before the medical board, where I had to produce evidence I wasn't still too crazy to see patients."

She suspected she would have faced the same scrutiny here in New Jersey if Shoreline hadn't been so desperate to get a doctor to fill their emergency-department shortage. As it was, she'd been watched carefully until her supervisor saw for himself that she was capable of handling even the busiest of shifts.

"You weren't crazy," Harris told her, taking her hand and raising it to his lips to kiss it. "From what I've read, postpartum depression's a chemical thing, triggered by hormones from the baby's birth. That, combined with stress and grief, no sleep, and—"

"And with whatever mental illness is really in my DNA," she finished, pulling her hand away from his.

He shook his head. "So that's why you hired a private investigator two years ago. You wanted to know."

"I *had* to," she insisted. "It wasn't just random curiosity, either. I had to know whether I was—whether Lilly could be safe with me. Whether I should risk whatever had led my biological mother to abandon us. Because there was something wrong with her. I know that. Something more than drugs—it's right there, at the edges of my memory."

"But you never found a trace of her, never heard a thing?"

Until my daughter spoke to me using her words—or the cruel words she'd given Renee every opportunity to plant in Lilly's mind. "That's true," Christina said.

"Did you ever consider that your mother might've been suffering from postpartum depression, too?"

"Please don't sugarcoat it, Harris. It wasn't just postpartum depression. It was full-blown psychosis I was diagnosed with, bad enough to send me to a mental hospital." The words, after all, were right there on paper. Words that meant that Lilly would never have a biological sibling. Because whatever the doctor had said about going forward *with proper support and supervision*, she couldn't force herself to take such a risk again. And Doug had been even more adamant that there would be no more children. *What if you were to pass something like this on? Or even hurt the children?*

"All right, then," Harris said with a nod of agreement. "Postpartum psychosis. Annie was only a few months old, then, right? Your birth mother could've been hearing voices herself. Maybe she abandoned you to keep herself from doing worse. Did you ever think of that? That she might've saved you both that night."

Coming to her feet, Christina started pacing. "You weren't there. You don't know. It was so damn cold and dark, and Annie—no matter how hard I tried, I couldn't keep her warm."

Raising his head from his paws to watch her, the greyhound gave a plaintive whine.

Harris grimaced. "I'm not saying it was a good decision. But maybe, in her state, it was the only one she was capable of making."

Christina had never thought about it that way. Had never allowed herself to feel compassion, let alone appreciation, for the woman who had left them that night.

"Especially if she was self-medicating with street drugs," she added, "like that woman claiming to be her told my sister." *Or could that have been Renee, too, somehow altering her voice?* Because now that Christina thought about it, she remembered that even on the baby monitor, the woman's words had sounded strange . . . as if they might have been digitally altered.

Altered to disguise a voice she and Annie would've recognized at once?

"The important thing," said Harris as he came to his feet, "is that you and Annie were saved, that you had a better life. And when you were sick, Christina, you got help, and you're better. You're fine."

A bubble of bitter laughter erupted. "You know I'm not fine, Harris. I've never felt less fine in my life."

He winced. "I didn't mean—I only—"

"It doesn't matter," she said, knowing there was nothing he or anyone could do to ease her pain. "I should've told you my history from the start. Told you all of it before you—before we—"

"Yeah, you should have," he agreed. "It's made my job tougher, your keeping things to yourself."

"At first, I didn't trust you," she explained. "And then I thought—I worried you might think I was hearing things again, th-that you'd report me to child welfare, try to get my daughter taken from me."

He went to her and folded her into his arms, stroking her hair and back and shoulders. "I would never do that."

She pulled away, pain from the arm she'd left free of its sling shooting to her shoulder. "Don't lie to me. If it came down to Lilly's welfare, you'd do your job. You'd have to. And I couldn't live with that. It's the one thing I could never—"

"Shh. Don't talk like that, please—"

"Or what? You'll have me committed?"

"I'm not your enemy. I swear it. And I wish you'd consider that maybe, more than most people, I understand what it's like to go through something like—"

"Just tell me," she interrupted, raising the papers in her shaking hand. "Who gave these to Renee? And what could she hope to achieve by bringing them to you?"

He blew out a tired sigh, his handsome face lined with regret. Or was that the same heartbreak she'd seen in Doug's eyes as he'd emotionally backed away from the bond they'd shared before her illness? "I'm willing to bet that it was money. And you aren't gonna believe who paid her off."

As Zach Fulton passed the little café where they used to meet, tension knotted in his shoulders at the sight of her vehicle parked a few doors down. What the hell was she doing back in this pissant little town? Christ, she must have texted him to meet her. Instantly seething, he went to work extracting his phone from his jeans. He'd *told* her they were through with this place. And she must be smoking crack if she thought he'd waste another precious hour holding the hand of some chickenshit bimbo, especially now, with the window of opportunity about to slam down on both their heads.

But there was no text, no voice mail, no missed call from her number. Why else would she be back in here, if not to meet him?

He weighed his options, feeling the pressure to get out of there, to figure a way to finally finish things—to finish both of his targets—without getting himself thrown in prison. Or did cop killers get death row in Jersey? But then, he'd almost rather die than end up rotting behind bars while that gutless bitch soaked up the spoils of his ideas and his courage—something that could happen if he didn't keep reminding her that there could be no turning back. She'd forfeited that right, just as she'd forfeited the right to flaunt and tease and entice him with her body. It was damn well *his* body now, every curve and crevice bought in blood and flame. He had earned the right to use it—to use her—whenever and however he chose, no matter how these last few times had scared her. Especially when he'd pulled out his knife and used it to saw off an eight-inch lock of her hair.

He kept it in his pocket, wound around the knife's haft, a reminder of the power he would never back away from. A power he would use to take down anyone who stood in his way. Hadn't he already learned that a man with a knife could move far faster than a cop could pull out his gun . . . at least from behind?

His mind made up, he waited for the light to turn green before grabbing the first available parking spot. Halfway out of the car, he froze when he caught sight of a pair of uniformed officers striding toward the café's door, their backs already to him. Lean and hard-muscled, the tall male cop hesitated, then glanced over his shoulder, as if some sixth sense had warned him how close he was to danger.

Zach tightened his grip on the knife's handle, still inside his jacket. His muscles coiled as he weighed his options: jump back into the car and take off, or make a run straight at this bastard?

The cop, though, looked right past him before returning his gaze to his partner. Even taller, the slimmer officer pulled open the door and held it for the guy with an *after you* wave and a mocking half smile.

A woman, Zach realized, surprised both by her height and how freaking hot he found her, with those big, green eyes and high cheekbones. What would it be like to dominate such an Amazon, to unpin that shiny, dark hair, grab a handful, and force her to her knees before him? Preferably still dressed in those blues she was wearing—or at least she'd start out dressed before he used his knife to slice away her uniform.

As the fantasy unspooled, her partner hesitated and said something he couldn't make out, though the smart-ass edge in the cop's voice carried well enough. An exchange followed. *Flirting,* Zach thought. He felt sure of it, even from this distance. Something was going on between these two. The male cop was aching to slip his nightstick between those long, lean legs. He was working her, set on charming her over some coffee and the daily special.

That was it, Zach told himself. Their visit here was nothing but a coincidental meal break. The bitch—*his* bitch—hadn't arranged to meet up with them here. She wouldn't dare do that to him, as deep into this as she was.

Climbing back into his car, he pulled out his phone. But he didn't try to reach her—couldn't—not with some instinctive apprehension gnawing at his gut.

Is she just about to call me, beg me to meet her here? Or would she have the fucking nerve to hook up with some other guy, right under my nose?

A blaring horn jerked his head toward the street, where a delivery truck slammed to a stop, courtesy of some idiot bicyclist who'd darted out between two parked vehicles. He shook his head in disgust, thinking the truck driver should've run down the Lycra-wearing yuppie—a thought that burned to ash when the truck rolled away from in front of a car he hadn't noticed.

The white Crown Vic was a mess, coated with grime and eaten up with salt corrosion just behind the wheel wells, but its light bar and its markings sent alarm jolting up his spinal column—markings telling him those hadn't been just any cops he'd spotted. They were *Seaside Creek Police.*

Which meant the cops' presence here couldn't possibly be random.

"Goddamn it," he said, sweat popping out like a rash beneath his jacket and stocking cap. Adrenaline blasting through him, he fought to steady his breathing, fought to convince himself she hadn't called them. Hadn't arranged to meet the two of them here, setting him up to be arrested.

But in his head, Zach saw her tears, silent tears on her face when he'd sawed at that lock of her hair. Like a mist rising off the water, words floated back to him from a previous conversation. *You've gone way too far. As always. That's why, this time I'm done. With you.*

Rage flashing over him, he bailed out of his vehicle, no longer caring about being caught. Not caring about anything but punishing her unthinkable betrayal. A few steps, and he caught sight of her through one of the café's windows, her face in profile as she sat talking. She was wiping at tears with a fistful of tissues as she spoke to the Amazon cop across the table from her. Probably sniveling over how he'd abused her, *forced* her into a plot to—

But wait, where was the male partner?

Looking around wildly, knife clutched inside his pocket, Zach reminded himself it didn't matter where the cop was. Nothing mattered except the bitch thinking she could get away with talking to the cops about him, could get off scot-free with all the money *he* deserved.

Stepping past him to get to the door, a dark-skinned man wearing a stocking cap hesitated before looking back his way.

"Sorry if I—were you heading inside?" the guy asked, his gaze uncertain as he held open the door.

As the blade slipped free of its leather sheath, Zach answered, "You're fucking right I am."

CHAPTER TWENTY-FOUR

"You have to understand. Renee's in a real financial jam," said Harris. "I offered to help her out, but she said she had it covered. I should've asked more questions, pressed her for details."

Christina's gaze bored into him. "I don't want to hear excuses. All I want to know is who? Who's paid her to do this to me?"

He grimaced, but the time for stalling had passed. "That young guy you saw her with? The description you gave me sounds a lot like someone I have reason to believe is tangled up with your husband's daughter, Ashley."

"Ashley?" Christina burst out. "You don't think—you really think she's mixed up in this?"

Harris shrugged and gestured toward the couch in the hope that they could sit again, rather than watching her continue to wind herself up by pacing.

With a grudging look, she switched on a lamp against the evening gloom before perching on the edge of a cushion.

Harris nodded his thanks and sat beside her, explaining, "I actually figured the girl's mother for it. I'm not sure you're aware, but

Evelyn Paxton and her daughter have spent the last few months in Philadelphia . . . just a bridge away from New Jersey and the Parkway."

Her forehead creased. "What're they doing there?"

"Evelyn's mother was in hospice there," he said, "and from what I understand, there was the added benefit of getting Ashley away from this boyfriend the family thought was trouble."

Christina nodded. "She's always been so trusting. It worried her dad, too."

Harris agreed, recalling how surprisingly open Ashley had been with him that morning he'd met her. "I didn't think a whole lot of it, until I saw from the tollbooth screen grabs the authorities sent me that Ashley, not her mother, had made several suspiciously timed trips into Jersey driving her mom's car."

"Was she with him? This bad-news boyfriend?"

Harris shook his head. "Going to meet him would be my guess—once the afternoon before your car was vandalized, and then again the day before the house burned."

Shaking her head, Christina said, "But Ashley—she's the sweetest of them, the one who always had a big hug for me, at least before her mom decided that her visits to our house in Texas were too *confusing* and *unsettling* for a sensitive girl like her."

"Stands to reason her mother's done her best to turn the kids against you, maybe even convinced them it's your fault their father's dead."

"*My* fault?" A flush bloomed in Christina's cheeks. As if maybe she, too, believed it on some level.

"I know it's nuts," he said, wanting to assure her he didn't buy it for a second. "But I saw Evelyn the morning after her mother passed away. She was too emotional to hold back anything."

Christina sighed. "And now she's poisoned her daughter's mind against me, too."

"Or maybe I was right before, and it all really does boil down to greed—because I've gotten some more info on this kid Ashley was seeing, and he's even worse than her family suspected. Way worse. I found records of past charges: aggravated assault, robbery . . . and he likes to watch things burn."

Her eyes widened, as her hand went to her injured arm.

"He and a buddy were prime suspects in a string of fires, including one that badly damaged a school outside of Pittsburgh. The arson-squad guy I spoke with said they were close to making an arrest when this kid—his name's Zach Fulton—vanished a few weeks back."

"Then it was *him*," she said. "This lunatic was the one who tried to burn my daughter and me alive. But I don't see how this tracks." She laid a finger across her chin, her mouth tightening in a look of concentration. "Why bother with the car thing or using this paperwork to try to run me out of town if they were going to turn around and try to kill us?"

"I'm guessing Fulton's off his meds—the arson cop told me the kid's mom's worried because he left without them.

"What sort of meds?"

"Cloza—cloza-something?" he guessed, digging out the small pad he'd used to take notes during the call.

Before he could flip to the right page, she supplied, "Clozapine. It's an antipsychotic, used a lot with schizophrenics, among other things. Which means this kid—" The color drained from her face.

"What is it?"

"He killed her, didn't he? My mother. And Fiorelli, too."

"I have two officers meeting with Ashley Paxton as we speak. We'll get this Fulton, too. I swear it. And then we'll get our answers."

"But what if he—my God!" Christina blurted out. "My head's been so messed up today. How could I let my sister go anywhere alone with Lilly? And I gave her my keys, too. She's driving my loaner."

"Settle down. It's okay. I asked her to go to the mall security office, where I sent an officer to meet her for an escort home."

"You—you're sure?"

He looked into her eyes, his gaze never wavering. "I promise you, Christina. I'll do whatever it takes to get you through this. I'm not going anywhere."

He'd scarcely gotten the word out when his phone vibrated in his pocket. Pausing to pull it out, he glanced down at a lit screen reading *M. Del Vecchio*. Probably letting him know he and Zarzycki were on their way back from a little café in Millville, a small city about halfway between Philadelphia and Seaside Creek, where Ashley Paxton had suggested meeting when he'd spoken to her earlier by phone.

With an apologetic nod toward Christina, Harris rose and turned away to answer. "Bowers here. What d'you got for—"

"He—he stabbed her!" Del shouted. "I just ducked in the restroom for a minute and heard screaming and he—this Fulton guy knifed Ashley Paxton three or four times before I—I shot the bastard, but I—I hit—"

"Marco—Marco, calm down!" Harris barked, hoping to shock his officer out of his emotional reaction and get some sense out of him. Not that his own body wasn't vibrating with the rocket fuel of the adrenaline ripping through him. "Just give me the facts. Is the scene secure now? Are you safe?"

He was vaguely aware of Christina coming to stand beside him, her eyes huge. Even Max was on his feet.

"Yeah. The—the suspect's down and disarmed," said Del Vecchio over the sound of some commotion close by. "The girl, too, and Alex, I mean Zarzycki—I shot her, Chief. One of my bullets passed right through the perp and—I didn't mean to—"

"Is she breathing?" Harris demanded, the blood pumping through him ice-cold. "Can you tell me? Have you called an ambulance?"

"I—I think she is. Yeah. Rescue squad and Millville PD en route. And I'm—I'm applying direct pressure. It's her—her shoulder, Chief, but there's so much blood and she's—what if I killed her?"

"You can't think about that now. You just think about keeping her from bleeding out in the next few minutes. What about the girl? Is she—"

"There's a Good Samaritan here with me, former army medic. He's doing what he can. The waitress—she's brought us cloth napkins and clean towels."

"And the suspect?"

"Hasn't moved, and—and there's what looks like brain matter spattered—hell, Chief. It's a freaking bloodbath."

As the background noise of approaching sirens swelled, Harris wanted to tell Del to preserve the scene, but he knew it would be impossible to control with people working frantically to save the injured. Because the living always came first, including the traumatized officer on the line, Harris told him, "You know what to do here. Your priorities. Just focus on your training, and let the local cops take the lead."

Feeling Christina clutching his arm, he glanced toward her white face.

"Rescue Squad just rolled up," Del Vecchio said, relief in his voice. "More lights right behind 'em. Everybody's here."

"I'm on my way, too," Harris told him. "And I'll need you need to be there with the PD when I arrive."

"I—I understand," Del Vecchio choked out, aware as Harris was that his duties as an officer and witness must take precedence over his emotional need to ride with Zarzycki and the young woman who'd been stabbed. "I'm just—I'm so damn sorry. I was trying—just trying to stop him from slashing both of them. Alex—Zarzycki was going for her gun, but it all happened so fast—"

"I trust you did the best that you could manage," Harris assured him, knowing a knife-wielder could do a lot of damage in close quarters before a cop could draw. "You and Aleksandra both. You be sure to tell her for me—tell her she's gotta live, and that's an order." *I'll be damned if we bury another of our own.*

"Will do," Del managed before ending the call.

"I caught some of that, but what is it?" Christina asked, her eyes pleading. "What's going on, Harris?"

"A freaking nightmare," he said, quickly explaining as he headed for the door.

"Millville?" she asked. "I don't have my medical bag, but let me come with you. I can help with triage and—"

"You have to stay here. I can't take you."

"Sore arm or not, I'm an emergency doctor and a damn good one."

He shook his head. "The paramedics'll have 'em at the local hospital by the time we get there."

"Then I'll meet them there. I have to—your officer—and Ashley's my husband's daughter. She's—"

The girl whose greed or rotten taste in boyfriends most likely got your mother killed—and nearly you and Lilly, too. But this was no time for a debate, so he defaulted to command mode. "Absolutely not. You need to stay here. I'll have the officer escorting Annie and your daughter wait with you until I give the word."

"Because you think I'm too unstable?" she accused him.

"Less than twenty-four hours after finding your mother's body? Yeah, I do, as a matter of fact—and who could blame you? And I won't have you jeopardizing this case—or whatever justice your family can hope for by coming within a mile of Ashley Paxton or Zach Fulton."

She opened her mouth to argue, but he shut her down.

"Give me your word right now, Christina, that you'll wait here until you have my say-so. Otherwise, your family's going to come home to find you handcuffed to the arm of this sofa. Got it?"

She nodded stiffly. But the hurt and anger in her eyes told him that, fragile as she was, he'd just hurt her deeply. But with one of his officers fighting for her life, another devastated, and both of his prime suspects dead or badly injured, he put damage control aside for later.

After all, at that moment he was still certain he would get another chance to make things right with her.

~

Furious as she was, Christina knew Harris was right. She didn't have privileges at the hospital nearest Millville, so there was no way she would be allowed to treat any of the patients. And she was well versed enough on medico-legal issues to know that having anything to do with Ashley's treatment could go very wrong—whether or not Doug's daughter survived her injuries.

How in the hell could you get yourself mixed up in something like this, Ashley? Did you know what this boyfriend of yours did to my poor mother? What he tried to do to me and your own half sister, too? Did you want that?

A spasm of grief hitting her, Christina popped the heel of her hand against the door Harris had closed behind him. Startled by the banging sound, Max tucked his tail and sprinted to safety up the staircase.

Guilt for scaring the poor greyhound only made her feel worse. She felt like a stranger to herself, a shadow of the model daughter her adoptive parents had lavished with so much love. Parents she hadn't been here for when each of them had needed her most.

But then, since she'd fallen ill, everything she touched was tainted. Christina knew that Evelyn was right in part, that the disappointment Doug felt in his young wife had driven him to pull away from her, to immerse himself in the training that would eventually lead to his death. Oh, they might have remained married, out of Doug's inherent decency and whatever sense of duty he'd felt toward his toddler daughter, but things would never have been the same between them . . . just as they would never be between her and Harris now that he knew all about her background.

You have to stop this, Christina warned herself. It was over now for her, at least. With Ashley heading for the hospital and Zach Fulton either critical or dead, she, Lilly, and Annie would all be safe here. Safe to grieve and process what had happened before Christina and her daughter packed up what little they had left and—

Sitting on the sofa, she pulled out her phone to call her sister to see how far she and Lilly were from home. The phone rang several times and went to voice mail. Christina sighed, wishing that for once Annie would answer.

She hesitated to text, deciding it wasn't worth the risk of having her sister take her eyes off the road—because she had to face it, Annie didn't have the patience to pull over to read or talk. But surely, she and Lilly couldn't be much longer, could they? Or was she still back at the mall, begging her officer escort to explain what was going on?

In an attempt to distract herself, Christina coaxed Max back downstairs before scooping out some food for him and refilling the pan she was using for his water. After he ate, she took him out into the front yard, glad the snow had melted. But the growing darkness made her nervous; the first few stars were multiplying with each passing minute.

As she opened the door to bring the greyhound back inside, she heard her mother's landline ringing. Hurrying to the desk nook, she wondered, would it be another family friend offering condolences or assistance, or fishing for details Christina couldn't bear to speak of? She felt a surge of gratitude when she saw "Not Available" on the caller ID. A telemarketer, at least, she could deal with.

Scooping up the handset, she said, "Whatever you're selling, we're not interested."

"You didn't come and find me like I told you, Katie-baby," said a voice that sliced straight to her marrow. The same female voice she'd heard over the baby monitor and on the telephone what seemed like so long ago.

"You're not my mother," Christina shouted, tears springing to her eyes. "My real mother's dead now. *Dead*—and if find out—if I find out you had one thing to do with it, I swear I'll choke the life out of you!"

"Oh, but I'm already dead, my darling," said the woman. "That's been the trouble all along."

"Who the hell *are* you? Why are you doing this?" Christina demanded.

"I already have your sister and your daughter with me," came the icy words. "Now all I need is you."

CHAPTER TWENTY-FIVE

As Harris approached Millville on tree-lined Route 55, the phone calls never stopped. Once again, he buried any worries over the budget—between arresting Edgewood's son and having a second officer injured, he figured he'd be out of a job before it caught up with him—and called in extra officers to make sure Seaside Creek had coverage while he and the three other cops scheduled to be on duty were out of their jurisdiction. There were also status calls to and from his dispatcher, as well as an update from the hospital where Zarzycki, Ashley Paxton, and Zach Fulton had all been transported.

Fulton was DOA, he quickly learned, and both of the women had been taken to surgery. A snapped "Critical condition" was all Harris could get out of the ER nurse he'd spoken with, even after he'd identified himself as law enforcement.

At some point, someone from the ER or ambulance crew had contacted Ashley's mother, and Evelyn Paxton was practically blowing up his phone with increasingly frantic calls and texts demanding information. So it didn't much surprise him when Maya radioed to ask whether Pete Washington, the officer he'd sent to accompany Annie and Lilly from the mall, had ever managed to get through to him.

"No, why?" he asked as he turned onto Millville's High Street and spotted a number of police vehicles, their lights flashing, a few blocks ahead. A thin sliver of moon had risen over the little downtown, with its brick-faced buildings, and people were standing on the sidewalk, most in uniform.

"He needs to touch base with you."

"Now's a bad time," Harris said, as he eyed a parking spot. "Tell him I want him to sit tight at the Wallace house with Christina Paxton and her sister until he—"

"He's there now," said Maya, her young voice strained, as it had been ever since she'd learned about Zarzycki's shooting. "And he's alone."

He felt the throbbing of his own pulse. "What? What are you saying?"

"He couldn't find Annie Wallace and the little girl at the mall. Security there said they'd never checked in at their office. Since Pete had been held up in traffic, he'd figured that maybe Annie had gotten impatient and driven home on her own. When he couldn't reach her on the cell number he had, he hurried back—and nobody was home."

The beat picked up speed. "You're sure of this?"

"No cars at the house, and no one inside except the dog. The front door was unlocked, too."

His gut dropped through the floorboard. *Unlocked?* After what had happened to Christina and Annie's mother? "Has he tried Dr. Paxton's cell, too?"

"Yes, I believe so. I just got him her number."

Harris used a choice word, forgetting for the moment that he was on the radio. A gut instinct insisted this wasn't going to turn out to be something easy, like Christina going to help her sister change a flat or meeting her someplace to deal with funeral arrangements. With the vandals behind bars and Ashley Paxton and her psycho boyfriend no longer a threat, he'd figured all three would be safe from any further danger, but what if he'd been wrong? Had his leaving Christina alone given someone else a narrow window of opportunity? *How the hell many of them could there be, and what was it he was missing?*

His mind rocketed back to the voice on the child monitor and the phone calls that had come after. Communications he hadn't yet accounted for from a woman who'd claimed to be Christina and Annie's birth mother. Could she have seen Christina and Annie's adoptive mother as standing in the way of some twisted plan for a reunion? Or could someone else entirely have been responsible for those calls, perhaps disguising her voice?

Her voice. He thought back to Christina's theory about the murder of her mother—her idea that a female attacker might have needed a multitude of blows to kill Elizabeth Wallace. At the time, he'd thought it unlikely, but was it possible Christina had been right?

"Sounds like you're busy there. What should I tell Pete?" Maya repeated. "Should he sit tight at the mall?"

"You tell him he'd damn well better find her. Find the three of them. Put out a BOLO and get everybody on it, and contact me the minute they're accounted for."

"Will do," she said. "You make it to the hospital yet? How is she?"

Knowing she was genuinely worried for Zarzycki—that everyone within their small department would be—Harris promised, "I'll be tied up at the scene for a while, but I'll check on Alex as soon as I can. And I promise you, I'll let you know how she and Del are. Then I'll head straight back to Seaside Creek as fast as I can get there."

As he ended the call, he prayed that his instincts were wrong, that Christina and her family would be quickly located and escorted home . . .

And that his responsibilities to his officers, his department, and his investigation wouldn't cost him the woman he had, against all odds and reason, allowed into his heart.

You'd best come quick. Tide's turning.

The woman's words had replayed inside Christina's head as she'd dug frantically through her mother's desk drawers, where she'd kept the spare keys to the Cadillac the police had discovered still parked in the detached garage. Failing to find them, Christina had hurried upstairs, the sounds of her daughter's weeping in the call's background playing on an endless loop inside her head. With her heart crashing against her chest wall, Christina found her mother's purse. A cry bubbled from her throat when she didn't find the keys there, either.

She found Annie's, though, in her sister's old room. Soon, she was pushing the battered red Kia flat out. Its aging engine screamed until she slammed the manual transmission—something she hadn't driven in at least a decade—into fourth.

She tried to think of how to get there, her mind struggling to dredge up directions to the once-familiar road. With the darkness closing in on her, she felt raw terror pressing the air from her lungs. What if she could no longer find it?

She gulped a breath of cool night air, cursing herself for not stopping to look up directions before she'd left the house—or leave a note telling Harris where she was going. *If you tell anyone, your family's dead,* the woman on the phone had warned her. But how would she have any way to know what Christina did?

She's depending on me panicking, losing my head and rushing to her. But knowing this was one thing. Tamping down the icy fear clawing at her throat was another. *Just how disturbed is this woman, really—enough to hurt them as she threatened if I don't make it in time?*

But staccato images flashed through her brain—the horror of finding her own mother's body last night around this time. Christina knew then that she'd do anything, take any risk, to keep the same fate from befalling Lilly and her sister.

Just as she was thinking of pulling over to check directions on her phone, her own unconscious mind kicked in as she passed a Y-style turnoff to her right. Though someone had taken down the sign pointing out the way to Willet's Point after the lighthouse had been abandoned, her instincts screamed that it was the right way, forcing her to slow to make a U-turn.

The car stalled—her own fault, since she hadn't thought to downshift. Shaking hard, she had to remind herself to breathe, to calm down so she wouldn't flood the engine.

"Thank you, God," she said when the Kia restarted on the first try. But she didn't put it into gear again yet, forcing herself to take her phone out and amend the error she'd made earlier. Because logic, not emotion, was what she needed to get through this—or, for all she knew, her own battered body could be the next one found.

As badly as her hands were shaking, she fumbled with her texting. Feeling time slipping away, she glanced at the half bar of reception and prayed it would be enough. Biting her lip, she hit "Send," trusting the autocorrect feature to make sense of things before she shoved the cell back into the pocket of the all-weather jacket she'd grabbed from the closet on her way out the front door.

After negotiating an awkward turn onto the pothole-ridden road to the lighthouse, she wondered, was this all for nothing? Some sick joke that would lead her to the dangerously slick rocks hours after a killing January tide had already rolled in, leaving her path underwater? Even if the caller had told the truth, and there was still time, Christina realized that risking the walk out there would leave her trapped by rising water, struggling to climb a ladder crusted with razor-edged barnacles and mossy slime, heaving on a locked entry hatch that had long since rusted shut. Why hadn't she brought thick gloves—or even a flashlight?

But as dangerous as this trip was, what choice did she have? Unless—what if the phone call she'd received—all of the communications from her biological mother—had really been hallucinations after all?

No. It wasn't possible, not when Annie, too, had heard from a woman issuing nearly identical commands. But as Christina forced the car over the ruts and rocks of the point, a sense of the surreal clung to her, along with the memory of those disappearing taillights reflected in Lilly's eyes.

The Kia's right side dropped with a bone-jarring thud, jolting her in her seat. She tried to steer out of the hole, to back out, but the car refused to budge. Shifting out of gear, she left the motor running and the headlights aimed farther down the pitch-black point, where the jagged tops of the spinelike slabs were just visible above the slapping surf. With over half a tank of gas, the engine should run for some time, keeping the battery alive to light her way at least partway across the rocks. Other than the car's light, there was no illumination, only the all-too-distant stars and a fingernail-thin crescent moon that rose behind the dark hulk jutting from the sea a half-mile ahead . . .

A lighthouse she must walk to, with the waves breaking around her and terror propelling every step.

As she opened the car door, a cold gust tore it open wide, submerging her in the smells of salt, seaweed, and the inescapable hint of decomposing dead things. Apprehension shuddering through her, she pulled out her cell phone one last time to check it, only to see the text she'd written to Harris still sitting unsent in her outbox.

But there was no time to delay, nothing to do but hope the message might get out at some point . . . and that it would be in time to lead him to her living, breathing little family, and not three more battered corpses.

CHAPTER TWENTY-SIX

Millville might be considered a small city, but it was still ten times the size of tiny Seaside Creek—a fact that its police chief, Charles Guthrie, whose thickly grizzled mustache and brows brought to mind an angry walrus, was quick to point out when Harris tried to speak up on Marco Del Vecchio's behalf.

"This is *my* damned jurisdiction you let your mess spill over into," Guthrie said, his face ruddy beneath the lights of the café, where he, Harris, and Marco stood beside the counter. "Which makes it *my* mess, now that young Dirty Harry here's shot up the damned Arts District."

Del Vecchio grimaced, his gaze straying to two more Millville cops who were carefully photographing the small seating area, with its crimson puddles, bloody footprints, overturned chairs, and pushed-back tables, several of which were covered with shards of broken window glass. Other cops and CSI milled about, some of the officers holding back a gathering crowd. Among those pushing toward the front, Harris had spotted at least one cameraman, who most likely belonged to the Philadelphia network affiliate news van that had arrived to document the mayhem.

"My officers didn't come here expecting trouble," Harris protested, though he knew he would have had plenty to say if a couple of Guthrie's officers had left a mess like this in his town. "Del Vecchio here took out a dangerous criminal—a cop killer who'd already stabbed one woman—before he could do any more damage."

"*Alleged* cop killer," Guthrie corrected him.

Harris nodded. "That's right. If we'd known for sure this was our guy or had any idea he'd show up for a public meeting we'd set up with his girlfriend, believe me, I would've gone through proper channels to ensure the public's safety—and my own officers'."

"Regardless, you still should've touched base with us. Instead, I end up with all this, right down the street from City Hall," Guthrie said, gesturing toward the north. "It's a freaking PR nightmare, Bowers."

"You're right, and I'm sorry. If you want me to, I'll step up, take full responsibility for the error in judgment." Why the hell not? Seaside Creek's city council could only fire him once.

Harris felt the vibration of a couple of incoming texts in his pocket, one after the other. But with Del Vecchio looking as if he might tell Guthrie to go screw himself at any second so he could rush off to Zarzycki's side, Harris didn't dare look away to check his messages.

But Guthrie held up his meaty palms. "Forget it. It's done now. Just fill me in enough that I can sound like I knew all about this from the start, maybe grab a share of credit for nabbing your cop killer."

Harris snorted, nodding. "I see department politics aren't restricted to *pissant little shore towns*, then," he said, quoting Guthrie's earlier assessment of tiny Seaside Creek.

The two shared a wry smile. The guy wasn't such a hard-ass after all, just another police chief doing his best to keep his job.

"Happy to do that, yeah," Harris agreed, "but how 'bout we let Officer Del Vecchio head over to the med center, while we're talking, so he can check up on his partner and our female suspect? Then after you finish whatever damage control you need to do here, you can have your detectives meet him over there to get his official statement."

Guthrie gave Del Vecchio a searching look. "You won't take off on me before we get all our questions answered, will you?"

"You have my word, sir," Marco said earnestly, extended a right hand still smeared with blood. Guthrie shook it before stepping back to give the young officer room to leave the café.

"He's a good guy, a good cop, and he's been through a lot tonight," Harris told the other chief as he watched Del jog toward his department sedan. "I'm trusting you to handle him like you'd want one of your own treated."

As Guthrie offered his assurances, the phone in Harris's pocket vibrated once again. Only this time, Harris murmured an excuse to check the incoming message.

"You look confused," said Guthrie moments later. "What is it?"

Harris shook his head. "It's not what's there," he said, studying the close-up photo Maya had sent showing a highlighted page from the cellphone records he'd requested last week. "It's what *isn't* that's the issue."

Had he gotten the wrong dates and times from Annie on the anonymous calls she'd received from the woman who had claimed to be her mother? Depending on how the originating number had been disguised or possibly spoofed using a third-party Internet application, these communications might not be traceable. But still, they should appear on Annie's bill detail pages, giving him the opportunity to do further research.

But these questions, he decided, could wait a few more minutes. With Guthrie taking notes on dates and names, Harris finished briefing the man on the critical events leading up to the café incident.

"You'll be there with me for the statement?" Guthrie asked, probably thinking that the public would find the appearance of unity comforting.

But by that time, Harris was once more staring at his cell, his heart stuttering as he opened and read a message that had gotten lost among so many others . . .

The text, from his ex-wife, read: `Need you over here NOW. She's gone—Jacob too! —Mom`

What the hell? *Mom*, he knew, was surely Renee's mother, who rarely carried her own cell phone. What was she doing texting him on her daughter's phone? And what in hell was Renee doing without the iPhone she'd been all but glued to since he'd bought it for her last year? Especially considering his belief that she was somehow tied up with Zach Fulton. What if the crazy bastard had decided to silence her before coming to deal with his pink-and-blue-haired girlfriend? And if Renee had happened to have Jacob with her at the time . . .

With Christina and her family, too, among the missing, his head spun with possibilities—each one more alarming than the last.

"What's going on, Bowers?" Guthrie asked.

"It's my kid and my ex-wife," Harris told him, "so you go ahead and run your dog and pony show any way you want to. Take the credit, blame it on me—I don't give a damn right now."

"Slow down," Guthrie ordered. "Tell me, what can I do to help?"

"I have no idea," said Harris as he headed for the exit. "All I know is, I have to get back to Seaside Creek fast—because it's starting to sound like all hell's breaking loose."

Relief flooded through Christina when she saw the spine of rocks still visible above the waves, the carved surfaces that formed the old path evident as far as she could make out. No, she hadn't missed the tide yet, but her teeth pinched her lip at the sight of the churning water lapping greedily only a few feet—or was that inches?—below where she'd be walking. If she fell, what then? Would she smash her head on a submerged rock or drown fighting to swim against the treacherous currents?

"Don't think about it. Think of them," she said aloud, focusing on an image of Annie holding Lilly. Drawing a deep breath, Christina swallowed back her fear, then took her first tentative steps onto the mossy rocks.

"Please don't let me fall," she prayed, tears in her eyes as she forced herself to move faster. "Don't fall. Don't fall. You can't."

Within moments, cold seawater had swamped the workout shoes she wore, and the spray had her face, hands, and legs dripping wet. Her mother's all-weather jacket, with its insulated hood, protected her head and torso, though. And her pounding heart—especially when she slipped as she jumped a watery gap where part of the ridge had collapsed—kept hypothermia at bay.

As she approached the lighthouse, she heard a hollow banging against the lighthouse base but couldn't yet make out what was causing it. Then her eyes were drawn to the dark cylinder that loomed above, and at the level of the living quarters, she spotted a light inside the window and gave a cry of pure relief. She hadn't risked drowning here for nothing; someone was definitely waiting for her here. But had this someone really brought her baby and her sister out here? Could they have made it, walking this same treacherous path?

As she reached the level of the ladder to the door hatch, she spotted the source of the banging sounds: an older, open-bowed boat tied nearby, a smallish runabout being repeatedly bashed against the lighthouse with the rising water.

The hull wouldn't last long moored like that, Christina thought, wondering if the person who'd left it tied there knew much about boating. The woman who'd phoned her might well be trapped as she was, if she didn't get out of here before the vessel was destroyed.

Taking a deep breath, Christina rubbed her hands together and looked back to where the Kia still offered its weak—and distressingly distant—illumination. "I'm bringing them both back," she told the little hatchback.

The wind snatched away the promise as she began to climb.

"I'm heading back from Millville fast as I can," Harris said after putting his cell phone on speaker and calling Renee's mother's landline. "What can you tell me, Kathleen? When did you last see Renee and Jacob?"

"What's that?" she asked. "I can barely hear you."

He turned off the Tahoe's siren but left his emergency lights flashing as he goosed his speed to eighty—as fast as he could reasonably drive this stretch of highway. "Sorry," he said before repeating the questions he'd just asked.

"It was—I think it was just after lunchtime." Though Renee's mother sounded breathless, he could tell she was making an effort to hold herself together. "I had to run some errands that kept me out for a few hours. When I came back a while ago, she wasn't here, but I found the phone between the sofa cushions when I heard the little chime."

"Could be she was in a hurry and she'd just misplaced it," he suggested. A huge hurry, if she'd left without bothering to try to locate the cell phone by ringing it from her mom's landline. "Is her purse there? What about the Jeep?"

"Both gone," her mother said, "but—but she'd been acting funny."

He flipped on the siren long enough for it to emit a single whoop, waking up the left-lane driver who'd failed to yield at his approach. "Funny, how?" he asked as the pickup pulled to the right.

"Nervous, I think. This job she's interviewed for. It's not the day-care center like she told us. It's a full-time teaching job in Wilmington," she said, naming a city more than an hour and a half away.

"She's thinking of moving to Delaware?" The terms of their custody agreement wouldn't allow her to take Jacob out of state, not without

Harris's permission. That explained why she would have lied about it—at least until she had a solid offer.

"It wasn't just that, Harris. She kept saying she'd made a terrible mistake, that she needed to talk to you."

"To me?" Did his ex-wife have regrets about what she'd gotten involved with? Had Zach Fulton tricked her somehow, possibly by striking up that conversation at the store she'd mentioned, before using violence to control her, too?

"Yes, and I think—I could be wrong about this, but I believe it had something to do with her friend, Christina."

"They're not speaking anymore."

"I know they had a falling out, but when I went to text you—my calls kept rolling over to your voice mail—I found a message from Christina, sent just a little while ago."

Had all of them met up someplace in an attempt to hash out the differences between them? "What message? Can you read it to me? This could be incredibly important."

"I'm afraid it doesn't make sense. It's all garbled."

"Just read it verbatim. Please, if you ever want to see your daughter and my son again."

"*What?* You think they're in danger, Harris?" Kathleen asked, her voice high and tight with panic. "Oh my Lord—I heard about Christina's mother, h-how they found her dead at her house. Could my sweet babies—could they be—"

"I don't think so. In fact, I'm sure not—I'm sorry for upsetting you," he said. "I just need you to read the text from Christina."

"All right. Here it is." She sniffled and then cleared her throat, clearly fighting to pull herself together. She read the message to him, but it made little sense, even after he had her spell out some words. "What could any of that mean?" she asked.

"I'm not sure," he admitted, his attention partly on the traffic. "But could you forward it to my phone, so I can see it?"

"How would I do that?" she asked.

He talked her through it and then thanked her, promising to call her the minute he knew anything.

"I'm t-trusting you to bring them home," she said, her words shaky.

"I swear to you," he answered, feeling nothing but affection for the woman who'd always treated him so kindly, "I won't rest until I know they're safe." *All five of them,* he thought, his mind drifting from Renee and Jacob to Lilly, her aunt Annie, and the woman who had commandeered his heart.

CHAPTER TWENTY-SEVEN

By the time Christina reached the level of the lower gallery platform encircling the lighthouse like a belt, her stitched left arm was throbbing, and her hands were a bloody mess from the corroded metal rungs. Unable to feel her feet in her sodden sneakers, she used the outer railing to haul herself upright.

Her strength failing, she stumbled to the double doors. When she came upon the padlock that must have secured them lying broken on the galley platform, her heart pounded at the sign that someone might well be waiting inside, just as the caller had claimed. Queasiness slithered through her stomach, a reminder that the same fate that had befallen her mother could be waiting behind the peeling red paint of the entrance.

But turning back was not an option, so she grabbed the right-hand door and pulled. Hinges creaked—a cry like a woman's scream—and she stumbled inside. Seeing no one, she collapsed to her hands and knees, shaking with exhaustion.

As she fought to catch her breath, her gaze went first to the floor a few feet ahead, at what appeared to be an antique lantern. Behind its grimy windows, the lantern's flame painted ash-coated walls in shifting shadows, and the stink of charred wood and ocean dampness reminded her that the place had been abandoned for more than twenty years.

Beyond the lantern, a spiral staircase dominated the dark space. Its metal rails and treads dared her to climb to where the living quarters had been. It made sense that the woman holding her family would have them there—more sense than dragging Lilly and Annie to the very top, where the light had once been housed.

Hauling herself to her feet, Christina stumbled to a salt-filmed, porthole-style window, where she looked back in the direction of the Kia. Disoriented with exhaustion, she couldn't find its headlights. She saw no sign, either, of the rocky spine, the path—along with her escape route—already erased by the rising tide.

Did her tormenter know she'd made it? Or had she given up on her?

"I'm here!" Christina shouted, her cries echoing up the tight coil of the stairs. "I've come, just like you asked me. Where are they? You promised!"

She heard a sound from above, a harsh clatter on the staircase.

With her heart doing its best to beat its way free, she picked up the lantern by its wire bail and called the words she guessed her tormentor wanted most to hear. "I'm coming for you, Mother. I'll be right up. You'll see."

As she began to climb, Christina noticed the ash clinging to the brick walls and metal stairs seemed thicker. The air felt heavier as well, chilled and tainted by the burned wood of the living quarters, where she'd heard the fire had started.

Against the overall gloom of the steps above her, something white and rounded stood out on one of the steps. At first she took it for a broken bowl—an artifact of the men who'd once lived here for weeks or months at a time.

It wasn't until she'd nearly reached it that she realized she'd been wrong. What she was seeing wasn't the curved wall of any kind of crockery—but a skull, certainly human, lying on its side.

Harris had nearly made it back to town when Maya's harried-sounding voice blasted over the radio. "Answer your cell, Chief. I've got some news you're gonna want to hear."

Harris's pulse ticked at his throat as he slowed the Tahoe. The moment he heard the phone vibrate, he thumbed the "Answer" button. "What is it, Maya?" he asked, worried she might be calling with bad news about his injured rookie—or any of those missing, including his son.

The thought had him pulling to the shoulder. "Please tell me it's not—"

"Kym Meador just called, scared out of her wits. She found Lilly Paxton sleeping in her bathtub—someone had made a little nest of blankets for her and left her there—with a half-empty bottle of liquid cold medication nearby."

Alarm sucker-punched him. *Drugged.* "Is she okay?"

"Pretty groggy, but Kym was able to rouse her while I had her on the line. She's getting her checked out at Shoreline ER just in case. But she's terrified for Annie, said she'd never do something like this willingly."

Agreeing, Harris asked himself, "Where the hell has she gone?"

"No one's found her yet, or Christina Paxton, either," Maya told him.

Heart sinking, he asked, "What about Renee and my son?" The moment he'd finished his conversation with his ex's mother, Harris had called in to report their disappearance, his gut telling him that finding the two would lead him to Christina and her family.

"Give it time. They'll turn up," Maya assured him. "How far from the station are you?"

"Be there in about ten minutes," he said before wrapping up the call.

Despite the urgency he felt, though, he sat there for a minute, unable to escape the suspicion that he was missing something crucial. Opening his phone's texts, he studied the garbled message Renee's mother had forwarded from her daughter's phone.

`Will it's point,` he read aloud, desperate to make sense of the jumble. `Calms has Lilly and anniversary. Hurry, Hair is.`"

The final two words jumped out at him, *Hair is.* He'd seen them before—when his own first name fell victim to someone's hurry and a smartphone's autocorrect feature.

Hurry, Harris, Christina had meant to write. But why send such the message to his ex-wife—especially considering their recent falling out?

She never meant to text Renee. Christina must have accidentally messaged the other Bowers whose contact information she'd stored in her phone. Had Renee seen it before rushing out—and pieced together the intended message?

"Not *Will it's point,*" he told himself, tension tightening his jaw. "*Willet's Point*, you idiot. The lighthouse." Keeping autocorrect in mind, he pieced together the rest of the intended message: *Claims had Lilly and Annie.* That was it—they were all there, at the lighthouse. The same abandoned lighthouse Christina, Annie, and Renee had visited during their childhood.

But had Renee gone to try to save them—or was she more involved in Zach Fulton's and Ashley Paxton's plot than he wanted to admit?

Enveloped by an icy sense of unreality, Christina stared with her jaw unhinged as her pulse pounded in her ears. But she didn't cry out, telling herself instead that the skull was no threat to her. The dead, at least, were past inflicting pain.

But what about the person who'd sent it rolling down the stairs? The person attempting to shatter her mind with cruel threats and crazed demands? *That's what these games are really meant for—not to kill me, but to drive me to another breakdown.* And the only way to beat her enemy was to keep her grip on reason. To hold fast despite the fear threatening to swallow her alive.

Forcing herself to slow her breathing, she grabbed the railing and bent forward, holding the lantern close enough to give the disembodied head a better look. It was real, she knew at once, with a few leathery scraps of flesh clinging to ivory-colored bone—even strands of hair. Blonde hair—or maybe white, with one side of the mandible hanging loose to give the face the appearance of a crazed grin. But that damage could have easily been done when the skull came crashing down.

The damage to the back of the head—the parietal bone—was another story. She was no forensics expert, but she knew a depression fracture when she saw one, and this one—a round spot a little large than a quarter, with cracks radiating outward from the center—could have easily been the cause of death of the skull's owner.

Christina shivered at a vision: a woman with her back turned, a man swinging a pipe or brick with all his might. *Maybe,* she thought, guessing from the finer facial bones, with their lack of brow ridges, that she really was looking at the skull of an adult female.

Or it could be instead that she'd been thrown off by the length of those pale strands, along with the words of the woman who'd lured her here. The woman who'd been playing games with her—was she really upstairs, holding Lilly and her sister?

Christina's rational mind kicked into gear, followed by her fury. "So where are they?" she shouted up the stairwell. "Because they can't really be here, can they? Lilly could never climb that ladder, and Annie would be screaming and fighting you with every step."

The only answer that came to her was the echo of her own words, and doubts crept in. What if Lilly and Annie were both silent because they'd been killed, just like her poor mother?

My mother . . .

Christina's scalp prickled as she remembered Lilly looking up from her cereal to point out the painting of the lighthouse. "Gramma's house," she'd announced, absolute certainty in her voice.

But which grandmother? Christina stared back down toward the skull, a lump aching in her throat as it hit her that this—this could be her . . .

Murder me. Bad people. Wasn't that what her daughter had been trying to tell her all along?

"She's—she's *not* my mother!" Christina shouted, memories of the battered body she'd found last night crowding into her head. "She's not!"

"She *is!*" shrieked a female voice above her. A voice Christina knew too well. "She *was*, because she came back. Came back for us before that heartless bitch and the man we called our father killed her!"

CHAPTER TWENTY-EIGHT

"That *bitch*?" Christina cried, reeling with the comprehension that this skull belonged to the birth mother who had apparently come looking for them—and with the idea that the loving woman who had raised them could possibly have been involved in that woman's death.

Then reeling once again with the sudden understanding that her own sister—poor, sweet, deluded Annie—had attacked and killed their adoptive mother in a fit of rage when the horrible reality of their birth mother's end had collided with the fantasies Annie had built around that unbalanced, absent figure . . .

A biological mother who had passed on her legacy of instability not to Christina, as she'd feared, but to her younger daughter.

"Oh God, Annie, what have you done?" Christina said as she headed up the stairs.

"No more than they did to her." Annie's voice reverberated off the brick. "Daddy—he told me himself when I was taking care of him while he was so sick two years ago. He asked me to forgive—to forgive them both. He claimed she was still messed up when she showed up, higher than a kite the day she tried to make him give her money for stealing her kids."

As she rounded the curve leading her into what had been the living quarters, Christina got her first glimpse of her sister standing, wild-eyed and filthy, with a pair of bolt cutters in hand—probably the same tool she'd used to break into the lighthouse. Lit by a second lantern, the room behind her was so badly burned, from wall to floors to ceiling, that it looked like a black cave.

"When?" Christina managed, her gaze darting everywhere as she searched for any sign of Lilly. "When did this happen?"

"I only know we were still just kids," Annie said, her voice distorted by sobbing. "You were going to your therapy for the nightmares, and they thought—he said she would've only hurt us. They didn't care that she really wanted us, that she wanted to take us to our real home. They didn't even—didn't even ask her what my name is, Katie."

Christina fixed her with a hard stare. "Where's my daughter? What have you done with Lilly? You didn't hurt—"

"I'd never hurt her. Never," she insisted, shaking her head. "But I need you to understand. They killed our mother. *Murdered* her. He said it was an accident, that he never meant to, except—except she kept trying to go upstairs where we were sleeping, and he couldn't—wouldn't—let her."

"So this happened at our house?" Christina asked, sidestepping Annie to peer into another fire-ravaged room. On the floor she saw what looked like burlap, partly unwrapped, more bones jutting from it. As if the body inside it had gone to pieces.

"*Their* house. In that horrible basement, where they took her so we wouldn't hear them talking," Annie told her. "But later on, they moved her—he hid the body out here. He still had a key at the time, even though this place had been condemned after the fire."

Seeing no sign of Lilly, Christina once again turned to her sister, who was blocking her path to a second doorway. Her sister, whose assurances about never hurting her niece now meant nothing. "I need you to let me past you."

Annie didn't budge. "You have to understand," she said. "I—I thought it was just him at first. It's what he told me on his deathbed. Until, two weeks ago, that bitch was on me again, lecturing me again over money, calling me irresponsible and childish and—and accusing me of whoring myself with a married man."

Christina grimaced at the bitterness she heard—and the realization that things had been far worse between her sister and their mom than she'd imagined. That they had both hidden the truth because they thought of Christina, who'd overcome childhood night terrors, postpartum psychosis, and the death of a husband, as too fragile to handle it? "Edgewood, you mean?"

Annie nodded, tears spilling as she explained. "She wouldn't believe me when I told her I've never slept with him. That men—men aren't even on my radar right now. And then, when she told me how our—how that man I always thought of as our father—would be ashamed, I just—I told her straight out that I didn't give a damn what that murderer thought of me."

Christina stopped looking for a way around her sister and looked at her, through the mask she'd worn for so long. It came to her that Annie had dealt with their dad's deathbed confession—maybe buried it—for more than two years all on her own. But at what cost to her sanity—and her relationship with their adoptive mother?

"And then what happened?" As Christina set the lantern on a partly burned projection that might once have been a shelf, her stomach turned. Because she knew, or thought she did, already. Had found the horrible evidence last night, wrapped in that makeshift tarp.

"She—she slapped me," Annie said through tears. "Slapped me and told me that it wasn't him. *She* was the one who did it, with some tool off his workbench. He'd lied for her about it. Lied to me when he was dying. And I just went—I went crazy. But you have to understand, Christina. I don't want you to be mad."

Christina felt both brows rise as she stared, gaping, at her sister. "You—you didn't want me to be *mad* at you? That's why you've been telling Lilly—why you've been faking the calls and—it was *your* voice, wasn't it? On the monitor and the phone? You disguised it somehow?"

Annie's gaze dropped, as if she were too ashamed to bear Christina's scrutiny. "You're all that I have left. And I'm all that *you*—"

She cut herself off, the bolt cutters rising as she noticed Christina had gotten out her phone. "What are you *doing*?"

What I should've done—and would have, if I'd been thinking halfway straight—the moment you called me to come out here. Christina pressed to connect, praying her phone would have enough of a signal at this elevation to get the call through. "I'm calling Harris, Annie. Maybe you'll be willing to tell *him* what you've done with Lilly."

"No! You can't!"

As Annie advanced on her, Christina stepped backward, her elbow toppling the lantern she'd set down. As glass shattered, the flame went out, halving the already-dim illumination.

Alarmed by her sister's approach—and her maniacal expression—Christina dropped the phone back inside the pocket of her jacket.

"Then tell me, where's my daughter, you delusional little—" Christina launched herself at Annie, meaning to grab her by the shoulders and shake the truth out of her. Because if she'd hurt Lilly, too—

Annie gasped and jerked back, swinging the bolt cutters in her hand straight at her sister's face.

"No!" shouted Christina, backpedaling to avoid the blow—

Then crying out in panic, her arms windmilling as she pitched backward down the same steps she'd ascended.

"Christina? Christina, are you all right? Say something if you hear me," Harris shouted into his phone over the sound of the dark water lapping at the hull. But it was too late. The call had dropped already, leaving him with only the memory of her scream.

His stomach pitching with the light chop, he tied off the little johnboat, with its pull-start motor, that he'd cut loose from its dock at the small natural harbor sheltered by the submerged point. Smacking up against the lighthouse's base was a smaller craft beside it—another boat that shouldn't be here. Did it belong to Christina's tormentor, or had she *borrowed* this boat the way he had?

Feeling his phone vibrate again, Harris snatched it from his pocket, praying it would be Christina calling back to tell him she was fine at home, that the message she'd sent Renee had been nothing but a huge misunderstanding.

Instead, he saw a text from Maya. He hesitated for a moment and then clicked it open.

RENEE & JACOB SAFE WITH OFFICER WASHINGTON,
FOUND WAITING FOR YOU AT YOUR HOME.

"Thank God," Harris said, relieved beyond measure that both were unharmed—and that he wasn't about to confront his ex-wife as he'd feared—or find her standing over Christina's lifeless—

Unable to finish the thought, he put away the phone, then reflexively checked his shoulder holster before scrambling for the ladder. The climb was awkward, scar tissue stubbornly hampering his right hand's ability to grip. Thrusting his right elbow through the rungs and using his strength as a lever, along with his capable left hand, he managed to fight his way up, rung by rung.

By the time he made it to the double doors, he was breathing hard and bathed in sweat. He stepped cautiously through the right-hand door, which stood open, and into the darkness, with the echo of Christina's scream shadowing his thoughts.

But he knew that rushing in was a good way to get someone killed. So he stood in silence for seconds that felt more like hours, straining his ears and eyes for the slightest sound or flicker of light, and inhaling air that tasted faintly of burned wood.

Slipping a hand beneath his jacket, Harris reached for the SIG Sauer. He left the small flashlight he'd brought in his pocket, unwilling to give away his presence, though he knew it was possible that his approach by boat had been observed. As his eyes slowly adjusted, he made out a faint light above him to his right—a light that led him, with careful sliding steps, to the bottom of what he quickly realized was a spiral staircase.

But was there anyone alive to find above?

A sharp metallic clang from overhead answered his question.

Step by step, he climbed, praying that he wouldn't find Christina's battered body—murdered as her mother had been. That she wouldn't be lying beside the sister she'd fought so hard to protect for so long—the sister who . . .

His mind ticked back to the missing records for Annie's cell phone. What if she hadn't gotten the dates and times wrong, but instead had *lied* for some reason? What if—

He again heard something overhead, this time a soft, fleeting sound. Scarcely daring to breathe, he strained his ears to be sure. Yes, there it was again—another soft gasp, the sounds of someone weeping. Someone female, he thought.

Christina—she's still alive.

Hurrying to find her, he noticed the charred scent growing stronger a moment before he caught the glimmer of light off a railing.

"Please don't—" came the woman's desperate whispers. "Don't be mad at me. It isn't my fault. You weren't there. You didn't hear the awful things—she could be so hateful—"

Hell . . . Harris's foot knocked into something with a hollow thunk, sending the hard object clattering downward. The sound against the metal steps was as loud as an explosion.

A frightened shriek rose. "Who's there? Who is it?"

"Annie?" he called, recognizing her voice. And putting the words he'd overheard into the context of the calls she'd never actually received, and the decision to leave her beloved niece behind tonight, alone in that tub. Putting it all together with the years she'd spent living in her smarter, more successful older sister's shadow . . .

Years that had undoubtedly done nothing for her relationship with the adoptive parents trying to shape her in Christina's image.

"H-Harris?" Annie cried. "Harris, help my sister! He's—he's hurt her!"

"*Who* hurt her? What's happened?" he asked as he spotted a silhouetted form through the metal grating of the treads above him. Hurrying to reach it, he found Christina motionless on her side, her head and arms pointed downward and her hair across her face. He spotted Annie a few steps higher, squatting beside her sister's legs, which curved upward with the staircase.

"Please, you have to help her," she pleaded, looking every bit as desperate as she sounded.

"Christina, can you hear me?" Harris's heart jerked as he noticed the odd angle of her neck, from where her head—now at his eye level—was leaning against one of the metal rungs supporting the railing.

Was he already too late?

"She's out cold," Annie said. "He shoved her—knocked her down before he ran off. He—he's gone now."

"Ran off? Who did? Who did this, Annie?"

She wasn't making any sense, but still he set his weapon on the stair beside him and reached for Christina's wrist to find a pulse. Nothing—no, there it was. Swift but strong, except . . . He brushed the hair off her face and then ran a hand down the column of her neck, terrified of what he might find there. *Please, Christina, wake up.*

"The man who took me, the kidnapper," said Annie, the story gushing from her now. "A big, nasty-looking guy—I've never seen him before in my life."

No bulges or sharp angles on Christina's neck, thank God. But Harris's hand came away damp—bloody from the back of the unconscious woman's head. He pulled out his phone, needing to add to his earlier request for backup a call for a medevac crew—or maybe the coast guard would be better—to get her down from here and onto a chopper without further injury.

But first, he fixed Annie with his sternest look. "A *stranger*?" he asked. "A complete stranger did this to your sister?"

Her gaze darted away, like a school of minnows evading a hungry egret's beak, and she retreated a step higher. "Come to think of it, I've seen him. Hanging around the Shell Pile a few times, staring. And I think—yes, he was following my car the other day, too. I think he's, like, a stalker."

Do you *think that's what I want to hear?* "So this *kidnapper*," Harris asked her, "he made you drop off Lilly. At a place where you had reason to think she'd be safe."

"That's right," she said, her voice quavering a little as she scooted back another couple of steps, retreating to the solid flooring that must have comprised the former living quarters. "Because he didn't want her. But then my sister showed up and he—he grabbed her, too, and—I think he meant to, you know, rape us. But then—then Christina fell, and I guess he panicked."

"Annie, stop this. Okay?" *At least until I've gotten you in an interview room, where I've read you your rights and the conversation can be recorded.*

"Stop what?" she asked nervously.

"Let's just stay focused now on helping Christina, shall we? Come back down here, will you, and hold her hand." *So I can see where you have both of yours.* "While I call for the right help to get her to a hospital. You want to her to be all right, don't you? You want her to forgive you."

"For-forgive me?" Panic threaded through her words. "For what?"

"Well, for getting her kidnapped," he said, not wanting to escalate things any further, though he was keenly aware of the SIG Sauer he'd laid on the step, and the covered handcuff holster on his belt. "That *is* what you said, right? Not purposely, of course. I know you'd never want to hurt her, as close as you two are."

"*Were,*" came the whispered response—not from Annie but from Christina, who was pushing herself into a more comfortable position. "Not—not anymore. She—Annie was the one who—"

"No! You can't!" her sister shouted, leaning back to grab something from the floor behind her. Something that in the dim light looked to Harris like a rifle or shotgun as she swung it into place to—

Practice, training, and the instincts of a man who'd learned to trust them came together, his left hand grasping and raising the pistol as adrenaline blazed a hot path to his brain. Raising and firing, the deafening reports of two shots ringing off the curved brick, before Annie could silence the woman he would gladly give his life for.

Christina jolted, pushing herself upright, her shrill screams mingling with her sister's as his hearing returned. As the long-barreled object slid from Annie's hands, he lunged to grab it, only to realize, as she slumped, that she'd grabbed bolt cutters rather than a firearm . . .

And only realizing, as he attempted to stand, that just one of the hollow-point bullets he'd fired had struck Annie Wallace.

The other must have ricocheted off either brick or the steel railing—only to bounce back and hit him in the throat.

CHAPTER TWENTY-NINE

Since they wouldn't let him leave the hospital—not after the surgery to repair the artery ripped open by a red-hot fragment of the .40 round that had nearly killed him—Harris gradually refashioned the room into Command Central. Three days after the shooting, he was strong—or at least stubborn—enough to use his laptop and his cell to read reports and issue orders, and causing more than one of the nurses assigned to his floor to roll her eyes in irritation.

Though his memories from the first twenty-hour hours were foggy, he was aware that most of his officers and staff had come by to check on him—except for Aleksandra Zarzycki. Alex, as everyone was now calling her, had been released and was now recovering in an extra bedroom at the home of Marco Del Vecchio's mother, since she had no family of her own to help her out. Yesterday, however, Alex had called to ask how he was doing and assure Harris, her tongue firmly planted in her cheek, that "I'm not letting my pretty-boy partner's rotten shooting scare me out of coming back to work."

"Don't be too hard on the guy." Though the Millville cops had cleared Marco of all wrongdoing in an act that had certainly saved

Ashley Paxton's life, Harris knew he was racked with guilt about it. "In a confined space, heat of the moment like that—"

"This, coming from the chief who managed to shoot his own damn *self*," she'd said, causing Harris to laugh so hard, he'd had to ask for morphine for the resulting neck pain.

As he was settling in to read a witness statement for the fourth time, Stella Bradford came in, dressed in a colorful jogging suit that had surely never seen athletic service. Plump as she was short in stature, the mayor's blue eyes danced as she raised a silvery eyebrow.

"What happened to the sexy gown, Chief?"

He smiled, feeling a hell of a lot more comfortable in the jeans and long-sleeved T-shirt one of his guys has brought him. "Nurses kept complaining there was too way much testosterone on the floor." When Stella laughed, he added, "Seriously, I'm getting discharged in about an hour. Just waiting on the paperwork."

Grinning, she pulled a large green bottle from the tote she carried. "Then I guess we have two things to celebrate."

"Is that *champagne*?"

"Relax, you prude," she said. "It's just a nonalcoholic screw-top. But I thought this moment deserved some bubbles."

"What moment?" Closing the lid of his laptop, he set it on the wheeled tray table.

She cracked open the bottle, then poured some of the pale gold beverage into a pair of plastic flutes and pressed one into his hand.

"The moment I tell you that Reginald Edgewood's just resigned from the city council to, *ahem*, spend more time with his family."

"Really?"

"Hell no. That's just what he's telling people to save face, letting them think he's dedicated to looking out for his poor wife's health and getting his son back on track, now that Eric's out on bail." She tossed back her glass and drained her drink with gusto.

But Harris waited, sensing there was more to come.

"I'm sure it's just coincidence," she said happily, "that word's just come down that the great Reg Edge has been indicted by a federal grand jury—for trying to bribe his way around those permit problems on his development."

Harris snorted and raised his glass.

"Oh, come on," Stella said. "I thought that'd get a smile out of you, at least. Your job's safe—as it sure as hell should be, after solving the worst crime wave Seaside Creek's ever known. Or is it—" She frowned as she appraised him. "You aren't in pain, are you?"

"It's not that. I was just thinking about Christina Paxton." The witness whose statement he kept rereading, and whose absence weighed on him more heavily with each passing day. "Everything she's been through, everything she's lost. She saved my life, you know—making that pressure bandage from her shirt to keep me from bleeding out on the spot. But I can't help thinking, if that fragment hadn't nailed me, if she hadn't had to work on me, she could've—could've somehow—"

"Saved my sister?" asked Christina as she stepped through the door. "I'll never know that. I think not, but . . ."

She shrugged as if it didn't matter, though the haunted look in her eyes told him that it always would. Along with the fact that his other round had struck Annie's chest dead center. A bullet he had fired after mistaking the bolt cutters for a gun.

As Stella's eyes darted between the two of them, her ebullient mood faded visibly. "I—I'm so sorry for your loss—your *losses*, Dr. Paxton."

"This is Mayor Bradford, Christina," Harris said quietly, feeling the thud of his own heartbeat. *Has she come to say good-bye?*

She nodded at the older woman. "Thank you. I'm afraid I've b-brought a lot of trouble to your town. So you—you might be glad to know, my daughter and I won't be staying." Christina glanced at Harris before she dropped her gaze. Her cheeks went pink, the only color in her otherwise pale face. "Too many ghosts here. Too much—I *can't*."

"Christina," he said, the emotion in the single word drawing a look of surprise from Stella.

"From everything I understand," the mayor said gently as she turned her attention toward the younger woman, "not a bit of this was your fault. If you change your mind at any point, home will always welcome you—"

"Thank you for that." Christina's voice was flat and lifeless, the light in her once-warm brown eyes gone cold. "But the memories alone—" Shaking her head, she cut herself off before repeating, "Thank you."

Stella responded politely, then abruptly remembered an appointment back in town. After an awkward good-bye, she gave Harris one last look, one silver brow raised, before closing the door behind her.

She knows. The realization jolted him. *Am I really that easy to read—as pathetically obvious as Del Vecchio is around Zarzycki?*

"How are—how are you feeling?" Christina asked him.

"You came," he said, smelling the faint vanilla scent of body wash. Though she wore not a trace of makeup, and her hair hung straight past her shoulders, he was struck by how beautiful she was as she stepped into the soft winter sunlight coming through the window.

Or was he only memorizing every detail out of fear that he would never see her again?

"I thought I should," she said, shrugging off her jacket. Underneath she wore a soft-blue sweater with a pair of darker jeans. "I wanted you to know I don't—it wasn't your fault, about Annie."

"I was sure she meant to hurt you. To shoot you—the light in there was—"

"I know. And she would have—would have beaten me the way she did our—our mother. Her voice, her face—she wasn't the person I thought I knew." She crossed her arms as if to hug herself. "Or maybe she was, if I'd only been willing to see it."

"I've read the statement you gave, and I'm sorry."

"People keep saying that, but what does it mean?" she asked. "What do I do with it when my family, my whole family—"

"Lilly—Lilly's all right?" he asked, though he knew she'd recovered from the drugging unscathed, just as he'd learned that Christina had refused to be admitted the night they'd been brought in, though she'd been warned that she might have a concussion.

"She asks for Annie all the time. She says she wants to hear more stories about Katie."

"Who's with her now?"

"Kym's watching her."

"You trust her?" he asked.

Christina nodded. "This has been as big a shock to her as anyone, but I think that helping us is helping her in some way, and maybe one day she'll forgive herself for not seeing what we both missed."

"People hide things," he said. "They get damned good at it. And Annie was carrying a lot of secrets for a long time." If what he'd read in Christina's statement was true, she'd carried her adoptive father's deathbed confession for more than two years in silence before she'd finally snapped.

Christina nodded. "Until those secrets broke her somehow. Or maybe she was always broken . . ."

She moved close to his bedside, close enough to touch him. Yet only her eyes reached his, a flicker of warmth in them like a memory of summer. "You never told me how you're feeling."

"Alive, thanks to you."

"Beyond that?"

"Could be better," he said, aching to reach out to her, to drag her close enough to pull her into his arms. But when he pushed aside the wheeled table, she tensed visibly, convincing him to take things slower. Much slower, or she'd bolt like a startled deer, leaving him forever.

"But I'll be fine—at least I'm heading home," he continued. "I'm a lot more worried about you."

"Renee came by to see me last night."

"Did she?" he asked carefully, still mulling over what Renee stopped by the hospital to tell him yesterday. What she'd gone to his house to confess the night he shot Annie Wallace. "What did she say?"

"She begged my forgiveness for letting Zach Fulton charm her into passing you my private information."

"He didn't *charm* her into it. He played on her vanity. Then, when that quit working, he flat- out bribed her," Harris said, still furious that his ex had allowed herself to be drawn into a relationship with the most manipulative young psychopath he'd ever come across, who had, according to Ashley Paxton, set up the grocery meeting after spotting her coming out of the Victorian where Christina was living. It could have ended up a lot worse, he knew, having learned from the Millville police chief that Ashley had been used and badly abused by Fulton when she had tried to put the brakes on his increasingly dangerous behavior. Once she recovered from her stab wounds, Ashley faced serious charges—charges that could range all the way up to accessory after the fact in the murder of Frank Fiorelli.

Whether she would be convicted was another story. From what he understood, her mother had hired a team of high-priced lawyers to paint her as another victim. And maybe in a way she was. That was for a judge and jury to decide. Harris was just grateful that Zach Fulton had been put down like the mad dog that he was.

"Renee fed him information, too," he told Christina, "about your schedule, where you went, even the key code to get into the garage door that night he messed up your car—"

"She told me all of that, too. Told me how ashamed she was, that she didn't deserve my forgiveness."

"That may be the most honest thing she's ever said."

Christina blew out an audible breath. "I'll never be her friend again. I could never pretend her betrayal hasn't hurt me. But she's still your son's mother—a good mom, a mom Jacob loves and needs. I wouldn't take her from him."

"You mean you're—"

"I don't want her charged for what she did. She doesn't need to go to jail." The barest of smiles lifted the corners of Christina mouth. "Besides, it'll grate on her forever having to live with knowing I'm the bigger person."

With a smile of his own, he nodded. "Especially now that we've all seen her at her smallest." He didn't doubt for a moment that this would prompt her to accept the job she'd been offered—and would be free to accept if she wasn't facing charges. It would mean a longer drive to see his son, but Harris was more than willing to put in the miles.

"Besides, what does it matter now?" Christina said. "As soon as I get past the—the funerals and figure out what to do about my mom's house and her business, I'll be heading back to my old job in Dallas."

Unable to restrain himself, he reached out and captured her hand, squeezing it tight in his. "Please don't, Christina. Don't let them win by driving you away."

Her hand began to shake, and he saw her blink back tears.

"It's not anything to do with winning," she said. "They've already lost, all of them. Even my mom and dad, who thought they could protect us by—"

"They were wrong—of course, they were wrong—but they clearly wanted you raised with love and care, to grow up to be—"

"And look how well that's worked out for us." Pulling her hand free, she wiped her eyes. "Annie gone, my parents, even that sad wreck of a woman who abandoned us. And me—will I ever stop seeing it in my head—my mother dead? My sister dying? If I—if I wasn't crazy before, how will I ever find my way through this without screwing up as badly as they did? How will I ever do this, Harris?"

Unable to hold back any longer, Harris climbed from the bed and went to her. Enveloping her in his arms, he bent his head to press a kiss just above her ear. And lowered his voice to whisper, "With someone who will always love you at your side . . . if you'll only let me."

EPILOGUE

Floating against the sapphire sky, the white gulls seemed to laugh at them, as well they might, having knocked the cone of french fries from the little girl's hand and scattered them across the sun-bleached boards, where the food vanished in a flurry of brazenness and feathers.

Sending up a howl of protest, Lilly began crying, until Jacob took her by the hand and led her from the mayhem, saying, "It's okay, Lilly. I'll share mine with you."

As Christina, who had been moving to placate her daughter as best she could, watched in amazement, Lilly stopped midsob and gave the curly-haired four-year-old an angelic smile before she threw her arms around the boy she proudly called Big Brudder.

"Those have to be the cutest kids in the free world," said Harris, looking at ease on a rare off day in late June in his worn cargo shorts, an old-school Springsteen T-shirt, and the kind of tan that made her wish they were alone so she could check out its borders . . .

Not that she didn't know every inch of him by now, six months beyond her harrowing off season. But fine as it was, it hadn't been his body that had convinced her to put the brakes on her stubborn—and oft-repeated—plan to return to Dallas once she finally had things settled. It had been his steadfast help with everything she needed—from the painful packing away of so many memories at her mother's house, to his refusal to leave her side even on those days when she was at her very worst—that had finally convinced her he'd meant it when he'd told her he wanted nothing more than to make a life with her.

And thanks to his insistence that she see a licensed professional to talk through her doubts and fears and self-recrimination, she had come to trust herself again—and believe that she—that *they*—deserved this chance at happiness.

A warm wind ruffled her hair as they stepped out of the flow of tourists strolling toward the entertainment pier, with all its rides and games and carnival music set to the soothing cadence of the breaking surf. This late in the afternoon, most of the sun worshippers were packing up their blankets, totes, and coolers and abandoning the white-gold sands. She caught the warm scent of tanning lotion, along with a hint of something—maybe gyro meat or pork roll—that had her forgetting she'd just put away a big chocolate-and-vanilla frozen custard cone.

But the shore, this season, and the man at her side were all about allowing herself to give in to temptation. Allowing herself to believe that she—that both of them—deserved to.

As they sat down on a bench, they watched Jacob lead Lilly to the railing and hold their cone of fries while she settled in beside him so they could dangle their bare legs over the sand.

"I'm so glad Gentleman Jake's going to be staying for the summer," Christina sighed. "Maybe some of his good manners will rub off on Lilly before he has to go back to start preschool."

"What're you talking about?" Harris said. "My girl's just a little spirited, that's all."

"*Your* girl?" Christina asked. "And what are you, her official apologist these days?"

She grinned, knowing that even before they'd moved in together, Lilly had wrapped Seaside Creek's police chief around her finger—from the moment she'd conned him into allowing her to paint his nails and watch the latest princess movie with her for the umpteenth time.

"My girl . . . yeah, about that," he said. "I have something else to ask you. Something serious."

"I'm not sure you could top last night's question," Christina said, extending her hand to admire her beautiful new ring. Though the diamond wasn't as large as the one she'd put aside to someday give to her daughter, she couldn't stop smiling every time she looked at its sparkling facets—smiles that eased the sting of her still-healing heart. "But if your bad knee's up for more kneeling—"

"It's not quite that kind of question." He pushed his aviator sunglasses on top his head to look at her with serious hazel eyes. "I'm not asking because I think I can erase Doug or take his place, or that I want anything to do with Lilly's trust fund. But after everything your daughter's gone through, I think she's going to need a father. A dad and a family that she really feels a part of."

"And we'll have that—I know we will."

"What if we made it official?" he asked before a rare look of uncertainty troubled his handsome features. "After the wedding, I was wondering—and feel free to say no if you in any way feel weird about this—but I'd like to adopt Lilly so she and Jacob and you and I can all be a family forever."

Blinking away tears, Christina looked at the two preschoolers on the boards' edge, giggling over nothing with their chubby elbows resting on the bottom railing. Her gaze moved beyond them to the blue-gray expanse of the sun-warmed Atlantic, and then back to the man whose words, whose love, and whose healing had finally brought her spirit home.

Instead of answering, she kissed him, a sweet kiss full of everything she was feeling. Because at this moment, words were nothing . . .

And not even ten eternities could ever be enough.

AUTHOR'S NOTE AND ACKNOWLEDGMENTS

Growing up near the southern New Jersey shore, I came to love the small beach towns, with their wonderful old houses, lively boardwalks, and sandy beaches. But I have to admit, I especially loved the quiet and cold of the off season, where the seaside neighborhoods stood eerily empty, and the deserted beaches were perfect for long walks in warm coats . . . perhaps with hot chocolates in hand, if we were lucky enough to find someplace open.

Seaside Creek is a fictional community, inspired by places such as Wildwood, Ocean City, and, of course, Cape May, New Jersey. The lighthouse at Willet's Point, too, is an imaginary locale, though some might notice that it bears a strong resemblance to the conical red-and-black light at Miah Maull Shoal in nearby Delaware Bay.

I'd like to take time to thank my first readers, talented authors Barbara Taylor Sissel, Kim O'Brien, and Joy Preble. Your insights and encouragement greatly helped to shape the story.

Agent Nalini Akolekar of Spencerhill Associates has championed *The Off Season* since its inception. Thanks as always for being there—and for putting the proposal in the hands of acquisition editor Alison Dasho of Montlake. Her thoughtful fine-tuning, along with the brilliant work of developmental editor David Downing, have helped the long journey from manuscript to book. Thanks, too, to the rest of the Amazon team, including the amazing Jessica Poore for everything I know you do—and all the stuff I haven't figured out yet.

Closer to home, I want to end with a special shout-out to my husband, Mike, who's always been incredibly supportive of my work—along with my tendency to adopt sweet-but-needy dogs from pounds and rescues, including a couple of retired racing greyhounds, whose cherished memories inspired the creation of Max in *The Off Season.* Thanks, Mike, for understanding when I text you all those grocery lists from my deadline cave!

ABOUT THE AUTHOR

RITA Award–nominated author Colleen Thompson cut her teeth writing historical romances under the pseudonym Gwyneth Atlee. But she couldn't resist the draw of intrigue, and neither could her readers. Together they've traveled the twists and turns of her many tales of romantic suspense. A native of New Jersey, Thompson now calls Texas home. When she's not out and about exploring the Lone Star State with her husband, she's at home writing, or playing with her two rescue dogs.